continued . . .

"Filled with history, romance, and passion, a story that pulled me in and held me captive."

—Romance Reader at Heart

Mystic Guardian

"Extraordinary characters . . . subtle touches of humor and clever dialogue."

—*Romantic Times* (Top Pick, 4½ Stars)

"Will enchant readers."

—The Romance Readers Connection

"A fine, fresh series kickoff, Rice's latest is passionate, rich in historical detail, and peopled with enough captivating secondary characters to pique readers' curiosity for many volumes to come."   —*Publishers Weekly*

The Magic Series

Magic Man

"Never slows down until the final thread is magically resolved. Patricia Rice is clearly the Magic Woman with this superb tale and magnificent series."

—*Midwest Book Review*

Much Ado About Magic

"The magical Rice takes Trev and Lucinda, along with her readers, on a passionate, sensual, and romantic adventure in this fast-paced, witty, poignant, and magical tale of love."   —*Romantic Times* (Top Pick, 4½ Stars)

This Magic Moment

"Charming and immensely entertaining."

—*Library Journal*

"Rice has a magical touch for creating fascinating plots, delicious romance, and delightful characters, both flesh-and-blood and ectoplasmic." —*Booklist*

The Trouble with Magic

"Rice's third enchanting book about the Malcolm sisters is truly spellbinding." —*Booklist*

Must Be Magic

"Very sensual." —The Romance Reader

"Rice has created a mystical masterpiece full of enchanting characters, a spellbinding plot, and the sweetest of romances." —*Booklist* (Starred Review)

"I love an impeccably researched, well-written tale, and *Must Be Magic*, which continues the saga of the Iveses and Malcolms, is about as good as it gets. I'm very pleased to give it a Perfect Ten, and I encourage everyone to pick up this terrific book."

—Romance Reviews Today

Merely Magic

"Simply enchanting! Patricia Rice, a master storyteller, weaves a spellbinding tale that's passionate and powerful." —Teresa Medeiros

"Like Julie Garwood, Patricia Rice employs wicked wit and sizzling sensuality to turn the battles of the sexes into a magical romp." —Mary Jo Putney

"One of those tales that you pick up and can't put down.... Brava!" —*Midwest Book Review*

PATRICIA RICE

The Wicked Wyckerly

THE REBELLIOUS SONS

WITHDRAWN

A SIGNET ECLIPSE BOOK

SIGNET ECLIPSE
Published by New American Library, a division of
Penguin Group (USA) Inc., 375 Hudson Street,
New York, New York 10014, USA
Penguin Group (Canada), 90 Eglinton Avenue East, Suite 700, Toronto,
Ontario M4P 2Y3, Canada (a division of Pearson Penguin Canada Inc.)
Penguin Books Ltd., 80 Strand, London WC2R 0RL, England
Penguin Ireland, 25 St. Stephen's Green, Dublin 2,
Ireland (a division of Penguin Books Ltd.)
Penguin Group (Australia), 250 Camberwell Road, Camberwell, Victoria 3124,
Australia (a division of Pearson Australia Group Pty. Ltd.)
Penguin Books India Pvt. Ltd., 11 Community Centre, Panchsheel Park,
New Delhi - 110 017, India
Penguin Group (NZ), 67 Apollo Drive, Rosedale, North Shore 0632,
New Zealand (a division of Pearson New Zealand Ltd.)
Penguin Books (South Africa) (Pty.) Ltd., 24 Sturdee Avenue,
Rosebank, Johannesburg 2196, South Africa

Penguin Books Ltd., Registered Offices:
80 Strand, London WC2R 0RL, England

First published by Signet Eclipse, an imprint of New American Library,
a division of Penguin Group (USA) Inc.

First Printing, July 2010
10 9 8 7 6 5 4 3 2

Dedicated to the late Edith Layton, one of this country's greatest Regency writers, an even better friend and person, and guardian angel of all creatures large or small. Your smile is remembered in every ray of sunshine and glitter of amber.

Acknowledgments

Hats off to Sherrie Holmes for her hilarious list of epithets, from which I've blatantly borrowed. (Check out the comments to http://patriciarice.blogspot.com/ under "Epitaph/epithet" for a chuckle.)

And blessings to Connie Rinehold, who lifts my spirits while checking my grammar.

As always, my gratitude to the Cauldron for turning my whines into hilarious plot twists and character foibles.

I'm always amazed at how so many people are there when I need them. To all the usual suspects—I appreciate you more than you can ever know.

1

John Fitzhugh Wyckerly, newly styled seventh Earl of Danecroft, tilted back his late father's wooden office chair and plopped his muddy boots on a towering stack of yellowed invoices. From that position, he contemplated the gun collection on the far wall, left to him by his freshly departed brother.

If guns were the solution to his problems, he had a vast array from which to choose.

Outside the estate office, a clamor arose among the creditors waiting there. With any luck, the hue and cry signaled the arrival of a servant with the coffee he'd ordered.

Whiskey would have been preferable under the circumstances, but it was only noon, and drinking spirits so early in the day would be disrespectful to the brother who had just been laid to rest in the family vault. On second thought, the old boy would have encouraged a swallow of good malt, or two, or the whole bottle, regardless of the hour. George had arrived at the pearly gates in the same manner in which he'd lived—well pickled. Fitz understood the compulsion to reach for a bottle, but unlike his simpleminded brother, he wasn't inclined to follow orders or urges.

Until now, Fitz had supported himself with his skill for cards. As a younger son, he'd had no obligation to family or estate. His affable charm and a peculiar gift for numbers had provided financial freedom. Now—he rolled his eyes in disgust—as far as he could tell, his family's general incompetence and selfish indulgence had dug a hole deeper than a king's treasure house could fill.

An earlier scan of the invoices and dunning notices scattered across the desk had produced the depressing calculation that if he could organize the meager family assets well enough to produce ten thousand pounds a year, the Danecroft estate would be out of debt in approximately a hundred years.

The Wicked Wyckerlys had ridden the road to ruin to its inevitable cliff. At least, in previous generations, there had been a few branches dedicated to saving the estate, but that had ended when his grandfather and great-uncle had come to blows. Perhaps his grandfather shouldn't have wagered his brother's marriage settlement on a cheese-rolling race, but the rabbit hole that had broken the champion cheese-roller's ankle couldn't have been predicted.

The younger branch of the family had gone on to amass a fortune in trade. Apparently all the earldom's luck had gone with them.

Bracing his hands behind his head, Fitz watched with admiration as Bibley maneuvered the door open and slipped through the narrow slot carrying a tray, effectively blocking any sight of the inner office from the angry hordes in the outer one.

"You have perfected evasive action to a science, Bib," Fitz complimented the aging family retainer. "I deduce you have had much experience in dodging creditors."

"Yes, my lord." With palsied, spotted hands, the shrunken butler carefully lowered the wooden tray.

The silver had been sold long ago, despite the entailment requiring that it remain with the estate. The earls of Danecroft generally believed themselves above the boring details of law, even when they protected the welfare of uninteresting and often odious offspring.

"And bailiffs," Bibley continued as if asking if he'd like sugar.

"Bailiffs?"

"Your brother's debtors sued and won. They're here to take him to Newgate."

Fitz returned his boots to the floor to reach for the steaming cup of coffee. "Did someone point out the cemetery to them?"

"They weren't amused, my lord."

"No, I suppose they wouldn't be." Fitz straightened the neckcloth knot that had suddenly tightened around his throat. "I don't suppose there's a groat to be found among the cushions or a bottle of wine in the cellar worth selling?"

"Mice ate the cushions, and the late earl was brewing ale in the washtub," Bibley said with all the dignity of his exalted position, despite the fact that his frock coat was shiny with age and his linen threadbare from laundering.

"Which late earl, Georgie or Pops?" Fitz spun his chair to look out upon the estate's neglected weed field. *Lawn* was much too refined a word for the overgrown pasture beyond the terrace. But what did he know? He was a product of the beau monde, not a farmer. He thrived on London's society. He would sell the land and return to the city if he could. But he couldn't, or his ancestors would have already done so. Selling land no doubt required lawyers who understood the niceties of entailments.

He ought to feel sorrow at the recent losses of his only family in drunken accidents. He supposed, once he recovered from the shock of their sudden deaths, he would dig out a pleasant memory or two to mourn. But in truth, he hadn't seen either his brother or father in what? Five years? Six? Along with being above the law, the Wicked Wyckerlys lacked family instincts. Or was that family affection and nesting instincts? Anyway, cuckoos would fare better.

"Viscount Wyckerly experimented in brewing," Bibley replied, reverting to the sixth earl's former title. George had managed to break his neck tumbling down inn stairs only a few months after inheriting the title—hardly time to be remembered as an earl.

"Enterprising of the old boy," Fitz said absently, turning back to regard the piles of unpaid—and previously unopened—bills. "Don't suppose he planned to sell the results of his ale experiments to pay your wages, did he?"

"Unlikely, my lord," the butler said stiffly, pinching his wrinkled lips in disapproval.

"No, I thought not." Pensively, Fitz drained his cup and regarded the gun collection. "Despite the family differences, Cousin Geoff really would be a better earl, wouldn't he?"

Bibley took the empty cup and refilled it, a certain sign that he approved of the conversation's direction. "Mr. Geoffrey Wyckerly runs his family's woolen industry and has experience in managing accounts," he agreed.

"*My* experience makes me a damned fine gambler." Fitz spoke his thoughts aloud. It wasn't as if anyone else knew his dissolute family's affairs better than Bibley. "I won a Thoroughbred stud the night before last. I was on my way to Cheltenham to claim him when word reached me."

"Very fortunate the solicitors found you, my lord."

"Is it?" Fitz sipped the second cup. The uproar outside the office subsided to an angry buzz. He had a suspicion the estate office teeming with bailiffs and creditors wasn't the best place for him to contemplate his future. "It might have been more fortunate if I had seen fit to be hit by a mail coach while on my way to claim my prize. Cousin Geoff would have been most grateful, as would all those angry men out there."

"Your cousin is a wealthy man who would like to be earl," Bibley agreed, polishing the gold watch he'd no doubt appropriated in lieu of wages at some earlier date.

He was surrounded by scoundrels, Fitz mused. A fitting environment for the likes of him. A deep and abiding respect for mathematics, and a fascinating but wholly useless knowledge of insects, did not qualify him to be an earl. "A stud as valuable as the one I won can provide a handsome return," was all he revealed aloud. "I could have lived comfortably off the stud fees alone. I could have gambled the race prizes into greater wealth."

"Not as great as Mr. Wyckerly's," Bibley said in the same agreeable tone as earlier.

"True." Fitz listened for any indication that the estate's creditors might be preparing to batter down the office door. "Geoff's father married a wealthy Cit. His blood isn't as blue as mine. He *works* for a living. In mills. And warehouses. And sundry other filthy holes."

Bibley pursed his wrinkled lips and said nothing. A master manipulator was Bibley. Having lived on his wits and the cards for years, Fitz possessed a strong understanding of human nature. He recognized the butler's mannerisms well enough.

"I sympathize with your plight, Bib." He sat back and sipped his coffee, still eyeing the impressive gun collection. "And like you, I agree that while Geoff is no doubt as wicked as any Wyckerly, he might be a better earl, one who could make some inroads in paying the estate's debts, anyway. The bailiffs are unlikely to haul him off to Newgate."

The doddering family retainer tucked his watch back into his vest pocket. "As you say, my lord."

"Unfortunately"—Fitz drained his second cup—"I'm not inclined to blow out my brains for the benefit of my tenants and staff."

Bibley nodded as if that was to be expected of a degenerate, inconsiderate Wyckerly. "If I might be so bold as to suggest, my lord . . . ?"

"Have at it, old boy. I've not yet reached wit's end, but the signpost is on the horizon."

"With all due respect, my lord, evidence suggesting your death might come to light."

Listening to the distant toll of a doorbell announcing the arrival of still another creditor or needy tenant, Fitz nodded in understanding. "Excellent ploy. Fake my death, put the bailiffs off, let Geoff think he inherits, and see what happens. Dishonest, but intriguing."

"I would see that he paid the staff, of course."

"Of course." Fitz's gaze found the portrait of his mother hidden behind the stacks of deteriorating estate ledgers his brother had evidently moved so as to more effectively display his gun collection.

"Perhaps you could build a better life elsewhere," Bib suggested, staring over Fitz's head at the unproductive fields beyond the window.

"I think not, old man," he said thoughtfully. "Awful hard for an earl to disappear. Strange as it may seem, I have responsibilities." And one rather important one that he couldn't neglect any more than he already had. But now was not the time to mention the result of his youthful indiscretions.

Raised by ill-paid servants, Fitz, now the seventh Earl of Danecroft, had never known affection, or owned more than the suit on his back, but he hoped he had the character to attempt to crawl out from under the family woodpile and become a better person.

His greatest fear was that in his incompetence he would be the earl to complete the destruction of what his ancestors had wrought. "No tales about my death, Bib," he warned.

"Yes, my lord," Bib's pursed lips of disapproval returned.

"I daresay it wouldn't hurt if I disappeared for a bit, though," Fitz said thoughtfully, tapping his fingers against the desk. "Buy a little time. Figure out what to do next.

Find Croesus and see if he has a daughter I could marry. This being earl isn't something I was trained for."

Old Bib almost smiled. "Perfectly understandable, my lord. I believe your cousin could be persuaded to loan a small sum for wages in your inexplicable absence."

Fitz knew to be wary when Bib smiled, but his mind had already traveled to his next port of call. "I knew I could count on you, Bib. Tell my visitors I've stepped out, will you?"

Dusting off the curly-brimmed beaver hat he'd worn to the funeral, Fitz opened the floor-to-ceiling-length mullioned window behind the desk, ducked his head beneath the peeling frame, and stepped over the rotten sill.

The tall grass parted as he strode in the direction of the weed-smothered shrubbery where he'd heaved his baggage from the mail coach on his way to George's funeral.

Dignity belonged to butlers, not to Danecrofts.

2

Abigail Merriweather drove the sharp blade of her hoe into the weed that was daring to invade her rhubarb patch. The thick green leaves and red stalks of the rhubarb grew with a lushness that made a mockery of her arid existence since her half-siblings had been taken away.

"The house is so quiet!" She cried her despair to the tailless squirrel perched on the fence.

The squirrel chattered his agreement, reaching with his little paw to grab the nutty reward she offered for his company. The tickle of his nails against her palm might be the only small hand that touched hers this day. She almost burst into tears.

"I cannot go on like this," she told her sympathetic friend. "I've written to the marquess asking for help and waited and waited, but he does not answer my pleas."

She didn't whine to the servants. That would be undignified. And her friends in the village thought she ought to be *relieved* to be rid of four rowdy young children. Certainly, she'd already sacrificed enough on their behalf. She had been twenty-three before she finally found a suitor in the local vicar, and twenty-four when he ran away rather than adopt the rambunctious half-siblings whose responsibility she'd assumed upon her father's unexpected death. Her minuscule dowry hardly covered the expense of such a ready-made family. For a vicar hoping to advance his position, she had become a liability rather than an asset overnight.

She understood why Frederick had left, but she'd been crushed all the same. Losing both her papa and her fiancé in a single year had been devastating. But she loved the children and had given up marriage to keep them. Except now they were gone, too, shipped away by Mr. Greyson, her father's executor, to the safekeeping of a guardian *who could provide more effectual male guidance.* Tears welled at the still-fresh sting of the insult. A veritable stranger was more suitable because he wore trousers!

"They're all the family I have left," she told the squirrel, who would have switched his tail in approval had Miss Kitty not deprived him of it when he was just a nestling.

Brushing her short curls from her forehead, Abigail leaned on the hoe handle and surveyed the rhubarb bed with a sharp eye for nefarious dandelions and wild garlic. Soon, both rhubarb and strawberries would be plentiful, and Cook would prepare the tarts the twins so dearly loved.

But Cissy and Jeremy wouldn't be here to eat them.

"I need a man," she declared so decisively that the squirrel leaped from the fence and hid under the hedge. "I need to marry a rich solicitor," she amended. "A gentleman who loves children and would take my case to the highest courts. An upright, respectable man with enough money not to worry about the expense!"

Rather than cry more useless tears, she was stubbornly contemplating the solicitors of her acquaintance—which amounted to exactly none—when the mail coach rattled to a halt on the treelined road. The mail wasn't delivered personally to Abbey Lane, but Abigail couldn't prevent her heartbeat from skipping in hope. Perhaps a letter of response from a marquess required hand delivery. She wouldn't know. Her father's distant, titled cousin had never sent one.

Please, let him say he would help her fetch the children back. Jennie and Tommy were older than the twins, but they were still too young to be away from home. If she couldn't find a rich solicitor to marry, she needed a respectable, wealthy London gentleman, like the marquess, who would be willing to fight for her cause.

The coach lingered, and she hurried toward the gate, hoe still in hand. Perhaps their guardian had relented and sent the children home for a visit. The mail might stop out here for young children—

"Keep the demon bratling off my coach until you've tamed or caged her!" a cranky male voice bellowed.

"I hate you, you bloody damned cawker!" a child screamed.

Despite the appalling curse, Abigail hurried faster. She did not recognize the voice, but she knew hopeless desperation when she heard it. She would not let harm come to any child under her notice.

"Your generosity will not be forgotten," a wry, plummy baritone called over the thump of baggage hitting the ground.

Sophisticated aristocrats with rounded vowels and haughty accents were not a common commodity in these rural environs. Abigail's innate social insecurity kicked in, rendering her immobile while she tried to decide upon a course of action.

A small figure darted through the hedgerow, dragging a ragged doll and shouting, "Beetle-brained catch-farts can't catch me!"

"Penelope!" the gentleman shouted. "Penelope, come back here this instant."

Oh, that would turn the imp right around. With a sniff of disdain at such incompetence, Abigail intercepted the foulmouthed termagant's path. Crouching down to the child's level, she placed a hand on her arm. "If you run around behind the house," she murmured, "he won't find you, and Cook will give you shortbread."

Tearstained cheeks belied the fury in huge, long-lashed green eyes as the child gazed warily upon her. With her heart-shaped face framed by golden brown hair that was caught loosely in a long braid, she could have been a miniature princess, were it not for her threadbare and too-short gown. And the outrageous expletives that had polluted her rosy lips.

"Hurry along now. I will talk to the rather perturbed gentleman who is opening the gate."

The child glanced behind her and, setting her jaw in mulish determination, raced across the lawn toward the three-story brick cottage that Abigail called home.

"Penelope!" The fashionably garbed Corinthian caught sight of the child and strode briskly up the drive after her.

Abigail gaped at the intruder's manly physique, accentuated by an impeccably tailored, long-tailed cutaway, knit pantaloons, and Hessians polished to a fare-thee-well. She thought her heart actually stumbled in awe—until alarm startled her mind into ticking again.

She might be inclined to be generous and reserve judgment for a man who made a child cry. Children cried for many reasons, not necessarily rational ones. She did not know a man alive who could deal successfully with tearful children, including her late, lamented father. But the gentleman's expensive frock coat and Hessians in the face of the child's pitiful attire raised distressing questions.

Abigail was even less inclined to be forgiving when he seemed prepared to race right past her as if she did not exist. She was painfully aware that she was small and unprepossessing, and she supposed her gardening bonnet and hoe added to her invisibility in the eyes of an arrogant aristocrat. But she wasn't of a mind to be treated like a garden gnome.

She stepped into the drive and wielded the hoe so it would knock the elegant stranger's knees if he didn't acknowledge her. He might be large and formidable, but no man would intimidate her into abandoning a hurt child. He halted with the quick reflexes of an athlete and gazed at her in startlement.

She scarcely had time to admire his disheveled whiskey-colored hair and impressive square chin before he ripped the hoe handle from her grip and flung it into the boxwoods. For a brief moment, she stared into long-lashed, troubled green eyes, and she suffered the insane urge to brush the hair from his forehead to reassure him. Except he was so formidably masculine from his whiskered jaw to his muscled calves, and smelled so deliciously of rich, male musk, that she trembled at the audacity of her impulse. Reverend Frederick had always smelled of lavender sachet.

"The little heathen first, introductions later." The Corinthian broke into a ground-eating gallop that would have done a Thoroughbred proud.

Discarding her disquiet, Abigail hastened up the drive in the intruder's wake. Dignity and her corset prevented her from galloping. As did her short legs.

She arrived at the kitchen door to behold a scene of chaos.

Plump and perplexed, Cook stood with a tray of shortbread in her hand while the threadbare princess darted under the ancient trestle table, shoving a sweet in her mouth.

Miss Kitty yowled and leaped from her napping place on the sill, knocking over a geranium in her haste to achieve the top of the pie safe. The scullery maid cried out in surprise and dashed into the pantry, whether to hide or to secure a weapon was not easily discerned.

And the gentleman—

Abigail thought her eyes might be bulging as she regarded the captivating view of a gentleman's posterior upended under her kitchen table. She had never particularly noticed that part of a man's anatomy, but garbed in knit pantaloons, his was extraordinarily . . . muscled. And neither her insight nor his action was pertinent to the task at hand.

She sighed in exasperation and yanked the green coattail as the gentleman attempted to squeeze his broad shoulders between the table and Cook's favorite chair in an effort to retrieve the child. "Honestly, one would think you'd never seen a child have a tantrum before. Leave her be. She won't die of temper."

Unprepared for a rear attack, the intruder stumbled sideways, caught Cook's chair to steady himself, and knocked over a steaming teapot. He gracefully managed to catch the pottery before it crashed to the brick floor, but not before scalding his hand with the contents.

Abigail winced and waited for the flow of colorful, inappropriate invectives that the child had to have learned somewhere.

The gentleman's throttled silence was more evocative. Dragon green eyes glaring, he returned the pot to the table, clenched his burned wrist and ruined shirt cuff, and, ignoring Abigail's admonitions, again crouched down to check on the runaway.

If she had not already noted the family resemblance of matching forelocks that tumbled hair in their faces, Abigail would have known the two strangers were related by the identical mulish set of their mouths.

Bumping his head against a kitchen table while holding his scalded wrist, Fitz tried to recall why he'd thought learning to be an earl required turning over a new leaf. The moldy, crumbing old foliage he'd lived under all his life had been perfectly adequate for the lowly insect he was, although he must admit his impulsive actions in the past might occasionally give the flighty appearance of a butterfly. He snorted. In the past? If kidnapping his own daughter wasn't flighty, it was the most ill-conceived, most absurd, and possibly stupidest thing he'd ever done, as even the child seemed to recognize.

"I want my mommy." Beneath the table, Penelope stuck out her lower lip.

He peered in exasperation at the whining, scrawny six-year-old bit of fluff he'd accidentally begot in his brainless years, when he'd thought women would save his wicked soul.

The child had his thick brownish hair and green eyes, so he knew she was his, right down to the unruly swirl of hair falling across her forehead. The petulant lip and constant demands obviously belonged to her actress mother—may the woman be damned to perdition.

And yet, he was stupidly drawn to this imp of Satan who so resembled his neglected childhood self. He suffered an uncomfortable understanding of her rebelliousness. After all, she'd been ignored for years by a mother who had run off to marry a rich German and a father who thought good upbringing required only servants. He still preferred servants, but he obviously needed to find more competent ones.

"I will find you a better mother," he recklessly promised, if only to coax her from beneath the table.

"I want *my* mommy!" Big round eyes glared daggers at him.

"You have a daddy now. That ought to be enough until we have time to look around and pick a pretty new mommy for you." What in hell did she expect him to say? That her mother didn't want her? That was one truth that wouldn't pass his tongue, even though the damned woman hadn't seen her child since infancy.

"Mommy says you're a worthless toadsucker. I don't want you for a daddy," she declared.

Her real mother would never have lowered herself to such a common expression. Understanding dawned. "If you mean Mrs. Jones, she is a slack-brained lickspittle," he countered, "and she is *not* your mother. Do you think I'd pick dragon dung like that for your mother?"

He ignored the choking laughter—or outrage—of his audience in his effort to solve one problem at a time.

The child's mother had chosen the nanny. He should have paid closer attention when he'd approved her choice, but at the time, Mrs. Jones had seemed affable and maternal, with all those qualities he imagined a good mother ought to have. Not that he had any experience with mothers or children, good or bad.

He couldn't remember even *being* a child. An undisciplined hellion, yes, but never an innocent. What the devil had he been thinking? That he wouldn't repeat the mistakes of his father? And his grandfather. They hadn't been called Wicked Wyckerlys for naught. Berkshire was littered with his family's bastards. Given the Danecroft debt-ridden habit of marrying for money, producing legitimate spawn had been more of a challenge.

Still, he tried another tactic, plying the silver tongue for which he was known. "But I need a daughter very much, Penelope, and I would like you to live with me now."

No, he wouldn't, actually. He'd always assumed the child would be better off almost anywhere except with him. Therein lay the rub. There was nowhere else for her to go.

He suspected the banty hen breathing down his neck was prepared to dump the entire pot of steaming tea on him, if her tapping toe was any indication. If he'd learned nothing else in his wastrel life, he'd learned to be wary of vindictive women, which seemed to include all pinched, spinsterish females with time on their hands.

"If you will remove yourself from my table—" Right on schedule, the hen attacked, kicking at his boots in a futile attempt to dislodge him.

"I want my mommy," the child wailed in a higher pitch, rubbing her eyes with small, balled-up fists. "You *hate* me!"

"Of course I don't hate you," Fitz said, too appalled to pay attention to the hen. "Who told you that I hate you?" Gobsmacked by her accusation, he could only be blunt. "You're all the family I have. I *can't* hate you."

Sensing she'd shocked a genuine reaction from him, Penelope wailed louder. "You hate me, you hate me. I hate you, I hate you—"

"If you will give her time to calm down . . . ," the increasingly impatient voice intruded.

He didn't listen to the rest of her admonition. "Do the theatrics usually work with Mrs. Jones?" he asked the child, deciding on a nonchalant approach that generally shocked furious women into momentary silence.

At his unruffled response to her tantrum, Penelope fell quiet and stared, taken aback. Fitz crooked an eyebrow at her.

"While this is all very entertaining," the little hen behind him clucked, "you are preventing Cook from preparing dinner."

He winced at the reminder of the utter cake he was making of himself instead of impressing the household with his usual currency of sophistication and charm. Having been abandoned by the mail coach, they had nowhere else to go. Cheltenham and his prize stallion were still over a day's hard journey to the west.

The hen ducked down until Fitz was suddenly blinking into delectable blueberry-colored eyes rimmed with lush ginger lashes. A halo of strawberry curls framed dainty peach-and-cream cheeks. Whoa, why had she hidden such lusciousness beneath that ghastly bonnet? His gaze dropped to her ripe, cherry lips, and he nearly salivated as he inhaled the intoxicating scent of cinnamon and apples. He must be hungrier than he'd thought.

Ignoring him, she looked pointedly at Penelope and barked like a field sergeant instead of in the syrupy voice he'd anticipated. "Young lady, if you will refrain from caterwauling like an undisciplined hound, you may wash your hands and take a seat at the table."

Apparently expecting to be obeyed, the pint-sized Venus stood up, and her unfashionable but sensible ankle boots stalked away. Fitz stared back at his daughter. Over their heads, he could hear the exquisite little lady commanding her troops.

"Cook, I believe we will need your burn salve. And, sir"—she kicked his bootheel just in case he didn't realize he was the only man in the room—"if you will step outside for a moment, we will have a little talk while the salve is prepared."

"Just keep remembering, she eats sweets, not people," he whispered to Penelope before backing out to face his punishment.

3

After the way the elegant gentleman had stared at her as if she were a Christmas pudding and he a starving man, Abigail was too shaky to meet his eyes again. Perhaps her loneliness had simply conjured that look. It had felt entirely too good to be *seen* by a man for a change.

She threaded her fingers together against her apron and set her glare on the pearl pin with which he had fastened the folds of his neckcloth. He seemed even more dashing than the prince's friend the infamous Beau Brummell. And she had kicked his boots and admired his posterior!

She wanted to sink through the kitchen step, but she would not allow her insecurity to get the best of her. She had inherited her magistrate father's keen sense of duty but must work hard to find the courage to carry it through, especially now. A vaporish spinster would have no chance of reclaiming and properly raising four rambunctious children.

"Allow me to introduce myself," she said stiffly. "I am Abigail Merriweather, and this is my home." She had discarded her bonnet upon entering the kitchen, but now she wished she'd left it on. She'd had her unruly locks shorn when she'd lost patience with taming the frizz, assuming no one cared how she looked anyway. She feared the bonnet had left her curls squashed flat.

"My sincerest apologies for the behavior of myself and my daughter," the stranger responded in a mellow baritone that could melt her bones in the same way good organ music elevated her spirits. "As you may be able to tell, I am not accustomed to dealing with her."

The gentleman hesitated long enough for Abigail to wonder why and dare a glance upward. He was slicking his unruly forelock back from his high brow, and his sculpted features frowned as if he was as agitated as she. Or at least aware of the awkwardness. The gesture almost melted her resistance as well as her bones.

But instead of offering an honest admission of failure, he donned a deceptive smile of assurance designed, she was certain, to charm susceptible females. "I am called Jack Wyckerly, and my daughter is Penelope. I have just removed her from an unsuitable situation, and she is justifiably outraged at being taken from the only home she's ever known."

Abigail was having a hard time thinking straight while his green eyes lingered admiringly upon her. Men did not often look at her, much less with appreciation, so she did not believe his charm for an instant.

His plummy accents and stylish garb did not deceive her either. True aristocrats did not ride in mail coaches. Nor did they escort children about without nannies. Or leave them in *unsuitable situations.* Jack Wyckerly was a fraud, not a nobleman. At best, he might be an impoverished gentleman or a tradesman, which made him much easier for her to deal with.

Besides, his incompetent attempts to deal with the little girl invoked her protective instincts. She could not refuse her aid. "Children tire easily. She needs to be fed and put down for a nap."

"She does?" He blinked in astonishment. "She isn't a babe."

Oh, dear. The way his intelligent eyes lit with interest created an abnormally warm sensation in her breast. She focused on the unshaven whiskers shadowing his high-boned cheeks to remind herself of his deceit.

"Age matters only in the hours of sleep needed. Babies may slumber most of the day. Young children require as much as twelve hours or more each night. If you've been traveling, I wager she's not slept at all."

Fitz drove his hand through his hair, resisted admiring Miss Merriweather's bounteous bosom, and absorbed the interesting bit of knowledge she offered. "You mean, maybe Penelope doesn't hate me? She's just tired?" Oddly, for the first time in his selfish life, his daughter's opinion mattered. Losing his immediate family must have skewered his usual detachment.

"Oh, she may hate you," the adorable little hen said with equanimity. "I can't answer to that, not knowing what you have done to make her suffer. But children are very adaptable. They respond well to love and trust and security."

She spoke with the voice of experience, although he saw no evidence of any children about. Fitz desperately wanted to believe her, though. He needed a brief respite to order his thoughts and work out his next step. Aid with his hellion offspring would be appreciated.

He hated lying on general principle, and he was supposed to be learning responsibility, but he couldn't in all good conscience declare his true identity, not with bailiffs on his heels, and not until he'd worked out some financial solution that didn't involve Newgate.

"I seem to be in a bit of a pickle here."

Miss Merriweather's cheeks pinkened delightfully as she waited for him to express himself. He was always a sap for a pretty face, and the farmer miss was exceptionally adorable, especially when she tried to force her plump lips into a scowl. But he never preyed on the innocent, so he knew not to look at her as any more than a convenient reprieve from his difficulties.

"I have no experience in raising a child and wasn't prepared to take on Penelope just yet. My investments are currently . . . tied up." Well, he assumed the prize stallion waiting for him in Cheltenham had to be tied to a post occasionally, so that wasn't too much of a stretch. "I need some time to learn to deal with a child before we continue our journey."

And even though he'd only reached Oxfordshire, this remote farm looked like the end of the world to a city man like him, an excellent place to hide from creditors. He had traveled with Penny from Reading, not far from his ancestral ruins in Berkshire, and he'd already realized that even another day in a coach with his daughter would be a hair-raising, death-defying experience. Besides, he couldn't carry her on the stallion from far western England back to his estate southwest of London, even should he dare set foot there again without pockets full of gold.

He needed a place to leave Penelope while he retrieved his horse and sold it. He scarcely dared hope that providence had supplied such a miracle. He would study the situation instead of making another impulsive decision.

Miss Merriweather hesitated, as she had every good reason to do. Fitz wondered if there were any males about that he could speak with man to man, but even as vulnerable as the lady seemed, she didn't appear to answer to anyone. He was barely aware that such freedom for women existed, but that's what came of spending his life in the rarefied atmosphere of the city's upper echelons—the familiar society that he most strenuously wished to return to, if he could figure out how.

"I don't suppose you could put us up for a few days until Penelope learns to mind me?" he continued, forcing her decision.

"It would be very improper for you to stay in the house with me," she said, indirectly answering his question about men. "Even though we have a nursery that isn't currently in use."

Fitz tried to puzzle out the sadness that caused her pretty lips to droop, but he didn't want to distract her with too many questions. "Perhaps you have some chores that require a man's hand?" he asked, even though he knew his hand was skilled only with cards and women. "If Penelope could use the nursery, I could stay in your stable and earn my keep."

She looked skeptical. "I can't ask a gentleman to sleep in a stable. Don't be absurd. Do you know anything of estate management?"

How galling of her to nail his most damaging failing in a single stroke. Fitz cleared his throat and, under her impatient gaze, tried to look wise and knowledgeable. "I mostly leave management to others more qualified than I, but I would be happy to be of assistance."

"You would take orders from a woman?"

Fitz tugged at his neckcloth. He took orders from no one. Gritting his teeth, thinking of Penelope and turning new leaves, he did his best to look lofty. "I'm certain you know your grounds better than I do."

Had he just heard a feminine snort of disbelief? Quirking an eyebrow, he gazed down on her halo of sunset curls. How did a rural nonentity acquire the latest London hairstyle? At least she had returned to staring at his linen instead of giving him the evil eye.

"I'm certain I know my land better, too, since I have lived here all my life. For your daughter's sake, and against my better judgment, I will let you use the gardener's cottage behind the stable. It is only one room and not in good repair. There is little point in installing a bed for Penny just for a few days, so she may stay in the house. Everyone knows I've been searching for a head gardener, except they will not believe you are he while wearing those clothes."

He glanced down at his second-best frock coat, the one he'd hoped would impress his daughter with his importance. He'd looked quite the dandy when he'd set out yesterday. Penelope had promptly smeared meat-pie grease on his sleeve. And tea now stained the once pristine cuff of his good shirt. His scalded wrist still stung, but not so badly as his pride. He would have to retrieve his baggage from the roadway.

"I fear I have only my city coats with me," he admitted. Over the years, after paying the meager stipend for his daughter's upkeep, he'd invested his winnings on clothes and women and keeping a roof over his head. Appearance and family name were his entrée to the wealthy society from which he earned his upkeep, since the Danecroft estate had never provided an allowance for its spare heir.

"I'll see if I can alter a few of my father's clothes to fit," Miss Merriweather said, eyeing him thoughtfully. "Some garments were too old to give away to charity."

Lovely. Fitz tried not to roll his eyes at the thought of any other earl wearing a country bumpkin's discarded rags. He obviously hadn't achieved nobility yet.

"You will not regret your generosity, Miss Merriweather." And that was not a lie either. He had no good way of repaying her, but he had connections. He would think of something.

"That remains to be seen, Mr. Wyckerly. Come along, Cook should have that salve ready. I'll have someone show you to your quarters. Dinner is served at noon, supper at six. If Penelope does not object, I'll give her a bite to eat and show her to the nursery."

She marched off like a soldier to war. Fitz tried not to wonder what he was getting himself into, but the proper earl he must be still struggled with the predicament brought on by his former louselike existence.

"My little sister Jennifer likes this bed." After their meal, Abigail had led Penelope upstairs to the nursery, where she patted the quilted cover of a child's bed. She'd personally appliquéd the flowers and rabbits from Jennie's favorite old dresses. Penelope seemed to be studying them favorably.

"I'm not tired," the child said, hugging her ragged doll.

"Of course you're not. But if you hide up here with some picture books, your papa won't know where you are unless I tell him."

"Picture books?" Her gaze slid to the shelves stacked with slender volumes beneath the window seat.

Abigail opened a wardrobe, pretending not to watch the girl's every expression. She had been studying how children's minds worked since she was fifteen. At first, it had been only to keep her privacy from being invaded. But as she'd come to accept her stepmother, she'd gradually learned to love the joy and energy her half-siblings added to her father's household.

She swallowed her tears at the ache of their absence. In the past three years both her beloved father and stepmother had died. She could not—would not—accept any more losses.

"I think Jennie outgrew this frock. You might want to try it on later." She carefully laid out the pink and green sprigged muslin. "If that fits, I'm sure we can find others."

Standing on the braided rug in the middle of the room, Penelope looked torn between the books, the bed, and the pretty frock. Good. They would keep her occupied for a little while. Not expecting a reply from a distraught, tired little girl, Abigail reached for the door handle.

"Thank you," a small voice whispered.

Abigail smiled in relief that the child wasn't totally untutored. "You're welcome, Penelope. Have a nice rest."

She walked out—smack into a worn twill shirt and open waistcoat that she recognized as her father's. Except her father didn't have muscles so hard that she nearly bounced off them.

Flustered by her encounter with such overt masculinity, she stepped sideways while pulling the nursery door closed. "She should be asleep within minutes."

"Are you a professional nanny?" Mr. Wyckerly asked. He hadn't bothered fastening the worn leather waistcoat, as if he'd hurried to watch how she dealt with his daughter.

She would have smiled at his question had she not been so skittish at having a tall gentleman standing so close. "Four younger siblings," she murmured, trying to think of a polite way of maneuvering around his intimidating figure to reach the stairs. She could take the back steps to the kitchen, she supposed.

"When will they be coming home?"

A perfectly normal question, although his tone hinted at an unusual level of consternation that Abigail chose to ignore, just as she brushed off a reply that would only make her weep. "They're with their guardian now. Come along, the strawberry bed needs tending, and my tenant needs help with hoeing. I'll introduce you around."

She bustled down the hall, expecting him to follow.

He seemed to hesitate, but his long strides broke the silence of the upper hall as he hurried after her.

She wondered if Mr. Wyckerly might know any wealthy, unmarried solicitors who wouldn't mind acquiring an instant family.

4

"And this is the rhubarb bed," Miss Merriweather announced.

Bored, and uncomfortable in his uncouth attire, Fitz gazed at rows of thick, wrinkled leaves and tried to link them with his hostess's tone of admiration. "You grow weeds on purpose?" he asked, just to produce a reaction from the placid female. He'd offered smiles and charm and flattery during this tour of duty, and she'd yet to flap a flirtatious lash in his direction. Must be the clothes.

How daunting to think women admired him only for his dashing attire.

"Weeds?" Finally, she looked at him, but not with delight. "Have you never had rhubarb jelly? Or strawberry-rhubarb tarts? Or rhubarb relish? Or—"

He hastily interrupted the list of atrocious delicacies. "My pardon. I jested. I promise not to do that again."

She narrowed her eyes, possibly aware that he was having fun at her expense.

"Did you know that you have twelve freckles across your nose?" he asked, to distract her. "If you acquired a new one every two years, I could guess your age." They were adorable freckles, and if he were a true scoundrel, he'd wonder how many more he could count if he removed a few articles of her clothing. But he tried not to reveal that lascivious interest.

She covered her nose with her hand as if he might steal her freckles, then gave a huff of exasperation as she recognized his ploy. "I will leave you to tend the strawberry bed." She nodded at the neat rows of healthy plants on the far side of the fence. "I must walk into town, but Cook and the maids will keep an eye on your daughter."

He would rather walk to town than hoe a field. Fitz fiendishly sought any excuse to exchange tasks. "Is there a stationery shop? I have correspondence to keep up. I could walk into town after I'm done hoeing and save you a trip," he declared blithely, as if he weren't aware the shops would close before he could perform such feats of magic as hoe a field.

She glanced at what appeared to him to be pristine rows, then threaded her fingers in the nervous mannerism he'd noted earlier. She seemed to have two modes of speech—bossy or tongue-tied. She was an intriguing combination of conflicting traits that he would enjoy unraveling. A pity she was the rural sort. And not wealthy.

"It *is* late," she finally answered. "The shops will close shortly. Would you mind going now and delivering my letter to the inn while you are there? And pick up a packet of thread so I may take in the seams of some shirts for you."

He was a right, proper villain, but he'd wear even more of these disgusting garments if he could avoid revealing his incompetence at farming. "I would be delighted. And perhaps I could finish the field after supper."

The darkling look she bestowed upon him said he had not yet charmed her into believing his plumpers, which disgruntled him more. If he weren't currently dealing with the results of a prior error in judgment—namely, his daughter—he'd employ his considerable charm to win the little lady's heartfelt smiles. Unfortunately, wooing a farmer was not among the options a responsible earl could choose among.

"Give me a moment to freshen up, and I will be delighted to run your errands," he agreed with all sincerity.

Finding her guest waiting at the front door, looking more distinguished than her father had looked while wearing that tweed coat, Abigail handed Mr. Wyckerly a shilling for the thread and another letter addressed to her father's distant, aristocratic relation. Perhaps the first two letters had gone astray.

Perhaps a marquess could convince Mr. Greyson, the executor, that the children would be far better off in the home they knew than with distant cousins. Although she was none too certain a marquess would listen either. Her father really should have overseen the writing of his will himself instead of allowing a stiff-necked solicitor to do it, but admittedly, her father had not counted on dying so soon after his wife. He'd been too grief-stricken to consider the effect his death would have on a motherless household.

So, as usual, the consequences of her father's carelessness were now in her inadequate hands.

Mr. Wyckerly had rakishly tilted his borrowed leather cap, which added boyish appeal to match the twinkle in his eye. But the crinkles at the corners of those same eyes belied the boyishness, and he carried himself with the superiority of someone years older and more sophisticated than herself. At supper, she would have to question him more thoroughly.

"Do not forget that supper is at six," she said abruptly, then bit her tongue. She had no right to treat him with the familiarity of a family member.

He looked amused and a dash condescending—until he noted the address on her letter and his eyebrows disappeared under his hat. "The Marquess of Belden?"

She drew herself up as tall as she was able. "My father's second cousin on his grandmother's side." She owed him no explanation, but she did not like to give herself airs, pretending she frequented exalted circles.

When she did not say more, he looked dubious. "You realize the new marquess lives in Scotland, don't you?"

"The *new* marquess?" Her voice faltered.

"Old Chucklebottom died a few months back. Apoplexy, I heard. He had no immediate heir, so some distant branch inherited." He offered the letter back to her. "The dowager is still in London, if you would care to redirect it?"

"Chucklebottom?" she asked faintly. With plummeting hope and growing despair, she accepted the return of the epistle.

"Forgive the shallow humor. He was a dour old man. Shall I wait?"

Mr. Wyckerly knew London aristocrats well enough to use their nicknames! Somehow, that was not very reassuring.

Abigail crumpled the precious letter in her grip and shook her head. A woman, dowager marchioness or not, would not have the influence with Mr. Greyson to convince him to remove the children from their new guardian and return them to her. Whatever would she do now? "No, please, go on. I must compose a letter of consolation for his widow."

"I doubt the dowager mourns his passing. He left her in charge of his fortune, a source of much amazement at the time." He was laughing at her again, although he tried to hide it.

It must be exceedingly pleasant to be left a fortune. Perhaps the new widow had been too busy or griefstricken to answer her earlier letters. Abigail was immensely grateful that the farm had been part of her mother's dowry so that she would always have a home, but the estate of a marquess would be a great burden.

"London gossip is far more entertaining than that of my small village," she said quietly. "Thank you for bringing me up to date."

He tipped his cap, winked audaciously, and sauntered down the drive, a self-confident man in command of his corner of the world. Abigail wished she possessed that kind of assurance.

She carried the crumpled letter back to the study. She refused to let her lack of boldness hold her back. Closing the door, she rubbed fiercely at the tears in her eyes, while scanning the shelves for her father's family genealogy. She didn't know the name of his cousin's heir, but if she could find it, perhaps the new marquess would help her.

Did it matter that he lived in Scotland? Surely a marquess wielded influence no matter where he lived. Although—would he even know of her tiny branch of the family? At least her father had personally known his London cousin.

For the first time since the older couple the executor had appointed as guardians had arrived to take the children away, Abigail faced the possibility that her siblings might never return. Tears poured down her cheeks as she found the book she sought.

She would never give up trying to bring them home. Unfolding Tommy's last unhappy letter as incentive, she sat down with the list of family connections.

Hurrying into the village, Fitz brushed off the image of Rhubarb Girl's sad countenance. He was scarcely in a position to help himself, much less anyone else.

That he actually *desired* to help the prickly lady was incredible. Perhaps a tankard of ale would squelch that inclination.

But he was a man of his word, and he owed the lady labor in her field, even if he had no intention of doing it himself. Flipping the shilling she'd given him, he entered the rural tavern and perused the inhabitants, looking for a likely mark. The golden-haired young farmer with brawny shoulders should do.

Picking up his ale at the counter, Fitz took a seat not

far from the young man and spread his small array of coins across the table. Parlor tricks were child's play. He reserved his true genius for relieving the rich of their heavy pockets, but the wealthy were few and far between out here. His rural opponents would merely pay the price of entertainment.

He slid the coins about, rearranging the coppers and frowning as if in hopes that a different pattern would produce a greater sum. When he knew he had the farmer's attention, Fitz palmed a ha'penny and replaced it with the shilling in a sleight of hand he'd practiced since childhood. Chortling at his new wealth, he signaled the barkeep for more ale.

Looking around as if noticing his surroundings for the first time, Fitz smiled congenially and pointed at the farmer's empty mug. "And fill a round for the lad here. I'm feeling lucky today."

The barkeep shrugged and filled both mugs. "You didn't come in on the mail coach."

"We're visiting with Miss Merriweather," he said with a careless wave, as if he had a sister or wife accompanying him. "She has some need of assistance." Her idea to pass him off as a gardener wasn't credible, but if she had a marquess in the family, he could be a distant relation. He scattered the coppers across the table again and began rearranging them.

"Now that the young'uns are gone, she ought to marry up. Right fine land she has out there." The barkeep threw a knowing look at the blond farmer.

A crude giant and dainty Miss Rhubarb Girl? Had these people no eyes in their heads? Fitz hid his disapproval and pondered the reference to "young'uns." There was a mystery there. Had she been married and lost her children? No wonder she looked so sad!

"She's a tartar, that one," one of the older patrons commented, coming to stand beside the table to observe the moving coins. "She'd have a body working sunup to sundown."

"You'll remember you speak of my hostess," Fitz admonished genially, while shuddering at the thought of physical labor. "Anyone willing to wager I can turn copper to silver?"

"Don't take him up on it," the young farmer warned. "I just saw him do it."

The older man cuffed the younger. "Ain't possible to turn copper to silver, no more than you can turn wood to stone."

Fitz had arranged his coins in a circle with a large penny in the center. "Petrified wood becomes stone. Anything is possible." He gestured at the circle. "You just have to find the right combination of ingredients."

As his sleeve swept back to his tankard, the penny became a shilling again. The older man leaned over and tested the coin against the table, frowning.

"Betcha can't turn two of them," the farmer said cynically.

Fitz raised his eyebrows. He usually judged his marks well, but rural charm held hidden depths. "A challenge, excellent! That might take a few more coins, but we'll see what happens. Care to throw some in to speed the process?"

The lad added two ha'pennies, and the older man added three. An audience began to gather.

Fitz wanted to inquire more about his hostess, but if he meant to pass himself off as part of the family, he had to be more circumspect. "What's our wager, gentlemen? Miss Merry could use some help in her strawberry field. An hour of your time if I produce two silver coins? And a shilling to each of you if I don't?"

"Aye, that's fair," both men agreed.

Fitz calculated the minutes he'd have to spend playing games in return for the hours he could avoid spending in the fields and deemed the odds very fair, indeed.

"Papa forgot me," Penelope said, carrying her doll to the kitchen table, where Abigail helped her into a chair.

Abby feared Mr. Wyckerly might have more than forgotten the child. She feared he had absconded altogether. It took half an hour to walk into town, and it was now after six. He'd been gone half the afternoon.

"No, he forgot supper," she told the child, tying a towel around Penelope's neck to protect the pretty frock. "He will be very sorry when he goes to bed hungry."

The child regarded her through eyes far older than her years. "Papa forgot me forever. It is what papas do, Trudy says."

Oh, dear. Oh, double dear. She wanted to beat Mr. Wyckerly about the ears for his criminal neglect, but she was not naive. Gentleman of the *ton* expected armies of servants to care for their children, so perhaps instead of being a tradesman, he aspired to the fringes of the aristocracy. She'd met a few of the penniless young men at Oxford who had learned to pass themselves off as their betters.

She gulped and hoped her half-siblings' new guardians did not aspire to the *ton*. The children required the attention of more than servants. She had only Mr. Greyson's promises and one stilted meeting with the Weatherstons to reassure her that they would be respectable parents.

Perhaps if the strawberry crop was very good, she could earn a sufficient sum to take a coach to Surrey and visit. Tommy's letters of woe with Jennifer's scrawled addenda had been plaintive, but that did not mean they were being mistreated so much as they were homesick. She hoped.

"Fathers are often busy earning money to buy their daughters pretty frocks and sweets," Abigail replied matter-of-factly, scooping fresh spring peas onto the child's plate. "And sometimes it costs a great deal for the roof over our heads and good nannies."

"Not my papa." Penelope looked askance at the peas. "Mrs. Jones says I'm a bloody bastard and my papa is 'shamed of me."

Behind them, Cook and the scullery maid froze. Abigail removed the bowl of mashed potatoes from the maid and added a spoonful to the child's plate. "I believe you may have misunderstood. I'm sure she said he was ashamed of himself. Have you ever made a ship of your potatoes and populated it with little green people?"

"Green people?" Easily distracted, Penelope turned to her food.

Throughout supper Abigail alternated among wanting to box Mr. Wyckerly's ears, hoping to teach him to appreciate his daughter's worth, and fearing he would take Penelope away if she did either. The child obviously needed love and attention, and her dashing guest equally obviously did not know how to provide it.

She had worked herself into a state of high dudgeon by the time she tucked Penelope into bed, still with no sign of the miserable scoundrel's return.

5

"What are these letters in this drawer, Maynard?" Isabell Hoyt, the youthful Dowager Marchioness of Belden, ran her hand over stacks of yellowing correspondence, some neatly tied with disintegrating ribbon, others lying loose and unopened.

"That's the Poor Relations drawer, my lady," her late husband's assistant said with a sniff, showing no evidence of irony. A scarecrow of a man who'd worked with the marquess for years, he'd no doubt been hired for his lack of both imagination and humor.

"Yes, I daresay he had poor relations with anyone whose correspondence was left unopened for years," she mused, choosing to unfold a sheet that was less yellowed than the others.

"One cannot indulge all those who believe they are owed funds for no better reason than their name," Maynard intoned. "The estate would be bankrupt in days."

"Yes, Edward having such a large and prolific family," the dowager said with a hint of the irony that Maynard lacked. She glanced up from the heartfelt plea in her hand. "This one does not request funds. Did anyone even read this correspondence, Maynard?"

He tugged on his neckcloth. "Only if his lordship requested."

Which, of course, her gouty, miserable clutch-fist of a spouse had not. Really, she hoped Edward was having a good long talk with his Maker about now. The man may have been a charmer in his time, but age and illness—and possibly his infertile wife—had turned him into a bitter relic well before his death.

She glanced up at a polite scratch on the office door and sighed. "Yes, Butler?" She lived surrounded by irony. Her butler's name was Butler.

"The Honorable Lord Quentin Hoyt has arrived to offer his family's condolences."

"Dashitall." She stood and shook out her mourning gown. Dust blended nicely with the dove gray. "It took his family three months to send a representative down from Scotland?"

Maynard cleared his throat. When she glanced at him with annoyance, he lifted his invisible chin high so that his scrawny chicken wattles stretched above his collar. "I believe the Scots relations were the reason for the refusal to parcel out funds, my lady."

"Yes, of course, because they were poor and had many children and actually had reason to *need* funds, while Edward only needed his port. Yes, indeed, I understand that logic perfectly. I do hope the new marquess's heir is not carrying a dirk and broadsword."

"Younger son, my lady," Butler offered. "The new marquess and his heir are both still in Scotland. Lord Quentin is the fourth eldest of the ten children and does business in London."

She knew that. But she was feeling peevish, and she had every right to be as querulous as a dowager, since she was one, with all the privileges and honors that rank disposed—like having no man in her bed and no social life.

At the ripe old age of thirty-three, she hardly considered that fair, so she found her amusement where she could, though she supposed tormenting her servants wasn't a good habit to develop.

Her heels *click-clack*ed down hollow halls, following Butler to the front of her town residence. She owned all this now. She was possibly the wealthiest lady in all London to be fully in charge of her own fortune and future. After years of living under Edward's thumb, she found it a strange situation.

Edward had never allowed any of his distant relations inside his home. Perhaps she ought to learn if there was any reason for that, other than snobbery.

Lord Quentin stood hat in hand, his broad shoulders and height diminishing the narrow entrance. He appeared elegantly handsome and perfectly at ease inside the town house that would have belonged to his father had the Hoyt wealth been entailed. Which it was not. The title was merely attached to worthless hills in the north and the new marquess and his Scots family had inherited next to nothing.

The new marquess had waited a long time for the title. His younger son was older than Isabell and far more darkly handsome than Edward had ever been, but she was not enamored of ambitious men these days.

"Good afternoon, sir," she said crisply, leading the way into the formal parlor, the only room in the house that Edward had allowed her to decorate. She was fond of the gold damask draperies. The Persian rug with hints of gold and blue among the ivories and crimsons thoroughly satisfied her. The cost had nearly given dear Edward an apoplexy ten years before his time—perhaps the reason he'd never allowed her to decorate another room.

Lord Quentin possessed a full head of dark, windblown curls and a healthy bronze color that spoke of a life spent outdoors. Given the extreme poverty of his large Scots family, he'd had to work for a living, unlike his peers who preferred to exist like vampires, rising only when it was dark to frequent their clubs and stagger home at dawn. For his efforts, he'd been scorned by the *ton* and was seldom accepted in the best homes.

She had heard that he'd done extremely well at trade—shipping and mining and things in which she held no interest. Now that his family held the title, and Lord Quentin provided the coin, they would want to partake of the society that had scorned them.

Edward would roll over in his grave if she encouraged his poor relations, she decided with relish.

"I have come to offer my family's condolences, my lady," Lord Quentin said formally, following her into the feminine room and overpowering it with his size and masculinity.

"Very good." She tugged her skirt into place and settled on the crimson velvet settee. "I appreciate your vanquishing your grief for the sake of propriety, but please do not carry the hypocrisy too far. I am suffering a strong sense of irony today and cannot vouch for my behavior."

He didn't smile. She had hoped at least one Hoyt possessed a sense of humor. Oh well, tedious family traits would win out. She'd learned her lesson about admiring dashing men with no humor. They turned into controlling old misers who prized money more than people.

"I apologize for my tardiness in paying my respects," Lord Quentin said. "I have been away and have just come home to run afoul of mortality twice over. Edward was a decade younger than my father. His demise was unexpected. And I have also lost a good friend years younger than myself. It is a cruel reminder that life is short."

"Wasn't it Samuel Johnson who said *'Life is hell, and then we die'*? If he didn't, he should have." Isabell gestured at her hovering servant. "I believe Lord Quentin requires something stronger than tea, and I would not mind a brandy myself. And perhaps something a little more filling than pastry to go with it, please."

She'd hoped to shock her husband's relation with her tart tongue, but he was still squeezing his hat brim and looking into the distance as if he truly was affected by morbid sentiments. She'd heard he was a serious gentleman. One had to be as a younger son in a barefoot horde. Even choosing between the military or the priesthood, as most younger sons did, had to have been impossible, since he'd had no funds with which to build a career. That he'd dared to scorn tradition and take up trade had been a bold, and perhaps foolish, decision. Society frowned on men who actually *worked* for a living. So common, after all.

"I did not mean to burden you with my gloom, my lady. I apologize." Hoyt rose, as if preparing to leave.

"Sit down," she ordered. "I am trapped in this house day in and day out, doomed to listen to old biddies prosing and posturing, asking when I'll begin entertaining again. I haven't decided if I shall. I would appreciate some good, honest talk."

Politely, if rather absently, Lord Quentin returned to his seat, setting aside the hat he hadn't relinquished upon entering. His broad shoulders overwhelmed the slender chairback. "I am at your service, as ever, my lady."

He did not seem excessively appreciative that he was the first Hoyt outside of Edward's sisters to cross the threshold. Nor did he seem the obsequious type inclined to flatter her generosity. Annoying man. "Isabell. My name is Isabell. If we are to be friends, we must speak as equals."

"Are we to be friends?" he asked quizzically, rightfully so.

"I hold nothing against you or your family." She gestured as if waving away decades of old grudges. "Although I suppose you have every right to hate me. Do you?"

"Hate you?" He blinked, and for the first time since he'd entered, he actually focused on her. A decidedly male interest sharpened his dark gaze.

She preened, if only just a little. It had been a very long time since she'd felt like a woman, much less an attractive one. Perhaps she wouldn't bury herself in blacks and caps just yet. "My husband and I have not been considerate toward your family."

He shrugged. "You are the one who had to live with the curmudgeon all these years. You've earned your wealth the hard way."

She snorted indelicately. "On my back? Granted, it ended up that way, but I was young, foolish, and thought myself in love at first. Love is highly overrated."

"Possibly, but in our world, marriage can be beneficial in many ways. Your family gained from the marquess's connections."

"If saving my father from debtors' prison and shipping my younger sisters to the Americas can be called *gaining,* then I suppose your argument is correct. But I do not consider selling my soul for money a wise choice, particularly since I have not seen my family since."

He nodded his understanding. "But yours was an unusual situation, and you must admit, your current circumstances are better than they might have been otherwise. Had my friend Fitz found a lady of wealth, he might not have so readily committed the heroic deed of dying for the benefit of his estate." He returned to looking miserable.

"Fitz? The younger Wyckerly, you mean?" she asked, appalled. "The lovely gambler? I sincerely regret his loss, but the man never committed a heroic deed in his life." She gestured for Butler to set the tray down in front of her. "I find it hard to believe that he would die for anyone. Not that I find anything heroic in death."

"They discovered his clothing and a fired pistol beside the river on the grounds of his estate." Quentin swirled the brandy in the glass she handed him. "His father and brother were notorious wastrels, but Fitz always lived within his means. He must have despaired at being left an estate so mired in debt that he could not possibly have paid his way out in two lifetimes. I don't think it's a coincidence that his cousin and heir is a man of fortune. No, I believe the evidence speaks for itself. Fitz did the honorable thing. He took his own life for the sake of his tenants and creditors."

"Absolute balderdash. I daresay Danecroft's tenants or creditors shot him down as they may have his antecedents in hopes that someone with sense and money would inherit. Or given the family's general notoriety, perhaps his heir helped him depart this mortal coil. If memory serves me, his cousin Geoffrey has been courting a duke's daughter. Even a bankrupt title would sway the tide in his favor."

Like Lord Quentin, Geoffrey Wyckerly was also in trade. Without a title, he did not stand a chance as a prospect for any heiress among the *ton*.

Her guest possessed a refined air of intelligence and accomplishment as he considered her words. Isabell sat back and enjoyed the view. Now that she was wealthy and independent, perhaps she could start collecting cicisbei, as women did in her mother's time. She would have to take a good look at herself in the mirror one of these days, but she feared what little beauty she'd once possessed had faded with age and disillusionment.

"If Fitz was murdered, then we must discover the murderer," Quentin declared with a flash of outrage that was more pleasant to look upon than his earlier gloom.

"A blessing he wasn't married, or I'd suspect the wife."

Wrong thing to say. Quentin returned to his dismals. "I should have steered him toward the marriage mart, but he was doing fine on his own. I never anticipated that he'd inherit his family's mistakes so soon. Or at all."

Isabell rolled her eyes heavenward. "For pity's sake, do you hate women so much that you are determined to snare some poor innocent in your Machiavellian coils? Can you think of anyone who would be happy married to a feckless gambler? As you are well aware, I know whereof I speak. He'd run through her dowry and leave her barefoot and pregnant. It would take the wealth of a duke to save the Danecroft estate. I will miss Fitz's smile, but I would have shot him myself if he'd tried marrying for money."

Quentin set down his glass, and his lovely brandy-colored eyes flashed again. "Fitz was a good man burdened by circumstance. Someone needs to come to the aid of the younger sons who have been raised to live as idle nobility but left with no means of support."

Amused, Isabell sipped her brandy. "And you will find them all wealthy women to drag down with them?"

"If they are good women, they will provide a steadying effect, while their dowries would offer opportunities for advancement that young men need."

Isabell enjoyed his outrage, so she politely refrained from snorting. "If they are good women, I would rather see them keep their fortunes to make lives of their own choosing. Why do they need irresponsible, impoverished husbands?"

"So they won't become selfish harridans?" Snapping his hat back on his lovely curls, Lord Quentin stalked toward the door. "Instead of wasting time here, I shall look further into Fitz's death."

Oh, the man had a temper. She liked that. Showed spark, unlike Edward, who merely growled and closed the door when she expressed an opinion. "I don't think it at all selfish for women to look after themselves and their families as men look after their own!" she threw after him. "The misfortune is that we are even more limited than younger sons in the ways society will allow us to do it."

He halted in the doorway to glower at her. "Which is why women need men to take care of them! If Fitz had married well, he'd be doubling his wife's fortune by now, whereas a female would fritter it away on fripperies."

"I am female and I have no intention of frittering away my fortune on fripperies," Isabell exclaimed, feeling the excitement of a challenge for the first time in a very long while. "I will show you that women can manage their wealth wisely."

"How?" he asked cynically. "You have enough for ten lifetimes, so there is small chance you could squander it all."

Happily remembering the letter she'd just read, Isabell smiled. Saving innocent young women from Quentin's would-be predators suddenly seemed an excellent place to start. "I will give dowries to deserving young women so they may have the freedom to choose their own paths to happiness. I challenge you to find matches for your friends that can do the same."

His dark eyes bored fiercely into her. "I say your young women would be happier married to my friends. I accept your challenge."

"I will not see the dowries I provide go to your feckless friends, sir!"

A fiendish smile brightened his dark visage. "Would you care to make a wager?"

"I don't gamble," she said crossly. "That's a fool's game." To which her father had been addicted, much to the despair and cost of his wife and daughters.

"We'll exchange no money," he agreed. "If one of my friends marries one of your heiresses, you will agree to provide one of my younger sisters entrée to society and the wherewithal to do it in style."

She liked what little she'd seen of his sisters. Now that Edward wasn't there to object, she would have sought them out anyway, so she could scarcely lose. "Agreed," she said with a simpering smile. "But I warn you that I shall see my *heiresses,* as you style them, well prepared to fend off fortune hunters."

"My friends are *career* hunters. I wish you well of your silly heiresses." He tapped his hat and strode out.

Isabell felt exhilarated. She'd been left bored and

all alone for far too long. Lord Quentin had shown her that she needed a project to occupy her. She finished her sandwich, shook out her skirt, and marched back to the office. It was time someone helped her husband's neglected relations—the female ones.

6

Still wearing her robe, Abigail brushed out her curls, then touched her nose and wondered if Mr. Wyckerly had actually counted all her freckles. She didn't think it possible.

Even more irritated that she'd let her thoughts drift, she brushed harder. If she was to spend the rest of her life as a spinster, she must not be led astray by idle men.

She had never planned on being a spinster. Although her father was the least ambitious man she knew, he'd been generous and loving in his own way. She had thought if she could find a man with a little more purpose, she would be very happy married. Unfortunately, there were few interesting single men available in her limited surroundings.

So she'd fallen for the wonderful new vicar who had ambitions to rise higher than a small village. She would have made a fine vicar's wife. Men of the church were seldom wealthy, but she was good at pinching pennies. She was educated sufficiently to converse with the wives of bishops and squires. With some effort, she might have even learned to accept living in a town as large as Oxford. She would have made an excellent partner.

But then her father had died. And now she was losing hope. And patience.

She set down her hairbrush and rose to take off her robe. She was no longer a naive child who believed men would solve her problems. The law was such that she required their aid, but they weren't to be relied on in domestic matters.

Mr. Jack Wyckerly was certainly evidence of that. As far as she was aware, he'd never come back last night.

Setting her lips in a tight line to hold back her temper, she tugged a dowdy brown morning dress over her petticoat and tied the drawstrings. It seemed she would have to tend to her strawberry patch on her own. Perhaps she should meditate on how to save Penelope from her dastardly excuse of a father.

She took the back stairs down to the kitchen. Since the children had been removed from her *ineffectual female guidance*, she'd begun taking all her meals in the kitchen, where she at least had stoic Cook and shy Annie for company. They weren't great conversationalists, but they listened when she talked.

As Abigail entered the kitchen, Penelope squealed, and both child and kitten dived under the sideboard. A pretty pink gown and ruffled petticoat had been left out for her to wear, but it appeared that Penelope disdained petticoats. And her stockings were dirty enough to be yesterday's.

Abigail bent over to peer under the sturdy oak cabinet. "This kitten belongs in the stable with the others, Miss Penny."

"I know! I'm trying to catch him. Papa thought I'd like to play with him."

Rolling her eyes, Abigail scooped up the mewling runaway. Apparently the wayfaring stranger had found his way home sometime during the night—just long enough to disrupt the household, since there was no sign of him now.

A bowl of fresh strawberries and a pitcher of cream

waited on the table. The aroma of cooking ham made her stomach rumble in anticipation. But she couldn't eat until she'd straightened out Mr. Wyckerly. She'd tossed and turned all night, seething with fury at his neglect of his daughter, at his complete disregard for her fears—or for her shilling, for all that mattered. She *refused* to be treated as an insignificant female whose thoughts and concerns were of no relevance.

Carrying the squirming kitten, Abigail marched out the kitchen door. She had to assume her guest was up and about if he'd left a kitten for Penelope. The stable was empty since she'd sold the horses, but it was the first building in her path that might hide a man.

She entered to discover unfamiliar horses finishing off the last of the winter hay. Was that Billy's pony trying to chew his way out of his stall?

Confusion didn't eliminate her righteous anger. She let the kitten free and set out for the fields, primed for a showdown. Men who abandoned their children ought to be shot.

She found Wretched Wyckerly not hoeing her field but in the orchard, idling away his time by staring into an apple tree. Too angry to untie her tongue, she picked up a handful of small green apples and flung one at his broad back, clad only in a shirt. She didn't want to know what he'd done with her father's tweed coat or waistcoat. Probably sold them. The view of his muscled shoulders was practically indecent. She flung another apple as he turned to see who was pelting him.

He caught the second apple and juggled it from hand to hand while studying her with that infernally condescending look of puzzled amusement.

"Target practice?" he guessed. "Is there a prize for apple throwing at some rural festivity?"

She flung her third apple directly at his flat abdomen. If he would dress properly, she shouldn't be able to *see* that he did not have a soft, paunchy stomach hanging over his belt like most gentlemen she knew.

He was fortunate that the fallen apple hadn't rotted yet. It merely bounced off his taut muscles. His smile brightened.

"Good shot! May I suggest a smaller target next time—say that tailless rodent on the branch up there? I wager you can't hit him."

"That squirrel is my *friend*." She launched the last of her ammunition at his fat head, but he easily dodged the blow. "You, on the other hand, are a rotten, no-good scoundrel who deserves whipping."

He continued tossing his apple back and forth, pretending to ponder her accusations. His hair looked as rumpled as hers, but it fell in a handsome wave across his brow that gave him more appeal than a Roman god. She itched to run her fingers through the thick locks and push them from his eyes. Which made her even angrier.

"I don't doubt that I'm a scoundrel," he said with an appearance of thoughtfulness, "but I cannot see how I deserve whipping for missing my supper."

"Your daughter thought she'd been abandoned! *Again.*" She threw up her hands in disgust and wished for a dozen more apples. "You could have been *killed*, and we had no way of knowing it. You cannot promise to return, then disappear instead!"

He grimaced. "I didn't mean to cause concern. I was trying to be helpful."

"*Helpful?*" She would be shrieking like a hawk if she didn't recover her temper. Taking a deep breath as her stepmother had taught her, she squeezed her fingers into her palms and refrained from hunting down a hoe with which to bash some sense into his frivolous head. "In what world is disappearing for hours *helpful*?"

This time, she could swear he looked slightly embarrassed, but she refused to be fooled any longer. He might be lovely to look at, but so were stinging nettles.

"I am not accustomed to accounting to anyone for my time," he admitted. "If I caused undue distress, I sincerely apologize. But I brought you better labor than I would be." He gestured toward the strawberry field.

She had assigned him the strawberries because tending them was a woman's simple duty, and she assumed he couldn't do much damage to them. In his place, three strong men in shirtsleeves were hard at work.

She blinked in astonishment. That was Billy gathering the first fruits of the field. And Harry, the grocer, awkwardly hoeing grass from under the leaves. And ... she swallowed and shook her head in disbelief. John, the barkeep, setting runners into mounds?

"How did you persuade them to help?" she asked, incredulity replacing her tantrum. "Billy's so shy, he won't even speak to me."

"Golden boy?" Mr. Wyckerly studied his laborers. "He's the one telling the others what to do. He is enamored of you. He'd probably crawl through mud and eat bugs if you asked it of him, but I'd recommend leaving him his pride. Men need something to get them through the humiliations of their day. Sometimes pride is all we have."

Startled by such candor, she cast him a glance, but he seemed content to juggle his apple and study the work being done. She couldn't think of any conniving scheme that would benefit from his declaration, so she had to accept it at face value. For now.

"Pride is a pretty poor substitute for substance," she said. "Billy is two years younger than I am. He'll inherit his father's farm some day far in the future. In the meantime, he expends much energy arguing over how things should be done and sulking if he doesn't get his own way. He may grow up in time, but he has little to be proud of now."

Mr. Wyckerly nodded as if he understood. "We are not all of us born heroes, I fear. Women expect us to be wealthy and well-mannered and sophisticated. To be witty and thoughtful and honest. To be tender to children, loving to spouses and parents, and tough to bullies. Veritable saints, but . . ." He slanted her a look. "Pardon my bluntness, but women also expect us to be exciting, mysterious devils in the bedroom. Perhaps a contradiction?"

She blushed, not at all certain how to respond. No man had ever spoken to her in such . . . intimate . . . terms. Worse yet, he had to be speaking more of himself than poor Billy, who would never be witty or sophisticated. And now Mr. Wyckerly would have her thinking about what happened in beds, which was no doubt his intention. "I don't believe I should like mysterious and exciting," she announced. "I think I prefer honest and prompt."

He laughed. "That shows your inexperience, Miss Merriweather."

"I know myself fairly well, sir." She drew her spine straight and glared at him with hauteur. It wasn't as if she were entirely ignorant. She nodded at a rooster chasing a hen into the bushes. "I am not a silly city miss who is unaware of the inclinations of males of every species."

He turned to observe the rooster's mating behavior. "And here I thought myself more stallion than rooster," he said mournfully, belying the amusement firmly plastered to his sculpted lips. "I am crushed by your low opinion of me."

He didn't appear crushed. He appeared attractively confident, stirring adolescent desires that she'd thought she'd suppressed by now. Salivating over devilish good looks was a recipe for disaster.

"I have no more opinion of you than of a male donkey, Mr. Wyckerly. My concern is with your daughter." Or ought to be. His overly warm gaze and conversation stirred unwelcome thoughts. Why couldn't the mail coach have dumped a wealthy solicitor instead of a deceitful fribble on her lawn?

"I tried to apologize with the kitten," he said defensively.

"Children need to know that their fathers can be relied on far more than they need kittens or gifts. One cannot buy love, respect, or security. I trust you managed to buy my thread?"

"I did at that. I left it in the kitchen with the kitten."

"And how long will you have the able-bodied men of Chalkwick Abbey working on my strawberry field?"

He pinned her with a wary glare, finally grasping that she was on to his ploy to avoid physical labor, even if she didn't know how he'd accomplished it.

"An hour each," he said cautiously. "I did not want to be greedy, just useful."

"You are a very odd man, Mr. Wyckerly. Tell them to come up to the house for breakfast before they leave."

Uncomfortably aware that he was watching her, Abigail attempted to walk away at a sedate, ladylike pace, but she wouldn't have been female if she hadn't added just the slightest extra sway to her hips. Just to keep him looking.

7

After the laborers had completed their task in the fields, Fitz took Penelope for a walk and watched her race around the pond, quacking like the ducks she was chasing. Rather than ponder the intricacies of fatherhood, he wondered how much an acre of land could earn if planted in strawberries. If he estimated his father's estates at two hundred acres of arable land—he pulled a number out of the hat since he had no idea—earning ten pounds each a year, he could pay off a few hundred thousand in debt at one percent interest a year in ...

He did the math easily. He'd be old, dead, and moldering in his grave, and his heirs would still be paying their way out of the hole. He really ought to take Bibley's suggestion, fake his death, claim his stallion, hie off to the Americas, and let his wealthy cousin inherit the mess.

He would need to claim and sell his prize stud if he was to go anywhere. If he told the delectable Miss Merriweather that he was an earl, raising his insect self higher in her all-too-knowing eyes, perhaps he could even borrow fare to Cheltenham, where the stallion was housed. If she didn't know her own relation was dead, she probably hadn't heard the sordid tales about the notorious Danecroft earls. She might even think him noble.

He rather fancied the notion of the lovely pocket Venus gazing at him with the respect due an earl—instead of pelting him with apples and disgust. Perhaps she would even be amenable to a stolen kiss or two. Unfortunately, no matter how delicious stolen kisses sounded, they would be an extremely bad idea, since he hadn't had a woman in longer than he cared to remember. Unslaked lust was probably the reason he was drawn to a bossy little hen who would prefer to cackle and peck his insect carapace. Cancel any notion of kisses.

His daughter ran perilously close to the pond's edge, and he panicked at realizing that she probably couldn't swim. Neither could he. Loping in her direction and wondering how he would pull her out if she went under, he shouted, "Penny, get away from the pond!"

Of course, she instantly waded in, muddying her shoes and splashing on the edge, giving him shudders of sheer terror. Would he ever get the hang of this fathering business?

Probably not, he concluded, striding down to the water after her. There wasn't any profit in being a father. And if he was to keep Penny from starvation, he had to use his mathematical skills to generate profit during his every waking minute. Instead, he was wasting time wondering why his hostess thought he was a useless scoundrel and a jackass—he hadn't missed the male donkey reference—when every other woman he knew swooned at his feet.

Well, maybe not swooned, and maybe not *every* woman, but enough to convince him that the ladies thought him pretty and worth keeping around. But not Miss Merry. She thought he ought to have *substance*.

Squelching through the muddy quagmire, he retrieved his recalcitrant offspring. "Pretend you are a butterfly and flap your wings while I remove these wet shoes."

He threw her headfirst over his shoulder and let her scream and flap while he pried off her soaked shoes and stockings.

Just keeping them both in clean clothing would eat up what few coins he possessed. He was pathetically grateful to Miss Merry for supplying Penelope's attire now that he realized Mrs. Jones had neglected his daughter's wardrobe.

Which meant he had to take the lady's welfare into consideration as well as his own, dammit all.

"Butterflies don't roar," he reminded his daughter as they approached the quiet, pristine farmhouse.

At least he'd managed not to be late for what was apparently the highlight of the day—noon *dinner*. Not accustomed to using a servants' entrance, he carried Penelope in the front door and noted the elegant settings on the dining table. Silver and crystal sparkled in the sunlight pouring through the broad windows, and a bouquet of lilacs scented the air.

And he was filthy head to toe from Penny's kicking feet. "Upstairs and wash, my little duckling. Scrub all over and put on a pretty gown. And *petticoat*," he added sternly.

"Miss Abby doesn't mind if I'm dirty," she protested, her rebellious bottom lip emerging.

"She won't let a dirty duck sit on her nice chairs," he warned, nodding at the cream damask cushions.

He watched her race upstairs before he dashed back outside again. If they were to dine in state instead of the kitchen, he also needed to change. Keeping up appearances in a rural environment was a challenge. In London, he was normally just contemplating meeting the day at this hour.

Whom was he fooling by playing out here in pastoral splendor? He glanced down the drive. He had enough coin to gamble his way to Cheltenham if he didn't have to watch over Penny. Perhaps if he left a note explaining that he would return at the quickest possible moment . . . ?

The elegantly set dining table warned that he would not only crush the lady's expectations but also cement her disgust of him, and for some unfathomable reason, he didn't want Miss Merry to think less of him than she already did. He would leave after dinner. Perhaps he would even think of a good explanation for his departure.

Penny would bite him before listening to his excuses.

Uncomfortably—and damned inconveniently—aware that he'd just had several responsible thoughts, he had no idea what to make of them.

Abigail was scratching out another line in her plea to the new Marquess of Belden when she heard Mr. Wyckerly and his daughter enter. She almost smiled at the pounding of bare feet racing up the stairs. She had desperately missed that racket.

The letter to the marquess wasn't going well. How did one explain to a stranger that an unmarried, impoverished, rural female could better raise four young children than a wealthy older couple like the Weatherstons?

She watched out the study window as Mr. Wyckerly strode across the lawn toward the gardener's cottage. The diversion of setting the formal dining room with her family heirlooms had been more pleasant than her morose thoughts, but it had been vain of her to want to show off to a London gentleman.

Of course, she did not think he was a *real* gentleman, not the wealthy respectable sort, at least. Remembering his complaint about women expecting men to be heroes, she thought perhaps he might be a trifle sensitive about his lack. Unlike most of society, however, she did not care if he was in trade.

What if . . . ?

She shook her head to knock out that wholly ridiculous speculation, but once the notion lodged in her brain, it grew roots. She had so very few choices. . . .

What if Mr. Wyckerly was actually respectable enough

for the children's executor to accept him as their foster father?

Of course, she knew he was no such thing. Men who spoke of devils in bedrooms were far from decent. She capped her inkwell and stood up to prepare for dinner.

But what if the guardians the executor had chosen did not know how to be parents any better than Mr. Wyckerly? Perhaps they were already looking for any excuse to be rid of her noisy, mischievous brood. Even she must admit, her siblings weren't the best-behaved children in the world. After her stepmother died giving birth to the twins, her father had allowed them a great deal of freedom.

That thought was much too wayward. She knew nothing of Mr. Wyckerly except that he was a very bad, extremely awful father. No, far better that she visit the children and confirm for herself that they were safe and happy.

And if they weren't? She had so few options that she was grasping at straws.

In agitation, she glared into her bedroom mirror and attempted to tame her wispy curls. Earlier, she'd foolishly changed from her frumpy morning gown into a high-necked pink muslin that flattered her coloring. She would have to change again if she meant to carry a letter into town. The muslin was much too frail for anything except parlors. As an afterthought, she added a small rope of seed pearls her father had given her for her sixteenth birthday.

She felt decidedly overdressed as she stopped to check on Penelope. People in the country did not dress for their midday meal. It was foolish to do so, since there was always work to be done while the sun was up. It seemed equally foolish to dress up for soup and cold meats later. But she so seldom had a chance to wear this gown. . . .

"I don't like stockings," Penelope said defiantly when Abigail entered the nursery. She wore one crumpled white stocking twisted up to her knee. The other dangled from her fingers.

"Well, we could pretend you are a kitten who doesn't need shoes and feed you in the stable, but I think you'll like Cook's rhubarb tarts better than mice." Briskly, Abby straightened out the crooked knit stocking, tied the ribbon, then smoothly tugged on the other. "Perhaps you would like them better if the ribbons were pink?"

"I want to wear boots." Her lip still stuck out, but she didn't wiggle away when Abby buckled her into Jennifer's old shoes.

"Boots and pantaloons?" Abby suggested, taking the child's hand to help her jump off the bed. "I tried that once. I looked silly. I think one must be tall with long legs to wear boots."

Penelope eyed her disapprovingly. "Girls don't wear pantaloons."

"What if they did?" Abby asked, swinging the child's hand as they descended the stairs. "What if daddies wore dresses?"

Penelope was laughing at this fanciful notion as they reached the foyer and her father entered. Wearing a neatly folded—although not starched—neckcloth, bottle green cutaway, and yellow waistcoat over impeccable buff stockinet pantaloons, Mr. Wyckerly appeared as if he'd just stepped from a fashion plate.

Abby tried not to let her jaw drop in awe.

The gentleman seemed to be fighting the same inclination as he observed his daughter's laughter. "What a pretty pair you make," he declared. "I should like to have a painting of the two of you in your matching gowns and ribbons."

Astonishingly, his flattery actually made Abby feel feminine and attractive. She knew his words were mere gallantry, except—even her father had failed to notice that she'd made up these gowns so she and Jennifer would match.

"You are looking uncommonly elegant yourself," she

admitted with a flirtatious flutter of her lashes. It couldn't hurt to practice. "This is scarcely a London repast."

Mr. Wyckerly's dragon green eyes fastened on her, and he appeared momentarily taken by her coquetry, but he recovered rapidly. "Thank goodness," he said, shuddering with comic exaggeration. "City dinners are so *banal*. I far prefer this more exclusive society."

Even though she could have scarcely understood a word, Penelope giggled at her father's antics. "You look pretty, Papa."

"Will you stop hating me if I continue to look pretty?" he asked, widening his eyes hopefully and offering his arms to both of them, although he had to lean over to set Penny's hand in the crook of his elbow.

"Maybe," she agreed with all the solemn grace of a queen.

Their foolish byplay relieved Abby's nervousness at encountering the solid, ungiving muscle beneath his coat sleeve. Mr. Wyckerly was considerably taller and much more . . . physically developed . . . than the vicar. "I believe the two of you missed your calling. You should be on the stage."

"My little drama queen should be in theater," he agreed, seating Abby on the right-hand side of the table, "but the only stage I belong on is a coach." He pulled out a chair across from her for Penny, before taking the place at the head of the table between them.

Her father's place. How easily he usurped the position of head of household, even though he was no more than an encroaching guest. An appallingly attractive one whose subtle bay rum scent caused her to surreptitiously study the masculine stubble shadowing his jaw.

"A stagecoach?" she inquired casually, fearing the reference meant he planned to leave.

"A topic for another day." As Cook arrived with the soup tureen, he removed a letter from inside his coat. "A local delivered this as I was walking up to the door."

With suddenly shaky hands, Abby took the dirty,

wrinkled page. She smiled fondly at the sight of her half brother's scribbled penmanship. He didn't dip his ink often enough. It was a wonder anyone could read it.

Out of politeness, she ought to set it aside, but these letters were far too infrequent and precious for her to eat a bite until she was certain all was well.

"Go ahead. We will simply eat all this delicious soup while you read." Mr. Wyckerly gestured grandiosely before catching Penny's tilting spoon so soup didn't spill down her front.

He tucked a napkin into his daughter's gown while Abigail hastily scanned the scrawled note, then returned to the beginning and tried to read between the few lines. Tommy did not say enough. She needed to know if they ate well, if they had good tutors and were being taught manners. If their guardians were kind to them. So many things she needed to know . . .

Tears welled up in her eyes as she translated the few brief sentences. *How are you? We are well. Cissy ate a bug. Can we come home when I am eleven?*

Such simple words tore at her heart, and she couldn't prevent great heavy sobs from emerging. She rose hastily from the table and rushed to the front room to blow her nose in a lace-edged handkerchief.

A moment later, a much larger plain white linen square was held before her, and a solidly reassuring hand grasped her shoulder. "If there's any way I can help . . . ," he offered.

She wanted to crawl into Mr. Wyckerly's strong arms and pretend this devastatingly handsome man could wield a magic wand and return her world to normal. Instead, she used his linen to wipe her eyes. "It would take lawyers and courts, or a man of great influence, I fear. I am being silly. I'm sure they're fine. It's just—" She teared up and couldn't continue.

"You miss them," he said gravely, as if understanding.

She nodded and dabbed her eyes dry again. "They're

all I have left. I didn't think I was raising them badly. We aren't wealthy, I know, but we've never gone without. Only—"

"Someone took them away? Why?"

She took a deep breath, taking strength from his pragmatic question. Pity would have broken her, but Mr. Wyckerly seemed as bewildered as she had been.

"Because I'm not a man. Tommy will inherit my father's small estate. Mr. Greyson, the family lawyer who is in charge of the estate, thought it better if a childless couple raised them. He seemed to think he was doing me a favor, even though I have protested vehemently. Now he thinks I want Tommy's money!"

"Most generally, the child's executor must provide an allowance for the upkeep of the children. Is there some chance he wishes to keep those funds for himself?" he asked sensibly.

Returning Mr. Wyckerly's handkerchief, taking strength from knowing he did not agree with Mr. Greyson, Abby marched back to the dining room. Penny watched anxiously from the doorway, and Abby caught her hand, forcing a smile as she returned her to the table. "I am just missing my little brothers and sisters," she told the child. "Hop back in your chair before Cook's dumplings get cold."

She sank into the chair Mr. Wyckerly held for her. She couldn't eat a bite, but his masculine presence reassured her in ways she could not explain. She would dearly love a strong shoulder to cry on, but she wasn't one to indulge in fantasy. Knowing his shoulder was available was a kindness she hadn't expected, and it weakened her will.

"I have no reason to believe that Mr. Greyson means to do more than see the children suitably placed. My father wasn't a wealthy man. His income came from his father's trust. He made a few shrewd investments, and they provided us with some luxuries. The children's mother had a small dowry, nothing extravagant.

We would have fared fine. But I am not a man," she repeated bitterly.

It seemed Rhubarb Girl had problems as grim as his own and with equally little chance of solving them, because she was right, Fitz concluded glumly after seeing Penny in bed for her nap. Miss Merry was all feminine delicacy, and no right-minded male would believe her capable of raising four young children on her own. They wouldn't even believe she would *want* to. He certainly couldn't, not after one pint-sized hellion had given him multiple gray hairs in a few short days.

The superb strawberry-rhubarb pie he'd savored for dessert still tingled his tongue with sweet and tart as he returned downstairs, pondering solutions to their mutual dilemmas.

He wanted his daughter to be strong like the woman waiting at the bottom of the stairs. He knew Miss Merriweather was as worried as he was, but she wore competence around her like a cloak of invulnerability, while he groveled in ignorance.

His father and older brother had viewed book learning with distaste. They had believed riding the fields and talking to tenants provided sufficient knowledge of estate management, but as a younger son, Fitz had been left out of their activities and denied further instruction. He despised his lack of useful education.

"I want to show you my gratitude but don't know how," he said. He offered his arm and led her back to the table, where the maid had set out cups and saucers for tea. His hostess's head barely met his chin, and she glided so lightly beside him, he thought she must be made of air.

He was almost glad Miss Merry didn't wear the distractingly low bodices of the city, except the formless bit of cloth she covered herself with didn't do justice to what appeared to be an extravagant figure. One he shouldn't be admiring.

"You owe me nothing." She briefly squeezed his arm before he seated her at the table. "Your daughter has given me a welcome distraction, and you have provided information that might be of use. I think I will sell all the strawberries this year instead of preserving them so I might take a coach to Surrey to visit the children. Once I am assured they're well, everything will look better."

She was letting him off too easily—because she expected a man without the funds to properly care for his daughter to be nothing more than a bankrupt scoundrel. Fitz gritted his teeth against any protest. It wasn't as if she were wrong.

"Regardless of how it looks, I *can* help," he insisted. "I have friends in London. I could even borrow a private coach-and-four to take you to Surrey once I've solved my quandary of how to travel with my unruly daughter. Which I'll do shortly."

She looked up from her teacup with amusement. "Of course you will, as soon as you tame Penelope."

"Is that like saying as soon as I prove the moon is green cheese?" he asked in disgruntlement.

Her eyes danced, and Fitz almost made the mistake of falling into their cerulean depths. He had to remind himself that he did not have time for women unless they came accompanied by boundless wealth—and immense stupidity. Miss Merry did not qualify on either count.

Seeing no choice, he opted for bluntness. "I need to fetch a stallion in Cheltenham. I simply had not realized how perilous it would be to travel with Penny."

"Leaving her with an unqualified nanny was equally perilous," she pointed out. "But you are right. You have a lot to learn about children before you'll be able to travel safely with a child as strong-willed as your daughter."

"We're not known as a biddable family," he said gloomily.

Rhubarb Girl looked adorable considering his predicament when she had so many of her own problems to solve. She had a lusciously red, moist mouth that invited tasting as much as the strawberries she grew. The idea of kissing strawberry-flavored lips aroused him in unacceptable ways. The idea of her kissing him back . . .

It screamed of wedding bells and vows he couldn't make. There were reasons men and women shouldn't dine alone together, even with servants trotting in and out.

He discreetly adjusted his breeches and turned his gaze back to his tea.

"I don't suppose you count among your friends any powerful solicitor who might persuade the children's executor to return them to me?" she asked, her train of thought so far from his that it caught him by surprise.

"I know solicitors," he agreed warily. He was fairly certain the estate's solicitors would be biddable should he find the funds to pay them. The prestige of having an earl for a client inevitably influenced even the thorniest of lawyers into forgiveness. "I have friends who could give me the names of the best one."

She nodded thoughtfully. He could almost hear the gears of her mind spinning. That wasn't feminine interest behind her lovely blue stare, much as he would like to think it. He might long to run his hands through the enticing fluff of her strawberry curls, but he was starting to learn that countrywomen hid spiky spines of steel. Or this one did, at any rate.

Accustomed to the simpering ladies of the *ton*, he was uncomfortable with the knowledge—and intrigued. He waited with anticipation to see what conclusion she reached.

"If I agree to take care of Penny while you take care of your business in Cheltenham, is there some way I can legally bind you to find a good solicitor for me in return?"

He almost snorted out his tea. "Legally bind? As in an IOU for a solicitor?"

She studied him the same way he studied her—warily. "I would probably need documents declaring you intend to return for her and any other assurances that might be useful should you unexpectedly . . . not return. I would not wish the authorities to believe I've kidnapped her."

"No, of course not." He could barely swallow the lump in his throat. She regarded him as a termite so low that she thought he would *abandon* his daughter.

She was absolutely right to doubt him. It merely grated that this bit of fluff recognized the depths to which he'd burrowed. "I dislike leaving her," he said, honestly enough. "She doesn't deserve to be treated like that."

"I agree that she needs to know she won't be abandoned, so you would have to return quickly. Once you've established that you will always return, she will eventually accept that you must occasionally leave on business."

He nodded, not reassured yet seeing no other choice. He couldn't believe he was discussing his uncouth behavior with a lady of obvious gentility. A woman who was little more than a stranger to him. How could he think of leaving his daughter with a near stranger?

Yet he'd left her with Mrs. Jones for years, and they didn't come any stranger than that.

Swallowing the lump in his throat, he reached for his tea to wash down his doubts. "I will write any document you specify, Miss Merriweather, with the understanding that I will crucify you should anything happen to Penny."

Her smile brightened the room better than a dozen chandeliers.

8

"Penelope, no! Not the pigsty!" The morning after her uneasy accord with Mr. Wyckerly, Abigail dropped the chicken feed she was distributing to chase after her new charge. Penny was following the kitten into the hog enclosure. "It's dirty!"

As if Penny cared. The child tumbled over the fence and hit the filth on the other side, then valiantly picked herself up and stalked the wicked kitten, ignoring the unholy stench.

Abby gave the child credit for resilience and hoped Mr. Wyckerly had half as much. Obviously out of his depths with child rearing, he must learn to be both adaptable and firm to handle his daughter all by himself.

At Abigail's cry, Mr. Wyckerly dropped the basket of strawberries he was carrying in from the field. In a few long strides, he reached the sty and stared in dismay at his filthy offspring. "I think she's found her element," he said with exasperation.

Watching Penny fall to her knees and wallow in the mud with the animals, he yanked out his handkerchief and held it to his nose. "Come to think of it, she may just be reverting to her family origins."

Abigail laughed, then glanced mischievously at the snow-white cravat he'd persuaded Annie to scrub, starch, and press for him that morning. Earlier, Mr. Wyckerly had ascertained the mail coach schedule, and he was now dressed for his departure. He plainly enjoyed clean clothes and high fashion—neither of which was practical in rural abodes.

"Pigs are extremely intelligent creatures," she told him. "They know mud packs are good for their complexions. But our hog does not have a pleasant disposition. We need to pry Penelope out of there before he becomes territorial." She glanced expectantly at Mr. Wyckerly.

He glared back. "At what point does she become your duty?"

"When you leave," she arbitrarily decided. "This is my best morning gown. I can't go out there."

"Penelope!" he roared, in apparent optimism that his daughter would listen. "Get your skinny posterior out of there before a hog eats you."

"He'll eat Kitty!" she called back, intent on her pursuit.

"Well, at least she answered." Abigail added a positive note to his scowling curse.

Muttering, Mr. Wyckerly leaned against the fence to tug off his polished boots. Abigail watched in horrified fascination as he peeled off his stockings next, revealing long white feet, and . . . she gulped. Hairy, well-shaped calves.

He rolled up his pantaloons to his knees, cast off his coat and waistcoat, and then, with a look of regret, neatly untied his neckcloth, laying it carefully over the other garments on the grass, well out of reach of the filthy pigsty.

Abigail thought she may have stopped breathing. If she'd ever seen a man stripped to naught but short breeches and shirt, she couldn't remember it. And she would have remembered had the man looked as superb as this one did.

Smelling of strawberries and woodsy shaving soap, without benefit of his elegant attire, Mr. Wyckerly was all raw male. His open shirt revealed a curl of manly hair on a wide, muscled chest. His shoulders bulged at the seams of his patched cotton shirt. Powerful arm and thigh muscles surged as he climbed the fence and reluctantly lowered his bare feet into the filth.

Abby was in a state of captivation over her guest's well-shaped *posterior* when the clatter of carriage wheels and squeak of harness rattled up the drive, startling her back to the real world.

The last time a carriage had arrived at the house, it had been the Weatherstons to pick up the children.

The racket jarred the half-asleep hog into waking. "Watch out, Mr. Wyckerly!" she shouted before abandoning him to his fate.

In heart-thumping excitement, she picked up her skirt and raced for a glimpse of the vehicle rolling around to the front. She doubted anyone in all Oxfordshire, short of the Duke of Marlborough, owned a polished berlin and matching carriage horses. Someone must be bringing the children to visit, thank all the heavens!

The elegant berlin drew up to the front steps. The gold crest on its door caused her to stumble, but the thought of seeing the children again overcame her trepidation. Let London society scorn her lack of sophistication. No one could love the children more than she did.

"Penelope!" At the wild male cry of fear and fury emanating from behind her, Abigail skidded to a halt. She glanced over her shoulder in time to see Mr. Wyckerly grab for his daughter and the kitten just as the hog charged.

"Oh, botheration!" Switching directions, she ran back to the fence, and caught Penelope and her kitten as Mr. Wyckerly swung the pair over. With his hands free, her guest scrambled onto the rails just as the hog butted the back of his knees.

With a shout of surprise, he fell sideways into the muck.

Penelope wiggled, and Abigail set her smelly charge on her feet, while clinging to her hand so she could not escape again. She held her breath until Mr. Wyckerly stood up. As he vaulted the fence in a powerful surge of muscle, she sighed in relief. He was dripping filth, smelling of hog feces, and scowling at his daughter as if he'd heave Penny back into the sty when a melodic feminine voice called from the drive.

"How very bucolic, Danecroft. I see you have finally found your proper milieu."

Danecroft?

In startlement, Abigail swung to confront the new arrival.

Wiping his face with one of the cleaner patches of his filthy shirt, mentally grinding the hog's snout into sausage and calculating the price per pound for pork, Fitz regarded the Marchioness of Belden with frustration. He'd almost got clean away. It was his cursed bad luck that society should come calling before he could escape.

He didn't know Lady Belden well, but he knew not to count on the dowager to leave him with any secrets. Discovering an earl in a pigsty was simply too juicy a bit of gossip. Once she notified all London of his whereabouts, he was a doomed man. Apprehensively, he glanced behind her just to be certain she hadn't led bailiffs and half his London creditors to him.

No bailiffs, but Miss Merriweather had frozen in place, still clutching Penelope's hand.

"It appears one of your letters to the late marquess has been answered," he muttered, standing at a discreet distance, since he reeked of pig filth.

His normally tart-tongued hostess fell speechless as the slender marchioness advanced across the lawn in a cloud of expensive French perfume, trailing delicate, pleated muslin skirts of blue gray, and wearing a ridiculously useless navy velvet spencer that matched the ribbons of her bonnet. The lady had obviously tired of wearing heavy mourning and was amusing herself by skirting propriety.

"My lady," he replied, offering a muddy bow that would have graced the best parlors—except for his bare knees and lack of proper attire.

Abigail dipped a curtsy beside him. He'd never seen Rhubarb Girl forget her manners, but she didn't smooth over the awkward scene with explanations as would most females of his acquaintance. Was he now in *her* black books, too? He'd thought he'd behaved cleverly and responsibly by fishing his daughter from danger. He'd expected to be lavished with praise, but both women were ignoring him.

"Introductions, Danecroft," the marchioness demanded.

With a heavy sigh of regret, Fitz whispered in his daughter's ear, "Take the kitten back to Cook and tell her she has guests who will appreciate her rhubarb tarts. Tell her I said you could have one, too, even if you are a nasty little pig."

Penelope slipped from Miss Merry's hold, and raced for the house before Fitz was forced to introduce her as well. He didn't expect the approaching confrontation to be pleasant, and the child may as well be out of it.

"Lady Belden, may I present the estimable Miss Abigail Merriweather, my hostess. Miss Merriweather, I believe I mentioned the dowager marchioness to you."

Abigail made another stiff curtsy but said nothing.

"Very prettily done, my lord," the dowager said with obvious sarcasm. "You do realize all of London believes you dead?"

It was his turn to be shocked into silence. *Dead?* What the devil had Bibley done? Fitz had specifically told the old man not to play the fraud. He wanted to be a *responsible* Wyckerly, not a wicked one. He glared at the blasted woman for dashing his few fragile hopes of escaping to retrieve his stallion and turned to a very pale Miss Merry, who seemed about to faint.

"I can explain," he hastily told her. "Not about the dead part, but the rest." He caught her elbow but she shook him off. Bad sign. He turned back to the Machiavellian marchioness, who was gloating over the gossip fodder he was providing. "Since I am very much alive and intend to stay that way, why would anyone think I'm dead?"

"Because your gun and clothing were found on the bank of the Thames where it runs through your estate." Isabell displayed all her dainty teeth in a broad smile. "Your heir has gone into hiding and your friends are devastated."

"The fools think I *killed* myself? They think so little of me?" He didn't have to ask *why* anyone would set up a scene of suicide, since Bibley had already proposed it as a means of escaping his creditors and wasn't always scrupulous about following orders. And if Geoff had any idea of the estate's condition, he couldn't blame his cousin for hiding. But he couldn't believe his friends hadn't beaten the river looking for him, knowing he would never be so henhearted as to take the easy way out.

"Well, now that you are found"—she glanced at the pigsty—"in all your glory, I'm sure you can correct their error. What interests me is why you would be dallying with my husband's little cousin."

Miss Merriweather paled even further, if that was possible. He could see the freckles across the bridge of her nose despite the shadow of her bonnet. Where before she had laughed and treated him as a friend, now she eased away from him. Rejecting her rejection, Fitz firmly placed Abigail's chilled fingers on his shirtsleeve, and started toward the house. Only then did he remember his sleeve was filth-caked—but she continued to cling to it anyway. For once, the damned woman was acting as fragile as she looked. He didn't think he liked it.

"Miss Merriweather has been generous enough to offer me her guest cottage while I recover from the shock of George's death," he said blithely to the mar-

chioness, who had wisely taken her footman's arm and
preceded them, upwind from his stench. Fitz's mind
raced fast and furiously. He didn't want to compromise
the generous farm girl who had given him hope when
he'd despaired, but he wasn't at all certain that explaining Miss Merriweather merely cared for Penelope was
the best decision either. He stalled for time.

"I regret that it took me so long to respond to your
plea, dear, but Fitz is not a solution. He is up a tree with
nary a feather to fly with," the marchioness politely informed her *cousin*. "There are bailiffs on his doorstep.
You can do much better than him."

"The children?" Abigail finally whispered, watching
her aristocratic guest with hope.

Fitz bit back his amusement at her immediate dismissal of his embarrassing situation. Naturally, she focused on her main concern. Unlike most of society, she
knew children were more important than philandering
no-accounts.

"I'm sure your young relations are fine. I've sent my
man of business to check on them. I apologize for taking
so long to settle my late husband's estate, but his death
was sudden, and I wasn't prepared."

"Lady Bell can outmaneuver a general," Fitz whispered into Miss Merry's ear, trying to warn her, although
he had no idea of what.

"I am sorry for your loss, my lady," Abigail murmured,
ignoring his aside but still steadying herself on his arm.

He was covered in pig filth, but it was the back of his
neck that itched in discomfort as he realized she was so
shaken that she was actually relying on his support. He
wasn't accustomed to supporting anyone but himself.
And Penelope.

"Well, my loss is your gain," the marchioness said
cheerfully, examining the neat brick house and trim
beds of ivy and yew surrounding it. "Edward has left you
a substantial inheritance. I've come to take you under
my wing until you've decided how best to use it."

"Inheritance?" Abigail whispered, shocked. "What kind of inheritance?"

Her fingers gripped Fitz's arm so tightly that he could feel the pressure in his bones, but he also felt relief. She didn't need his aid after all! How large an inheritance? And was he a complete ass for wondering?

The marchioness swept through the doorway as if she owned the place, aiming directly for the drawing room and taking the best chair by the hearth. "A monetary one, of course. Approximately a thousand pounds a year."

An extravagant sum, but still insufficient for his needs, Fitz acknowledged with regret.

"You will stay with me while we purchase your wardrobe," the marchioness continued. "The season has already begun, but I'm sure we have time to introduce you. It will require time and planning to find someone suitable to take your claim to the children to court."

She cast Fitz a glance, reminding him that he was no such thing. And she was right. He wasn't suitable to take care of the one child he already had, much less four more.

Reluctantly, he escorted his stunned hostess to the other hearthside chair. He needed to find Penny and be on his way. He couldn't leave his friends believing him dead. But where could he go with a small child?

"I only wish to have the children home," Abigail replied faintly, finally recovering her voice.

"Nonsense," the marchioness said firmly. "First, you will see the larger world outside this pitiful one to which you've been confined. An heiress cannot make uninformed decisions. You will need to consult with my man of business and learn about investments. You will need to meet the people who can help you make decisions. If it becomes necessary to take the children's executor to court, you may need a husband who will stand up and claim them. I'm here to tell you that money will not solve everything."

It would solve a damned lot, Fitz thought, but he could see the lady's point—and that Miss Merriweather no longer had need of his connections, not when she had the wealthy marchioness on her side.

Better to consider his own predicament. Now that his hiding place had been revealed, all London would know his whereabouts. He had to return and face the music. And the bailiffs. And the creditors. And whoever in hell had planned to make him look suicidal.

Had Bibley really thought Fitz would take the escape his fraudulent death offered? Possibly. Fitz had had a great-uncle return from the dead once. It had been a source of much amusement over the dinner table when Tobias Wyckerly had returned from years in darkest Africa to find his supposed widow married to another man. But surely Bibley would not have gone against Fitz's express wishes—unless he'd felt pressured by unforeseen circumstances.

Geoff's ambitious branch of the family had taught his cousin to appreciate an extravagant lifestyle. Had Geoff decided to add a title to his wealth by taking advantage of Bibley's suggestion of fraud?

In any case, Miss Merriweather would retrieve her young relations much easier without a Wicked Wyckerly tarnishing her reputation.

9

"Fitz is a gallant blade of the first order," the marchioness murmured in Abigail's ear as she poured the tea, "but like so many younger sons of society, his pockets are to let."

Abigail didn't care about pockets or blades. Aside from learning of her incredible fortune, she was still reeling from learning that her handsome, elegant guest was on familiar terms with a *marchioness*. Had she known Mr. Wyckerly was actually a respectable part of the London *ton*, she would never have been able to stutter a word in his presence. And she'd asked him to pick her strawberries!

Mr. Wyckerly—or Danecroft, or whoever he was— had refused to sit down in his filthy clothes and had made his excuses earlier, abandoning her to this elegant lady's machinations. Abby supposed she deserved to be abandoned, but she stupidly missed his reassuring bows and gallantries that eased communication between the lady and her own simple self. Mostly, she needed his charm and presence to shield her while she contemplated the enormity of what the lady had told her. She needed time to think things through. She didn't respond well to surprises.

Inheritance? Her father's distant cousin had remembered *her*?

"Are you certain that I was named in the will?" she asked tentatively, because too much weighed on the answer, and she could not afford to be backward. "Isn't it more likely he remembered my father, and it would go to Tommy?"

"No," the lady said firmly. "The amount was specifically set aside for females of the family. I regret that we were not introduced earlier."

Abby's heart thudded in her chest. Surely a thousand pounds would allow her to hire a solicitor? She didn't care about society's seasons or new wardrobes. She was country born and bred, with no training for the beau monde. All she wanted was to reclaim the children.

The possibility that she might have to *marry* some stranger before she could have the children terrified her. Surely, that wouldn't be necessary now?

She didn't know how to express her doubts to the self-confident woman complacently occupying her dull front room. The marchioness had sweeping dark eyebrows that rose and fell with her volatile temper. She wore her rich chestnut hair in an elegant chignon pinned with what appeared to be small sapphires. Her blue eyes smiled, so she did not seem unfriendly, although Abby detected a hint of sadness in their depths.

She thought the lady might have character, but the marchioness disguised it well with city mannerisms, sipping her tea and haughtily observing her surroundings.

"Mr. Wyckerly has been helpful," Abby said, returning to their earlier topic, defending him for no reason except that she didn't know what else to say. He'd waded into a *pigsty* after his daughter. She didn't know many men who would do that.

The marchioness's rouged lips curved and a soft chuckle escaped them. "He is that. The dinner-table stories I'll tell of the *ton*'s most charming Corinthian consorting with pigs will be well worth the journey. Fitz's survival has depended on his being helpful to the right people. I must remember to call him Danecroft, although it's hard to. His father and brother were such dull clods, they should have buried the title with them."

"Title?" Abigail felt like a parrot. Perhaps too many surprises at once had bludgeoned her wits.

"Earl of Danecroft, m'dear." The grand lady looked on her with a dash of pity for her rural ignorance. "He's just come rather suddenly into his family's bankrupt estate. But enough of him. We must get to know each other better so I can judge the best gentlemen for you to meet."

An *earl*. She'd let an earl muck about in her pigsty. She'd given him what amounted to a storage shed to sleep in these last few nights! An earl's daughter had been bathing in her kitchen. Abigail wondered if she could excuse herself to go bash her head against a wall, but she decided it was not her fault if an earl had decided to make a fool of her by arriving incognito. From the start, she'd known he was a deceiving charmer, so she wasn't a complete idiot. Only a partial one.

"Is marriage my only choice?" she finally found the wit to ask. "Couldn't I just consult a solicitor?"

The marchioness frowned and tapped her teacup impatiently. "I gather from your letters that your main concern is retrieving the children, is it not?"

Abigail nodded.

"Then unless we can find evidence that your father's executor or the children's guardians are incompetent, you must prove that the children will have the proper guidance of a man before there is any possibility whatsoever of reclaiming them. It's how the world works."

The lady was right, of course. And honest, which gave her hope that she might trust her. The lady had arrived in a carriage with a crest, unlike deceptive Mr. Wyckerly, who'd been thrown off a mail coach. She knew about Abigail's letters to the marquess. She knew Mr. Wyckerly— Lord Danecroft—and he knew her. Abby couldn't find anything to distrust except her own remarkable good fortune. And if the lady could help her reclaim the children, how could she not do everything within her power to do so? Wasn't this exactly what she'd prayed would happen—that a wealthy, titled person would come to her aid?

"Of course, we will have my man of business investigate the children's circumstances," Lady Belden continued, "but in the meantime, you should prepare yourself for a battle. It helps to have powerful allies, and all the better if they're men. For that, we will need to spruce you up."

The lady observed Abigail with a critical eye until Abby was ready to squirm in her seat. She didn't know whether she liked the marchioness. She was simply attempting to digest her abrupt change in circumstance. She had spent her entire life in Chalkwick Abbey. She did not know how to go about elsewhere. And the thought of trusting this stranger to teach her . . .

"Good bosom. You must display it to better effect," the marchioness announced. "Your hair is all wrong, but I'll have my hairdresser fashion it for you. With the proper headdress, no one will notice the unsuitable color. You're well past the ingenue stage, so I think we can dismiss white and dress you in colors," she said with all the power and authority of an aristocrat. "You'll do just fine."

Abigail didn't want to do fine. She didn't want to go to London. But recalling Tommy's pleas, she knew she would do whatever it took to make her siblings happy again. She straightened her shoulders and sipped her tea as if she were in perfect agreement.

She would faint dead away when she reached the privacy of her room.

"You will do splendidly in London," Fitz said with false joviality as maids scurried to and fro, packing Miss Merry's bags under the curt commands of the marchioness in the upper hall.

Even standing there in shock, Miss Merry managed to bleed him with her glare. "I trust all London isn't filled with lying earls, then. I have an unfortunate tendency to believe people are who they say they are."

"I didn't lie to you," he protested. "I've been an earl for less than a week. And I'm dashed uncomfortable with it."

She relented enough to scan the kitchen doorway for some sign of Penelope, who had grown miraculously quiet after screaming foul curses during yet another bath.

"I'm sorry for the loss of your family," she said. "I know how difficult that is. I hope you find someone suitable to look after your daughter. She deserves a good home."

Fitz would rather she bled him with glares than twist a knife in his heart as she was doing now. "I have no choice but to take her to London with me while I straighten out the gossip mill. It might be convenient to be dead, and perhaps my heir and tenants might wish it so, but contrary to your belief, I do not lie."

She nodded absently. "Lies of omission don't count in your world, I suppose. Do you have any relations who might help you with Penelope?"

He snorted and tapped his thigh impatiently. She was the most annoying prig of a female. "If you demand complete and open honesty, then I must point out to you that Penelope is the result of an illicit liaison and won't be welcome in the homes of what few relations might still claim me as family."

"Her mother . . . ?" his prim hostess inquired without any sign of condemnation for his wayward youth.

"Was an actress who married well and moved to the Continent," he said more sharply than he'd intended. It was still hard to believe he'd ever been so young and desperate as to believe in love when all evidence was to the contrary. "Penny has never known her."

"That's her mother's loss, then," Miss Merry said in apparent disapproval of Penny's mother. "If I had a choice, I would be happy to look after her, but for now it seems my future lies in hands other than my own."

He ought to despise her rural bluntness. He certainly resented her backing out of their agreement for her to take Penny while he claimed his stallion. But had he been she, he would have done the same. They were in accord on one point—the children had to come first. "You give me hope that there are other sane, sensible women who will think the same as you. I don't believe I'm qualified to cope with Penelope on my own." And he hadn't the funds to hire anyone. He hid his desperation behind a smile.

The marchioness swept down the stairs, trailing a maid, a groom, and her carriage driver carrying band-boxes and trunks. "Most of these clothes are outdated and will have to go to your maids later, but they're good quality and will suffice for now. If we leave immediately, we can be in Oxford before dark and in London by tomorrow. Fitz, are you traveling with us?"

He'd rather be gnawed to death by rabbits. Nevertheless, he bowed gallantly. "If you would be so gracious as to accept our company, I would be delighted."

"*Our* company?" Although she was half a head shorter than he, Isabell managed to convey the impression of looking disapprovingly down on him. She'd seen Penelope earlier but had no reason to recognize her.

The patter of little feet arrived just in time. Fitz grinned and turned to the imp racing down the corridor, green eyes wide with interest. Her hair had been braided while still wet, but already the unruly forelock was escaping. He didn't know where Abigail's efficient servants kept finding new clothes for her, but Penelope was now properly garbed in pretty cloth slippers that matched her spring green muslin. She even wore a frilly petticoat and a lacy white scarf that would no doubt be smudged with snot and her luncheon within the hour.

"My lady, my daughter, Penelope. Can you make a curtsy, Penny?"

He nearly crowed with pride when she performed a perfectly correct bob of respect.

"I want to go with Miss Abby," the pestilence demanded the instant she stood straight again. She was a Wyckerly—staying silent wasn't in her nature. Fitz lifted his eyebrow to the dowager but didn't voice the challenge.

"As my niece says, this just gets interestinger and interestinger." The marchioness glanced from Fitz to Penny, confirming the likeness, and shook her head in disapproval. "I thought you smarter than that. Oh well, come along, then, we will be a merry party."

Feeling as if he rode to his doom by returning to London, where Newgate and creditors awaited, Fitz lifted Penny to his shoulder and followed the ladies out to the oversized berlin.

He glanced at Miss Merriweather, who appeared to be doing her best imitation of a doorlatch. He'd rather hear her laughing with joy at her newfound fortune. Instead, she looked pale and frozen. And still she bussed her weeping maid on the cheek, quietly gave instructions to her cook, and climbed into the berlin without a word of protest.

He wanted to growl and tell her that she needn't listen to Isabell if she didn't want to go to London. But Miss Merry's unusual timidity wasn't any of his business.

He had approximately a day and a half to figure out how to hire a solicitor without money, and dodge bailiffs and Newgate until he could sell his stud, while taking care of a six-year-old diva.

When all was said and done, being dead held a certain peaceful appeal.

Late the following day, the berlin rumbled down London's Oxford Street and turned into an older section just outside of Mayfair where once elegant townhomes now appeared to lean tiredly against one another. A sedan chair carrying an old woman wearing the powdered wig of another era plodded slowly in front of the weary horses.

All the way through town, Abigail had gawked at the tall buildings they passed. They'd traversed streets packed with carriages, wagons, scurrying servants, and idle gentlemen. She'd seen monumental edifices she was certain would have encompassed all of Chalkwick Abbey. Holding Penelope in her lap, she pressed her face to the window just like the child. Penny clung to her doll, and a book she'd taken from the nursery, but she'd not once looked at either.

The lumbering coach maneuvered down a street no wider than an alley, and Abby covered Penny's ears as a street urchin shook his fist and cursed a leaking fish wagon. When the carriage halted in front of a narrow brick house with blank, dark windows, she glanced over at Mr. Wyckerly—*Lord Danecroft*. He looked exceedingly elegant in his cutaway coat, pantaloons, Hessians, and tall city hat. She should have known he was an earl just from his attire. But the earl wasn't looking very happy to be home.

No housekeepers had hung lanterns out the windows in this dark neighborhood. No mourning wreath adorned the house's faded front door, and no knocker indicated the family was at home. A precariously leaning rail scarcely protected passersby from falling down the stairway to the kitchen. Leaves and other debris littered the filthy stairs up to the main floor. Penelope still looked fascinated.

"No bailiffs on the doorstep," the marchioness said gaily. "Talk to Lord Quentin first, Fitz. He was bemoaning your demise and castigating himself for not aiding you sooner."

The new earl appeared surprised to hear that, but he nodded silently, all his gallant charm submerged in this crash with reality.

Abigail wanted to catch his sleeve and urge him to go home with them, to a place filled with light and servants and warmth, but he was an impoverished earl who needed to marry great wealth, and she was a nobody. She knew better than to plant her hopes for the future on him, but she hated the idea of never seeing him again.

"Have someone bring Penny to see me sometime, please?" she whispered as the driver opened the door.

Lord Danecroft donned a cheerful smile and lifted his daughter from her lap. "We are most grateful for your generous hospitality, Miss Merriweather. I'm sure we'll see you soon."

"Want Miss Abby!" Penelope said threateningly when it became apparent that Abigail didn't intend to leave the carriage with them. The child hugged the book to her thin chest as if someone might take it from her.

"I think you get to pick your own bedroom, Miss Penny," Abby called to her as Lord Danecroft leaped out. "Find a pretty one, then look to see if there's a good place in the kitchen for a kitten!"

"Don't wanna!" Penny cried as the berlin began to roll away.

Abigail dabbed her eyes with her handkerchief and waved out the window for as long as she could see them. It appeared the earl had no servants to open the door for him. Her last glimpse was of his tall, wide-shouldered figure carrying a screaming, kicking Penny down the kitchen stairs.

10

Hanging on to a struggling Penny, Fitz braced his shoulders against the crumbling stairwell and slammed his boot against the rotting kitchen door. The whole damned panel fell inside. It wasn't as if anyone had ever given him the keys to his own home, and it was a trifle late in the day to hunt down the family lawyers.

Even Penny fell silent in awe at the damage he had caused.

"This is what Wicked Wyckerlys do, my girl," he said cheerfully, walking over the fallen door and setting her down so he could hunt for a candle stub in the growing darkness. "I had a cousin once whose wife ran off with the keys. They say he crushed every locked door in the house. I've always wondered if that was possible or just a tale. Guess we know now."

He was actually glad to have the child with him. He hadn't set foot in the earl's town house since he'd turned seventeen and his father, having learned about the funds Fitz had saved from his gambling, insisted that Fitz hand them over, claiming real Wyckerlys didn't need books. Apparently real Wyckerlys needed a wine cellar more than an education.

Fitz told himself he would never have made a scholar anyway. Professor Fitz, moldering away in the mathematical department, wouldn't have suited him. It had been far simpler to find his own rooms, gamble for a living, and stay away from the dissolute sots he called family.

He could understand why Geoff's branch of the family would give his a wide berth. The earls would only hit the tradesmen up for loans. Then renege on them.

And now the sots were all gone, and the house echoed with their ghosts. He didn't think his father or brother had lived here anytime recently. The place should have been rented out long ago—just one of many examples of the family's selfish incompetence. He'd no doubt find a crumbling lease agreement amid the debris of neglected paperwork in the estate office. Surely the family solicitors would have attempted to earn income off a valuable asset, if only to ensure their own payment.

Fitz lit a candle stub, found another, and lit it, too. A rat scurried into hiding. Dark shapes skittered up walls and under baseboards. No decent cook would come near this kitchen. His fascination with entomology did not lean toward *living* with roaches.

He should have taken Penny to the rooms he rented, but they were on the third floor of a tenement in a far less respectable area of the city. And creditors probably slept on the doorstep. At least no one had thought to look for him in this long-deserted property.

It was a far cry from Miss Abigail's clean and cozy home, but at least he now knew what cozy ought to look like. "Don't touch anything, Penny," he warned as he carried in their bags, then raised and braced the door with bars to hold it in place.

"Want Miss Abby," his little charmer replied, sticking out her flexible lower lip and clinging to the purloined book the lady had gracefully called a gift. He could scarcely condemn his daughter for stealing books, since he'd done the same in his youth.

Fitz wanted Miss Abby, too, but probably not in the same way Penny meant. He wanted Miss Abby's laughter and her sensible voice telling him his home would simply need a little work. And then he wanted to take her fairy figure up to bed and find solace in her jolly bosom. Damned good thing he wasn't a rake. "What would Miss Abby do if she saw this mess?" he asked, more of himself than of Penny.

"Say *'Ooo, yuck,'*" Penny answered.

Fitz laughed. "You are absolutely correct, my precious. Let us see how much *ooo yuck*ing we must say before we find a place to lay our heads. Grab that broom over there. I fear we'll need to fight for our claim to the beds."

Apparently delighted with an opportunity to wreak mayhem, Penny set down her few belongings to grab the broom and whack anything that moved in her path. And some shadows that didn't. He hadn't begot any squeamish, insipid miss, but a warrior child. Idiotic pride swelled in his chest.

Fitz led the way up the stairs, sweeping aside cobwebs with his hat and stomping anything that looked like a cockroach. He'd seen cleaner homes in the stews of Seven Dials. The last servant must have abandoned the place over a decade ago.

Upstairs, anything that could be sold had been. Even the lighter-colored areas where paintings had once hung were now coated in a thick layer of London soot. The expensive satin wall covering of some prior generation hung in tatters, rotted by age and damp. The house had been in the family since before Mayfair had first been developed in the late sixteen hundreds. The Wyckerlys had acquired an earldom shortly after that, in reward for their successful piracy, which had filled the king's coffers.

It would cost another fortune to repair the place sufficiently to rent it out. It was a pity piracy was frowned upon these days.

At least they'd eaten not long before they'd arrived here. All he had to do was find a bed that was not too bug-ridden for Penny to sleep in. In the morning, he would seek out Quentin and see if he would accept the prize stud's papers as collateral. Quentin was a businessman, not a gambler or a horseman, but he was good for a properly secured loan.

With a little exploration Fitz discovered that the linen closet was empty. The beds had apparently been sold, too, all except the king's bed that was too huge to be moved without removing walls. Charlie Stuart had reportedly slept in it, probably with half a dozen women. The first Earl of Danecroft had gained his title from scandalous royalty. The passive, boring Hanovers had dismissed the Wyckerlys as frivolous. Imagine that.

The mattress on the king's bed had been made of doeskin, practically bug proof. Fitz threw his coat over it and wadded his waistcoat into a pillow. "No napping," he told his daughter as she wandered around the room, swatting at shadows. "I absolutely forbid you to lie down and sleep until I say so."

His little contrarian glared at him suspiciously. "Miss Abby says I'm supposed to take naps."

"Well, I'm not Miss Abby. I say you need to swat roaches and clean cobwebs for another hour or two."

"Will not! I wanna nap!"

"If you nap, it better not be for more than half an hour," he warned, calling on the threatening tone that had raised his hackles and made him rebel when tutors had tried it.

"I'll nap as long as I want!" she shouted back, climbing up on the bed and snuggling down into his coat.

"Then don't you dare take those shoes off!"

She promptly sat up, took off her shoes and stockings, and threw them on the floor. And then she wiggled out of her petticoat and skirt, leaving on only her bodice and chemise. "So there!" She crawled into his coat again.

Bemused at his success, Fitz swept her garments off

the filthy floor, folded them, and set them inside an armoire that was equally too large to cart off. He didn't think Miss Merry would approve of child rearing that invited open rebellion, but his daughter was a Wyckerly. No one ever followed orders in his family. Defiance seemed to light their wicks. A point to ponder some other time when he was feeling philosophical. For now, he had to plot his survival.

Abigail was too tired and nervous to do more than gape at crystal chandeliers, marble floors, silk wall coverings, and indecent statues that belonged in museums as she traversed the halls of the marchioness's townhome to the guest room she'd been assigned. The dowager had departed on some matter of business, leaving her guest in the hands of silent, well-trained servants.

She might as well be sleeping in a museum. Gilt-framed oil paintings covered the walls of the bedchamber to which they'd taken her. An old-fashioned Chippendale table served as a writing desk, adorned with onyx and gilded inkstand and pens. Heavy maroon velvet draperies guarded her tester bed from nonexistent breezes. The stuffy air stank of coal smoke seeping beneath the mullioned windows. An immense floral carpet adorned the wooden floor, and a maid in crisp white mobcap with dangling ribbons dropped striped maroon and green draperies over the windows to enhance the vaultlike effect.

A brass bed lamp illuminated a marble-topped dressing table and a gilded wall mirror. Two more maids shook out her clothes, folded them, and placed them in a tall cherry armoire.

She was surrounded by bustling servants, yet felt all alone.

And scared, although she would not admit that even to herself. She would walk deserts and swim oceans to see the children. Elegant loneliness was luxury in comparison.

"We breakfast at ten, ma'am," the housekeeper informed her after shooing the maids from the room. "Would you like hot chocolate before then?" At Abby's tongue-tied nod, the servant curtsied and slipped out, closing the door behind her.

Left alone, Abigail opened the drawer of the writing table, found stationery, and sat down to write to the children. She had to be very careful not to raise their hopes too much—or her own—but the first thing she must do was to let them know where to find her.

Our cousin the Marchioness of Belden has agreed to help us. I am staying with her in London while her man of business checks on you. I hope very much to find a way to see you soon. I am sending all my love and kisses, so everyone remember me until I arrive.

She folded, sealed, and addressed the letter. She didn't know if a dowager marchioness could frank it, but she assumed not. Perhaps the lady would know someone who could. Abby wasn't certain how many miles it was to Surrey, so she couldn't calculate the postage, but she hated for the children to have to find the pennies to pay the cost when it arrived.

Her one duty done, she glanced around her elegant prison and her heart raced in trepidation. Could this be real? Had she truly inherited enough money to hope she could hire a solicitor?

And if so, how long would it take before the children might be returned to her, and she could revert to her familiar routines?

Perhaps she could worry about how Lord Danecroft and Penelope were faring.

She'd dined with an *earl*. After that, she should be able to survive anything society presented.

Lord Quentin Hoyt, younger son of the recently installed fourth Marquess of Belden, was the man of substance that Fitz had never been. Although Quentin was only a few years older, Fitz tried not to fidget in his imposing presence when he and Penny were granted entrance to Hoyt's study the next morning.

Fitz's skill at talking commerce was nonexistent, but he knew he must present a businesslike demeanor while making his case to a man with the education and determination to have acquired a fortune in shipping and industry over the past few years. But keeping an eye on Penelope as she wandered the limits of Hoyt's study tested Fitz's concentration.

Lord Quentin was a large man, known at Gentleman Jackson's for his methodical technique of pummeling his opponents until they surrendered. He'd expressed momentary shock and relief when Fitz had been introduced from the dead, but he wasn't given to conveying more than polite curiosity at the best of times.

He didn't raise his voice or tap his fingers now as he listened to Fitz's explanations. With any other man, Fitz could have leaned back in the chair and offered a cigar, a wink, and a blithe tale, and he would have been satisfied. Not Quentin.

Besides, Fitz had too much respect for the man to give him anything less than the truth.

"So you told your servant that you were going to pick up the stallion, and he knew perfectly well that you were alive?" Quentin steepled his fingers and looked thoughtful.

"Bibley's an old family retainer who probably hasn't been paid in a century. I daresay he no longer takes orders from us but captains his own ship. Perhaps he hoped to convince Geoff that he was heir and liable for wages."

As if to confirm Fitz's ruminations, Quentin nodded. "I've met your cousin through a few trade associations. Seems a sensible man, but his tastes are on the lavish side, and he's a little too aware of his consequence. I heard he applied for admission to Almack's when we thought you dead."

Thunderation. The bastard was celebrating Fitz's death by joining the fashionable party set? That was execrable even for a Wyckerly.

Because of an old feud, Fitz's family and Geoff's had never been close. They traveled in different circles, but he'd never heard that his cousin was an encroaching mushroom, mooching off the family name, what there was of it. Was there any chance Fitz's absence had given Geoff ideas? If he and Bibley had plotted together . . . Bibley would most certainly have taken Geoff's suggestions if money was involved. The butler liked his creature comforts.

"Encouraging honesty was never high on my family's scale of virtues," Fitz said, dismissing speculation until he could investigate further.

Quentin snorted. "Your *family's* virtues might be lacking, but you could have charmed Lady Bell into lying for you, disappeared for a year, and stuck your cousin with the title's woes until you were ready to return. The temptation to do so even now must be tremendous."

With a weary sigh, Fitz rose from the comfortable leather chair and crossed the room to pry Penelope off a shelf. He clapped a hand over her mouth before she could emit any epithets, and scanned the shelves until he found the book he wanted.

He handed Penny a large portfolio of colored lithographs of birds and set her beside his chair. "As you can see, I have acquired a complication. She is the main reason I'm here. I need funds to hire a good governess and decent rooms while I straighten out my affairs. I can give you the bill of sale on the stud as collateral, but I cannot tell you how soon I can pay you back."

Quentin drew his eyebrows down in thought, and Fitz quailed at the prospect of his request being rejected. He couldn't take Penny into the gambling hells where he earned his living. He couldn't take her into the ballrooms where he needed to woo and win an heiress. He was developing some understanding of why widowers with children often married in haste.

"Why the devil didn't you leave her where she was?"

Fitz had asked himself that a dozen times, and always came up with the same answer. "I had no choice. After the funeral, I had to travel north through Reading on my way to pick up the stallion. So I stopped to give her nanny her monthly fee and check on how Penny was faring. I had some foolish notion that once I had some funds, I may as well bring her back to the estate and pay one of the servants for her care. But I found her locked in a corncrib, crying and screaming, while Mrs. Jones tippled and dawdled with her gentleman caller. I fear I behaved badly."

He'd nearly destroyed the room in a fit of temper. Had he the wherewithal, he'd have removed all the children the woman kept, including her own. Instead, he'd left the nanny quivering in her shoes in fear of every authority Fitz had summoned. Her charges would have watchdogs now, and the gentleman caller wouldn't be returning.

Quentin gave another inelegant snort, this one apparently of approval. "Temper is a bad habit, but I see the justification. Since all London has heard of your demise, what are the chances that your cousin will object to your rising from the dead?"

"I hadn't given it any consideration," Fitz acknowledged. "Both my brother and father were young enough to marry and have sons, had they lived. The odds of Geoff inheriting have always been slight. He had no expectations until this past week. If I had any choice, I'd hand him title, estates, and the whole rats' nest and walk away."

"A pity death is the only means of doing so." Quentin rocked his chair back and regarded Fitz with sympathy. "I'll keep mum if you want to sail away and never return, but I'll never sit still for it if you decide to reclaim your title once your cousin straightens out your affairs."

Fitz thrust his hand through the unruly hank of hair falling in his face. "You tempt me, I'll admit." He glanced down at Penelope. "But I just can't do it. I have friends of sorts, and a few elderly female relations. To fake my death would mean lying to them all, as well as to the servants and tenants. I suppose I'm a villain for placing my pride over my tenants' welfare, but I just can't give up without trying. If it ultimately comes down to faking my death or facing starvation, I would at least like to know that I did my best."

Quentin nodded and stood to remove a painting from the shelf behind him, revealing a small wall safe. "I told Isabell I regretted not investing in my friends, and she all but laughed in my face. Let's find you an heiress and prove to the lady that all we younger sons need is an influx of cash and an opportunity to make our way in the world."

Fitz hid his surprise that anything the mischievous marchioness had said might affect a hardheaded businessman like Hoyt. He himself certainly wasn't one to scorn a soft spot for a pretty face. He actually missed Rhubarb Girl's calming pragmatism, but he'd overcome sentimentality before. He could do it again. Penny and the estate were his priorities.

He took the bill of sale for the stud from his coat pocket and exchanged it for the heavy purse of coins that Hoyt handed him.

"I have two marriageable younger sisters," Quentin said casually, "and four nieces coming along. You couldn't find better elsewhere, although their dowries are modest compared to your needs. Still, between them, they know every female in town. We'll have you sorted out by next week."

"Have you booked some wager with Lady Bell on how fast you can marry me off?" Fitz asked, trying to sound nonchalant but feeling as nervous as a cat in a kennel.

Quentin laughed off his suggestion, leaving Fitz to assume the man never gambled.

He could be married by the end of the month. He

glanced down at Penelope, who had just smeared a dirty thumbprint on the picture she was admiring. Was she worth it?

He had no idea, but unlike the mess his father and brother had left him, he'd begot her, she was his responsibility, and he would show the world that there was one Wyckerly who knew what duty meant.

And duty meant seeking the largest dowry at the least cost, which left out the intriguing Miss Merry's thousand pounds and her expensive battle to acquire four young hellions that he couldn't afford.

He wished life calculations were as simple as mathematical ones.

11

Pretending to be sweet and complacent was taking its toll on Abigail's limited patience. After days of chafing under the marchioness's constant flow of commands, she had begun wearing a locket containing wisps of the twins' baby hair to remind her why she must listen to the lady and not go haring back to Oxfordshire.

"The apricot sarcenet for the lining under the lemon yellow georgette," the marchioness decided, fingering the fabrics the modiste presented. "With the yellow ribbons and no lace."

Abby added up the cost of the fragile, impractical gown and forced a smile, trying to appear as if she squandered such riches every day. Since the bills were being charged to an account in her name, she would be fortunate to have a dowry left by the time the dowager tired of spending it. "I really think I should learn the expense of the solicitor first," she demurred as the modiste scurried off to find a different bolt of silk. "I will never wear these gowns after this season. It seems a waste."

"Nonsense. Experience is never wasted. You must see life to know what you want of it. I refuse to let you incarcerate yourself in rural oblivion with four young heathens until you have experienced the world beyond your limited horizons."

They'd had this same argument in different variations for days. Now that Abigail was appropriately attired in a fashionable walking gown, boots, and bonnet, the marchioness had finally allowed her out in public. Abby had hoped that meant she might finally visit the lawyer, but apparently it only meant she could acquire more clothing.

She fiddled with her artfully coiffed curls and glanced down at the long lines of her new gown that—along with the heels on her new boots—almost made her appear tall and slender instead of short and frumpy. Under her hostess's discriminating eye, she'd been transformed. She loved the femininity of pretty heels and soft gloves, but they were scarcely sensible.

"I am not the frivolous sort," she reminded her hostess again. It was very forward of her to argue with her betters, she knew, but polite demurrals had not worked. Nothing seemed to anger or deter the lady.

"Buried in the country as you were, you had no opportunity to discover what sort you are. Believe me when I say you would come to regret that." The marchioness waved a dismissive hand. "We will have the report on the children this afternoon. Then we may decide how to proceed. In the meantime, you will need evening gloves to go with the ball gown and proper lingerie. Come along."

The horrible part was that Abigail suspected her hostess was right. She had no experience. She gaped like a hayseed at the gaslights going up in Pall Mall, at Gunter's ices, and at high-perch phaetons rolling behind prancing, matched horses.

How could she be expected to navigate the narrow paths of society to deal with executors and solicitors, or find a man who could do so, if she didn't learn to walk bravely in the marchioness's world? She wasn't certain how far she could stretch her inheritance, but she knew she was being offered an opportunity beyond her dreams.

She had no desire to visit Almack's or ballrooms or rub elbows with nobility—especially if they were all as autocratic as the delicate dowager—but she *would* love to take the children walking along the Serpentine, or to see the lions in the Tower.

She was too ignorant to even know what to do if she ran into the earl. Curtsy? It seemed odd after she'd loaned him her father's clothes. She longed to know how Penelope fared. That Danecroft had not made good his promise to visit in these last four days had hurt her far more than it should. She'd hoped to have one friend in town. But to think of an earl as a friend was probably presumptuous.

They were preparing to cross a busy intersection to visit still another milliner when Abby heard her name being called in familiar childish excitement. Pulse accelerating, she glanced behind her, looking for broad shoulders in a bottle green coat, certain she would see Lord Danecroft's handsome presence well before she could find tiny Penny in this crowd.

Instead, she heard shouted curses and a neighing horse, and froze in horror as she watched Penny dash into the busy street. The marchioness grabbed Abby's arm and dragged her back onto the walk before she could dart into the road after the child.

At the same time, a familiar long-legged gentleman in black and gray loped between carriages and wagons, grabbed his irrepressible daughter, and reached the curb with no more than mud splattered on his polished boots.

Once she could breathe again in relief, Abby was so happy to see Danecroft that she almost imagined the earl's eyes lit with equal pleasure. But he quickly recovered, properly setting his daughter back on her feet, removing his hat, and making a dashing bow before the marchioness, without acknowledging Abigail's elegant transformation.

"My lady!" he called as if he had discovered gold. "It is a true pleasure to see you again." Only then did he turn to Abby and let a flicker of appreciation appear as his gaze traversed her high-waisted periwinkle blue gown. "Miss Merriweather, I trust you are enjoying your visit to our fair city?" He sounded as formal as if they'd only just met.

His gaze lingered a shade too long on the tight fit of the spencer over her breasts, and she quivered, not knowing how to react. The marchioness wore an identical garment, and he hadn't seemed to notice. But otherwise he was being so very proper. . . .

"At least there are no pigsties." She spoke as she might have at home. Then biting her tongue, she retreated to comfortable routine by crouching down to hug Penny while hiding her reaction to the pain in her chest. She was, indeed, extremely foolish to think a farmer's daughter could be *friends* with an earl.

"You must not cross the street without looking both ways and holding your papa's hand," she scolded, hugging the child. "I almost had a failure of the heart. And look what you have done to your pretty shoes!"

Penny glanced down at her kid slippers and shrugged. "I don't like shoes. Papa says I am to have a nursemaid. I'm too big for a nursemaid."

The child was quite right. She needed a governess. But it wasn't Abby's place to say so. She stood and raised a questioning eyebrow, just in case this aristocratic stranger wished to explain. She might be reticent in unfamiliar situations, but she wasn't shy. Danecroft wore his suit of mourning with all the panache she would never possess, right down to the pearl stickpin she remembered first admiring, but he still didn't know what was best for his daughter.

The earl shrugged in the same careless manner as

Penny. "Governesses require rooms and servants, who require more rooms. All very tedious."

He had an entire town house full of rooms—and no money. Abby nodded, fighting the urge to offer aid, for Penny's sake. She could hire a cook *and* a governess for the cost of the gown and accessories she'd just bought.

"I hear Quentin has snared you into escorting his legion of female relations," the marchioness said blithely. "They have no wealth. You can do better."

"I'll inquire at Tattersall's as to the price of a good earl these days," Danecroft responded with smiling archness.

"A stud with a pedigree like yours surely will bring a handsome price," Lady Belden cooed.

Abby winced. She truly disliked society's habit of demeaning one another in the name of wit, but apparently this was how the *ton* communicated. She gritted her teeth and remained silent.

"The Hoyt chits are acting as my secretaries, sorting through the unusual flood of invitations. It seems my charming presence has suddenly become fashionable."

Abby heard soul-deep irony behind that observation and wondered if he could be callous enough to accept a society that appreciated him only for his title—and wouldn't want his daughter at all.

Unaffected by Danecroft's caustic tone, the marchioness laughed.

Leaving the two elegant aristocrats to flirt and exchange insults, Abby retied Penny's bonnet ribbons and tucked her braids inside her pelisse. She was concerned for the child, that was all. Why should she consider the earl's feelings when he had refined, wealthy ladies at his beck and call? It didn't matter one jot to her that he could be escorting elegant beauties to balls and soirees. A fortnight ago she hadn't even known he existed. Just because she was lonely and had wept in his arms and dreamed of far more didn't mean that he had ever thought of her at all.

"Do you have at-home hours?" Lord Danecroft inquired of the dowager. "I would like to call, if I would be welcome."

The marchioness tapped him with her fan. "Bring Quentin's sisters, and you will be welcome. I will employ their organizational abilities in launching Miss Merriweather into society."

The earl beamed, appropriated Penny's hand, and, with no more than a wink in Abby's direction, sauntered away.

As they progressed down the street, a ruffian approached the earl with loud complaints in an incomprehensible accent. The earl insouciantly held up his walking stick to shield Penny, and the pair were soon gone from sight.

"Pockets to let," the dowager reminded Abby, resuming their journey to the milliner. "Excellent for occupying space at the dinner table, but totally unsuitable for your purposes, and he knows it. Your inheritance would be merely a drop in the bucket of his obligations, and any executor worth his salt would object to your siblings living in poverty."

Abby swallowed her protests. Since the earl had absolutely no interest in her, there was no use in arguing the benefits of her frugality. What did she know of an earl's debts? Her inheritance sounded like a grand fortune to her, but she was learning that living in society cost far more than she could afford.

"Really, my lord," the tall, blond miss beside Fitz said disparagingly as her footman knocked on the marchioness's door the next day, "it is most improper to take a child on a morning call. Now that she has a nanny, she should stay home."

In his still-roach-infested house. He knew better than

to mention that objection. He helped Penny from the lady's carriage as the marchioness's servant answered the door. "Call me Fitz, Lady Sally. And you will understand my impropriety shortly."

"Danecroft," she corrected. "I am ten years your junior and it would be disrespectful to address you with familiarity."

But it wasn't disrespectful to correct his etiquette. Ah, the flagrant genius of youth! Quentin's sisters had been drilled in the formality of the position their father would one day inherit. He doubted there was a duchess alive who took her rank more seriously than the daughters of a newly made marquess. He hoped they'd lighten up in a year or two. They seemed pleasant enough chits otherwise.

Their naïveté made him feel old. And jaded. And dissolute.

Awed by their entrance into Lady Belden's home, Penny gaped at the towering hall with its Adam ceiling, ornate wall sconces, and abundance of bigger-than-life-sized paintings. He diverted her gaze from a fig-leafed statue in a wall niche and pointed out the enormous bouquet on the chest where guests left their cards on a silver platter.

"I want a flower," she whispered, gazing longingly at the colorful array of roses and other blooms Fitz couldn't identify.

"I will buy you a posy later, if you behave," he promised.

She nodded solemnly, her eyes as wide as saucers and her tiny hand squeezing his. At times like this, he knew he was mad to even consider raising a child on his own. Bringing the unpredictable brat into these exalted echelons proved his ignorance.

But Penny needed the attention of a woman, and Miss Merriweather was singularly silent when his daughter wasn't present. He didn't dare enter Miss Merry's presence without her.

"Miss Abby!" his daughter cried in delight the instant she discovered her idol setting aside a book in the echoing, high-ceilinged tunnel that the marchioness called a drawing room. "I'm gonna get a posy!"

Jerking her hand from his, she flew across the carpet and dived into Miss Abby's arms.

Fitz would gladly have done the same. He had almost publicly swallowed his tongue the other day when he'd seen her in that revealing walking dress.

Today, his pocket Venus looked almost ethereal in a dainty green frock that hugged her bounteous breasts and draped seductively over her lovely curves. Bereft of horrendous bonnets, her sunset curls were held back by a ribbon. The locks had been fashionably trimmed and curled to frame her petite face in a manner that begged caressing.

Fitz fisted his fingers and resisted testing curly silkiness. At Lady Sally's tug, he remembered his manners, and bowed over Lady Bell's hand. As the daughter of an Irish earl, she had once been known as Lady Isabell or Lady Bell. According to gossip, she claimed she'd married Lord Belden so she wouldn't have to change her name. Fitz hadn't been in town long at the time of her marriage and knew little more than society hearsay about her circumstances.

At the dowager's invitation, he accepted tea and wished for brandy. He watched Penny and Miss Merriweather whisper to each other on a distant sofa while Sally and Isabell charted his course and Abby's with all the expertise of generals plotting a campaign. He had not thought Lady Sally moved in the dowager's circles, given that Sally's brother dealt in trade. Of course, Fitz could scarcely afford the society frequenting Almack's to know who was accepted or not.

"Excellent," he heard Isabell murmur. "Danecroft's attentions will draw the notice of other gentlemen to Abigail. And the matchmaking mamas will not see him as so much of a gazetted fortune hunter if he's entertaining my protégée. Your brother must keep him from the gaming tables until he's formally attached."

Their voices lowered, and Fitz grimaced and sipped the weak tea. He made an honest living at the gaming tables. He needed funds to keep up appearances if the women meant to drag him about like a prized Thoroughbred. Gratuities to the servants, impromptu ices and ribbons, flowers after the dance—all required coins he didn't possess. The loan he'd acquired barely paid his solicitors to keep the bailiffs at bay while they sorted out the estate's inventory and entailment and debts. He didn't have enough left to pay for decent rooms for Penny and her nanny.

His heir had been ominously silent since Fitz's arrival had squelched the suicide rumors. An expression of delight that the head of the family had returned from the dead would have been polite, but Fitz supposed that would be too much to ask from a man to whom he seldom spoke. He'd asked the family solicitor to send a note round to Geoff, asking for a word, but he'd not heard back.

Penny dragged Miss Merriweather from her seat to investigate a large floor globe that had once adorned the late marquess's study. Fitz wondered at its placement in this feminine room and, without conscious decision, rose to investigate it as well.

"It is good of you to bring Penny to see me, my lord," his Rhubarb Girl said stiffly at his approach. "She tells me her nanny snores, and she has swatted two thousand million spiders."

There was the clever little hen he knew. He couldn't wait to hear her opinion of the *ton*. "I have promoted Penny to chief bug swatter and awarded her the copper badge of courage."

Penny proudly peeled back her spencer to reveal the silly ha'penny pin he'd found in the gutter. "See? It says I'm a big girl."

"Big and strong," Miss Abby agreed solemnly. "As

chief bug swatter, you must instruct your papa to sprinkle the corners with pennyroyal after you have swept out all the cobwebs."

"Pennyroyal?" they both asked at once. Fitz was rewarded by the light of laughter in Miss Merry's eyes.

"Like father, like daughter," she said with what almost sounded like approval. "You really make a bad earl. You should be appalled at my suggestion. You should be over there scheming with the marchioness, choosing the perfect plum to pick from the wealthy orchard of society."

"I prefer tart rhubarb with my sweets. You have ruined me for all time." Fitz immediately bit his tongue. After all the years of practice, flattery came naturally to him, but he had no right to encourage her to think of him as any more than a tool to be used, just as he would use her.

Unfooled by his glib phrases, she eyed him with a trace of that tartness he so admired. "As I understand, you were ruined long before I came along."

She handed Penny a snow globe containing an elaborate miniature of Hyde Park, then stepped toward the window seat, where the clatter of traffic outside would hide her speech. "Is the house really that bad that she must swat spiders?"

"Worse," he admitted grimly. Miss Merry had seen him flailing in a pigsty and could see through his affections of charm with her eagle eye, and still, she did not reject his shallowness. She might be the one person on earth to whom he could speak honestly. "It's been uninhabited for a decade or more, but staying there saves me the cost of rent. Will the pennyroyal work?"

"After every room is thoroughly cleaned, perhaps. The stench of lye will drive out most creatures. I don't suppose the nanny is of any use in sweeping and scrubbing?"

"I can't ask it of her. She's had a few too many years of eating nursery bonbons. She's good with Penny, but if she got down on her knees, she couldn't get up again."

Abby shook her head in disapproval of his careless insult, while watching over Penny and the glass globe. "You mentioned you had servants elsewhere. Would they come to London?"

"Not unless I paid them. Their homes and families are in Wycombe."

"Lady Belden is spending the better part of my inheritance on clothes so I may *experience the world.* I dislike wasting my funds when I'll need them for the children," she whispered, darting a look to the two women cozing over tea. "Maybe we could help each other."

Fitz waited, puzzled, unable to follow her thoughts. He would like nothing better than to feel useful instead of like a frivolous fribble, but he couldn't see how he could help her.

She looked embarrassed and folded her fingers into her skirts. "The marchioness has not given me access to my inheritance. The bills are sent to the solicitor for payment. I thought . . . if I send back an occasional ribbon or bonnet to the shops, I could ask for a refund in coin."

"Clever," he said admiringly. "It's not normally done, but if the bills are promptly paid, a little persuasion might do it. If it's funds for a carriage to take you to see the children that you need, you don't need to resort to trickery. I can get you there."

"Thank you," she said in relief. "I had hoped you would say that."

Fitz thought he might buy her carriages and fling roses in her path if it meant basking in the glory of her respect again. Respect wasn't a sentiment to which he was accustomed. Nor did it fit comfortably, yet he was averse to giving it up.

"If I have coins to pay you," she continued, "then you could pay your servants, and Penny won't have to be chief bug swatter for long."

"You may have just outmaneuvered the two generals," he said in disgruntlement at realizing he had become a charity case instead of a conquering hero. "I can borrow a carriage without any expense to you. I owe you that much."

Penny attempted to roll the snow globe across the carpet.

"We'll talk later." Abigail dashed to rescue the globe and lead his daughter to another enticing object.

Fitz scowled and felt more than ever like a worthless fribble.

12

"You need to find a better neighborhood, Atherton. I nearly had to cosh a rather insistent babblingruffian who accosted me on the corner." Fitz threw down his ace to win the round of *vingt-et-un* and removed the stack of coins in the table center to his side.

"Your pretty phiz attracts them like magnets. Or your debt collectors grow bolder." Unconcerned, golden-haired Nicholas Atherton lounged in an easy chair, one long leg flung across the arm. He had led the sheltered life of aristocracy, rural estates, Eton, all those time-honored traditions that had bypassed Fitz, but like other younger sons, Nick had no occupation beyond seeking amusement.

"Your tact surpasses your concern," Fitz said drily as Nick dealt a new hand. "On a completely different note, where does one buy pennyroyal, Montague?"

With an odd streak of silver accenting the black of his thick hair, Blake Montague was a lethal combination of dangerous intensity and steadfast loyalty. Fitz had gravitated toward the baron's son when he'd first come to town simply because Blake was willing to impart his vast array of knowledge. Montague could have been a professor, but he had an athlete's need to beat his competition into the ground, which didn't suit the ivied halls of education. Fitz refused to go up against him in the ring on the days Montague was spoiling for a fight, but he'd happily race curricles against him when they could borrow the rigs.

They'd become friends the day Blake had laid his older brother flat in an altercation on Bond Street. Fitz had spirited Montague from the scene and bought him a round of ale without questioning. Fitz had often wished to punch his own brother in the snout and admired Blake's willingness to physically express his ire with the Montague heir. They shared a common bond of frustration with a feudal system that left them idle and penniless.

"A penny royal?" Montague said with a sniff. "No such creature. If the expenditures on our royals amounted to mere pennies, England would have sufficient wealth left in our coffers to raise ten armies." He shuffled the cards before passing them on.

"I think pennyroyal is some form of herb," Nick informed them, ignoring his friend's punnish sarcasm. "At some point, I had a nanny who indulged in pennyroyal tea."

"Pennyroyal, a class of perennial mint with small, aromatic leaves said to repel mosquitoes, ants, and other insects." Having proved he'd known the definition all along, Montague threw his wager into the pot. "Why do you ask?"

"One ought to know more than the servants one hires," Fitz said vaguely, wondering if he was one of the insects the mint would repel. "Do you still have access to that cabriolet? I'll wager all I've won against the use of it. Here's your chance to win back your losses."

Even though he was only a younger son, Nick had an allowance sufficient to keep him in linen neckcloths and finance his entertainment, but he had no head for sums. Nick borrowed from Fitz as often as Fitz won Nick's allowance, so Fitz felt no qualms in occasionally relieving his wealthier friend of a few coins by way of cards.

Montague, however, had an allowance so minuscule he couldn't save enough to enter the military as an officer, although he'd threatened to join the navy as a seaman until his father had warned he'd cut off even his small allowance should he do so. Fitz preferred making use of Blake's family's resources and picking his brains instead of his pockets. In return, Fitz did his best to tame Blake's more reckless behavior.

Montague grunted. "I accept. Courting a wealthy Cit who wishes a spin around the park, are we? Or hitting Almack's since you've acquired the title?"

"He's accepted an invitation to my mother's ball. My sisters are all atwitter," Nick declared, throwing his hand in with disgust.

Rather, Lady Sally had accepted for him. Fitz sure the hell wouldn't have done so. Nick's sisters twittered— constantly. Atherton's languid, oblivious attitude had apparently developed as a means of childhood survival. Fitz decided that if he had to marry birdbrains to pay for his family debt—faking his death might not be such a blow to his pride after all.

"Ever find out how the rumors of your death got started?" Montague asked, undoubtedly following the path of Fitz's desperate thoughts, since he had also been encouraged to court the aforesaid twittering sisters.

Fitz shrugged. "Servants at the estate found the clothes and pistol and notified my father's man of business. Haven't gone out there to question anyone yet."

"No chance your cousin contrived the scheme?" Montague asked offhandedly.

"Any reason to suspect he did?" Fitz drew another card.

"Last week when we still thought you dead, my father overheard him at the club inquiring as to the best man for painting crests on carriages. He didn't appear to be mourning your demise."

"M'sisters say he's angling for Lady Anne Montfort." With disgust, Nick threw down the king he'd just drawn, and Fitz once more won the round.

"Lady Anne? A duke's daughter? I hadn't thought Geoff ran as mad as the rest of the family." Fitz raked in his winnings. "His mother is a Cit, and His Grace would choke a Cit's son before letting one near Lady Anne."

"Your mother was a duke's daughter. *You* could court Lady Anne," Montague pointed out. "She's nearly on the shelf. With your charm, you could have her compromised and her dowry in your pocket within a month."

"She's nearly on the shelf because she has more sense than to notice termites like me, and wealthy enough not to care about marrying." Fitz contemplated his memory of the tall, commanding Lady Anne. She owned a stable that would benefit from his stud. She would spend all her time at the racetrack or riding to the hounds. He could stay in London—doing what? Gambling for the rest of his life? Living off her wealth?

He needed to start considering what he wanted of a wife before he fell for the machinations of the well-meaning Hoyts. He pocketed Nick's coins and gestured at a disgruntled Montague. "I'll send word around when I need the carriage."

Pockets jingling with blunt enough for another day, hoping the Atherton ball would have a decent gaming room, Fitz left Nick's rooms after supper. Penny would be tucked into the bed Quent's loan had bought. Her nanny would be snoring. He smiled to himself at how quickly Miss Merriweather had learned the details of his daughter's life. He doubted Lady Anne could do that.

The idea of bedding the duke's horse-mad daughter to beget an heir was daunting enough without wondering if she would keep the children in leading strings until they were housebroken. Geoff was welcome to her.

"Fitz, wait up," Montague called, taking the stairs to the street two at a time.

Lingering, Fitz heard an unintelligible shout, followed by a brick exploding—just where his head would have been had Montague not called out. Instinctively, he dropped into a crouch that tumbled his expensive beaver hat into the gutter. A round stone rolled across the paver at his feet. *What the devil?*

Accompanied by more furious shouts, another shot hit the paver, splintering into pieces of baked clay. A *marble?* Someone was trying to kill him with a clay *marble?*

"Back inside!" Montague shouted, gesturing for him to return to Nick's apartment.

There was nothing for him to hide behind if someone meant to try another shot. Catapulting marbles could put a man's eye out! Fitz snatched up his hat and hit the stairs running.

Opening the door to let him in, Montague peered around the doorjamb, searching the street for activity. "It looked like he had a *sling,*" he said in disgust. "What kind of man uses a child's toy?"

"A drunken one. Could you hear what he was shouting?" Disgruntled, Fitz checked his hat for damage.

"His brogue was too thick, although '*You owe me*' is a possible translation."

"Creditors can't collect if I'm dead," Fitz objected. Slinging marbles at his head to catch his attention was not logical and bordered on being murderous. Surely his cousin couldn't have . . . No, he'd rather believe a creditor had grown frustrated.

Nick sauntered down to join them in the foyer. "What the devil is going on?"

"I warned you this was a rough neighborhood," Fitz complained, although even he knew that street ruffians did not normally shoot catapults.

"Someone slung marbles at Fitz," Montague explained. "If they had hit his temple, they could have killed him. I'll go out the back and sneak around for a better look."

"That's absurd," Nick protested, leading the way to

the back hall and the servants' exit to the mews. "Slings and marbles are children's toys."

Which might have made Fitz's death look accidental.

Blake, chess player and master problem solver, had already leaped to the conclusion that Fitz was trying to avoid. There wasn't much point in stating their theory to Nick, who thought all the world revolved around pleasure. Fitz left his costly hat with the intention of retrieving it later. Shrugging off Montague's staying hand, he slipped past a still-protesting Nick into the kitchen garden.

"I won't believe my heir is insane enough to want my worthless title," Fitz argued with Blake's unexpressed thoughts. The back gate creaked in the otherwise silent night.

"It's not unheard of," Blake murmured. "Your brief demise could have made him realize how close he was to being a member of the Lords and winning the right to Lady Anne's hand. You're risking your life needlessly by providing him a target."

"For a sling?" Fitz asked in incredulity. "You want me to run from marbles?"

"Or exploding bricks." Undaunted, Montague entered the filthy alley, leaving Nick watching from the doorway.

Following, Fitz grimaced at the smelly spurt of a horse pile beneath his boot sole. He needed a lantern.

"You can't cross the street without being seen," Montague argued. "I hope you left a will if you try."

Penny. He needed to ask someone to take Penny should he depart this mortal coil. He'd do that in the morning, right after he strangled whoever had tried to take a piece of his head.

Wondering whom he could ask to look after his daughter kept him occupied until they'd taken the alley to the corner and crossed the intersection without incident.

"He had to have been behind those columns," Montague whispered, leaning one shoulder against the wall of the corner house and peering down the street. "There's nowhere else to hide."

"If I admit that the shot was deliberate, I'd have to admit that he followed me to Atherton's and hid behind those columns all evening," Fitz complained. "I'm thinking it's far more likely some child was playing with a new toy."

"Then we should have seen him running away. He's probably gone by now, but let me take a look first."

"You can play spy. I just want to teach the brat a lesson." Disregarding caution, Fitz strode down the quiet residential street, swinging his walking stick. To shoot again, anyone hiding behind the column would have to step out where he would be easily seen. Fitz assumed his reflexes were good enough to drop to the ground if that happened.

He'd seldom been angry enough to engage in street-level fisticuffs, but the possibility that the blackguard could have left Penny fatherless enraged him beyond measure. He hoped his assailant was full grown, because he *needed* to hit someone. Unfortunately, there was no one about to hit.

"He ran," Montague said, examining the narrow ground behind the columned gateway. "One shot might have been accidental, but two was deliberate. He'll target your rooms next."

Fitz still considered the attack ludicrous, but for Penny's sake, he had to be cautious. How many people knew he'd moved into the family tomb? His invitations still went to his old bachelor flat. He'd told no one of his new direction except Miss Merriweather and Lady Bell. If even his best friend hadn't heard the rumor, then chances were good the ladies had been silent. Perhaps he should keep quiet about his place of residence for as long as possible, as a precaution.

"I'll talk to my cuz, see if he's up to mischief," Fitz said, slapping his friend on the back. "Thanks for shouting at me. Saved me a nasty headache."

"I suggest you take an armed guard with you if you visit Geoff," Montague said drily, heading across to Atherton's to let Nick know all was well. "Desperate men commit desperate acts."

As Fitz well knew. "I'll keep that in mind. In the meantime, why did you call out to me?"

Montague shrugged uncomfortably. "Just wanted to ask if you'll be taking your seat in the Lords. I'm seeking a position in the War Office and thought you could put in a word for me. They're all complacently waiting for Napoleon to own the world, and someone needs to make them sit up and take notice."

More concerned with his own survival than that of the Continent, Fitz shook his head in dismay at this new responsibility. "Devil take it, that bunch of stuffed shirts is my lot now, ain't it? Although I daresay faces would freeze should a Danecroft darken their exalted assembly."

"You could make a difference, Fitz," Montague argued.

He snorted. "Not very likely. The family ermine is too moth-eaten. But should I rub shoulders with any dukes, I'll put in a word for you. Your father dead set against politics, too?"

Montague rubbed the silver streak at his temple. "My mother wants me to be a vicar and take over the local parish, and my father takes orders only from her. You know how it is."

"Actually I don't, old boy." With their farewells said to Nick, they stopped at the corner. "Can't remember ever seeing my mother," Fitz admitted, "and my father never did anything he didn't want to do. I need to take up studying how marriage works if I'm to take a wife."

Montague laughed. "From what I've seen, you just wed them, bed them, pay their bills, and go back to your usual routine."

"In my case, they'd have to pay *my* bills first." Rather than see the other man's pity, Fitz waved farewell and, swinging his walking stick, strolled down a main thoroughfare filled with carriages and pedestrians hurrying home from the theater and other entertainments.

Wondering why anyone would be taking potshots at him kept him from contemplating his lonely, wasted life and what the future held in store.

Some blocks away from the street containing his doddering town house, he stepped into a door front to scan the nighttime strollers. Deciding no one appeared to be following him, he took no chances but blended in with a rowdy gang of revelers until he reached a connecting alley, where he slipped away under cover of darkness. If nothing else, he would keep creditors from following him.

He couldn't believe Geoff would be stupid enough to want the title so badly that he'd kill—with a sling!—to obtain it, but he wasn't taking any chances with his life until he knew Penny would be loved and sheltered.

Now that Rhubarb Girl had given him a glimpse of what it meant to be cared for, he damned well wouldn't allow any child of his to grow up with the same neglect he'd known.

13

"You've heard the report," the marchioness scolded the next morning, glancing over the top of the newssheet she was perusing. "The children are well tended. There is no reason to hare off to Surrey and have them begging to leave with you. We're attending the theater tonight, and I don't want you red-eyed from weeping."

End of discussion. The dowager could be as charming as Lord Danecroft in public, but Abigail was learning she was often cool and aloof in private. Perhaps she was still mourning her husband. It was a pity the lady never had children of her own to teach her tenderness or sympathy.

Abby pushed her kippers around on the plate. She'd always wanted to visit a real theater instead of the amateur theatricals the village put together. But how could she enjoy herself until she saw the children and knew for certain how they fared? The marchioness's solicitors had verified only that they were being fed and kept well, not that they were loved.

It was much too easy to be tempted into believing her desires were more important than her siblings and to accept the easy assurances that the children wouldn't care.

And maybe they wouldn't. Maybe she was wrong about stubbornly wishing to see them. But she had to *know*. Unfortunately, she was too intimidated by her hostess and her elegant surroundings to fight back.

She was fairly certain the marchioness meant well. But the dowager didn't have children and wouldn't understand how deeply fear affected them. Her siblings had already lost both mother and father. Abby was quite certain that to be abandoned by all those they loved would harm them for life.

After the marchioness left for her office to attend a matter of business, a footman brought Abby a note on a silver salver. Surprised that he'd brought it to her and not the dowager, she opened it and admired the strong masculine scroll across the bottom—*Wyckerly*. Not *Danecroft*. It was as if he would always be an ordinary gentleman with her.

I have a cabriolet today. Would you care to take a small excursion into Surrey?

Her spirits lifted immediately. "Tell the messenger I can be ready within the hour. I'll be waiting at the park entrance."

She could scarcely believe her good fortune that Danecroft had agreed to take her on this *excursion*. She knew it was improper, but a firing squad couldn't stop her from accepting the invitation. She'd never had a need to practice deception, but desperation drove her. The dowager wouldn't approve of the earl taking her to Surrey, so she would have to pretend she was elsewhere if she didn't wish to seem ungrateful.

By the time she'd donned her new lilac-colored pelisse with the matching bonnet adorned in violets, Abigail had formed a plan. Carrying a reticule containing the few coins she'd brought with her, taking her new parasol as if she meant to stroll in the sun, she sailed down the stairs to the front door.

"Tell Lady Belden that I'm meeting Lady Sally at the

milliner's to look for some more hat ribbons. I'll see her this evening."

She wasn't a young miss who needed to take orders from anyone. That she'd startled the servant didn't worry her in the least.

Of course, propriety required that she take a maid with her if she meant to travel with the earl, but who would know or care what she did? She had no reason not to trust him and every reason to believe she was safe in his company. Besides, they'd have Penny for a chaperone.

She had triumphantly convinced the milliner to refund her ribbon money in coin and was waiting at the gates of the park when a lovely yellow cabriolet pulled up. Penny waved enthusiastically from it.

Holding the reins of his horse, the earl opened the low-slung door, and climbed down to greet her. Despite his hat, his hair had tumbled across his brow, and he sported a devilish grin that turned Abby's insides to mush.

"Miss Abigail, it's a pleasure to see you. I trust the ogre did not give you much trouble when you made your escape?"

Her fingers tingled with the solid grip of his gloved hand as he assisted her into the seat. She'd always been aware of Wyckerly's masculinity, but his proximity hadn't seemed so dangerous when she was on familiar ground. Tasting the forbidden apparently led to all manner of sinful thoughts. She squeezed onto the seat beside Penny and hoped she hid her flutter of anticipation.

"I'm a free woman, beholden to no one." She dismissed his concern. "This *excursion* will more than erase any debt you feel you owe me," she continued, clasping her hands around her reticule in some inane attempt to keep from floating with joy as the earl climbed in on the other side of Penny and set the carriage in motion.

"If only all my creditors were so generous." He

steered the horse with expertise around a broken flower cart. "I trust you have some idea of our direction and that we won't be spending the day wandering around Surrey. We're likely to get rained on." He glanced at the clouds as if he already regretted his mad urge to take her visiting.

"South of Croydon, off the Brighton Road," she answered promptly, so he had no excuse to back down on the offer that he had to know was beyond propriety. "I applied to the children's executor for directions. I was disappointed to learn that the Surrey Iron Railway requires use of one's own wagon. Wouldn't it be more profitable to provide the wagons? But it would have only taken me to Croydon, and I had no way to travel the rest of the distance."

Fitz's well-shaped brows rose. "You would have been brave enough to attempt a *railway*?"

She shrugged. "They are horse-drawn wagons. If they fall off the rails, it can't be at very great speed. Overall, it sounds smoother and less dangerous than a crowded turnpike."

"You would do better to hire a post chaise. And I'd rather you not travel alone at all. You have no idea of the dangers of the road," he said reprovingly.

"Now you begin to sound like the marchioness," she said. "I am not an utter gudgeon. I did ask for your assistance, you recognize. But had you not offered, I was prepared to do whatever it took."

"You terrify me, Miss Abigail," he said with what sounded like laughter, apparently brought back around to her way of thinking. "Is there nothing you will not undertake for your siblings?"

She gave that some thought. "I assume there must be, for I would not spoil them, but they are very young. I doubt that they could ask anything difficult of me."

"Is that how families normally behave?" he asked. "I had not noticed many older siblings looking after younger ones. Mostly, I've noticed them fighting."

"I'm all they have. And I was already well grown by the time they came along, so I've always been more of a mother to them. I am no saint. There have been days when I would have liked to lock the lot of them in their rooms and run away just for some peace."

"Mrs. Jones locks us up," Penelope said. "She said we give her no peace. I gave her a piece of my bread, but she threw it away."

A quick glance at Danecroft revealed his knuckles whitening on the reins and his jaw clenching until it twitched. He obviously had not known how his daughter had been treated. She could lecture, but it seemed he was beating himself up quite adequately.

She laughed at Penny's phrasing and hugged her narrow shoulders. "You need not worry yourself over Mrs. Jones ever again. You are a very lucky girl to have a daddy who will look after you. I think you will like meeting Jennifer. You're almost her age. Maybe the two of you could watch over the twins. They're not yet three and don't speak as well as you do."

"Mrs. Jones sometimes took care of babies," Penny said. "They stink."

That forced a chuckle from the earl. "You used to stink, too. I visited you once when you were very little, and you wet all over me."

"I did not," she said indignantly.

But Abigail could tell she was intrigued to know that her father had come to see her even when she was small and stinky. He wasn't a bad man, just one who didn't know how to be a good father. She knew many men like that.

And she would admire the gentleman's attempt to be a father to Penny more than was good for her if she gave his behavior any more consideration.

After they'd navigated the crowded city streets, it was a pleasure to traverse the country road through villages of pretty cottages and past fields of sheep. Enjoying the fresh air and the company and the freedom to be herself for a while, Abby did her best to ignore the gathering clouds overhead. The cabriolet's hood would protect them somewhat in a shower, she hoped.

Once they left the main highway, her directions were a little more vague, and they had to stop at a crossroads to ask for the correct turn. She was holding her breath by the time they found the low stone wall leading up to a three-story house constructed with a tile facade intended to resemble brick. The Weatherstons either were avoiding having to pay the brick tax or thought brick too old-fashioned. Either way, a fashionable new house grander than her aging country cottage was now home for her siblings.

Fitz cast his passenger an anxious glance as he pulled the rig to a halt at the front steps. Miss Merry had carried on a lively and intelligent discourse all the way here, but upon their arrival at the drive, she'd turned into a stone-faced sphinx.

He leaned over to squeeze the gloved hands she clenched in her lap. "I'm sure they're fine. Wait here, and I'll rouse the household."

She nodded curtly. He left her studying the ugly new construction while he pounded the knocker. *Nouveau riche,* he concluded, noting the knocker was painted iron and not the brass that required an army of servants to keep it polished.

A maid with mobcap askew answered the door, bobbed a startled curtsy when he presented his card, and rudely left him standing on the step. Somewhere beyond the wide-open door, he could hear children yelling. Or romping. Small feet pounded on wood floors.

He had no experience at dealing with an entire brood of imps, and he almost regretted his impulsive urge to take Miss Merry visiting. But he'd not been able to get an appointment with the family solicitor until tomorrow, and he'd thought it a good idea to take Penny to the safety of the country, where ruffians and creditors weren't likely to find them.

He glanced over his shoulder to the carriage, which Penny was attempting to escape. She'd been remarkably well behaved these past hours, but now it was her nap time. He dreaded the whining and screams that might shortly ensue.

From the sounds of it, four more rapscallions were scampering around upstairs, about to descend in a stampede. He was feeling overwhelmed and out of his element.

How had he thought he could ever be a *father*?

Unfortunately, if he married for money, wedlock rather required breeding heirs.

"Abby!" a shrill voice shrieked from the upper story.

"You stop right there, you little hooligan," a woman with a vaguely Irish accent shouted. "It's nap time."

Definitely bad timing. Fitz stepped back as he realized his petite companion had joined him on the doorstep. The brim of her annoying bonnet brushed his cheek as she peered inside. He'd much rather enjoy her expressive face than those damned violets, but he supposed it was safer if women hid their faces from slavering wolves like him. Now that he had a better idea what she hid behind her modest clothing, his mind wandered like an errant schoolboy's in her presence.

"Abby! Abby! Abby!" An onslaught of childish chants accompanied more pounding feet.

Penelope clung to his leg, creasing his trousers to peer around his knees.

Why the devil had he agreed to this insane expedition? He didn't owe Miss Merriweather that much for landing him in pigsties and strawberry fields.

Still, he'd definitely developed a taste for rhubarb tart. . . .

A fair-haired girl with a long braid nearly broke her neck racing down the stairs to fling herself into her sister's arms. His daughter gripped Fitz's leg tighter and stared, making him wonder if she'd ever had a friend of her own. And realizing it was pathetic that he didn't know.

Behind the girl, a tall boy with carrot-colored hair solemnly prevented a pair of toddlers from tumbling headlong over the last few steps. The boy cast an anxious glance at his half sister before donning a mask of insouciance. Fitz's heart nearly broke in two watching the lad attempting to appear like a man who didn't give a damn.

He painfully recognized the attitude that hid a world of fear and uncertainty.

Behind the children, at the top of the stairs, stood the maid who'd left him on the step and someone he assumed was a nursemaid, wringing her hands and looking frighteningly stern.

Miss Abby had knelt down to squeeze and kiss the toddlers, who were pulling off her bonnet and wrinkling her fashionable skirt and rubbing grubby hands on her expensive pelisse. The pure bliss on her face told Fitz she was oblivious of the destruction—which made him unaccountably ache even more.

"Miss Jennifer, I assume?" He donned a gallant pose and addressed the shy girl hovering on the far side of the door. "May I introduce my daughter, Miss Penelope? I believe you may both be of an age." Penny crept halfway from behind his knees, eyeing Abby and the twins with a hunger for acceptance.

Leaving the girls to work it out, Fitz turned to the young boy clutching his hands behind his back and watching the proceedings. "You must be Mr. Thomas Merriweather, caretaker of this lively brood. I am most pleased to meet you. I'm Fitzhugh Wyckerly. Your sister has twisted my arm until I cried uncle and brought her to visit."

The boy properly held out his hand and shook Fitz's.

"Pleased to meet you, sir. I thank you for bringing Abby to see us. The children have missed her greatly."

And Tommy would have missed her even more, Fitz would wager as he watched Abby grab Tommy's neck and hug him. The boy turned three shades of scarlet but still squeezed her back, however briefly.

Which was when Fitz knew he wanted this kind of affection for himself and for Penny. Which meant he had a bigger problem than any his notorious family had ever brewed, because in his experience, wealth and affection never went hand in hand. Expecting both meant achieving neither.

14

Abby cuddled Cissy on her lap and ruffled Jeremy's golden curls where he leaned sleepily against her knee. She desperately needed to hug Jennie and Tommy as well, but she could not keep an earl waiting forever, or disturb the nursery routine for much longer.

"I am so very, very grateful that you have allowed me to visit," Abby told the nursemaid. Sitting at the tea table, she offered her half of a biscuit to Jeremy, who stuck it all in his mouth and smeared crumbs across his face. "I have been desperate to visit, but the distance is difficult. I hope I will not cause you any trouble for this."

"The missus is out visiting. She'll be home directly, if you want to stay," the nursemaid said with sympathy. "The mister stays in the city most nights. It's her what wanted the children, and he gives her all she wants."

"I wish I could stay." Abby threw Lord Danecroft a glance. He'd been remarkably patient, not complaining when the twins attacked his impeccable gray trousers and slobbered on his polished boots. He sipped his tea some distance from her. Having taken a rocking chair, he cradled a doll the girls had handed him, and discussed insect lore with Tommy.

She didn't think there could be anything so virile as a man confident enough in his masculinity to lower himself to a child's level.

At first, the earl had looked doubtful enough that she feared he might flee back to London on foot. But he'd made a courageous recovery after Penny had tackled his knee. Abby might be ill-disposed toward shallow charm, but Danecroft's magnetism apparently worked on children.

"His lordship must return to the city shortly, and I fear it will rain soon. You will convey my apologies and my gratitude to Mr. and Mrs. Weatherston? I hope they will be so kind as to bring the children to visit upon occasion. I'm certain the marchioness would not mind. I will send a note around with a proper invitation."

Abby desperately needed to know the people caring for the children. She had sent lists of instructions, but did they bother to make Jennie lie down in a dark room when her head hurt? Or remember that the twins had bad reactions to bee stings and should be kept away from flowers? Did they even care or did they expect nursemaids to do it all? It didn't look as if she could satisfy her concerns today. At least she now knew they had a comfortable roof over their heads.

"Don't go!" Cissy whined when Abigail set her down and prepared to leave. Her twin immediately mimicked the cry, and Abby sent the earl a wry look over their heads.

Despite his height and the confinement of his clothing, Danecroft rose agilely from the low chair and returned the doll to Jennie. "We thank you for the luncheon, ladies, gentleman." He bowed to the pouting, crying children and spoke to them firmly. "You must promise to behave and listen to your nanny if we are to be allowed to return. You don't want your sister to worry herself to death if she can't see you again, do you?"

Tommy and Jennie instantly picked up the little ones and dried their tears.

"Brilliant," Abby murmured as they made their escape down the stairs and to the door. She was already fumbling for her handkerchief to wipe the tears spilling down her cheeks. "You learn quickly."

Above, she could hear Tommy's voice crack as he directed the twins to their bed.

"I wanna stay here," Penny said, trying to flee Danecroft's hand. "I wanna play dollies."

"If you stay here and play dollies, you can't have dollies at home," he said, picking up his daughter and again offering his arm to Abby as they descended the outside stairs.

"I want dollies at home!" Penelope cried, on the verge of weeping.

"All right, you can have dollies at home, but you can't sleep until we get there."

Abby fought a smile at Danecroft's ridiculous sternness.

"I will too sleep if I wanna!" Penny shouted back.

"Not for very long." He slid his recalcitrant daughter into the seat, then aided Abby up the step into the carriage.

"All day and all night!" Penny retorted, but even she giggled weepily, as if this was a familiar form of argument.

Sinking into the carriage seat, Abby simply wanted to cry her eyes out, and the banter between father and daughter made her ache even more. The earl might be as poor as a street urchin, but he had Penny, and his life was much the better for it, whether he realized it or not.

She would easily give up all the coins in the world if only she could have the children back again.

She cast a longing glance around the carriage's hood as the horse trotted down the drive. Four small faces crowded an upper window, waving frantically.

How would she ever know what was best for them?

Rain began to fall before they were an hour down the road. Fitz cursed his impulsiveness in asking Abby to take this journey on such a day. The wind slashed the downpour across the road in gray sheets. The carriage's hood kept the rain out of their faces and off their backs, as long as they didn't turn west, but the spray of water would soon drench them no matter which way they turned. He debated whether it was better to get soaked, or to infuriate Isabell for jeopardizing Abby's reputation by stopping at an inn.

A true gentleman would no doubt know the right choice, but all his life he'd lived for expediency on the rough edges of bachelor society. He would normally never be caught in the company of a respectable lady.

"Penny will catch cold," the topic of his internal debate said softly, pulling her pelisse around the child sleeping in her lap. "There was a decent-looking inn just ahead, was there not?"

"And how do you remember this?"

"I feared we would be caught in the storm and didn't want you and Penny to suffer from my foolishness, so I noted likely shelter on the way down." She spoke apologetically, as if the dilemma were *her* fault and not his.

"The marchioness will be furious if she learns you've been with me. What tale did you tell to escape her velvet trap?"

"I am five and twenty and don't need a chaperone to protect my reputation," she said stiffly.

"Five and twenty," he crowed. "That makes you a doddering ancient, and I must be one foot from my grave."

She shot him a sharp glance that said she saw through his diversion. "Lady Belden means well, but I am not a silly miss with stars in my eyes, foolish enough to believe I can find a husband among the pampered aristocracy. She would do far better to introduce me to lawyers in need of my dowry, who would be able to defend my claim without cost. Men such as that will not know or care that a woman of my age is independent."

Fitz lashed the horse into the innyard, feeling unreasonably irascible at her perfectly logical conclusion.

How could he tell the damned woman that most sane men ought to pay gold for a treasure like her? "You underestimate yourself," he said curtly, throwing the reins down to a lad who ran out to meet them.

She ruined her useless silk parasol covering Penny from the rain until he lifted his sleeping daughter from her arms. Together, they hurried through the muddy yard into the inn, which was crowded with other travelers seeking refuge from the storm.

"This won't do." He shouldered his way through the mail coach's huddled, dripping passengers until he located an officious man ordering servants about. "A private parlor?" he called over the bustle.

"Only the wife's left," the innkeeper called back. "Small, but there's a fire and a place to lay the wee lass."

Small, and costly. As he pushed his way toward the hall the man indicated, Fitz mentally totaled the coins in his pockets, the fee for stabling the horse, and the stableboy's gratuity. Even if Miss Merriweather paid for tea with her coins, he'd still have to abandon her for a while to earn their keep. He glanced down at her petite figure, but she seemed undaunted by the crowd or the offer of an intimate parlor. There were advantages to a woman of pragmatic mind.

Of course, an insipid miss would no doubt have insisted that they return to London without stopping, thereby saving him a great deal of blunt.

They followed the innkeeper's plump wife to a small parlor at the back of the inn. Two well-worn wing chairs framed the small coal grate. A slightly unstable round table filled the space between the chairs. Their hostess gestured at a faded fainting couch in a dark corner. "Me mam used to lie there in her last days. The babe should sleep well in it." She brushed Penny's sleep-flushed cheek with a callused finger. "The two of you are lucky to have such a one. We never had none of our own."

In minutes, she produced a pot of tea, cups, and a quilt to cover Penny.

"For the sake of appearances, I'll have to leave you here with her," Fitz said as Abby tucked the child in. His companion's damp muslin clung to her rounded figure in ways that made him all too aware that they were alone and the innkeeper thought them married. And that he *liked* the idea. "And come back when the rain lessens."

She was having difficulty unfastening her wet bonnet ribbons, and he delayed his flight to help her untangle the knot. The delicate scent of violets that had enticed him all day hadn't faded with the hours, and his hands lingered a little too long near the curve of her jaw as he wrestled with the ribbon. If he could slide his fingers through her curls, cup her cheek, turn her head until her eyes met his . . .

She lifted her glorious blue gaze to study him without need of his seductive moves. Fitz didn't stop to think but lowered his head for just a taste of moist strawberry lips—his reward for enduring the frustration of looking and not touching all day.

She gasped, her mouth parting on the exhalation. He dropped her unfastened bonnet and finally and at long last slid his fingers through her silken curls. He captured the back of her head to hold her still, caught up in the wonder of her ingenuous sigh. He knew better. He truly did. But his Abby was a foreign delicacy too rare for him not to sample. Just for one minute out of his dissolute life, he needed the approval of a good woman.

To his shock, she laid a hand on his chest, burning a brand through his wet linen clear to the skin, and then she tilted her head so he could better access the pure ecstasy of her shy kiss.

This was wrong, wrong in so many ways that even his mathematical mind couldn't calculate them, but he'd never felt so perfectly, joyously right in all his life. For one intoxicating moment, her artless seduction blended into a potent concoction he could not name or recognize. He simply knew her kiss was the missing piece he'd sought forever.

Fitz pushed Abby's wet pelisse off her shoulders, sliding it down her arms to the floor so he could stroke her bare skin with hands shaking to grab and hold. But even in his madness, he fought the temptation. That she curled her fingers in his waistcoat and returned his kiss with fervency was all the bliss he dared ask.

A loud rap at the door forced them apart. Abby covered her swollen lips with a muffled gasp and regarded him with eyes so round, he didn't know whether she looked on him as insect or hero. He knew which he was, but he rather hoped he could be her hero for just a little while.

"Lady here asks if she might join you," the innkeeper called, opening the door without invitation. "Says she'll pay for supper."

Fitz stepped in front of Abby to give her time to recover herself, then wished for a shield of invisibility when Lady Anne Montfort walked in, her riding habit dripping, her superior smile flitting about her lips until she saw him.

"Oh, it's you, Fitz," she said with what he could swear was disappointment. "Did I interrupt something I shouldn't?"

"I was just leaving for the tavern. Have you met Miss Abigail Merriweather, Lady Belden's protégée?" Briskly, he performed the social niceties, pretending Abby wasn't looking as if she wanted to sink through the floor or that a duke's daughter wasn't scowling at him—pretending he hadn't just been given a glimpse of heaven and must now pay the price.

"I didn't mean to intrude," Lady Anne claimed, throwing her hat on the table and checking her upswept black hair for loose pins, making it clear she had no intention of leaving, "but I saw the rig and was told the driver had taken shelter here. My groom wanted to warn about a loose spoke."

Balderdash. She recognized the carriage and had come seeking the owner—Montague. Fitz would have to ask his friend a few impertinent questions about unobtainable daughters of dukes when he returned. And if his cousin Geoff had his eye on Lady Anne, as rumor had it, then he could taunt his tradesman heir about his slim chances against Corinthian Blake.

"I'll take a look at the spoke, thank you. Miss Merriweather, if you'll excuse me?"

Abby nodded, retreating into that sphinxlike silence Fitz had noted before. He hated leaving her in the company of a noblewoman who could tie grown men into knots with her tongue, but lingering invited more scandal than he'd already created.

"Your child?" Lady Anne asked, looking at Abby and indicating Penelope as she appropriated a chair and propped her riding boots on the grate.

"Mine," Fitz said, his hand on the door clasp. "Miss Merriweather has been kind enough to offer to look after her while she sleeps."

He didn't linger to see the lady's smirk. He didn't give a damn about duke's daughters. He simply hoped the woman wasn't cruel enough to destroy Abby simply for the fun of a little gossip mongering.

15

"Looks like I interrupted just in time," Lady Anne declared, sipping from the teacup that should have been the earl's. "Fitz is a charming bounder."

"It wasn't like that at all," Abby managed to murmur, although how a word passed her sinful tongue was a mystery to her. She'd never known her lips could be used to produce such pleasure, and a thrill shivered through her at recalling what the earl's mouth had done to hers. The vicar had certainly never kissed her in such a manner.

The Earl of Danecroft had *kissed* her—as if he really and truly meant it. Did that mean he found an insignificant country mouse like her attractive? That was almost too incredible to believe. Or perhaps he was just bored and demanding payment for his wasted hours. She supposed she ought to listen when everyone, including Fitz himself, declared he was little more than a shallow cad, but he'd left her too bewildered to think sensibly.

"Wasn't it like that?" Lady Anne asked in amusement. "I don't suppose you have a very large dowry?"

The mercenary part of the aristocracy, Abby understood too well. "Not large enough," she answered bluntly, checking on Penny before taking the second chair. The earl had introduced the lady as the daughter of a duke. She didn't understand why such an exalted personage was galloping about the countryside unescorted by more than a groom.

The lady chuckled. "Whereas my dowry would pull him out of the soup and put him on firm ground again. The plot thickens."

Without the fashionable armor of her pelisse, Abigail felt very small and inconsequential next to the taller, elegant lady in her striking wine-colored riding habit, with her hat and coat tailored like a man's. Abby knew she would never be able to carry off a look like that with such grace.

And she had no idea what the lady was talking about. "The plot?" she asked tentatively.

"If you're a relation of Lady Belden, you must know her late husband's distant cousin Lord Quentin Hoyt?"

"I don't believe I've had the pleasure," Abby said faintly, at an utter loss as to the direction of this conversation. Of course, her head was still spinning in the stars, and she was having difficulty breathing. She didn't know whether to laugh or cry. She could still smell Danecroft's bay rum cologne on her fingers. She had touched his neck! She might never think straight again.

"Well, if you stay in town for any length of time, you will come upon Quentin. He's a mischief-maker, with his fingers in more pies than is good for him. Smack his hand for me when you see him, will you? He's really quite bad at matchmaking."

"I . . ." She couldn't agree to smack a gentleman's hand. Abby simply offered a general "Of course," and let it go. Surely the lady didn't mean it. And then her final statement sank in. "Matchmaking?"

Accented by a black widow's peak, the lady's features were cool and regal. "Lord Quentin led me to believe I would find a friend of mine, Mr. Montague, in the vicinity. He deliberately deceived me. He knows Montague is not a likely candidate as my suitor, but the bankrupt earl

ing he was deuced lucky at cards, and that they could have beaten him had they played long enough.

But in counting cards, playing through the deck meant he won more often than not. Best to leave some element of chance so he lost occasionally. He'd invented a system of staggered wagers that lowered his odds of losing all he earned, so even if he lost a hand, his money came out ahead.

He slipped his winnings into his pocket, and met up with the duke's daughter in the lobby. "The rig is at your disposal if you are heading into town, my lady. The clouds haven't entirely dissipated."

She slapped her gloves impatiently against her palm. "No, I'm riding back to my father's stable, but thank you for the offer. I assume you are already aware that your friend has her heart set on a houseful of children and is not the match you need. While I may be the opposite, having no need of children and possessing wealth to spare, I still refuse to be won by seduction or trickery. Don't let Quent manipulate you. The man is too sure of himself and needs to be cut down to size."

The lady spoke like a man, in peremptory terms that would confuse many, but Fitz had no doubt of her meaning. "I don't believe Quent meant harm. He might have thrown you in my path, but he didn't know I was with Miss Merriweather. She was kind to me when I needed a friend, and I'm only returning her kindness. I trust you will not speak harm of her for this incident."

"Of course not. I meant to threaten you if you intended mischief, but you are not that sort of scoundrel. Good day." She marched out the instant her horse was led to the door.

Not that sort of scoundrel. Damned by faint praise, and he'd almost forfeited that one credit had he been left alone with Abby much longer.

He didn't know what had got into him. He wasn't a rake. His one attempt in his youth to be a man about town had resulted in Penelope. Since then, he'd learned to be wiser, using protection and worldly widows and the occasional whore. He *never* seduced innocents. Had no interest in them.

And he'd almost thrown his hat in the marriage ring over a woman who was totally unsuitable for his needs— as he was unsuitable for hers. He had wits to let.

Steeling himself, he returned to the cozy parlor to find Miss Abigail fastened into her pelisse and tying her bonnet ribbons. She offered him a curt nod of greeting and bent to remove the quilt from Penny's still-sleeping form.

Right. She was sensible. He'd hear no missish noises from his Rhubarb Girl. They were in this together. Friends helping each other and all that.

Heavenly kisses were simply an idyllic side road they'd mistakenly taken. Back to the main thoroughfare now.

But he could still swear her bonnet smelled of violets, and even though he carried his daughter over his shoulder, his spare hand instinctively sought to protect the small of his companion's back as he led her through the departing mob.

Females must emit some potent perfume that drained a man of his wits and distracted him from his course. That's why family men weren't often found in bachelor havens. They'd had their minds snatched, their souls snared, their peckers hung with golden chains attached to the women in their lives.

Fitz winced and tried not to think of the kind of life he must lead after he was wedded. Once he had the where-withal to fund the estate, he would be too busy learning about rutabagas to fritter about town after women, he supposed.

They completed the journey into the city in relative silence, until Penny woke at the crash of empty crates hitting the cobblestones after a phaeton sideswiped a dray. She didn't wake pleasantly and growled most of the way to Belden House.

"You should let me off at the park," Abigail insisted when he passed the park entrance.

"I am not such a worm as to deposit you alone on empty streets in this fog and let you take the blame for everything, providing you even made it home safely."

Yes, he was such a worm and would have done so perhaps even as late as last week rather than lose the good graces of a marchioness. But the day had left him feeling recalcitrant for some reason, and he wouldn't let his soul be snatched by any slip of a female.

He could tell by the way her spine went rigid that he'd earned her disapproval. So be it.

Fitz made a grumbling Penny hold his hand up to the door. It was locked and they had to knock. Sweeping his hat off, he stepped out of the drizzle when the door opened, and escorted both of his ladies into the foyer.

Isabell slammed out of a back room, scowling and stalking toward him as if he were the menace of the universe. Fitz didn't even bother offering her his patented smile. He scowled back with the imperiousness of his rank—the refusal to please was unexpectedly liberating.

"Where the devil have you been? It's past time for tea, Abigail, and you should be upstairs dressing for the theater."

"Lord Danecroft generously offered me a ride home when the rain started." Abigail handed her ruined parasol and bonnet to the footman waiting to accept them.

Fitz had to admire the daring way she turned and curtsied to him in dismissal. He was the earl here. She was naught more than a Rhubarb Girl. And she dismissed *him*. Very good. He'd have to swat Isabell for teaching her that lesson in arrogance. In the meantime, he would top it.

"I took Miss Merriweather to see her family," he told the frowning marchioness, negating Abigail's protective half-truth. He'd be damned if he hid behind her skirt. "She's not a puppet whose strings you can pull and maneuver to your own whims. I give you good day, my lady."

He smacked his hat back on his head, lifted his wide-eyed daughter, and stalked out.

16

Emotionally exhausted, Abby donned the gown that had been purchased for the theater, and let the maid arrange her hair. She thought the result of tousled orange curls caught in a pink ribbon looked as if she'd just risen from her pillow, but she didn't care. She'd kissed an earl today. And enjoyed it entirely too much. And liked even better that the earl had stood up to her hostess in her defense.

But she couldn't deal with aristocrats any longer. She didn't know why she'd thought she could. They confused her entirely too much. She would simply spend her inheritance hiring a solicitor and visiting the children.

She was desperately planning her speech asking Lady Belden for her funds when she met the marchioness in the foyer. The lady looked her over with a sharp eye and strode out without a word. So much for Abby's determination to speak. Etiquette required that she not do so unless the lady spoke first.

Silence commanded the carriage interior as the horses broke into a trot. Abby hated being given the silent treatment as if she were a misbehaving adolescent. Taking a lesson from Danecroft, she refused to be intimidated any longer. She took a deep breath, clenched her fingers, and voiced her concern. "I ran a household on my own for three years," she stated, starting on firm ground. "I ran my father's farm for years before that. I can converse with stewards and bishops. I am not a child nor do I wish to be treated like one." She didn't know if she was trying to convince herself or her hostess.

"You are a foolish young woman who doesn't know the way of the *ton*." Lady Belden clasped the head of her beribboned walking stick and jabbed it against the opposite seat. "Your reputation can be ruined by simply speaking to the wrong man."

"On the farm, I speak to all sorts of men. Perhaps that is not done by sheltered misses, but I am trying to tell you that I am no such thing. You cannot pass me off as one."

The lady pounded the stick idly a few more times, creating a dull clatter. "I never had children. Never particularly wanted them, but Edward was disappointed."

Abigail blinked. She didn't relax her rigid stance, yet the lady's offhand remark had jostled her from her high horse, and she didn't know whether to get back on again. She'd never thought much about the marchioness or her life. Lady Belden was simply a powerful stranger with the world at her fingertips.

But she was also a woman.

"You are still young and beautiful," Abby said cautiously. "Perhaps another man . . . ?"

"No, I've had enough of men and their managing ways. I have no desire to surrender my independence or my fortune. I doubt that I have any affinity for screaming brats, so that's not a concern." She pulled the stick across her lap and glanced out the window. "But I have always thought I have much to teach young women that I wish someone had taught me."

"I see." Abigail relaxed slightly. If she thought of the dowager as a woman not much older than herself, instead of a stranger with the power to turn her life upside down, it was easier to converse. "I realize there is much I need to learn if I wish to see beyond my own small world, and I thank you for giving me that opportunity. But you must understand that my family has always been my life, and I cannot simply discard them because circumstances have changed. They are the only reason I am here."

The marchioness sniffed haughtily. "Are you satisfied that they are well cared for?"

The carriage halted in a long line of gleaming black vehicles, sparkling with moisture in the foggy light of carriage lamps. Abby let anticipation for the evening build now that the barrier was toppling between her and her hostess.

"They are looked after by servants," she said quietly, not wishing to argue over child rearing at a time like this. "It is not the same as a loving family."

"I wouldn't know," the lady admitted with condescension. Then her demeanor changed, and she rapped lightly on the carriage window. "There is Quentin. Let us depart here. I wish him to see what a *sensible* young woman you are."

Once descended from the carriage, Abby made her curtsy and studied the gentleman that a duke's daughter had called a matchmaker, but she could see no more than a large, forbidding gentleman who didn't smile much, although he gallantly held an umbrella over their heads.

She preferred all the vast variations of Lord Danecroft's smiles and charm to this older gentleman's stoic elegance, but she knew the earl wouldn't attend the theater unless he had been invited to someone's box.

What did a penniless lord do to entertain himself in the evening?

A penniless lord stomped cockroaches in the wee hours, pouring vinegar in cracks and spreading smelly herbs across the floors to prevent insects from encroaching on his new bedroom. Fitz thought it a fitting occupation on this damp evening when his body lusted for a woman whose innocent kisses had turned his head around—a woman he could never have.

God had a cruel sense of humor. As the bloody Earl of Danecroft, he could behave like every other damned Wicked Wyckerly, play the pirate, and take what he wanted and say to hell with the consequences.

Or he could do what was right and live a life of misery to pay for the sins of his father.

At the moment, he almost sympathized with his father's blithe ignorance of what was right and wrong. Fitz wanted Abby, but he was painfully aware that it was wrong to have her.

Over these last few days, he'd sent the nanny out to purchase decent bed linens because he knew that's what Abby would have done. He'd hired laborers to carry the contents of his old rooms to the town house and tote beds out of the attics of friends. He'd paid a seamstress to sew up fresh bedding and stuff it with cotton—because Abby wouldn't have let servants or children sleep on floors.

He'd even started calling her *Abby* in his head, as if they were intimate enough for him to do so.

Except all he'd accomplished with his lustful thoughts and efforts was to lead his creditors to his town house door. He'd been ignoring their pounding intrusions since he'd returned today, as he ignored the knocker now. And the damned fresh mattresses did little good in a house crawling with fleas and other lice left by whatever animals had taken residence in the years of vacancy.

He'd done well to study bugs so he knew the enemy. He'd cleaned out debris, mopped with lye, and perfumed with herbs the upper rooms where his daughter and the nanny slept. And now he was working on his own room. He had a distaste for insects chomping on his expensive attire. And he would rather not use his prized Bug Book to crush spiders.

He still had an entire estate in the country disintegrating to dust, and tenants probably deserting by the dozens, but he saw no resolution to his problems until he'd found a wealthy wife. And the selection was far greater here in the city than in rural Berkshire.

At least the creditors seemed to have gone home for the night. The knocking had stopped.

As he stomped and swept, Fitz pondered the type of woman he ought to be seeking—should he have a spare moment from bug crushing to look for one. He might not have a proper education, but he'd spent years learning which gentlemen he could take into high-stakes games and which ones were good for only occasional entertainment, so he had an idea which daughters had the richest dowries. He didn't know the *daughters* so well. Since they provided him no income and he couldn't bed them, he hadn't bothered to know them. But he knew Lady Anne had a fortune at her disposal.

Lady Anne was an attractive woman who would probably bite the head off her mate after intercourse. Lady Anne was definitely a praying mantis—slender, elegant, and independent. As she'd bluntly said, she didn't need a husband.

So, did he want a woman who needed him? Probably not. Any woman who needed a scoundrel like him would be weak, and she would undoubtedly faint if presented with his mad household.

Still, he couldn't imagine the duke's daughter in his bed. If he had to submit to golden chains in tender parts, he wanted them tugged by someone gentle and loving.

Fine, then he'd hunt for a *gentle* wealthy woman. He was sure they abounded among the fairer sex. He hoped there were some who didn't twitter like Nick's sisters. A *quiet*, gentle, wealthy woman, that's what he needed.

He'd start looking at the Athertons' ball tomorrow night. Once he found the right woman, it shouldn't take long to sweep her off her feet. He was an earl now. Everyone wanted an earl.

Only one without a brain in her head would want a penniless earl, but brainless should be easy to find as well.

And once he had a biddable, rich female in his bed, all thoughts of prickly Rhubarb Girl would melt away.

As he leaned over to sweep a pile of dust into his dustpan, the window above him imploded, scattering glass all over his newly swept floor and knocking over his last candle. Even in the dark, he could see the shape of a brick amid the debris.

Escalating in a split second from mild discontent to utter fury, Fitz threw down his broom and raced down the stairs to the kitchen garden. How had anyone noticed his one candle in a back room that looked onto a walled garden?

He hadn't used the back door since arriving. He had to slam the rusted lock with his bootheel to jar it free. Soon, he wouldn't have a damned door left standing.

His fists itched to maim the monster who was endangering his household. With his coat off, his white shirtsleeves ought to be a prime target. Let them come after him. He stalked into the rubbish that was his backyard, fists raised, ready to strike. "Where are you, you festering guttersnipe? I'll beat you into a piss puddle!"

A tomcat howled from the broken brick wall that rose between him and the dark alley.

He really, really needed to beat someone into a pulp.

Vaulting over a caved-in section of wall, he scanned the darkness, but an encroaching fog prevented him from seeing beyond the nose on his face. He halted, listening. Either whoever was out there had fled, or he was standing as still as Fitz. He heard only the rustle of vermin in the trash.

He slammed the side of his fist against the wall in frustration, and the rotten mortar gave way, tumbling more bricks into the yard. *Damnation!*

Sucking on his scraped hand, Fitz stalked back into the house and wedged the back door shut with a decrepit chair taken from his old rooms before he went upstairs to check on Penny in the front. She and her nurse had slept soundly through the whole incident. He'd have to move her bed away from the window in the morning.

Fitz felt his way back down the dark hallway to the room he'd claimed for his own. Damp air entered through the broken pane, but the windows were so leaky that there had been little difference in the temperature inside or out even before the brick smashing through his window had disturbed his serenity.

He groped among the glass shards until he'd located the candlestick, and struck a flint from his pocket to light the wick. Still simmering with rage, Fitz cut the twine holding a piece of paper around the brick.

FED WUTZ YERS OR OIL TEK EM BAK, read the painstakingly printed scrawl on the back of a poster from Tattersall's.

Oh, that explained a lot.

Oil? What the devil did that mean? Fitz read the note aloud and decided he sounded like a demented Irishman. *Feed what's yours or I'll take him back?* Or *them* back?

Maybe next time someone knocked on his door, he'd meet him with a punch to the jaw, if this was how the dastard meant to get his attention.

Had he driven his creditors to insanity? Had a crazed tenant followed him to town? The estate was all he owned, so he couldn't imagine what else he needed to "feed." Or was there some chance that his cousin Geoff was as ill educated as most of the brainless Wyckerlys? Who else would be angry enough to heave bricks at him and tell him to feed his tenants?

For the sake of caution, hunting down his cousin moved to the top of Fitz's agenda. For all he knew, the man was a lunatic.

"What do you mean, he isn't in town? He was in town just last week." Swinging his ebony walking stick, Fitz paced the narrow untidy office of the estate solicitors the next morning. Decades of pipe and cigar smoke had seeped into the wood of the floor and bookcases, creating a disgustingly unhealthy stench. He was glad his empty pockets hadn't allowed him to take up the tobacco habit. He wanted to fling open the windows, but he doubted they'd been breached since jolly Charlie sat the throne. "Leeches like him need warm bodies to bleed," he insisted. "Geoff's warehouses are in town."

His balding solicitor polished his spectacles, ignoring Fitz's rage.

"Mr. Geoffrey stopped in and inquired into the status of the estate as was his right when you were thought dead. Once you returned to London and he could see that you were alive, he had to leave on business in Yorkshire."

Fitz realized he might persuade himself that Geoff had slung a stone at him in a rage at not inheriting, but he couldn't have heaved a brick if he was in Yorkshire. Then who else would send a note saying *Feed what's yours or I'll take them back?* He wasn't starving Penny, so it must be the estate tenants that needed *feeding*, although he couldn't fathom how even creditors could *take them back*. Geoff's side of the family might have some bee in their bonnet about the title, though. He had no clear idea of what the argument was that had parted the different branches a couple of generations ago. Could his heir have hired assassins and left town to cover his tracks?

Geoff owned warehouses and mills. Ruffians worked for him every day.

"I want Geoff notified that I must speak with him," Fitz said sternly. The solicitor nodded and made a note. "And then I need a will." Unable to strangle his cousin or beat a villain into the ground, Fitz was left with no choice but to be practical.

The solicitor peered over the top of his spectacles. "The estate is entirely entailed."

"My daughter isn't." Dusting off a chair with his

handkerchief, Fitz took a seat, crossed his boots, and began tapping them with his stick. "She needs a guardian should anything happen to me."

"If you marry, your wife would be the logical choice," the dusty man of business argued.

"But as things stand, I may die before I marry. I want an executor who won't argue about a woman's suitability to raise a child, and I would like to ask Miss Abigail Merriweather to be Penelope's guardian. She's the only one I'd trust to look after my daughter, no matter what condition my estate is in."

Satisfied that he'd finally got something right, Fitz sat back and waited for the solicitor to take his orders. It was time he stepped over the glaring disadvantages of his accursed title and learned to exploit the benefits it provided.

17

"I believe Lord Robert Smythe was taken with you last evening." The marchioness swept up and down her bed-chamber, patting perfume behind her ears and dodging the maid who was attempting to adjust the bow above her train. "And Sir Barton would be an excellent match. He has his own land, even if it is in the Lake Country."

"I have my own land," Abby murmured, sitting at the lady's dressing table and allowing still another maid to powder her nose and fret over the elaborate head-dress of dangling ribbons and pearls arranged over her cropped hair. "And Sir Barton is too easygoing. The children would run rampant over him."

Rich chestnut hair upswept and adorned with a string of shimmering gems, Lady Belden straightened her slender figure into an aristocratic pose and glared. "You'll have no children to run rampant if you insist on being particular."

Even though she knew the dowager was right, Abigail refused to be intimidated. "Surely there are men out there who speak firmly." Men like the earl, although she preferred it when he teased Penelope into behaving. If one such man existed, there had to be others.

"Of course there are, but the more specific the qualities you seek, the more difficult the competition. Most men prefer young misses fresh out of the nursery. You cannot be too choosy if you insist on pursuing the return of your siblings." Her voice softened as she observed Abigail stand up and shake out her new ball gown. "Well, perhaps you can be a *little* choosy. You are a veritable Cinderella."

Abigail *felt* like a Cinderella. Instead of her usual lumpy woolens, she wore whisper-soft amber silk that floated over a scandalously translucent chemise. A froth of gauzy sarcenet trailed over the skirt and into floor-length ruffles around her feet, which were encased in delicately embroidered silk slippers—not glass, but close enough.

Her bodice—Abigail gulped and tried not to peer too long in the marchioness's rather terrifying cheval glass. Imported from France, the mirror tilted to reveal Abigail from head to toe. Since she'd never owned more than a wall mirror, she'd never given her full figure much notice. Now—she could see that the thin silk band of her bodice was scarcely wider than her hand, revealing far more of her bosom than she'd ever exposed. And the silk scandalously draped over curves that she hadn't known she possessed.

She almost looked as if she *belonged* in London.

Rather than acknowledge her embarrassment at the ripe figure she saw in the glass, Abigail watched the ribbons dance from her curls as she shook her head. Her throat felt exposed without a chemisette to conceal it. "My seed pearls?" she suggested, touching the hollow at the base.

"Nonsense. We are presenting you as an heiress. Lily, the amber and rubies, please." Garbed in dove gray shot with blue, the marchioness had added a stunning set of diamonds to her ears, throat, and wrist. She shimmered like an evening goddess.

With her petite size and sheared curls, Abby could

never aspire to her hostess's dramatic elegance or sophistication, but the necklace the maid drew from the jewel box made her gasp.

"Excellent," the lady said in satisfaction, admiring the result as the maid fastened the five-strand bib necklace around Abby's throat. "You will be no insipid miss, blending in with all the other ingenues. You will stand out as a lady in your own right. Never let a man think you are any less than his equal. You must command respect."

Command respect? She would be fortunate enough to find the strength to swallow.

Suffering seven degrees of trepidation, Abigail trailed after the marchioness to the waiting carriage. As the vehicle traversed busy streets and waited in line for footmen to help them disembark, she listened dutifully to the lady's list of instructions, people she must meet, dances she mustn't dance, men she must avoid.

She wasn't entirely certain city dances were the same as country ones. And she had most certainly mixed up the names of the desirable men with the undesirable ones. Names were meaningless without faces. Faces were meaningless unless she saw them with the children. She really did not have a mind trained for society.

Still, even with her head whirling with instructions, Abby did her best to smile pleasantly and not gape as they climbed stairs crowded with laughing ladies flirting with elegant gentlemen. The mob pushed them up, past a glittering chandelier, until they came to stand in the entrance of the third-story ballroom, waiting to be announced by a servant in livery that put her father's best Sunday suit to shame.

The ballroom sparkled with what had to be a thousand wax tapers. Smoke curled around a ceiling painted to look like a midnight sky. Fragile white silk fluttered over open French doors on a distant balcony. Matching white silk festooned the blue walls, draped and caught up in ribbons and red roses. The perfume of a stifling crowd in an enclosed space overpowered any scent from the roses.

Abigail's stomach churned, and she considered fleeing, but the mob behind her was too thick and shoved her forward. She didn't know anyone. She didn't have a thing to say.

Only gradually did she emerge from her own selfish fears to realize that, unlike Lady Belden, most of the ladies here had escorts. Perhaps . . . could the lady need Abigail as an excuse to appear in public for the first time since her husband's death?

The possibility that she might be useful to her hostess in some small way gave her the courage to move forward, but she still thought Cinderella had been smart to arrive late, after the crowd had thinned out.

She wished she could hope for a handsome prince somewhere in this vast ballroom, but if the gentlemen she'd met last night at the theater were any indication, they were no different from Billy or Harry at home, just better dressed and inclined toward giving themselves airs.

Using his size to advantage, Lord Quentin shoved through the crush to appear at Lady Belden's side. "You should have told me you were coming," he said with disapproval. "If I am the only family you have here, it is my duty to escort you."

"Family!" The lady trilled with laughter and tapped him with her fan. "You can scarcely consider yourself *my* family. You are two removes from Edward's!"

Determined to learn from her hostess, Abigail observed the byplay with curiosity. She didn't think Lord Quentin liked being laughed at, but if he was the insufferable sort who preferred to have things his way, he deserved taking down a notch, as Lady Anne had said.

"Nevertheless, you are a Hoyt," he insisted. "Never let it be said that my family treats you in any way less than is proper."

"I still intend to spend my fortune before I die," Lady

Belden said merrily as the servant announced their names. "There is no need for you to do me up brown."

Abby had thought Lord Quentin had been kind and considerate in his generous offer, not managing or insufferable, but from the lady's response, she thought otherwise. Abby thought she'd never grasp the nuances.

"Truthfully, you did not think I would attend, did you?" he asked.

Lady Bell flicked her fan and glanced around the ballroom. "That's hardly my concern. You are the son of a marquess now. No matter where you attained your wealth, society can scarcely ignore you any longer. Where are your sisters?"

Ah, now she understood some of the stiffness between these two. Society did not deem Lord Quentin a gentleman because he was in trade. Abby didn't understand why that must be so, but she knew that's how it worked.

"Sally is with my aunt. Margaret isn't properly out yet, but Sally has danced once with Fitz." He turned and belatedly acknowledged Abigail. "Miss Merriweather, if you will allow me the pleasure of the cotillion, I would be most honored."

She offered her dance card and allowed Lord Quentin to scrawl his name for one of the first dances. She understood he had no need of her dowry, and his attention was only a maneuver to attract notice for her so she might find a husband. She, at least, was grateful for his consideration.

"Most of Danecroft's friends are here," Lady Belden murmured in Abby's ear as a footman announced their entrance. "They all have pockets to let, but unlike Fitz's, their families are influential. I'll introduce you to Lady Atherton, our hostess. Her youngest son, Nicholas, is a worse fribble than Danecroft, but his mother will do anything to see him settled. His father has the wealth to hire all the solicitors and barristers your little heart can desire."

Abby was pretty certain she didn't want an idle fribble. She'd hoped to find someone with a little work ethic. But she had to admit—glancing around at the awe-inspiring decor—a family with this much wealth and prestige could command kings.

Lord Quentin broke through the throng to reach their hostess, who nodded approvingly at Abby as the introductions were made. "I heard you meant to look after some of Edward's relations, Isabell," said Lady Atherton. "That is most generous of you. I hope you will enjoy your evening, Miss Merriweather."

Enjoy? She supposed she might if she didn't think her entire future and that of the children rested upon this frivolous fantasy. She would prefer to spend the evening admiring the beautiful gowns swirling past her, or observing the fascinating mating dance of the *ton*. If the hubbub of voices didn't nearly drown it out, she'd love to sit on the sidelines and simply enjoy the music. But her lot tonight was to enter the jungle and hope she didn't become prey for the animals.

She was too short to see past the gentlemen crowding around the marchioness. Wealthy and beautiful, the lady was the honey who drew every eligible bachelor in the room. Abby wished she could see Lord Danecroft, just so she knew one person who liked her for herself, but she smiled politely and extended her hand and accepted introductions to men whose eyes were only on her benefactor.

When it became apparent that Lady Belden would not dance and that the only way the gentlemen could please her was to dance with her protégée, Abby began her test of endurance.

"What a wuvahly pin, my lord!" the charming chit in white simpered, staring at Fitz's chest even though she loomed an inch over his head.

How daunting to have an eighteen-year-old top him, although he must admit, her height would have given him a much better glimpse of her bosom had she possessed one. With a sigh, Fitz added another qualification to his list of necessary wifely virtues—short and round. He hadn't decided about the lisp yet. For ten thousand pounds a year, he might endure a lisp.

He led the child back to her mother and moved on to the next name on his card, striving hard to remember who she was and why he'd asked for a dance. His usually good memory must be afflicted by his concern over leaving Penelope alone with only a nanny for protection. He'd used more of his loan money to have new bolts and locks installed. He'd ordered the nanny to keep Penny away from windows. But it grated that he couldn't provide a household of bullies to discourage a repetition of last night's brick throwing.

He spotted Quentin leading a lady with short red gold hair off the dance floor and approved of Miss Merriweather's choice of partner, even though the pain of envy stabbed him. They would make an excellent couple. He would have realized that Quent was ideal for Miss Merry's purposes had he not been so wrapped up in his own selfish concerns.

When he saw Quentin leading the lady toward the balcony door, Fitz growled and started after them. He caught himself just as the pair reached Nick, and it became apparent that Quentin was merely making introductions.

Matchmaking.

Golden Nick wouldn't suit Rhubarb Girl at all. Nick didn't have a sensible thought in his head beyond which beautiful courtesan he'd bed next. The idea of Nick even falling out of bed in time to *see* Abby's strawberry field in daylight was too absurd to consider. Hoyt needed to be smacked for matchmaking without an inkling of common sense.

"Lord Danecroft?" A lofty—peeved—male voice intruded on his reverie.

He glanced around and saw Viscount Pemberley

bearing down on him. Fitz winced. *Right.* He was supposed to be escorting the darling of the family onto the floor right now.

"Pemberley!" he said happily, extending his hand. "Where have you hidden that beautiful daughter of yours? I believe I've been promised this dance."

The viscount's thunderous look eased. "Thought you'd forgotten. She's been looking forward to it all evening."

Now Fitz remembered who she was. Sir Barton had been trapped by Pemberley's arm-twisting into agreeing to dance with the wallflower daughter. Barton had turned around and bribed Fitz to dance with the reticent miss in exchange for ripping up some of the debts the estate owed him. When approached, Pemberley had been delighted to substitute an earl for a mere baronet on his daughter's card.

The wallflower's dowry wasn't as large as that of the towering chit without breasts, but once Fitz had Miss Pemberley on the dance floor, she didn't twitter, at least. And she was a nice height. And there seemed to be some indication of breasts, although one could never be certain, since her bodice was poufed out in ruffles and was too high to reveal anything interesting. Since she blotchily blushed at his downward glance, he returned to smiling into her eyes.

She had a blemish on her nose. A large, almost purplish one, which warned him that his thirty years were no doubt nearly twice her age, which would make him a cradle robber as well as a scoundrel and an insect. In another ten years, this could be Penelope dancing with a worm like him. And Pemberley had pushed the poor puss in his jaded direction? The man should be horsewhipped.

Despite all Fitz's smiling attempts to beguile, the girl appeared to be looking anywhere except at him. Hell, if he couldn't sweep a nursery miss off her feet, he was in more trouble than he'd thought. He'd hoped to pick a wealthy female tonight, propose tomorrow, and have the special license in hand before the end of next week. He couldn't neglect the estate much longer than that.

He followed the direction of the child's wistful glance and saw Miss Merry bobbing a lively curtsy and swinging on the arm of her dance partner. Fitz's eyeballs nearly rolled from his head at the entrancing image. The elegant redhead sparkling in jewels and sweeping down the dance formation wasn't a rhubarb of any sort. There was nothing remotely rural about the manner in which Miss Merry tilted her head and smiled flirtatiously, as if she pranced in aristocratic company every day. The ribbons dangling from her crown drew his gaze to the slender turn of her neck, and the glitter of gold at her throat. . . . What the devil had Isabell dressed her in? A *night shift*? He would have to strangle the man drinking in the luscious view of firm curves. . . .

Barton! The gall of the cockroach. The man hadn't a ha'penny to his name beyond some rocky fields in the north. His family was nothing and no one. A mere baronet couldn't possibly help Abby get her family back. Knowing the man, Fitz was sure he wouldn't even try. Barton had tailor bills greater than any dowry Abby might have inherited.

If mild-mannered Barton was the man Pemberley's daughter was drooling over, they belonged together. At least Barton wouldn't terrify the child as Fitz obviously did.

Setting his mouth grimly, he danced his wistful miss to the end of the line, and broke in beside Abby and Barton. "There you are, m'dear," he said cheerfully. "We've been trying to catch your attention all evening."

Sacrificing whatever debts Barton would have torn up, delighting Miss Pemberley, who looked as if she would expire of pleasure, Fitz caught Abby in a whirl of music and carried her off, leaving the baronet stuck with the wealthy wallflower.

18

"Is exchanging partners proper in London?" Abigail asked, not at all comprehending how she had suddenly traded a polite baronet for a glowering earl. It was no wonder his partner had looked relieved to be traded if Danecroft had glared at the child as he glared at Abby now.

"It's perfectly proper when you're wasting time on penniless fools." Now that he had what he wanted, the earl seemed oddly preoccupied. He glanced from her to the people around them as he led her through the remaining steps of the dance.

Why had he switched partners if he merely wanted to study the crowd? There for a little while she had foolishly thought she was succeeding at attracting noble suitors. She had hoped Danecroft had noticed, but she was coming to understand that he survived by scheming, so she must be part of some devious plan of his. It was unfair that he looked so handsome and artless while gulling others.

"I scarcely had time to judge Sir Barton as a fool," she said tartly. "And only penniless suitors are likely to be interested in me." Danecroft might be a toplofty earl, but he was the only person in this ballroom she had seen wallowing, half-dressed, in pig slop. Somehow, that made it easier to be herself with him.

"I cannot believe you're relying on Hoyt to choose your partners." His green eyes flashed as he finally focused on her. "He has about as much understanding of human nature as your rhubarb."

Abby laughed at his ill humor. "That may be so, but Lord Quentin speaks well, and he knows everyone, so he might be a little more useful than rhubarb in this matter."

"No, he isn't. If I planted him in a field, he'd no doubt produce a crop of little Hoyts, but he wouldn't produce a respectable suitor for you."

The music ended, and he swung her to the edge of the dance floor. Ignoring Lady Belden bearing down on them, the earl hustled Abby toward a crowded anteroom where tables of delicacies awaited hungry guests. He ordered punch for both of them, and expertly guided her toward a corner hidden by a massive armoire, while still not looking at her. She might think she'd developed warts and a rash from the way he avoided her resplendent appearance. This was *not* how the Cinderella story was supposed to go.

"This is rude," she objected. "I have promised the next dance to Mr. Atherton. Lady Belden will be exceedingly upset if I am disrespectful of our hostess's son."

"I know Nick. He's no doubt with his latest conquest at the moment. His mother would have to find him first, grab his ear, and drag him onto the floor. I'm saving both of you from the humiliation of a scene. If Quent set you up with him, it only emphasizes my point. He doesn't understand people."

"And you do?" she asked politely, trying to fathom his sudden interest in her dance partners. Or why he observed the room while he talked with her.

"Exactly. Let me see your dance card."

Out of curiosity, she offered it to him. Danecroft

looked so serious and concerned that she suffered an inappropriate thrill at his interest. It was almost a relief to hand the card to someone she'd like to consider a friend.

"No, no, and no!" He shook his head in disbelief, and the recalcitrant strand of golden brown hair fell across his brow. "They've collected a fine set of family names, admittedly, but none of these fellows will suit. I can't imagine one of them helping you win back your siblings."

Their gloved hands touched as she tugged the card away from him, and she fought a shiver of desire. She *wanted* Danecroft to look at her. She wanted him to see her as Cinderella and not a plain farm girl. And that was utterly absurd, as he was making quite clear by scarcely noticing her existence. "I could make the return of the children part of the marriage settlement," she said with what she hoped was confidence.

Finally, he glared down at her. She couldn't tell if the flare of his nostrils was fire-breathing anger or male lust as he glimpsed the scandalous amount of flesh revealed by the cut of her gown, but she felt the brush of his gaze like hot coals. Before she could catch her breath, he jerked his attention back to her face.

"Don't be ridiculous," he asserted firmly, not sounding like a man overcome with desire. "Once a man has your blunt, he can do anything he wants with it. You need a man who likes children and doesn't need your money. Come along, let's see what I can do."

In amazement, Abby set aside her empty cup. She knew she couldn't expect an earl to look upon her as marriage material. And maybe he had forgotten the burning thrill of their kiss, but she hadn't. She was nearly breathless from just touching his coat sleeve as he led her across the room. She had to fight an urge to swat him.

She swallowed hard and tried to divert her thoughts by hoping Danecroft could find someone for her who was a bit like himself. She liked that the earl didn't tower over her as Lord Quentin did. Danecroft was tall and broad-shouldered enough to make her feel feminine and sheltered, but not so large as to intimidate. And he seemed to have her interests in mind, which was more exciting than all the money and titles around her. If she must have a husband, she wanted one who could be her friend, she decided. She feared it might be difficult to form friendships with men who wanted only her inheritance. Danecroft was right about that.

"Ah, here is Longacre. His children are grown. In fact, the younger son has legal offices in the city. He even has property in Oxfordshire. You can talk rhubarb together."

A man with children her age was a little daunting, but Abigail eagerly looked for this paragon who might be the answer to her problems.

Danecroft led her to a rotund older man who was happily munching on *foie gras*. Abby tried to swallow her disappointment. She hoped she wasn't so shallow as to choose a husband by looks alone. And at least Mr. Longacre was no taller than the earl. But she had hoped . . . perhaps just a little more dashing? She was dismayed at the extent of her petty selfishness.

"Miss Merriweather, may I present Mr. Albert Longacre of Oxfordshire. He has only one daughter left to marry off, am I correct, sir? Longacre, this is Abigail Merriweather, Lady Belden's protégée. The marquess remembered her in his will, so she has come to see town before returning to her estates out your way."

"How'dye do, Miss Merriweather." Longacre wiped his greasy hand on his handkerchief and, rather than pull on his glove again, used the linen to cover his palm as he bowed over her hand. "Most happy to meet you. Believe I knew your father. Sad, that he was taken so young."

Mr. Longacre was old enough to *be* her father. Abigail didn't know if she could do this. Uneasily, she clenched her hands in front of her, trying not to bunch up her gown in the process. "He mourned the loss of my stepmother. I like to think he is happy to be back with her."

"Or with your mother, eh what? Wonder how that works, if a man has two wives precede him to heaven? Does he have to make a choice when he gets there?"

Abigail didn't want to be a man's second choice to find out. She liked that he wondered about such things but felt only relief when Longacre's unmarried daughter arrived, eager to be introduced to an earl, and Danecroft made their excuses and dragged Abigail away.

"Didn't know the old goat was so maudlin," he muttered.

"But you were right that he would otherwise be a good choice," she said, hiding her dismay. "He reminded me very much of my father, who, by the way, would infinitely prefer my stepmother to my mother if given a choice. My mother was a bit of a tartar. I believe he married her for the house."

Fitz sent her a look of frustration, and she tingled inappropriately at all that heated concentration on her. Despite his glare, for the first time all evening, she felt relaxed enough to smile and have a good time.

Fitz thought his head might explode if he didn't shake some sense into the prim little spinster who had turned his eyeballs inside out wearing a gown her mother would never have approved. He was having difficulty staying focused while his sweaty palms ruined his gloves. He had to look anywhere except at Miss Merriweather's bosom, or he'd be dragging her off the dance floor in search of a bed, and she was not the sophisticated type of woman one bedded without consequence. He tried to remember her vicious hoe and ugly bonnets, but her image in the ball gown was branded into the back of his skull.

Her smile nearly brought him to his knees.

"If your mother was anything like you," he said in a grim tone she didn't deserve, "I can assure you that your father married her for more than a strawberry field. Do you have any idea of how ravishing you look in that gown?"

"Did you notice that Mr. Longacre was more interested in the food than my gown?" she retorted.

The necklace on her plump, white bosom shook when she was irritated, and Fitz ground his teeth in frustration while trying not to look. "That's the whole point! Feed him rhubarb tarts, and he'll do anything you ask." Like avoid her bed, was his hope. A fat old man shouldn't have any interest in ravishing his young bride.

Just the thought of *any* man taking Miss Abby to bed really was enough to make his overheated head explode like a cracked kettle. So an old man seemed the safest choice to prevent his head from shooting off his shoulders.

"And I'll be back to raising four children alone again, after he eats himself into an early grave. I don't mind being married for my money and my managing ways, but is it so difficult to believe that I might marry someone who would at least *like* to accompany me into old age?" Dropping Fitz's arm, she picked up her skirt and started back to the ballroom. "You are no better than Lord Quentin, seeing only one part of the whole. At least his lordship's choices appear to be young enough to stay around for a while. Do you propose to marry a woman twice your age just because she's wealthy and her lands lie near yours?"

"I've given it some thought," he said crossly, "but I need heirs."

He caught up with her and slowed her down before she stormed into the ballroom with all flags flying and every male in the place went cross-eyed.

"And what if I want children of my own?" she countered. "I've always wanted a family. I think I would be a very good mother. Are there any barristers in here?"

"Barristers?" he asked in incredulity. "Dry old sticks won't give you children." Although now that she mentioned it, dry sticks wouldn't be interested in her bed either. His head was definitely in the wrong place.

"Must a man be old to be a barrister? What are the qualifications?" she demanded.

Now she was the one who sounded cross. This was not going well. He could usually twist a woman around his little finger with a few well-placed suggestions. But he kept trying to be *honest* with this one.

Quentin stepped into their path. "A little quarrel?" he asked silkily. "Miss Merriweather, shall I escort you to your next partner?"

"Why don't you match her up with Cox?" Fitz asked in exasperation. "All he wants is a wife to convince his family he doesn't fly light. Or maybe Dobbs, who has four brats of his own and probably won't notice four more."

When Abigail looked interested at the mention of Dobbs, Fitz wanted to pull his hair. He glared at her. "He has no funds of his own, and his salary at the ministry isn't sufficient to feed the four mouths he already has. Don't saddle the poor man with more."

Fortunately, she had the wisdom not to argue.

Quentin, on the other hand, looked smug, took the lady's hand on his arm, and nodded toward the dance floor. "Fitz, you are scheduled to dance the waltz with Lady Mary Barron. She has a generous trust fund from her grandmother, as well as any marriage portion her father will bestow on her."

"And she no doubt plans to donate it all to the church," Fitz growled. He bowed to Miss Abby, who sent him a look of concern that he resented. "Enjoy yourself, Miss Merriweather, but do not consider one of those fellows on your dance card. They're not worthy of you." He stalked off.

Lady Mary looked like the queen for whom she'd been named. Her thin lips were drawn tight like a prune, her hair was scraped back from her face, and he swore, she had no eyebrows. She followed his shoes and counted her steps as he attempted to steer her through the dance. He inquired if she was enjoying the season, if she'd met anyone interesting, if she practiced needlework, and by the time the music ended, he was desperately asking if she had any younger sisters. The only reply he received to his inquiries was a tight smile and a nod or shrug.

Well, he'd wanted a quiet woman. He ought to hare off right now and find her father. He had a strong suspicion the lady's family were closet Catholics willing to trade her dowry for his vote on the Irish question, but he didn't much give a fig if they were Buddhists and wanted a temple as long as he had money in his pocket and could take Penelope out of London.

Maybe he could call on Lady Mary in the morning and see if she was a little more lively at that time of day. Or if her tight smile hid snaggled teeth. Or maybe it didn't matter. She was female and presumably had all her working parts. Plus a dowry and a father wealthy enough to buy what he wanted.

He would have to spend a lifetime chained to a woman who probably prayed in bed. And by the time he spent all her dowry paying his debts, he wouldn't be able to afford a mistress.

He noticed Miss Merriweather laughing with the normally taciturn Blake Montague, and his brain finally reached the boiling point. Blake would use her money to buy his way into the army and get himself killed, and Fitz would lose both his best friend and the woman he wanted for his own.

Which was how he knew his brain had finally exploded. He wanted Miss Merry for his wife, in his bed, chatting about strawberries, cuddling *his* children. Why should any other damned man in this room have her when she could be his countess?

He'd still be bankrupt, but if her dowry was large enough for him to hire an estate manager and replant a few fields, maybe he could scrape by with his gambling income. What were his creditors going to do, sue the residents of the family mausoleum and put their corpses in Newgate? The lawyers had assured him that since his name wasn't on any of the debts, they couldn't fling him in debtors' prison, yet. If he didn't do the honorable thing and pay up, he would never have credit anywhere, ever again, but since he'd never had any to begin with, that would hardly hurt.

Of course, he'd have to repay Quentin. It would take one hell of a gambling stake to win that much. . . .

So, he'd have to use the dowry to win a game or two to pay back Quentin before he could go back to earning a living and finding an estate manager. It would work out.

It had to because, entirely against his will and better sense, he was about to walk over and bounce Blake against a wall if his friend didn't keep his damned eyeballs in his head instead of on Miss Merriweather's splendiferous bosom.

19

Abigail gasped as a strong male hand gripped her bare elbow and tugged her through the open French doors where she'd stopped to catch a breeze.

"I need to talk with you."

Danecroft's bay rum scent seeped through her senses, more potent than the aroma of strawberries and roses combined, and more masculine than she was accustomed to. His grip on her arm was firm and slightly intoxicating. Or perhaps that sensation was caused by the glass of punch she'd drunk earlier. She just knew her head swam oddly when the earl pulled her into a niche behind a marble column and all she could see was him.

She stared at his impeccable neckcloth and white silk waistcoat, and her mind wandered to the man she'd seen in shirtsleeves. She was having difficulty juxtaposing the imposing aristocrat in silk with the man soaked to his skin in filth and carrying his child. It occurred to her that perhaps she put too much emphasis on appearance.

"How would you like to be a countess?" he asked desperately, clutching both her bare arms and pinning her against the wall. She could feel the heat of his hands even through his gloves.

A countess? That wasn't very likely. She looked up at him with puzzlement. In the faint light from the lamps, she could see Danecroft's mouth drawn into a tight line instead of curved with his usual smiling charm. His gaze was intense enough to light fires. Was he angry with her?

"I don't think I'd like to be a countess very much," she admitted. "I don't seem to have a knack for giving parties or chatting idly."

Belatedly, he stepped back and ran a hand through his rumpled hair. He glared, and she wasn't certain if he wanted to laugh, or shake her. Whatever was wrong, it had caused the affable earl to abandon all his deceptive charm—which she perversely found charming in itself.

"You have a knack for bossing people about," he reminded her.

"Children and servants, I suppose, but what does that have to do with being a countess?"

"I am not doing this very well, am I?" Hands behind his stiff back, he paced two steps, then swung about and paced four. "I have an estate in Berkshire large enough for an army of children."

Shock froze her to the stone wall. How had she forgotten that *he* was an earl? A heart-stoppingly sophisticated one. Surely, she had misinterpreted his strange comment. She waited, striving to comprehend any other reason why he might mention his estate and children. Evidently, her mind and his were at odds.

Danecroft threw her a despairing look. "You don't intend to make this easy for me, do you? Any other woman in that room would be smiling triumphantly and saying, 'Yes, of course, my lord, whatever you say, my lord,' and I'd be on firm ground. Or my knees. Depending on how I felt about her, I suppose."

Abby wanted to smile at the image of this charmingly self-confident gentleman falling on his knees for a mere woman, but she wasn't certain what woman he had in mind exactly. "I'm not much inclined to agreeing to questions I haven't been asked, and I should hope you wouldn't ask them of women who are so blandly agreeable."

"Then let me put it this way." Danecroft grabbed her waist and hauled her up against his silk-covered chest and covered her mouth with his.

Abby nearly swooned. She dug her gloved fingers into his wide shoulders and hung on while he showed her that the kiss they had exchanged at the inn had been a mere matchstick flame compared with the conflagration he lit now. Heat engulfed her from head to toe. Muscled arms held her close, dragging her from her feet. He bruised her lips with his passion, and she could do no less than open her mouth to allow him inside. The sweet tartness of his tongue was better than any pie she'd ever tasted.

For a few blazing minutes, she was immersed in mindless sensation, with no thought to responsibility or propriety. His moan of pleasure melted her bones. His big body engulfed hers, making her feel strong, desirable, and feminine instead of small, managing, and boring. Crushed against the hardness of his torso, her breasts swelled and softened.

When his hand slid up her back to stroke her bodice, she gasped at the erotically tactile sensation and pushed away, afraid her heart would leap from her chest. Danecroft reluctantly lowered her to her feet but didn't release her. She rested her head against his shoulder, unable to stand on her own just yet. He held her tight enough that she could feel his harsh breathing.

My goodness, he would twist her head around to believe anything if he continued kissing her like that.

"Marry me, Rhubarb Girl."

Rhubarb Girl? To whom was he talking? Seduced by the unexpected solace of the earl's powerful arms around her, promising the invincibility she'd never possess on her own, she didn't want to move. If she could simply freeze time and stay here forever . . .

"Be my countess and come home with me and Penelope and show us how to plant strawberries," he whispered into her hair.

Oh, he had meant he wanted to marry *her*. She flushed with embarrassment at her stupidity. How could she have known he was asking *her* to marry him? She couldn't even fathom it now that he'd stated it plainly.

He was always making her feel simple and unworldly, probably because that's what she was. A rhubarb, indeed.

"I don't understand," she murmured, pushing away slightly, fearful he was making fun of her in some way she didn't grasp. "You must marry wealth and perhaps someone with an influential family who can help you."

"*Think*, Abby. . . . I may call you Abby, may I not? I can't keep calling you Rhubarb Girl and Miss Merry, which produce this absurd desire to hug you and pet you as if you were my own personal kitten."

"Rhubarb Girl?" she inquired, recovering some segment of her sense of humor if not completely overcoming her shock. "I daresay Abby would be preferable."

"And you must call me Fitz. Or Jack, which is my given name." His gloved hands slid seductively around her waist, and his thumbs circled at the small of her back. She didn't dare look into his tempting eyes just yet, for fear she would completely lose her head. Or her heart.

"You said your given name was John," she said with what she hoped was severity, teasing because she could not believe any of this.

"John was my father's name. I prefer Jack. Or Fitz. Or Doddering Fool. But I think I'm finally getting a little smarter. I don't have much book learning, but I know people. I really do. And I think we'll suit. Tell me you agree."

She couldn't resist; she had to look up. With his lock of hair falling over his brow, he looked so earnest that his smiling charm was entirely dissipated. Even his eyes failed to laugh. He looked nearly as startled as she was—but determined.

"You don't have much book learning?" she asked, studying his expression, hoping her heart would stop fluttering long enough for her to understand. She needed time to mull over even mundane choices such as deciding to preserve or sell her strawberries. She couldn't possibly make a decision so important as marriage with just a moment's notice . . . especially to a man who obviously made momentous decisions on impulse.

Danecroft—Fitz—*Jack*—cupped her face between his big hands and planted a kiss on her nose. And the corner of her mouth. And she shivered with the need for more.

"Tutors like to be paid," he explained. "Schools require money. My father didn't see the necessity. That's all past now, don't you see? I can change things. Slowly, perhaps, but with you by my side, I'll learn." He sounded eager and not the least terrified of such a future.

Abby swallowed hard. He almost made her feel . . . desirable. To dream of an aristocrat like Danecroft . . . was insane. "Why me? I don't like town. My dowry is limited, and I don't know anyone influential. I have no idea what you're asking of me, and neither do you."

The most elegant, charming man she'd ever had the pleasure to know released her face to run both his hands through his hair in a gesture of despair. The action boyishly disheveled his golden brown locks, making him even more heartbreakingly appealing than in all his polished sophistication.

"I know. You're perfectly right," he agreed. "But think about it, Abby. I may not know rhubarb from rutabagas, but I can hire an estate manager with your dowry, one who will know how to put the land back in order. How could any executor deny you if you're married to an earl? You could have the children back. And I would have my sensible Rhubarb Girl for wife instead of some twittering adolescent."

He needed her dowry and her managing ways, just like everyone else did, she told herself. She had been ready to accept that, for the sake of the children. But this . . . she placed her gloved hands on her face in a vague attempt to hold herself together, or seal in the heat of his touch.

He'd called her sensible. Was that a good thing?

He was talking about *marriage*. To an earl. To the most handsome, desirable man she'd ever met. Fairy tales did *not* come true. He must be scheming again, and she was too naive to understand the rules. She could lose everything she had and more if she decided wrong.

She shook her head, and Danecroft's expression was so crestfallen that she nearly cried. She touched his coat, knowing she courted danger in doing so, because his gaze smoldered.

"I need time to think," she murmured. "I cannot . . . This is so . . ."

"I know, I know. I think my brain exploded when I thought of it. It just seems so right, and I'm not known for doing what is right."

He crushed her hand in his, and for a moment, everything seemed remarkably clear. Then he placed it on his arm and propriety returned. "If I do not return you inside, Quentin will fling me over the parapet and Isabell will demand an immediate wedding, and I would rather give you time to be certain. I take that back. No, I don't want to give you time to think of all the reasons it won't work. I want to rush you off to Gretna Green. But I won't. I know I'm the impulsive one, and you're not."

She nodded uncertainly. "I do need time, thank you. There are so many things I must consider before saying yes. You are . . . so much more than any of the gentlemen I have met. I cannot put my mind on it. You could have any woman in London."

He laughed in self-deprecation as he led her back to the ballroom. "Miss Pemberley prefers Sir Barton. I don't fancy ignorant young things. And most of the smart women don't fancy me. Or need me. You, on the other hand, need me just as I need you, so we're well matched in that."

A marriage based on mutual need almost made sense, in the same way this glittering ballroom of exotic scents, beautiful people, and lavish clothing made sense. Abby feared that once she returned to the real world, however, the Cinderella fantasy would turn back into ashes. She needed to be in the familiar, simple surroundings of her home, preferably with the children—anywhere but here—before she could even *think* of such an enormous leap of faith.

She was too tongue-tied to explain any of that before Lord Quentin and Lady Belden swooped down on them, clucking and threatening, and sweeping them in different directions as if they were disobedient children.

"Whatever are you thinking?" the marchioness cried, towing Abby away from Fitz toward a gaggle of her cronies. "I have told you Danecroft is unsuitable. He is a shallow cad who makes his living *gambling*. He has no interest in children and rural pursuits. You need a man who shares your interests."

Gambling? The earl—Fitz—was a gambler? How had she not known that? Because in reality she knew nothing of him at all. How could she learn when she scarcely knew a soul? "How does one make a living gambling?" she asked cautiously.

"Does it matter?" the marchioness asked with a dismissive sweep of her hand. "Perhaps he cheats. Perhaps his friends are extraordinarily stupid. Perhaps he smiles at ladies and they hand him their jewels. Or all of that. But someday, sometime, he will lose more than he can afford. I know whereof I speak. Do you wish a man like that to have possession of your farm and dowry and your siblings' futures?"

She couldn't risk her farm! She knew she needed to think hard and long about his proposal, but basing their futures on the fall of a card . . .

Abby suffered the agonizing suspicion that the light had just gone out on her shining moment.

"What the devil are you thinking?" Quentin demanded, digging his massive fist into Fitz's upper arm and hauling him toward the smoking room, where a bar had been set up for the gentlemen. "You're a damned *earl* now. You can't be seducing country chits under the noses of all society if you mean to marry one of their whelps."

Fitz debated declaring his intentions, but he had the uncomfortable notion that Quentin would demand his loan back if he did so. He shook his arm free and brushed at the wrinkles in his coat sleeve. "I would not seduce Miss Merriweather. I was just giving her some advice. You shouldn't bully her into marrying where she has no interest."

She hadn't accepted him yet. He had made a perfect botch of his proposal. He couldn't believe he'd botched something so important. He needed to collect his wits before trying again.

"Since when have you become an expert on marriage?" Quentin asked, pouring a whiskey and scowling.

"Same time as you, apparently." Fitz helped himself to a brandy and scowled back.

Quentin might be large, but Fitz had watched the man box. Quent used his size to advantage, but his proper footwork and practiced punches were much too predictable. Fitz knew how to think on his feet and strike unexpectedly. He could take the larger man down if necessary. But he'd rather remember Miss Merry's sweet kisses.

The thought of bedding Abigail fogged his mind with such lustful images that it obliterated any chance of winning this argument. "I need to hire an estate manager," he declared, taking a new direction. "I assume it's not too late to plant some of the fields if I had the blunt to pay for whatever is needed."

"Did you win another stud for collateral?" Quentin asked in scorn.

"I will stop liking you shortly," Fitz warned. "I might not have your education, but I know people and I know how to win at cards. I make do with what I can. I can't blame you if you don't trust me for another loan, but you know damned well I'm not a fool. If I want to court Miss Merriweather, that's my business and none of yours."

"Isabell will have your head on a platter," Quentin said bluntly. "She won't allow it. If you must marry quickly, you need to look elsewhere."

There were no doubt ten thousand reasons why he should look elsewhere, starting with lust not being a good basis for marriage and ending with Abby being a rural farm girl who would despise the unwholesome life he led. And there was all that business about creditors and children he couldn't afford and didn't know how to manage and run-down estates in between.

And he still stubbornly clung to his instincts. "I don't believe Isabell has any say in the matter. Will you help me find an estate manager or not?"

Quentin sipped his drink and eyed Fitz as if he were a snake who might strike. Fitz felt wild enough to bite, but his shield of civilization was too thick.

"Did you ever find out who set up your suicide scene?" Quentin asked unexpectedly.

Fitz took a swallow of the brandy. There were some subjects he'd rather not discuss. "My heir is on his way to Yorkshire, so I can't ask him about it."

"How do you know if it is even safe to return to your estate? Could there be someone there who wishes you dead?"

"What the devil is this all about?" Diverted by the change of subject, Fitz studied his friend. "I don't appreciate being questioned like a truant."

Quentin produced a folded, dirty sheet of paper from his pocket. "This arrived via my window last night."

Fitz's heart sank as he shook open the note.

WIKERLY IS TAYVENG SKAHNDRL—HEV HIMSEF MAYT ME TO BE GAYVENG BAK WUTZ NOT HEZ ER AYLS.

"Tayveng?" Fitz said in incredulity. "What is this, Russian illiteracy?"

"I have Irishmen working at the dock who talk like that. *Thieving scoundrel,* I believe, is the translation," Quentin said, watching Fitz carefully.

"Have himself meet me to be giving back what's not his or else?" Fitz interpreted. "Well, it looks as if my admirer is not only Irish but spells about as well as I do," he continued cheerfully, crumpling the Tattersall's poster it was written on and throwing it at the empty fireplace. "I'll be heading home now. I have some more windows to board up."

And an illiterate Irishman to hunt down and strangle before the villain started flinging bricks at Abby or any more of his friends. He didn't know any Irishmen! *Tattersall's* was hardly a clue. He didn't have the kind of blunt needed for horse-trading. He'd send Nick around to take a look for a lunatic Irishman. Nick knew the men over there better than Fitz ever would.

If Irishmen worked in Quent's shipping trade, might they not also work for Geoff's woolen trade?

Minutes later, Lady Isabell slipped into the smoking room and located Lord Quentin puffing on a cigar and looking smug. "She will not have a gambler," she declared in satisfaction. "I will see to that." She waited happily for him to frown at his impending loss of their wager.

Instead, Quentin blew a smoke ring, undisturbed. "Wyckerlys are notorious for good reason, my dear," he said, politely setting the cigar aside and viewing her with the superior attitude of a man who knew everything. "They always do what they're told not to do, come hell or high water. Your heiress doesn't stand a chance. I'm happy to see that you and my sister get along so splendidly. She will enjoy your company next season."

Narrowing her eyes, Lady Isabell did not deign to express her disapproval. She merely swept from the room, leaving him to contemplate the wallpaper.

20

Leaving the salon, her assistant at her side carrying still another bouquet from one of her admirers, Lady Belden halted at the arrival of a footman with a calling card. She read the card, sniffed, and glanced over her shoulder at Abigail. "It is your gambling friend. Shall I have him turned away?"

Abigail had stayed awake all night, tossing and turning and feeling feverish, reliving Fitz's impulsive proposal. Just knowing how far her thoughts had traveled down the path of marriage beds brought a blush to her cheeks. She distinctly remembered the day he'd said he preferred to be compared to a stallion than a rooster. She would go to hell for considering the image that raised.

"Lord Danecroft is my friend," she said quietly. No matter what else was between them, she had to believe that much.

"You have never seen men win and lose fortunes at a gaming table, have you?" the marchioness asked, not unsympathetically. "They become obsessed to the exclusion of all else. He could lose your farm and everything on it. Perhaps we should hold an evening of cards so you can judge for yourself." When Abigail's expression of determination didn't waver, she conceded. "Very well, have him in. I'll send a maid to chaperone."

"That isn't necessary, my lady," Abigail protested.

"Balderdash. He's a fortune hunter. I applaud his good taste, but I'll not see you wasted on his cause."

Abigail closed her eyes and reined in her temper. She had too many crises on her hands and did not need to add an argument with her hostess to the collection. She owed the lady too much. "I understand. Thank you, my lady."

She might lack the courage to stand up to the dowager in person, but she did not have the temperament for subservience. Instead of waiting for the chaperone, Abigail grabbed a shawl and met the earl in the foyer. She led him through the house and out the back to the kitchen garden. An upper housemaid would never follow her into the territory of a mere kitchen servant, so she assumed they could avoid any chaperone here.

Amusement twisted Danecroft's lips as he regarded the carefully tended beds glistening in the fine mist of a gloomy day. "Ah, is this what a garden should look like? How very . . . tidy."

Abigail strode a graveled path past the herb beds to the more private cutting gardens to the rear. "The lady likes fresh flowers," she stated curtly, not knowing how to deal with the vast array of emotions the earl's presence engendered. She was unaccustomed to being assaulted by conflicting desires.

How did one speak to a gentleman she had tried to envision naked? One who had crushed her breasts against his chest and invaded her mouth with his tongue? She rather thought such intimacies required a proposal. But she wasn't certain they required her acceptance. And that was only the beginning of her confusion.

"You are out of sorts." He spread his handkerchief on a damp bench and gestured for her to have a seat. "And you have led me out here to avoid the dragon lady. What is wrong?"

She wanted to weep over his perceptiveness. He still wore respectable mourning for his brother, although he obviously disdained full black. She did not like the dark gray with his coloring, but the tailored fit emphasized his formidable masculinity. Was she so shallow that she was simply falling for a dashing, handsome man?

Abby suspected the earl was well aware of how his appearance affected the fairer sex. He had a solid streak of pride and vanity, deservedly so. But he had revealed too much of his vulnerability last night, and her heart ached at the possibility that she might truly wound him.

"You always know the right thing to do and say," she said, taking the seat he'd offered. "I wish I had that gift."

"It isn't a gift but a lesson learned of necessity." He broke off a perfect pink rosebud and handed it to her. "Be glad that you grew up in a household where honesty was respected."

He must have ripped another hole in his soul to reveal that to her. Abby's eyes teared up at the image of this proud man growing up in scorn and neglect. She bent over the rose to prevent his seeing how much she really didn't want to tell him no. "We grew up in very different ways, did we not?" she murmured.

He'd been prowling the gravel path, examining the topiary. He swung on his heel at her tone and took the seat beside her. She could feel the heat and size of him without looking up.

"Don't let our differences be the excuse to turn me down," he said urgently. "I have done nothing these past hours but examine all the arguments you can possibly make, and none of them can overcome the fact that we suit each other better than anyone else we can meet."

She couldn't resist lifting her head, and his impassioned gaze nearly ripped her heart out. "You don't regret your hasty proposal? You know I will not force you to honor it." It would make her life infinitely easier if he backed out now, but believing that he thought well enough of her to propose filled her with wonder. Of course, he was also being extremely impractical, which showed how well they would not suit.

He grabbed her hand. His was gloved, but hers was not. Her fingers lingered in his warmth, even though she knew she must pull away.

"I have never had anyone to rely on but myself," he said earnestly. "I know that is not much of a recommendation, but I have learned to trust my instincts, and I know we will suit. Will you marry me, Abby? Be my helpmate, mother of my children, and my better half? I practiced my speech all night, but the pretty words fled as soon as I touched your hand."

She knew what he meant. She'd practiced speeches, too, but his hand clasped around hers was so certain and strong. . . . She desperately wanted to change her mind. She wanted his strength, his friendship. She wanted *him*. And for the sake of the children, she couldn't be so selfish. She gently freed her fingers.

"There," she whispered. "We can think clearly again. We cannot be like a pair of mindless poultry. We have others to think of besides ourselves."

"You are classifying me as a rutting rooster?" he asked in amusement. "I think I deserve better than that. I behaved in almost perfect circumspection when we were alone. It wasn't until the madness of last night that I realized I would be a fool to deny what your kisses tell me."

"I wish I could rely on instinct as you do," she said wistfully. "But I cannot. I hope someday you will forgive me enough to still be my friend. Perhaps then you might tell me what drove you to believe an inarticulate spinster with no accomplishments and little dowry could be your countess. It is a leap of judgment I cannot make."

He gripped the bench with his hands as if to keep them from straying. Abby wished she could find some equal means of preventing her gaze from wandering to the magnificent man she was sacrificing. She had to remember that appearance wasn't everything.

Yet he was so much more. . . . Or so he seemed. She truly did not know him well.

"You think you cannot be a countess?" he asked. His voice expressed his incredulity. "Would you like it better if I were a farmer?"

His shock raised her confidence, making her smile through her tears. He was a very smart man, and she knew she was right to force him to look for a more suitable match. "You were born to be a noble, my lord. You could sway all Parliament with your silver tongue if you chose to do so. It would be a waste for you to hoe fields."

"Well, I'm glad you think so, but hoeing would be far more productive to my current concerns than swaying a bunch of pigheaded aristocrats to vote for more laws we don't need. So if it's not my incipient roosterhood or my worthless title that puts you off, can you give me some hint of the obstacles in my way?"

"Do you ever get angry, my lord?" she asked when he summarily swept away all her excuses and waited patiently for the truth.

"Oh, yes, I've been towering with rage several times lately, but mostly temper results in bruised knuckles and not much else. And no, I won't tell you why I've been angry until you tell me why you're about to turn down my very respectable proposal. Come along, my Abby, speak up."

She wanted to weep against his shoulder for being so understanding, but then she would never be able to say the words. Swallowing the lump in her throat, she threaded her fingers together and asked, "Do you gamble, my lord?"

He sat so still that she knew the answer was yes.

She stood and walked to the end of the garden path, feeling her chest crushing so badly she could scarcely breathe. That had been her one hope—that the marchioness was wrong. But she knew it had been a slim one. Gambling was the most popular sport in England.

It had brought entire families to ruin, as it had undoubtedly ruined his.

She felt Danecroft standing behind her. She could not bear his proximity, could not bear that she would never feel his arms around her again. That she might never feel *any* man's arms, because she could not imagine anyone but him holding her. Tears leaked past her lids.

"I make my living gambling," he said carefully. "I'm good at it, and it puts clothes on my back. I can hope one day that I'll return the estate to profitability so there is no longer any necessity for me to spend time at the gaming tables."

"Until then, though, that would mean you must spend your time in town, just as you do now," she said gently. "And instead of needing small winnings to support yourself, you would need higher and higher stakes to support a wife and children and tenants. You are unlikely to turn your estates around if you are not there, but far more likely to do so if you married someone like Lady Mary, with a dowry far greater than mine and a family able to loan you what you need."

Steeling herself, Abby turned to observe Fitz's expression. It was dark and forbidding, not at all the insouciance of the laughing gallant she had thrown apples at. Here was the indomitable man who had fought to survive and succeeded. Should he ever show this side to an insipid young miss like Lady Mary, she would run screaming into the street. But Abigail saw his strength and determination, and wept that she could not have him.

"I do not want Lady Mary," was all he said.

"And there is the difference between us, my lord," she said in anguish. "You risk nothing by going after what you want. I risk the future of four young children who have no power over what becomes of them. I must think of them first. I cannot gamble with what little security they have."

He clenched his fists, and from the way his cheek

muscles worked, she thought he might be clenching his teeth as well. She would give everything she had to see him smile again, but she refused to believe she had shattered his hopes. In reality, he destroyed *her* just by letting her think she could be the only woman for him, when she knew that was not true. An earl had an entire world of choices. He'd simply fastened on the easiest, fastest one.

"You do not trust me to do what is best for you or the children," he stated flatly. "That is understandable. I give you good day, Miss Merriweather."

He bowed and strode off, keeping his pride intact but leaving her grieving over the impossibility of dreams. She buried her face in her hands and smothered her sobs.

21

She *turned him down*. Rhubarb Girl had turned *him* down. Rejected. Crushed like a cockroach.

Still simmering with hurt the next evening, Fitz turned his back on the simpering misses at still another grandiose ball. At least his hostess had the sense to provide a decent gaming room. He flipped a card on the table and took another, carelessly arranging his hand while the other inept players struggled over their decisions. The stack of coins in front of him tonight shimmered in gold instead of silver. He was feeling furious enough to risk higher stakes.

He didn't think winning would change Abby's mind.

He was supposed to be out on the dance floor, wooing a wife. Quent was likely to grab him by the scruff of his neck and haul him out of the gaming room and back to courting, should he discover Fitz's whereabouts.

To hell with Quent. Fitz knew whom he wanted.

He wanted Abigail for mother of his daughter as well as for his own desires. He *wasn't* selfish. Maybe, just a little bit. He supposed there might be other women out there who would be good with children. He just had no way of knowing, and he didn't have time to find out.

He scowled and lost count of the cards when he looked up to see Blake Montague walking past with Miss Merriweather on his arm, the two of them chatting like old friends. He would kill the bastard.

He lost the damned round. Glaring in dismay as half his winnings disappeared into the pockets of a wealthy viscount, Fitz gathered up what he had left and rose from the table.

"Sorry, gentlemen, but my mind is elsewhere this evening. Perhaps another time."

He walked off with more than he'd had going in, but not with as much as he'd hoped. If Quent wouldn't loan him the blunt to hire an estate manager, then he must earn it with cards.

Pursuing Montague, Fitz shoved a hand into his pocket and pretended to saunter around the edges of the ballroom until he located the bounder, who was still talking earnestly with Abigail. Treading a toe or two to remove the obstacles in his path, Fitz tapped his old friend on the shoulder.

"Still considering that position in the War Office, old chap?" he asked with a threatening growl.

Not easily deterred, Montague narrowed his dark eyes. "Haven't seen you wearing your silver balls yet, *my lord.*"

If the Danecrofts had ever owned a ceremonial coronet with an earl's eight silver balls, Fitz didn't know where the hell they kept it, and he certainly wasn't paying to have one made. But that wasn't what Montague meant.

"You don't really think the Lords would appreciate my arriving in their holy chambers trailing bailiffs, do you? There's one sitting on my front step as we speak." Fitz turned to Abby, who was following this discussion, eyes wide with sympathy. He didn't want her damned pity. "Penelope asks after you constantly. Perhaps we could arrange a visit in the park someday?"

"Yes, yes, of course," she stuttered. "I should like that."

He smiled blandly. "Beware of Montague unless you have a desire to be a widow, Miss Merriweather. His goal in life is to get himself killed in battle." He bowed and walked off before Blake could cause a scandal by planting him a facer in the middle of the ballroom.

Lady Belden observed the meeting of her protégée and the bankrupt earl with satisfaction. "She will not have him, sir. She is far too astute."

Lord Quentin rocked back on his heels and studied the expressions of his two friends. "If you think Montague a better choice, you are seriously mistaken, my lady."

"Anyone would be a better choice than a gambler."

"You are damning Fitz for the faults of your father," he warned. "Fitz is not obsessed by the game."

Isabell waved a hand in angry dismissal. "It makes no difference. *You* gamble on ships and trade. Men like risks. Women do not. I will see that my protégées have security."

Lord Quentin grunted noncommittally. "And are *you* happier for having chosen security?"

She refused to reply to his implied insult to her late husband. Edward had been a decent man and deserved respect. Their private life was of no concern to anyone else. "If I could arrange to have the children returned to her without need of marriage, I would recommend that, certainly. But Abigail and I have both applied personally to the executor, and he still refuses to accept that a woman can be a single parent. So far, I've not had much luck in finding a lawyer with the good sense to agree with us either. So marriage it must be, but only to a man who will not waste her inheritance."

"*Your* inheritance," he corrected with intolerable arrogance. "By providing funds with stipulations, you are pulling her purse strings. You are inexcusably manipulative, madam."

"She is a naive country girl, sir. I am merely looking after her best interests."

Quentin shot Isabell a smoldering look that woke something she hadn't felt in years. *Heat.*

"Which leaves me to look after mine," he said. "Fitz owes me a great deal of blunt, and I am determined to have it back with interest. If he has his mind set on your country girl, then the country girl he shall have. As I understand it, her dowry is more than sufficient for Fitz to repay me."

"I will not allow you to obtain my husband's money through the back door, Quentin Hoyt. Abby's marriage to Fitz is completely out of the question." She glared at him in disapproval. "You would do far better to encourage him to court Lady Mary or Lady Anne. Your loan would be repaid and Fitz would have more than enough to begin restoring his estates."

"Will you deny the chit the promised inheritance if she chooses Fitz?"

"She won't. She has already rejected him," she said in satisfaction. "Your friends simply must learn to live without my fortune, because I fully intend to give it away to deserving females."

"Fitz won't have to live without it." He smiled slowly, studying her ire with amusement. "I rather like the idea that he will get ahead living on your blunt instead of mine. And if he will not suit, I have plenty of other friends I can help by matching them with your *heiresses*. Enjoy your evening, my lady."

He walked off, leaving Isabell fuming—and feeling alive for the first time in a decade or more. She needed a battle of wits to remember she no longer had to cater to a peevish husband. She was free to do more than nod and smile and chat now. Doing so with an annoyingly smug tradesman simply added a little spice to the challenge.

She would win his wager—Hoyt's idle friends would not benefit from the money she provided. She had been a tiny bit naive in thinking just money would give the heiresses the choices she had been denied. Her father's destitution was a subject she preferred to erase as ancient history, but the results were engraved in her memory.

Fortunately, she was in a position to see that her protégées had not only money but also experience and knowledge, so they would not fall prey to desperate circumstances and could make more informed choices than she had made.

"Miss Merriweather, if I might have a moment of your time?"

Leaving the retiring room, Abigail started with surprise at Lord Quentin's hand on her shoulder. "Yes, of course, my lord. What can I do for you?"

"I believe Lady Belden mentioned you have some knowledge of estate management?"

Women climbing up and down the stairs to the retiring room cast them curious glances, but Abby didn't know any of them well enough to speak to. It was daunting to realize how incredibly alone she was in this strange society. Oddly, she hadn't felt so alone until she'd turned Fitz away.

She continued on down the stairs to a hallway teeming with guests leaving for other entertainments. "I don't think my small acreage constitutes an estate, my lord," she said quietly.

"But you do know the difference between a rutabaga and rhubarb?" he asked with what sounded like amusement, although she didn't think the busy Lord Quentin was a man who would tease.

"Of course. I even have one tenant. That scarcely makes me an expert."

"But it makes you more of an expert than Danecroft, doesn't it?"

She almost stumbled over the last step. Lord Quentin caught her elbow and gently steered her down the hall, past the throng flowing toward the door.

"He tells me he wishes to hire an estate manager to oversee his estate," Lord Quentin continued, "but I fear he will hire an incompetent scoundrel instead of the knowledgeable man he needs. I would like him to have the expertise of a second opinion."

These past weeks had been like a journey to the moon. Abby was starting to believe anything and everything was possible if the *ton* declared it so. She cast Lord Quentin a look of incredulity. "And you have no opinion on estates and managers, my lord?"

"Me?" He looked genuinely surprised. "Hardly. I'm a businessman, Miss Merriweather. Ask me about coal mines and shipping, and I will gladly give you my opinion. Do not ask me of sheep and turnips."

"And there is no other man in all of London who can recommend a manager?"

"That is not the point, Miss Merriweather. Of course I will ask about for recommendations. The point is that Fitz needs to interview these men, and he will not accept that he requires aid in choosing one. I disagree."

"You want *me* to help him interview estate managers? Pardon my bluntness, but have you run mad, my lord?"

He chuckled. "Not entirely. You do not dissemble at all, do you?"

"I see no reason to do so. Once I leave London, I will never see you again, so your opinion is of little concern to me. You cannot be affected by my sentiments, so I see no harm in stating them."

"I would not be so certain that you will never see society again, Miss Merriweather, but that's neither here nor there. I agree that you owe me nothing, but if I arrange for Danecroft to interview managers in my home, with my sisters present, will you come?"

"If Lord Danecroft wishes me to be there," she stated firmly. "I will be delighted to visit with your sisters. I would like to see Penelope, also, if that's possible."

"That is easily arranged, although the brat is likely to singe my sisters' delicate ears, so I would thank you to keep her in hand."

Feeling oddly buoyant at knowing she would see Penelope and Fitz again in safe surroundings that would not involve exchanging dangerous kisses, Abigail allowed Lord Quentin to return her to the ballroom. "Let me know when and where, my lord, and I will do what I can."

He bowed over her hand. "I see why Fitz is so taken with you, Miss Merriweather. It was a mistake to think he would be happy with anyone with less sense than he."

"I cannot believe a gambler displays an incredible amount of sense, sir," she protested, before hastening toward Lady Belden, who was impatiently tapping her toe while speaking with Abby's next dance partner. She hoped the lady's glare was for Lord Quentin and not herself, but she was too happy to care.

She told herself it was because she would see Penelope again, but she knew she was lying. She was hoping she could find some way of being Fitz's friend again.

Blake Montague was supposed to be Fitz's friend, but he hadn't seemed very pleased with the earl earlier. She must ask the marchioness about Fitz's claim that Mr. Montague wanted to die in battle. He had seemed rather imposing and dangerous to her. And while the military was a noble profession, if she must marry, she would really rather have what her mother and stepmother had had, a husband at home.

A gambler would spend more time at the gaming tables than at home, she reminded herself sternly as she took the hand of the portly gentleman to whom she owed this dance—Lord Robert Smythe. She would do far better with a man who had grown up in the country, like Lord Robert. He would know how to deal with her small acreage. She just wished he could be a little less dyspeptic and a little more charming.

Perhaps once Lord Robert left the unhealthy environs of the city and spent his days walking or riding about fields, he would change. She could have Cook feed him fresh greens from the garden instead of dish after dish of greasy meats from society's supper tables. And she would find out what kind of jokes he liked, so he would smile more.

Plotting the alterations she would make to her partner if they were wedded carried her through the quadrille with only a few minor missteps. Burly Lord Robert looked ridiculous trying to be light on his feet, but an ability to dance was not essential in a husband. He simply needed to be stable and good-natured and wish to have children. He seemed to be interested in her. It was up to her to hold his attention.

She caught a glimpse of Fitz bowing to a lovely young lady who beamed at him as if he'd set the moon and the stars in the sky, and Abby snagged her foot in her hem and stumbled.

Lord Robert broke up the set and led her to the room's edge while he caught his breath. "Better this way," he sighed. "Can't keep that pace. Would you like to take the air?"

She could tell he needed air. Perspiration poured down his brow, and he sopped it with his handkerchief. Really, although her escort was good-looking and polite, she may as well have stayed in Chalkwick Abbey and danced with Billy.

With a sigh, she took Lord Robert's elbow and let him lead her to the narrow balcony. This was not a large house like the one where Fitz had proposed. There were no convenient columns for murmuring couples to hide behind. She supposed some of the guests were walking about the garden below, but she didn't think Lord Robert was interested in walking.

She wondered if Fitz might be one of the gentlemen taking advantage of the darkness tonight, and she hated herself for thinking it. She could not condemn him for looking elsewhere now that she had turned him down.

"Do you like children, my lord?" she asked, leaning over the rail while Lord Robert swiped at his brow.

"Not much choice in the matter, is there?" he said pragmatically. "But m'sisters say a good nanny is worth her weight in gold."

"I have four young siblings," Abby mentioned casually.

He tugged nervously at his high, tight neckcloth. "Lady Belden says they're with a guardian. Happy there, are they?"

"They'd be happier with their sister," a familiar voice said silkily from behind them.

"Oh, didn't see you there, Fitz. You know Miss Merriweather?"

"And her siblings."

Abby could swear the earl's eyes glittered like green gems in the darkness, and her breath caught in her throat at his magnificence. Not an ounce of fat blurred the contoured angles of the earl's tight jaw or softened the breadth of his gleaming white shirt and waistcoat. She had the mischievous urge to dirty her finger and imprint it on his immaculate linen.

"Lord Danecroft believes children are toys whose lives may be played with like the cards of which he's so fond. I am needed elsewhere, gentlemen. I'll see you inside."

She returned to the open doorway, feeling exceedingly proud of her suave departure, until she tripped on her hem and tore it. Swearing, she yanked off the useless frill, then marched into the glittering ballroom as if it were her strawberry field.

"The lady is a trifle opinionated," Fitz commented casually, watching the enticing sway of Miss Merry's hips

as she escaped to the ballroom with her chin held high.
"Not to mention bossy and managing."

"Had enough of that with m'sisters," Lord Robert
agreed. "Think I'll find the buffet."

Poorly done, old boy, Fitz told himself as Abigail's
peach gown disappeared into the crowd. But she could
do better than henpecked Robert.

22

"Good morning, bailiff. Fine day, isn't it?" Fitz asked cheerfully, leading Penny down the front steps of his town house to the street. "You do realize, don't you, that there isn't an item worth a farthing anywhere in my vast kingdom that isn't already accounted for?"

The bailiff leaning against the town house used his fingernail to pry his breakfast from between his teeth while managing to look basset-hound mournful. "If there's aught coming or going, I'm to report it, my lord. It's my duty."

"Well, let me know if the crown jewels arrive, although I daresay if my brother stole them, he played them on the ponies before he popped off."

The bailiff rightfully declined to reply to this sally. Fitz swung Penny's hand and strolled in the direction of Quentin's. At least a bailiff at the door scared off the other creditors. And brick throwers. Nick had not discovered anything interesting at Tattersall's. With only the clue of possible nationality to the ruffian's identity, it was hard to search. Horse barns were stuffed with Irishmen.

"I wanna see Miss Abby," Penelope said warningly.

The pink ribbons in her hair had already come undone, probably from all her head swiveling. The city was still a new and absorbing playground to his daughter.

"She has said she will be there, and if she is not, we will hunt her down." The only reason he'd agreed to this expedition was Abby's promise to be at Quentin's. He certainly didn't need any help in hiring an estate manager beyond recommendations of available men. He might not know the best crops to plant, but he understood what made men tick.

If only he had the same understanding of women! He knew how to charm his way into a woman's bed, but Abby was too smart to be wooed by crass flattery.

Still, she'd thoroughly shocked him when she'd turned down his suit. Most women would seize the advantages an earl offered, and he'd rather hoped she looked on him with enough fondness to ignore his disadvantages. He alternated between being proud that he'd chosen a woman with such high moral standards and irate that she didn't trust him or give him credit for having common sense. And even then, he had to acknowledge she was right to be wary—he *would* gamble her dowry. And possibly her farm. He didn't have much choice.

But he would never lose her money or farm or leave her in dire straits. And he didn't know how he could possibly prove that.

"Can Miss Abby be my mama?" Penny asked, her thoughts remarkably echoing his own.

"That's up to Miss Abby, my poppet."

"You promised I could have a new mama."

"I did at that, and I'm hard at work on it. You must promise to behave like a model of decorum so you don't scare off Miss Abby."

"Won't scare her," Penny insisted. "She likes me."

"Odd woman that she is, it seems so." Penny was another reason he had to convince Abby that gambling was his profession, not his obsession. He couldn't imagine Lady Anne or Mary even acknowledging the existence of his illegitimate daughter.

Scowling fiercely at the persistent creditor shouting and waving his fist from across the crowded street, Fitz lifted Penny and hurried up the stairs to Lord Quentin's front door before the nuisance could cross the busy intersection. He'd rather not subject Penny to the man's curses or learn what villainy his family had perpetrated to generate debts to dissolute scoundrels. He could solve only one problem at a time.

Potential candidates for the position of estate agent lined the rear hall, twisting their hats in their hands and gazing about with interest or trepidation. A few even nodded in Fitz's direction, as if they knew he was the man hiring. He applauded their shrewdness and remembered their faces.

He heard Abby's laughter and his palms began to sweat. He had to prove himself today. Or become a liar and promise to give up gambling. He didn't think he could do either, but perversely, he was determined to have the woman who fit his needs, not just his pocket.

The footman led them to a rear parlor where Abby was speaking with two of Quent's many sisters and nieces. All three women turned and smiled at his approach, but he saw real concern and interest in only Abby's eyes. She instinctively held out her hands to Penny, who raced to climb into her lap, despite the fact that her dusty shoes left imprints on Abby's muslin.

"A bouquet of posies couldn't be lovelier, my ladies," Fitz declared, bowing with a gallant flourish.

Lady Sally and Lady Margaret did their best to imitate their brother's aristocratic hauteur, but their dancing eyes gave them away. They would make very bad card players.

Abby, contrary creature that she was, did her best to pretend he was invisible, but Fitz wagered that was her way of ignoring that he'd kissed her. And that she'd liked it. If she'd taken a complete disgust of him, she would have to say so before he would endeavor to close his eyes to her many charms.

He was even ready to overlook the fact that she could be as irritating as a burr under a saddle. "Miss Merriweather, how good of you to assist me in my search. Will Penny be a suitable chaperone for us, or shall we bore the ladies and conduct the interviews in here?"

"Quentin says you may use his study," Lady Sally informed him. "He has a matter of business to conduct this morning, but he said we might leave the connecting door open so Penny and Miss Merriweather may come and go as they like. We will try not to intrude too often."

Fitz didn't know what Quent was about, but he thought the whole arrangement slightly outside proper. Still, he wasn't about to argue with one that so eminently suited his needs. "Excellent! Shall we begin before the busy men in the outer hall become restless and depart?"

He offered his arm to Abby, and removing Penny from her lap, she reluctantly accepted it. Just the touch of her hand stirred indecent thoughts in him. If he must marry, he preferred a wife he was eager to bed. Abby filled that requirement so well that he felt like the restive stallion he'd once called himself.

He seated her in an unobtrusive wing chair in a corner behind Quent's desk, where she could observe the candidates he'd be interviewing. With light from the tall window glaring over his shoulder, the interviewees would be partially blinded and not able to discern Abby so well in the dark corner. Having a woman in the room was highly unusual—and bound to be distracting.

"You do not have to do this, you know," she said, lifting Penny back to her lap. "Your daughter is not likely to sit still for long, and I'm sure your judgment is as good as mine."

For good luck, and because he appreciated her confidence, Fitz bent over and planted a swift kiss on her head. He was rewarded by Abby lifting an astonished gaze to him. He caressed her pert nose. "If Penny is a nuisance, I shall stuff her under the desk and tickle her with my boot. You, on the other hand, will tell me if they know rhubarb from rutabagas."

"Or turnips from rutabagas, since I would hope any farmer would know the difference between a fruit and a vegetable," she said with a swift smile, before ducking her head again.

"Turnips are fruit? What about mangel-wurzels?"

"*Rhubarb* is a fruit. And mangel-wurzels are beets. Now quit being silly." She unwrapped Penny's ribbons and began to straighten them out.

Fitz valiantly denied the urge to kiss her again, which seemed directly related to the warmth engulfing him at the sight of Abby cuddling his daughter.

He nodded to the footman waiting at the door, and set about his first official duty as earl—hiring an estate manager who would magically turn weed fields into profit-making crops.

"Mangel-wurzels, sir?" The current interviewee crossed one leg over his other knee and appeared comfortable in the rich London study. "They make good winter fodder for cattle."

Abby bit back a smile. Fitz had insisted on asking every candidate about beets—whether to show off his spurious knowledge or test his prospective employees was beyond her ability to surmise. But their various reactions had proved entertaining.

She checked on Penelope, who had fallen asleep out of boredom and from the effort of being on her best behavior. She'd spent some time under the desk being tickled by her father's feet, but even that activity had palled after a while. Abby certainly understood. Interviewing was a dull business in which only Fitz could find entertainment.

She approved of the current candidate. He seemed willing to explore different methods of returning fields to production and improving tenant crop yields. He grasped instantly that Fitz was unable to provide extensive cash investments, and had suggested alternatives.

When he departed, she leaned forward to speak as Fitz made notes. "Choose that one—Mr. Beemer."

Fitz finished his note and glanced over his shoulder at her. "I would, except he's already employed. He's simply seeking a position where he would have more control over the results."

"Is that bad?"

"Not necessarily, but I don't want all the control wrenched from my hands, leaving me in ignorance. Besides, there are other equally qualified candidates who don't already have employment. They're likely to be more eager."

She frowned, but before she could argue, Lord Quentin walked in.

"Sorry I was late." He took a chair instead of disturbing Fitz at his desk. "I see you've worked your way through the lot. Made any choices?"

"I have." Fitz tented his fingers as if he had interviewed employees all his life. "Applebee will suit. He knows Berkshire soil and is familiar with the extent of the estate's neglect."

"But he was let go from his previous position because he was drunk!" Abby couldn't resist interjecting.

"And he admitted as much," Fitz argued, pushing his chair back to include her. "He has a family to feed, and he swears he's not a regular tippler, that it was just one instance after he lost his son. He'll be desperate to prove himself and willing to educate me in the process."

Quentin looked as dubious as Abigail felt. "Beemer came highly recommended. You'll need someone who knows how to get the most for your coin."

Abby noted Fitz's mulish expression and sat back. Lord Quentin was about to beat his head against a brick wall if he thought he could change Fitz's mind once he'd made it up—which ought to give her pause if Fitz had truly decided on her for his wife. A decidedly sinful thrill swept through her at the possibility of Fitz chasing her until she gave in.

"Beemer is looking out for himself," Fitz declared with the decisive authority of an earl. "Applebee will look out for *me*. I want a man who is loyal to the estate, who understands the consequences to everyone who works there if he fails. Beemer won't care. He'll simply move on to a better position."

"Miss Merriweather?" Quentin lifted a dark eyebrow in her direction.

"Mr. Applebee is highly knowledgeable, and Lord Danecroft is correct that he would put the estate before himself—if he doesn't fall back on his weakness for drink."

Fitz grinned at her, and Abby felt a little thrill that her opinion mattered to him. She had the odd notion that both men had set this up to involve her for reasons beyond requiring her limited expertise.

"And Applebee knows the difference between mangel-wurzels and turnips," Fitz added with a knowledgeable nod.

"Mangel-wurzels?" Lord Quentin looked puzzled, and Fitz, delighted.

"Beets, old boy, fodder for cattle I don't have. You see, I am learning! I think I will have to buy cattle just so I might grow mangel-wurzels. What do you think, Miss Merriweather?"

"I think you'd better start a household account." She rose and glanced down at the sleeping child at her feet. "And that you might want to take Miss Penny off to her bed and reward her with the biggest ice Gunter's will sell you when she wakes."

"Accounts." He brightened perceptibly. "I keep them in my head now. Would you care to teach me how to keep them in books?"

"Me?" Abby studied him, perplexed. "I'm sure there are more informed people available. Lord Quentin, for instance."

Both men had risen from their chairs when she did. Lord Quentin bowed in her direction. "I know how to keep books for businesses, Miss Merriweather, but perhaps you could explain the details of farm accounts."

"He's matchmaking," Fitz whispered in her ear before lifting his daughter from the floor.

"Oh." She regarded the large man innocently standing with hands beneath his coattails, studying her with the same interest as she did him. "Danecroft gambles," she told him, thinking she'd put an end to further nonsense now. "He would have to risk my farm *and* my inheritance before winning enough to cover even a small portion of his debt. I cannot take that chance."

Not appearing the least shocked by her bluntness, Lord Quentin explained, "Fitz only wagers when he knows he'll win, and he wins more often than not."

Fitz countered with, "And Montague would spend it on buying himself into the army and Atherton would use it to find a mistress. Hire a solicitor with your wealth, my dear. It's a far more certain method than marriage."

Since he was carrying Penelope, Fitz could not offer his arm to escort her out. Abigail glanced from one man to the other, not at all sure what she should think. Lord Quentin was saying it was all right to gamble with *her* funds? And Fitz was telling her to hire a lawyer instead of marrying him. Where she had been certain before, now she was confused.

"Don't worry, my sweet," Fitz said cheerfully, heading for the hall. "We'll muddle along on our own. You need only let us know how we can help when you decide what is best for you and your siblings. Come along. Lady Belden will think you have run away."

Right about now, since she had no hope of thinking her way through this conundrum, running away seemed the best thing to do. She wanted to be home where she could pick her strawberries and straighten out her spinning head.

Except the one thing she was fairly certain of was that she could never sit at her dining table again without wishing that Fitz sat next to her.

23

"Thank you for agreeing with me, Miss Abby," Fitz said, carting his sleeping daughter over his shoulder so he might offer an elbow to the woman who brightened his day, even when she was being contrary—which was pretty much most of the time, he acknowledged. "Quentin knows even less than I do about farming, and he trusts you."

"I can't understand why," she said a trifle peevishly. "I own a few acres I let out to a tenant, and I harvest a few crops. I've never had wealth, and I have no notion how to go about investing my inheritance in my farm, even if I could. Although Lady Belden is in no hurry to let me take charge of it so I might find out."

"Then at least let me thank you for respecting my judgment." Fitz fought back a smile at her irritation. He was learning that she didn't like being confused or uncertain, and he hoped he was the reason she was feeling unsettled. That would mean she had not entirely dismissed him as worthless. He was still miffed that she'd turned down his perfectly good marriage proposal, but it was early days yet, and even he had to admit that he had little to offer her. "As far as I'm aware, no one has ever acknowledged that my brainpan holds anything more than fleas."

She sent him a sharp look. "Then you must hang about with the most tremendous dunderheads in existence. Witless men end up in the gutter. Intelligent ones survive."

"You continually astound me with your perceptions, Miss Abby. Why is that?" Astound and inflate him, more like. He felt his head swell two sizes larger because his observant Miss Merry thought he was intelligent. He would have to buy a new hat to fit.

"Why does it matter what I think?" she grumbled. "I'm a mere provincial with no pretensions to society or education."

"I think you need a nap," he said in amusement. "Did you not sleep well last night?"

Penny stirred on his shoulder. Knowing his daughter did not wake in a pleasant humor, he kept her firmly in place once she started to wriggle and whine.

"No, I didn't sleep well at all." Abby didn't explain but released his arm so he might better control his burden.

"Then let us do something about whatever is keeping you awake. Have you heard from the children again?"

"No, which worries me as much as if they complained. And Lady Belden insists I need more ball gowns, and I fear all my inheritance will be spent in finding a husband, when what I really want is a solicitor."

He could push her now, tell her he could hire solicitors, but his Abby knew it would be at her own expense. Still, he supposed it wouldn't hurt to show her a little of what he could do. "Shall I help you pry your funds from Lady Bell's hands so you may begin the process of interviewing solicitors?"

She shot him a dubious look. Fitz set Penelope on her feet, ignoring Abby's doubt. He chose to believe that she was more concerned about his method of persuading the dowager than his ability to do so. And he was pleased that he had found a woman in whom he could place that much confidence.

"Lady Belden is immune to charm," she said, confirming his belief. "I believe she is bored and keeping me here for her own entertainment."

Rather than acknowledge that insight, Fitz halted to pull his daughter from the filth of the street where she'd collapsed. "Penelope, if you wake up and stop grumbling before we reach Gunter's, we can take Miss Abby for an ice. Otherwise, I must take you home to Nanny."

She sent him a disgruntled look but clung to his hand and rubbed her eyes and quit complaining. Oddly, Fitz did not consider his daughter a nuisance but felt pride that he was learning how to deal with her. And that she actually listened to him.

When he glanced to Abby, she was beaming with delight. All in all, this might be the very best day of his miserable life, and all because two females approved of him. And now he was heading into dangerously foolish territory again, believing women could be the answer to his prayers.

But today he was a grasshopper, out to enjoy a summer's day with no concern for approaching winter. "Well, then, we must find some means of entertaining the lady that will accomplish what we want," he said. "Come along, we will have our ices, then descend upon Belden House with all our cannon primed and loaded."

By the time they rambled through the crowded streets from Gunter's Tea Shop at Berkeley Square to the dowager's mansion in a quieter residential area near Hyde Park, Penny had tired of their excursion.

"Let me carry her to the nursery, and then I'll return to help you confront whatever lion stands between you and your inheritance," Fitz promised, stopping at the mansion's doorstep.

"Lady Belden will simply declare that you are after my money. I don't know if she has the power to take it away, and I don't wish to insult her. She's been very kind." Abigail wrung her hands in indecision. It had been a lovely morning, and she hated to see Fitz leave, but she feared taking control of her inheritance was a problem she must tackle on her own.

"I will be back," he said firmly. "If you are to handle your own affairs, you must learn how to deal with the bullies who would deny you."

That was true. She knew where she stood in the village, knew the people, and how to work with them. In London, she was out of her element, and frightened as a result. Not to mention confused, uncertain, and entirely unlike her usual self. She needed a guide to teach her this new milieu, and she could think of no one better than Fitz.

"Very well," she said gratefully. "I will let you know what I have found out when you return."

"Wanna stay with Miss Abby," Penny warned, attempting to tug her hand free from her father's grip.

"You can't swat spiders here," Abby told her, biting back a grin.

"Can, too." She placed her free hand on her hip and stuck out her lower lip.

"But we have much bigger, squishier spiders at home." Fitz tipped his hat in farewell as a servant opened the door to allow Abby in. "And I think Nanny meant to buy a new broom with which to squash them." He led Penny down the stairs, discussing more instruments of insect torture to hold his daughter's interest.

Abby wiped a silly tear in the corner of her eye as she listened to Penelope's clear voice, pitched high enough to hear even as they turned a corner.

Lord Danecroft would make a wonderful father. It was unfair that the world expected him to shoulder the costly burdens generated by decades of his ancestors' abuse.

But life was seldom fair and seemed to be more about making warm quilts out of the ragged scraps one was given. And so she would do, once she had an idea of what scraps were hers. She handed her bonnet and parasol to the footman who held the door, and decided her first step was to confront the marchioness's assistant, Maynard.

She found the scrawny retainer bent over account books in the dowager's business office. "Maynard, I should like to see the accounts of my inheritance and expenditures," she said when he did not even look up at her entrance.

"I've not seen them yet," he replied, his quill scribbling rapidly across the book he was working on. "The solicitors are slow to send me the documents."

"Then give me the name of the firm so I may go there and see them for myself."

He cast her an appalled glance. "Ladies never travel within the City walls!"

"I am not a lady. I'm a country girl, and I'm accustomed to looking after my own accounts." She said it as firmly as she dared, since the notion of finding transportation into the center of the business district terrified her.

"I will send word to the firm and ask them to bring the accounts here." He returned to his work without a further glance, effectively dismissing her.

"If you will write the note now, I will hand it to a footman to deliver," she insisted.

She saw the pen hesitate, as if he debated ignoring her. She had been pleasant and patient long enough. Fitz was right. She should not allow bullies to deny her what was rightfully hers. She stepped forward and placed her hand across his ledger. "Now, please, Maynard. I would very much like to speak with the solicitors."

With a scowl, he produced a clean sheet of paper, dipped his pen in the inkstand, and scrawled a note that Abigail inspected before he folded and sealed it.

"Lady Belden will not approve," he warned.

"Then I will not approve of Lady Belden," she retorted, swinging on her heel and returning to the hall to find a footman to run her errand.

Perhaps Fitz was right. Perhaps learning to deal with

society was just a matter of asserting herself and not caring if people thought her provincial.

The dowager had returned from her morning calls by the time the clerk from the solicitor and Fitz arrived, but the lady disappeared into the upper stories without interfering in the business office. Abigail directed the gentlemen into the study and nervously hoped the marchioness stayed otherwise occupied. She truly didn't like scenes, and she suspected Lady Belden was capable of creating dramatic ones.

Introductions were exchanged, and Mr. Wisdom, the solicitor's clerk, seemed sufficiently awed by the company of an earl to explain the details in the documents he produced.

"Barbara?" Fitz asked, scanning her inheritance papers. "Your name is Barbara Abigail?"

Abby snatched the paper from his grip and sat down at the library table to struggle with the legal verbiage. "I was named after my mother. I don't use it."

"Rhubarbara," he whispered in her ear as he picked up the ledger the clerk had carried in.

The nonsense name tickled all the way down her spine, making her grin foolishly. Losing himself in account books, unaware of his effect on her, Fitz strolled about the room, flipping through columns of numbers. He whistled a time or two, laughed once, and spun the book on his finger before returning it to the table.

Abigail looked up from the ponderous document she was perusing to glare at him. This was her future he dismissed so casually. The sums involved might be minuscule compared with an earl's estate, but they staggered her and seemed very serious business, indeed.

"Your fortune will keep you in frocks for years to come, my dear," Fitz said, sliding the book across to her. "And it will even keep food on the table if you invest it for more than the paltry one percent you are now earning."

Abby opened the ledger, but the numbers trailing down the page meant little to her. She glanced at the neat labels for each entry and nearly choked at the horrendous millinery bill. "I cannot imagine any amount of income paying for expenses like these!"

Fitz chuckled, leaning over her shoulder, and she nearly stopped thinking entirely as the scent of bay rum filled her senses, and his hard, masculine chest brushed her back. She stared dumbly as his long finger swept down the page, past all the neat numbers to the bottom, then flipped to the next sheet and tapped the untotaled column.

Those long fingers had slid through her hair not so long ago. If she'd accepted his proposal, they would touch her even more intimately. Her breasts ached at the notion, and she blushed. As if he followed her thoughts, he propped one hand on her shoulder and circled a surreptitious finger at her nape while he scribbled a few numbers into the columns with Mr. Wisdom's pen. The ink stained a callus she hadn't noticed earlier.

"There is the total of your current expenses to date." He tapped the astounding, breathtaking sum of over one hundred pounds. "And here's your income to date." He tapped a smaller sum. "You will see that you are currently spending more than you are earning."

"Of course, my lord. There are always initial expenses." Mr. Wisdom hurried to explain. "And I was given to understand that the lady means to marry. The marchioness assured me Miss Merriweather did not need to worry about enjoying herself while she can."

While she could? Of course, all these great sums would go to her husband when she married. She knew that. She was simply gasping at how quickly Fitz had totaled them—and from his breath tickling the hairs at her nape, and his hand squeezing her shoulder as he stepped back.

"Of course," Fitz said. "Miss Merriweather should always enjoy herself. But she could do so without touching the principal if the funds were invested more wisely."

Abigail stared at the ledger while Fitz argued with the solicitor about risk and cent per cents and things she'd never had any reason to understand. Mr. Wisdom complained about gambling on stocks. She understood that much. Fitz's argument about rates of return flew well beyond her understanding.

How had he added those columns so swiftly?

She wasn't given the opportunity to ask. Apparently made aware of her guests, the dowager sailed into the library without warning, and Abby's heart sank to her stomach.

"Danecroft!" Lady Belden thundered. "I don't believe I invited you."

Mr. Wisdom rose hastily and made an awkward bow, which the lady ignored.

"And so you didn't, my dearest lady." One leg in front of the other, Fitz made a grand flourish with his arm and bowed deeply, as if to a queen. When he straightened, he ruined the effect with his mocking smile. "I shall correct that instantly by removing myself and Miss Merriweather to another location."

He tucked the ledger and file under his arm and held out his hand to Abigail. She glanced warily at her hostess as she accepted it.

"You will not escape that easily!" Lady Belden warned. "Sally told me about this morning's adventures at her brother's house. Quentin is naught but a mischief-maker."

"There we agree, my lady," Fitz said, tucking Abigail's hand into the crook of the arm not occupied holding the ledger. "But since I owe him a great deal of blunt, he is looking after his own interests as well as mine, so I must concur with his goals, if not his means."

The dowager tugged the ledger from beneath Fitz's arm and flung it to the table. "Abigail must be offered choices. You cannot claim her fortune simply because you met her first. You are not suitable marriage material."

"Abigail is a grown woman with a mind of her own," Abby said quietly. She disliked argument, but she especially disliked being disregarded as if she had no say in her future. Picking up the ledger, she tucked it under her own arm. "And I do not appreciate being fought over like a bone between growling mastiffs. Now, if you will excuse me, I'd like to study these on my own."

With as much dignity as she could muster in her confusion, she left the library and stalked toward the front of the house. Taking charge of her fortune wasn't much of a declaration of independence, but it would have to do. Behind her, she could hear Fitz offering teasing farewells and the marchioness buzzing like an angry bee.

She desperately feared her heart was telling her to trust Fitz while her head was shouting all the reasons why she shouldn't. And logic was failing. How could a professed wastrel sum those columns so rapidly when even the solicitor had not yet had time to total them?

An urgent knock startled her into halting before she climbed the stairs. A footman in formal knee breeches and black frock coat opened the door. She caught only a few hasty words before the servant accepted a folded note, shut the door on the caller, and turned to her. "Miss, I believe this is for you. The messenger is awaiting your reply."

She set the papers on the stairs and opened the note. All the blood rushed from her face as she scanned the handwriting, reading it twice to be certain she hadn't misunderstood.

The children have disappeared. We demand to know if they are in your possession.

It was signed by Mr. Weatherston, the children's guardian.

24

Closing the library door on the dragon lady, Fitz hurried down the hall after his valiant Rhubarbara. He was proud of her for standing up to the dowager, but not so proud of himself for putting Abby in a position where she must argue with her benefactor.

Seeing her in the front foyer, he increased his pace, prepared to apologize for being an overbearing scoundrel, when he heard her gasp and saw her catch the banister to steady herself. What could cause his steel-spined Abby to feel faint?

Covering the distance in two strides, he snatched up the note she was holding, and firmly caught her in his embrace. She sagged against him without protest, warning the problem was dire.

Scanning the missive, Fitz growled an expletive, released Abby to the tender care of the banister, and threw open the door. "Who are you?" he demanded of the lad still standing on the doorstep.

"Just the messenger, my lord," he said in terror of Fitz's fury. "I took the coach up all by myself. The mistress is beside herself, and everyone's running about shouting and crying, and they said I was to get Mr. Grey-son the executor to search your house if I must."

"Good luck with that. Tell your employers the children are not here, that they could not possibly have made their way here alone, and that we will be on the road shortly to tear the countryside apart in search of them. If this is some type of jest, someone will pay, and they will pay dearly."

He handed the terrified lad a coin, slammed the door, and turned to Abby, who was already tying on a bonnet with shaking fingers.

"You need to stay, in case they find their way here," he told her, rubbing his hand through his hair and thinking fast. What would he do if it were Penny who went missing? "I assume this is the address the children will seek, is it not?"

"They have this address, and it's closer than Chalk-wick Abbey, but I cannot believe they would be so foolish as to attempt coming to London alone. I invited the Weatherstons to bring them here for the twins' birthday. Could someone have stolen them?"

"I'll interrogate the servants when I get there. If my own youthful experience is of any use, children tend to run away when circumstances frustrate them. Has Tommy ever run away?"

She threw him a look of curiosity, but now was not the time for him to explain his wayward youth. At least the color was returning to her cheeks.

"He did once, after his mother died. My father was incoherent with grief and yelled at him for some trivial error. We were all terribly distraught, so it was perfectly understandable, and he did not go far. But he was only seven."

And now he was ten. In little over three years, the children had lost both parents and been removed from their sister, the only remaining source of stability in their short lives. Having had his own boots yanked out from under him a time or three, Fitz thought he might have some understanding of their insecurity.

"I assume they did not take horses, so they should be easy to trace," he said with a confidence that hid his knowledge of all the dreadful things that could happen to four very young children along ten miles of a busy thoroughfare. "Quentin's closest. I'll stop there first and have him notify all the men of our acquaintance. We'll cover every road between London and Surrey."

The footman had stood stiffly at attention some distance from their conversation, but finally he could not resist adding his admonition, "It's threatening to rain, my lord. The road south floods and forms a mud pit if the rain lasts long."

Fitz bit back his curses.

Abby took up her reticule. "Please tell Lady Belden I have gone in search of the children, and beg her to look after them for me if they return here before I do."

She might dither over her own choices, but she was not slow to make up her mind when it came to her siblings. Fitz didn't think he could argue with her after telling her she must learn to face up to bullies. She was likely to slap him silly.

The footman somberly retrieved her umbrella and pelisse from the cloakroom beneath the stairs. "Yes, miss."

"I mean to borrow a horse and ride hard," Fitz said, not letting Abby past him, attempting to force her to think. "You will slow me down."

"You will leave me with Lord Quentin and his sisters, then, so I may help him write notes to your friends. And then I will borrow a gig and driver and follow you."

She poked his boot with her umbrella point until he cursed a little louder and yanked open the door. "You heard what he said about mud pits," he warned. "You will be caught in some seamy inn, and I won't be there to look after you. Don't give me more to worry about."

"You need not worry about me at all. I am a grown woman, not a child, and it is my choice whatever happens, not yours."

She marched down the street so swiftly that Fitz had to storm after her. *Dammitall!* He caught her arm just as a hard object grazed his head and knocked his hat flying. With his wits already scrambled, he glared down at a rock large enough to stun that had bounced off the crushed beaver onto the cobblestones. Abby's sharp scream returned his senses, and he spun on his bootheel in time to catch sight of the cursed ruffian across the crowded street shouting at him. Realizing he'd been attacked again, in broad daylight, and in a manner that had also endangered Abby, he lost the last restraint on his temper.

"You puny pox-ridden pig, I'll pound you into pulp when I catch you!" Disregarding the potential of more stones, he raced after the culprit, who abruptly took to his heels at the sight of Fitz's raised fists.

Startled, Abby instinctively rescued the hat from the gutter, but that was all she knew to do while Fitz dodged carriages and drays to race like a berserker after the stone thrower.

He might have been *killed* if that blow had connected with his head instead of his hat. She stared in dismay at the size of the object that had crashed into the street, and realized there was a note tied about it. Avoiding a carriage horse, she stooped to grab the rock and opened the note to read: *MAYT ME WIT TA BLOONT ER AYLS GEEV UP YER PRIZ.* A large arrow pointed at the side of the paper.

Bloont? Was that like a doubloon? Did the writer lack the letter *H*?

Other passersby halted to see if more stones would rain from the heavens, then moved on when they saw that all was well. Fitz disappeared around a corner.

Abruptly abandoned and feeling lost, Abby shivered.

She didn't like London at all. She wanted her familiar farm and her family back. She hugged herself to keep from weeping, but no one stopped to offer help or even notice her fright now that the excitement was past.

She was terrified for the children. She didn't know what to think of a large, sophisticated gentleman who ran after trouble with his fists raised. Danecroft was likely to come to harm, and she didn't know how to help him.

The children were less able to take care of themselves than a grown man. Too shaken to even know what to pray for, she tucked the strange note in her pocket, took a deep breath, and marched in the direction of Lord Quentin's house, carrying Danecroft's hat.

By the time she had crossed two squares and picked her way around snarled intersections, the earl came loping up behind her, dusting himself off and using language she was happy the children couldn't hear. She wasn't even certain of the meaning of some of his colorful phrases. *Pox-ridden pig*, indeed.

She silently handed him his hat and the note. He shoved the battered beaver on his head and growled, "*Bloont?* If this is someone's idea of a jest, I'll pound him into jam." Shoving the note in his pocket, he grabbed her hand, and tucked it into the crook of his arm as if they were continuing a pleasant stroll.

"Are you often attacked in such a manner, my lord?" she inquired as they came within sight of Lord Quentin's town house.

"Only since I made the mistake of returning from the dead," he muttered. "The scoundrel is determined to force me to buy a new hat."

"I don't think it was your hat he meant to harm." Her heart still pounded at the thought of what that rock could have done to his head.

"Fortunately for me, that's all he ever comes close to hitting. But at least this time I saw enough to know the stone thrower is no bigger than a scrawny lad. I will look

for him after we find the children." With that cryptic remark, he rapped Quentin's knocker so loudly, it could
be heard in the next county.

After that, there was no time for better explanations.
Lord Quentin was out on business, and footmen were
engaged to find him. Lady Sally and Lady Margaret insisted on writing notes to be sent around to every man
of Fitz's acquaintance to aid in his search, after which he
rushed off to procure a horse and ride south.

Abby's prayers went with him. At least the earl knew
what the children looked like. All the men the ladies sent
dashing down the road would not. Just as she wouldn't
know half of Fitz's friends should she happen to run into
them, which she might do, because she had no intention
of being left behind.

Lady Belden arrived at almost the same moment as
Lord Quentin. Despite their equally impassive demean-
ors, the two aristocrats gave orders in clipped tones that
sent servants scurrying in their wake.

"Abigail, you will return with me at once," Lady
Belden said. "I will hire able-bodied men more ac-
quainted with this type of search than a careless lot of
Corinthians without a wit between them. Quentin, you
will have your ruffians report to us if they find anything."
The marchioness waited impatiently for Abby to leave
the parlor they'd turned into a war office.

"If you had hired someone to fetch the children when
the lady requested it, this wouldn't have happened,"
Lord Quentin said, gesturing for Abby to keep her seat.
"You have hidden in your velvet nest for so long, you do
not know how to deal with the real world."

"I do not have time or patience to argue." Ignoring
him, the lady turned imperiously to Abby. "Abigail, let
us go."

Before Abby could defy her hostess, a blustery wind
blew through the hall, and a moment later, Fitz's would-
be-soldier friend, Blake Montague, appeared. In a caped
redingote, his lean frame filled the doorway.

"I've brought the gig," he announced to no one in particular. "But the storm is moving in swiftly."

Abby leaped up and hurried toward him. "I'm so sorry I've asked you to drive in this weather, but I'm quite desperate enough to direct the horses myself, if you will let me."

Mr. Montague offered a barely perceptible bow to the marchioness and ignored Quentin's sisters. Without otherwise acknowledging Abby's request, he gestured for a footman to hold out her pelisse so that she might put it on.

"You cannot go out like this, Abigail," the dowager protested. "You will be ruined, if you don't catch an ague and die! Quentin, tell the little goose that she's being a fool and wrecking her future!"

"If you can wait another half hour, I'll have the coachman harness my landau and bring it around," Lord Quentin said. "It will be far more comfortable than Montague's open gig."

"That is a very kind offer, my lord," Abby said quietly, "but I'm anxious to leave before the road floods. If Mr. Montague believes we can reach Surrey in his vehicle, then I am not concerned about my comfort."

"This is appalling," the lady grumbled, pacing back and forth. "I was assured those children were well taken care of. I cannot imagine how one goes about losing children. Really, this is the outside of enough. Abigail, you cannot take leave of your senses now. The children will need you. Take my carriage. It's outside. Quentin, provide a maid for her chaperone. Someone must stay in London in case the children arrive."

Abby thought she saw the solemn Mr. Montague's mouth quirk slightly at the concern the querulous lady did her best to hide, but he bowed and handed Abby an umbrella without a word.

"Where is Danecroft?" the marchioness demanded. "It is all his fault for stirring things up. All was perfectly fine until he came along."

"He should be nearly in Surrey by now." Mr. Montague finally spoke. "He borrowed that hell horse of Barton's." He held out his arm for Abigail to take. "You may choose your ride, Miss Merriweather, but I will accompany you either way. It will be dark soon, and Fitz would have my head on a platter if I did not provide more than a maid for escort."

Hell horse? Fitz was riding an unruly animal in this wind and rain? Abby's terror escalated.

She trusted Fitz's choice of friend. She took Montague's arm and offered the marchioness a deep curtsy. "My lady, if you will allow us the use of your carriage, I will owe you everything I am. So please do not think I am unappreciative of all you have done for me. I am simply terrified and can think only of the children lost out there in the dark and wet, at the mercy of strangers."

Abby could swear tears glistened in the lady's eyes as she nodded her approval.

"Go, child, bring the rascals back with you, if you must. But remember that you are as valuable as they, and do not risk yourself." She gestured for the maid to follow, then turned a sharp eye on Mr. Montague. "And you, sir, need not fear Danecroft as much as you must fear me. I will have you drawn and quartered should anything happen to Miss Merriweather."

"Aye, aye, Captain," Abby thought she heard him murmur, but he merely bowed deeply and led her to the door in the wake of cries of good wishes from the people behind them.

25

Fighting to control the high-strung Thoroughbred he'd borrowed, Fitz galloped into Croydon just as the downpour broke. Maybe the physical exercise of restraining the beast aided his thinking, but somewhere along the way, he'd decided that if he had been in Tommy's shoes, he would have loaded the children on a convenient farm wagon. A wagon was more likely to be headed into the village than to London. That left all of Croydon to search while his friends traversed the byways between here and the city. In the gathering dark and storm.

He had utterly no idea where farm wagons went once they left the farm. Stopping at a sprawling inn where one or two empty carts sat about, he threw the reins to a stableboy, ordered the horse wiped down and fed, and sprinted through the innyard to the tavern.

If the farm was five miles out of town and the children had caught an oxcart that traveled five miles an hour, they would have reached Croydon before the messenger had time to travel ten miles into the city after catching a coach in Croydon, and before Fitz could cross the crowded bridge out of London and travel ten miles.... His habit of performing mathematical calculations didn't calm him as it usually did. As he elbowed his way through the rain-avoiding throng in the inn, he concluded the children could be anywhere by now.

"I'm looking for four young runaway children," he shouted, leaping on a chair to make himself heard over the hubbub. "They came from the Weatherstons' place a few miles down the road," he continued as the men around him fell silent. "They're on their way to their sister in London. Has anyone seen them?"

"Weatherston was in here a few hours back," the bartender said, producing a mug of ale and handing it up to Fitz. "Madder than a wet hen. Didn't no one know nothing."

"Does anyone know of a cart or wagon that might have stopped out that way earlier? Even if it just passed down the road?" Now that he had their attention, Fitz climbed down and drank gratefully of the ale. He flipped a coin to the barkeep to cover his aid as well as the drink.

"My sister's boy leases their lower acres," a farmer at the back of the room called. "Don't know if he was out that way today. I can check when this rain lets up."

Fitz held up a gold coin remaining from Quentin's loan. "This if you check now."

The farmer was out of his chair and heading for the door before he had to say more.

Suddenly, the whole roomful of men was eager to solve the puzzle of who might have traversed the lane that day.

"Hanes been shearing his sheep down yonder!" one man yelled. "He uses the iron railway to send the fleece up to London."

The railway! Of course. If Abby was fascinated with the railway, Fitz could only imagine the extent of Tommy's interest. The boy might even be naive enough to think it could take them all the way to their sister.

He pitched another coin at the man who had offered the suggestion. "Where do I find the railway?"

Three of the younger lads hastened to show him in hopes of earning more of his coins. Little did they know that the noble lord in his fancy coat and frills was down to his last few shillings.

Even though the storm clouds and rain diminished the dying light of a summer evening, Fitz could see that no wagonloads of sheepskin waited at the railway. Wagoners from the nearby brewery, loading kegs of ale, looked up in curiosity as he ran through the mud and drizzle down the side of the rails, calling Tommy's name.

"If ye're lookin' for the childern, they's scampered when old Hanes caught them in his wagon," one of the drivers called.

Fitz thought he might fall on his knees in gratitude. At least they hadn't been delivered up to the depravities of London yet. He handed over another of his shillings and studied the miserable rail yard through the foggy mist. Tommy might have got himself anywhere, but he had three younger ones with him. He couldn't go far.

"How long ago?" he asked, scanning the brewery, then past to the warehouses and cottages abandoned after the railway was built.

The driver shrugged. "Few hours ago. Before the rain started."

The lads who had accompanied him looked less interested in getting soaked now that he'd handed his coin to someone who had actually seen the runaways. Without money, Fitz couldn't ask them to help search their surroundings.

It was slowly dawning on him that earning coins by gambling was an occupation for an idler with no other responsibilities. Abby was absolutely correct. A man wouldn't have *time* for both gambling and children.

He stalked off alone through the downpour, shouting, "Tommy! Jennie!" in hopes they would trust him enough to come out from wherever they were hiding. Praying they were still hiding.

His boots squelched soggily as he walked. He hadn't

worn a cloak in the humid summer air, and now even his waistcoat was soaked through to his shirt, and his breeches were plastered to his skin. "I must be out of my mind," he grumbled, knocking at doors of empty warehouses, opening any that were unlocked. "She'll need her income to feed the brats," he muttered, scanning still another empty building. "What was I thinking of, asking her to marry when I can't feed one child, much less four others? Far better that she toddle back to her farm once I wring Tommy's neck and terrify him so he never does this again."

He was slogging through a mud puddle, debating whether to bother checking a house so derelict that it appeared the roof would cave in, when he heard a child's voice—and his pulse accelerated as if he held a winning hand.

"Thomas Merriweather, your sister will catch her death of ague hunting for you, so you'd best come out now before that happens!" As soon as he shouted this angry command, Fitz kicked himself for not promising bribes of food or hugs or whatever appealed to young children, but he was exasperated, worried, and ready to tear down walls with his bare hands.

"In here, sir," a small voice piped. "Tommy hurt his leg."

Fitz had spent the worst summer of his life propped in bed with a broken leg. Heart firmly embedded in throat, Fitz searched the blinding mist until he located a small hand waving from the doorway of an abandoned cottage. He waded through the puddles to the rickety steps.

If her watery smile was any indication, little Jennifer was happy to see him. The house was dark and his eyes had to adjust before he could find Tommy propped against a wall, wearing what appeared to be his shirt wrapped around his bare calf. Two toddlers slept on a sheepskin on the floor, thumbs planted in their cherub mouths.

The girl barely older than Penny hiccuped on her sobs and wiped at the tearstains on her cheeks. "Is Abby coming for us?"

Saying nothing, Tommy scowled defiantly, crossing his arms over a skinny chest clothed only in his coat. Their executor might have it right—Tommy needed a man's hand, but only if that man cared. As Weatherston apparently did not.

"If I know your sister, she has commandeered a carriage and is leading a parade to Croydon right now," Fitz said cheerfully, not letting them see his terror, which was only starting to subside. He still needed to figure out how to get them back to wherever they belonged.

"We want to go home," Tommy demanded.

Fitz was pretty certain he didn't mean home to his guardians. "You'll be lucky your sister doesn't tie you to a fence post and lash you within an inch of your life for endangering these little ones," Fitz countered. He knew nothing of caring for injuries and rather thought Tommy would scream bloody murder should he try to take a look at his leg. He had only one chance to do this right. And he was ruining it by unleashing his anger.

"Mr. Weatherston hates us," Tommy shouted in frustration. "It's the twins' birthday this week, and Abby invited us to visit, and he wouldn't let us go, so we decided to go ourselves."

All of Fitz's aggravation and panic abruptly drained out of him. They were children, helpless to change anything in their world, with no understanding of why they were being treated as they were. "You should have told your sister," he admonished, more gently this time. "She would have found some way of seeing you. How bad is the leg? Can you walk?"

"I banged it when they chased us." Suspicious and not totally mollified, Tommy watched for his reaction.

"It bled all over," Jennifer said. "It looks awful."

Fitz thought such sisterly concern would not be appreciated by this young boy trying so hard to be a man.

He maintained a stoic expression until he could figure out what to do. If he displayed the children publicly at an inn, the Weatherstons might hear of it before he could send word to Abby.

With an assurance he didn't feel, he crouched down beside Tommy to check the bleeding and test to see if the leg truly wasn't broken.

"Can we go home when Abby comes?" Jennifer asked. "The twins cry for her every night."

Her plea would have *him* weeping. "You will have to ask your sister." He retied the bandage and met Tommy's eyes. "It's chilly and damp here. I can take you over to the inn where there's a fire and beds and send word to London. I don't know how soon my message will reach your sister, who is probably on the road right now."

Tommy's lips trembled, but Abby's stubbornness shone brightly in his eyes. "The Weatherstons would find us first. He'd beat us."

"I won't let your guardians lay a hand on you," Fitz vowed. He had to resist the impulse to leave them here, find a card game, and win enough to buy food while waiting for Abby to come tell him what to do. He had only the vaguest notion of what a real parent would do, but if this were Penny in this derelict hut, he'd want her somewhere safe immediately. Decision made. "You will have to trust my word. I can't leave you here."

"I don't have much choice, do I?" Tommy said bitterly.

"Very few people do," Fitz told him. "The game is to pick the best option offered, and right now, trying to run on a bad leg is a bad choice. And keeping the babies in the cold and damp is not a very good one either."

Tommy nodded curtly, choking back tears.

Fitz woke the twins by lifting them from their smelly bed. They fussed as much as Penny would have done, but Jennifer and Tommy spoke to them, and they calmed down, laying a golden head on either shoulder and curling up against him. Their simple trust engendered such unaccustomed feelings, he paused a moment to try to sort them out. All he knew was that he understood why Abigail was so distraught at losing them.

"If you can't walk, I'll come back for you in a few minutes," Fitz offered. "I'll trust your word that you'll wait until then."

"It's not broken," Tommy insisted, pushing himself up the wall. "It just hurts, is all."

"I believe your sister would say it ought to make you think twice about trying this foolish stunt again. Do you have bags?"

"The grouchy old man wouldn't let us keep them," Jennifer said indignantly, following him without question, while Tommy trailed behind. "I wanted to show Abby my new hairbrush."

Jennifer's chatter provided a cover of normalcy as they walked through the fog and lessening rain toward the noisy inn at the end of the road. Fitz thought of iron neck collars and golden chains on delicate parts and listened to the soles of his ruined boots flap loose while the children clung close, trusting him with their safety. He scarcely had the blunt to wager in the lowliest game in the seediest tavern, yet the children would need food and beds.

He was out of his mind to believe he could do this. And he was doing it anyway. Somewhere in the wet and fog, he'd finally turned over his shoddy leaf, and there was no turning back to his old insect ways.

"How far ahead of us will Fitz be?" Abby asked as the carriage rattled down the turnpike.

In the seat beside her, the maid snored lightly.

Abby didn't care that Mr. Montague was cross from having muddied his boots while pushing the carriage out of the mud pit they'd fallen into twenty minutes ago, or that she'd revealed entirely too much by using the earl's name instead of his title. Her world had never been more than the children and her home. It was a simple matter to shut out the opinions of others.

"Fitz is a bruising rider, and the Thoroughbred was made for speed. He wouldn't have had to push a carriage out of mud," Montague said with barely concealed disgust. "He's been in Croydon long enough to search it from one end to the other. The real question is where we will find *him*."

In between imagining all the horrors that could befall young children among strangers, Abby had fretted over that same question. It was nearly dark. She wondered how many inns Croydon had. Surely Fitz would have had to stop at several in his search.

And then she had wondered how he would pay for an inn for the night, and the solution seemed obvious. "I doubt that Danecroft has much money with him, so I suppose we must go to where men gamble," she said quietly.

Montague cast her a glance. "What makes you say that?"

She twisted her gloved fingers and watched the lights appear in the first houses outside of Croydon. "That is what the earl does, is it not? My father once told me that gambling is for fools—and for those who can keep count of the cards. I don't believe Danecroft is a fool."

Montague sat silently for a few minutes. "Your father must have been a very wise man."

"My father wasn't an ambitious man, but he spent a great deal of time in London as a youth. I suspect he may have been a bit of a rakehell."

"Which is how he knew about men who count cards?"

"Yes. He always beat me at whist and tried to explain how it was done, but I never had much interest in learning. Apparently Danecroft knows the trick."

"I don't know whether to plant Fitz a facer, or thank him for not bankrupting me," Montague mused. "Perhaps I shall do both."

Abby tilted her head to study his saturnine features for the first time that evening. "I said something I shouldn't have?"

"No, you have merely proved how valuable it is to have wise fathers."

Montague turned and instructed the driver to stop at the first inn he saw.

26

Wearily, Abby almost didn't climb down from the carriage at their fourth stop in Croydon. They'd found Lord Robert swilling ale at the Crown, where he'd given up the search and taken cover from the deluge. A farmer at the Swan said he'd heard the children had been found but didn't know where. Abby didn't place much hope in rumor and insisted on continuing down the road. At the George, Nicholas Atherton had joined them, soaked to the skin but still willing to aid their search, especially from the comfort of the marchioness's plush carriage.

"How can there be so many inns in one town?" Abby complained, then bit her tongue at the weariness she revealed.

"It's the road to Brighton," Montague explained. "Dozens of coaches travel through here each day. And get stopped by mud holes," he added in disgust.

"Why don't you stay in the carriage while we check this one," Mr. Atherton said sympathetically. He was still wringing water from his lace as the horses pulled up to a large establishment that looked rather costly for a man with no purse. It didn't appear a likely choice, so it seemed practical for Abby to remain in the carriage with the sleeping maid, but her frantic thoughts wouldn't allow her to sit still. She dashed through the mud after them.

Abby lingered in the inn's lobby, hoping to find some understanding woman who might know the gossip mill better. If the children had been found, where were they? Shouldn't there be a jubilant celebration in progress somewhere? And would Fitz have tried to return to London if he knew the children were safe?

As if summoned by her wishful thinking, a child's voice piped from down a dark hall.

She glanced around, looking for the innkeeper, but he was apparently occupied elsewhere. She heard serving maids laughing in the tavern. A moment later, she recognized a familiar male rumble, and relief washed over her so thoroughly that she almost staggered with the force of it.

Not waiting for her companions to return, she wandered down the hall, listening for more voices. She assumed these were mostly private parlors on this floor, places for the wealthy to retire to a warm fire and quiet service while waiting for the rain to stop or a coach to arrive.

Light seeped from a crack in the third and last door. She heard more male voices, none of which she recognized. And then—she was quite certain she heard Tommy.

She touched the door, and it swung partly open. Daringly, she peered around the edge, and she thought she might fall on her knees and weep for joy. And laugh with giddy relief. And fling herself into Fitz's arms in everlasting gratitude.

Rather than have hysterics, she lingered to figure out just exactly what the Earl of Danecroft was doing with four children and four well-dressed young gentlemen and a pack of cards.

Jeremy was curled up in Fitz's lap, sound asleep, creating a puddle of drool in the still-damp linen of the earl's frilled neckcloth. She located Fitz's gray frock coat draped over a heap on a daybed that she assumed to be Jennie and Cissy, judging by size and golden curls.

Tommy sat propped against a wall with his leg bandaged and stretched out on the floor in front of him, wearily fighting sleep while he observed the men at the table.

"Remember," Fitz was saying impatiently, "there are only fifty-two cards in the deck. It's not difficult. All you have to do is assign a minus one to all the cards above ten, and a plus one to cards from two to six. That's twenty points on either end, with the cards in between having no value. When the point count is low, the high cards are out of play. When more than one deck is in use, you'll have to add faster and the calculations are a little more advanced."

"You have to be some kind of genius to figure this out," one youth said in disgust, swigging from his mug of ale. "I can't believe anyone can win this way."

"You paid me to show you how I do it," Fitz said with a shrug. "You can listen and learn or just watch the pretty cards on the table."

Despite her exhaustion, Abby couldn't prevent a smile. He wasn't robbing these young lordlings. He was trying to *teach* them. At their expense, of course. The chamber didn't come free, and from the looks of the tray shoved to one side, the children had been well fed. He'd had to earn the coins to feed them.

One had to admire a man who could think on his feet and produce gold coins from thin air.

One had to love an earl who was willing to step outside his element to rescue children who weren't his own. She was in head over heels and tumbling fast.

Mr. Montague slipped up behind her and leaned his hand against the doorjamb to glance over her shoulder. "He could have offered to teach *me*," he grumbled.

"If you weren't bright enough to figure out he was counting cards, then you're probably not bright enough to learn how," Abby retorted. "Perhaps you should find what you are good at and give up cards."

Even though she spoke softly, Fitz looked up. Instead of sending her one of his beaming grins, he studied her warily, waiting for her reaction to his introducing minors to professional card sharking.

She knew gambling was wrong. She knew people lost fortunes over the gaming tables. She didn't want Tommy thinking he could make a living at playing games.

But she couldn't fault Fitz for doing what he must to survive. He wasn't shallow, as everyone would have her believe. The man had so much compassion, so much energy and life—and very few options for expressing them. Her burden lighter by no small amount, she entered the room, pressed a kiss of more than gratitude to Fitz's hair, then knelt to hug Tommy.

Her heart was much too full to complain about Fitz's idea of child care. The children were safe, which was all that mattered now.

Fitz was certain a choir of angels exploded into song when Abby brushed a kiss on his head with the whole world watching. His chest tightened with unwarranted pride as he watched her with the children. He *had* managed the rescue rather well. Spending his youth as a perennial reprobate had taught him a few lessons.

He tried to act nonchalant when he noted Montague's questioning look at Abby's intimate gesture. He knew Tommy hadn't missed a thing, but Fitz simply didn't care who knew that Abby was *his*. To hell with propriety. His prim and proper Rhubarbara approved his handling of the situation, and all was momentarily right with his world.

"There aren't any rooms left in the inn," he told Montague, while watching the happy reunion. The child curled up in his lap hadn't woken, but the girls stirred when Abby pressed happy kisses to their cheeks. "You can join us, if you like."

"Nick's here, too. Do I have to pay for lessons?"

"Depends on whether you want to bleed Ath dry or give him a fair chance." Fitz supposed he ought to feel shame at having taken advantage of his friends, but he'd just used his brain, not done anything illegal. "The advantage is only slight."

Abby swooped in to reclaim Jeremy from Fitz's lap. "Your friends have been kind enough to spend the evening in the rain and mud to help me," she reminded him. "I will pay for their lessons."

Not caring who watched, Fitz slid his hand to her nape, dragged her head down, and planted a firm kiss on her lovely mouth. He liked a woman who knew how to use her tongue, in all senses of the phrase. Logic had fled the room when she had entered it.

She blushed and looked delightfully tousled as she lifted Jeremy and stepped away. Fitz seemed to have left her speechless, which made him even happier. Of course, with Abby that condition never lasted long.

"We will have to take them where the Weatherstons can't find them," she whispered in his ear, before taking a soft chair one of the young men offered and settling down by the coal fire.

Filth and feathers. She was right. But they couldn't go anywhere in the dark of night with the rain flooding the roads. At least he'd managed to hide them for a few hours.

"I'll see if there is a bed in the attic for your maid," Montague told Abby, before warning, "I'll be back with Atherton."

Fitz would have loved to dismiss his "students" in favor of Abby's company, but they had paid for supper and this room and deserved the lessons he'd promised. Without Jeremy cuddled in his lap, he could move more freely. He expertly shuffled the cards and scattered them across the table.

Even after Blake returned with Nick and a fresh round of drinks, Fitz was aware of Abby settling Jeremy in beside Tommy, speaking to the innkeeper about bedding, and otherwise turning the plain room into her own little nest. She had more food brought up from the kitchen so no one filled up on ale and got too boisterous. She stroked small brows when the children stirred in their sleep, and examined Tommy's leg to pronounce it badly bruised but not broken. Nibbling on cheese and bread, she lingered at Fitz's shoulder to watch his cards. She acquired pillows and a footstool so she might stretch out and doze in a chair if they played until dawn. And not once did she flirt with his imposing friends or wealthy students. *He* was the only man who won Miss Merry's cautious smiles. She was a gem among women.

And Fitz intended to make her his own. He didn't think it was foolish impulse to decide Abby was the best he could do for himself and Penny. *Logically*, it was the wrong thing to do. Even though he knew he could take care of her siblings, Abby would hate how he lived.

But in all other ways, he knew his decision was right. If only he could persuade her to agree.

Finally, his students gave up and went to their beds or to the tavern. Fitz checked to see that Abby was sound asleep in her chair, her cheeks flushed with the heat from the fire she'd fed earlier. Now all he had to do was decide how to persuade her to his thinking.

After the departure of their guests, Montague eyed him as if he knew what Fitz was contemplating. Straddling his chair with the lithe grace of his dark Norman ancestors, he rested his arms across the back and swilled the last of the ale. "I have Lady Belden's carriage in the yard. You can deliver the lot to her in the morning and let her figure out what to do with the children. I'll be happy to return on Barton's impressive steed."

Blond, elegant Atherton sprawled his long legs indolently from a wing chair in the far corner. Never one with a regard for propriety, he countered, "You'd do better to take them back to Miss Merriweather's farm.

Possession is nine-tenths of the law, and all that. Let the courts fight it out."

Fitz shuffled the deck. "The children were afraid Weatherston would beat them if he found them. I think I need to take them somewhere safe until the situation is sorted out."

"You're about to do something beef-witted, aren't you?" Montague asked, snatching the cards away and spreading them out, apparently trying to visually memorize the point counts Fitz had taught him earlier. Montague believed in law and order, but he also believed in staying out of other people's business. He wouldn't interfere with Fitz's decisions.

Fitz removed another deck from an inside pocket and tapped it against the table before shuffling. He thought better with cards in his hands. "Miss Merriweather needs to hide her siblings until her father's executor is notified of our complaint against their guardian. I'm thinking my estate is larger than her farm."

He had a number of other thoughts about Abby and his home, all of them prurient, but until he knew whether his staff had sold off all the beds to cover their wages, he tried not to get ahead of himself.

Atherton snorted. "You think she'll agree to abscond to your estate unchaperoned? She seems the proper sort to me. She may take the children back to the dragon lady, but hiding them? I don't think so."

Fitz glanced over at his sleeping Miss Merry and knew he was right and Atherton was wrong. Abby might look small and sweet, but she would fight tooth and nail to keep her siblings now that she had them. If they complained of being beaten, she'd go after Weatherston with a big stick and a horsewhip. Fitz had the more delicate task of preventing Abby from killing the man.

Other men might object to a wife as intimidating as Miss Merry, but Fitz was completely confident that he could handle her and enjoy every minute of it. His Rhubarbara had the appearance of an angel and the fierceness of a lion, and he wanted her contrary self for his own.

He knew how to do it. He simply couldn't decide if he had earned the right to follow his crass desires instead of what his extremely respectable wits told him society expected of him.

First, he had to be assured he could keep Abby and the children safe. "I'd like the two of you to go back to Tattersall's. This time, search for an Irish ruffian not much bigger than Tommy, wearing clothes that look as if he's slept in them. He's either a lackwit or Geoff may have hired him, although if my cuz hopes to drive me out of the country by having ruffians fling bricks at me, he's as dim-witted as the rest of my family."

Atherton and Montague perked right up at this appealing enterprise.

Beating cads into pulp held little appeal to Fitz with Miss Merry on his horizon. But if he ever got his hands on Geoff, he'd have a fist ready, if only for thinking Fitz was such a sapskull as to kill himself and for celebrating his death with *carriage crests*. His heir needed some sense beaten into him.

Abby awoke to the heavenly aromas of hot chocolate and bacon and the even more delightful sound of childish whispers. Her neck ached from sleeping upright, but joy was her first reaction. *She had the children back!*

"Shhh, Abby's sleeping," Jeremy whispered so loudly he could probably be heard in the next room.

"You took my toast," Cissy whispered back. "I want more toast."

"You may have mine," Jennie said to hush the quarrel. "It has jam."

Abby dreaded having to scold them for running away. She dreaded worse asking what had driven them to flee. This very minute, she basked happily in the familiar morning argument.

She heard the door open and Fitz's boots upon the

floorboards. Her hand rose instantly to pat down her hair and straighten her ribbons.

"More toast and hot chocolate," he declared in an exaggerated undertone that said he'd noticed her gesture and was humoring her pretense at sleep. "But you'd better hurry and finish your bacon or I will eat it."

Abby knew she had acted inappropriately familiar with Fitz in front of strangers last night, but she simply couldn't bring herself to care. She wanted hot chocolate so she could sweeten her breath and be ready in case he wanted to kiss her again.

She would do almost anything to have more of those kisses. And she ought to be ashamed of that thought, too, but she wasn't. She was a grown woman, and even if she was fooling herself that a handsome earl wanted her for more than her money, she adored the way Fitz's attention made her feel desirable for the first time in her spinsterish life. She simply prayed his kisses were sincere and not more evidence of his deceptive charm.

Hoping she didn't look a fright, she stood and faced the little breakfast table. The twins instantly tumbled from their chairs to hug her legs. Tommy ducked his head and stared at his plate. And Jennie grinned as if the weight of the world had been removed from her small shoulders. Abby knew that feeling.

She crouched down to tousle blond heads and peck jam-smeared cheeks before daring to glance at Fitz. He was watching her with admiration while buttering toast, proving he was a modern wonder, a man capable of accomplishing two tasks at once.

Abby hustled the twins back to their seats. She pulled up a chair between Tommy and Jennie and poured hot chocolate from the fresh pot that Fitz had placed on the table.

"I want to know what happened, and I want the whole truth," she said solemnly to the eldest children. "I'm relying on you two."

"Mrs. Weatherston doesn't like me and Tommy

much," Jennie said prosaically. "We try to tell her how you do things, and she sends us to our room."

Abby nodded and waited, knowing her opinionated siblings well. They hadn't been raised to be silent and accepting, and she couldn't imagine any woman would appreciate children telling her what to do.

"She babies the twins," Tommy said with disgust. "She feeds them candy and shows them off to her friends when they should be napping. Then they get all mean and bite people."

"Bite people?" Fitz murmured near Abby's ear, placing a plate of toast in front of her.

"I still have a scar on my arm where Tommy bit me when he was that age," she assured him. "They're like young animals unless taught otherwise."

Now that they had a sympathetic ear, the older two poured out a litany of woes, large and small, that painted a picture of a woman who wanted children because she was expected to have them, and a man who had no interest in sharing parental duties. Abby wasn't at all certain that a court of law, or even their executor, would listen to their woes. They were children, after all. They were being fed and housed and no one was overtly harming them.

They just weren't being loved.

Tears filled her eyes as she struggled to decide what she must do.

"The mean man said we don't have birfdays no more," Jeremy said, joining in the complaints.

"He hit Tommy," Cissy chimed in with three-year-old indignation.

A glance at Tommy confirmed some version of the twins' statements, and Abby's heart sank. She glanced to Fitz, who had remained silent while she'd quizzed the children.

"I sent Lady Belden's maid and carriage back up to London so she needn't worry about you. Hopefully, the Weatherstons will believe you took them to London, and perhaps from there to your farm," he said without inflection. "I've rented a post chaise to go in another direction. We need to go some place the Weatherstons won't know about."

"Yes, that sounds ideal," she said in relief. "Where?"

"My estate," he replied with a shrug that Abby could tell wasn't as casual as he might pretend. "My offer stands. Perhaps we could negotiate later."

Negotiate. Marriage. With a gambler and an earl, one who was being pelted with stones carrying cryptic messages. If she went with him, she almost certainly had to marry him. She couldn't rely on no one's ever discovering she was in his company. She would ruin her reputation and make it impossible for the executor to believe she was a proper influence. But then, she was already here with him, so what did it matter?

Did she know him well enough to believe he was being honorable, or was he simply manipulating circumstances to get what he wanted?

And if Fitz was actually being honorable, could she risk harming him by bringing down the wrath of the law and the marchioness on him?

Abby looked around at her eager siblings and back to the man who made her heart yearn for fairy tales that came true.

And she nodded, rashly trusting Fitz with her future and the children's.

27

Riding Barton's steed alongside the bright yellow post chaise spilling with excited, noisy children, Fitz tried to quell his anxiety by comparing the shilling-per-mile charge for the chaise with shillings per pound of turnips to see how many acres the journey was costing him, but oddly, his head seemed crowded with people instead of numbers.

He'd sent to London for Penny and her nanny. Montague and Atherton had accompanied Lady Belden's carriage, carrying Abby's note of apology and heartfelt gratitude. He rather thought that wouldn't be the last he heard of the dragon lady, but that wasn't his most immediate concern, the one that had him counting turnips rather than thinking about it.

His most immediate concern loomed on the horizon, looking properly noble and majestic from this distance— Wyckersham, the seat of the earls of Danecroft for the last century. He was going home to officially take possession of his title and place among his not-so-illustrious ancestors.

He couldn't say he loved the magnificent edifice and acreage. Or even that they had ever been a welcoming home. He'd left at seventeen and never looked back. But it was a grand estate he'd be proud to claim, if only the roof weren't about to fall on his head.

He wanted Abby to love his home. He wanted his Rhubarbara to see the potential—in him, as well as in the estate. If it weren't for his enormous debt, he liked to think he could be a proper earl someday. He knew little of farming, but he wasn't so overwhelmed by the daunting task now. Applebee, the estate manager he'd hired, should be on the job. A small influx of cash plus his wits ought to get him started.

He simply had to summon the courage to ask Abby, again, to lock her golden chains around him. Important questions were far easier to ask on impulse. That she'd accepted his offer to hide the children indicated she trusted him, but to be fair to her, he needed to let her see the immensity of the undertaking his estate involved before he asked again.

He didn't even know if he was taking her to a house with cockroaches in the kitchen or lice in the beds. He hoped not.

Swiping bad thoughts from his mind, Fitz began calculating costs: one guinea per male servant per year—perhaps they could stick with Bibley and not hire footmen. Six pounds per year for housemaids—or should he have them buy their own tea and sugar and pay them nine pounds? He didn't know the cost of tea and sugar. How many maids would it take to rid the place of pests and clean it to Abby's satisfaction? Would she need a lady's maid?

The sum for servants' wages hadn't quite reached unreasonable by the time the carriage rattled over the pothole at the turn into the drive, and Tommy shouted excitedly from his high perch at the back of the chaise. Fitz followed his gaze and tried to see the sprawling weed field as a young boy might.

The house couldn't be seen from this perspective, but the fields stretched to a wooded copse fed by a wandering stream. Frightened from their feeding by the galloping horses, quail cried and fled to the sky. Ducks swam about a slimy green pond in the distance. A deer bounded for cover. Fitz was certain rabbits and other creatures raced for their burrows at the racket of carriage wheels on the rutted drive.

As an adult, he saw only the work that needed to be done, but the estate was boy heaven. No wonder he'd never wasted time in a schoolroom.

His education may have been neglected. He may not have any memory of loving arms and family reunions or even a father who bothered to teach him what little he knew. But the Danecroft lands were carved in Fitz's heart as surely as if he'd always been meant to own them.

He could do this, he decided with a deep inhalation of relief. He could make this land his own. He simply needed the proper incentive to work himself night and day to achieve his goal.

Riding alongside the hired chariot, Fitz anxiously observed Abby's expression as the colonnaded portico of the house rose above the overgrown yew hedge. He thought he saw awe and a little fear. He wanted to leap down and explain that the earldom's fortunes had begun their long decline when the Wyckerlys gave up the sea to pour their wealth into that limestone and marble. Or perhaps the final blow had come in prior generations when the overproud earls had driven off their younger brothers and sons. Either way, the house was a monument to folly and not worthy of her fear.

It was a beautiful Palladian home, built from the ground up based on plans from Colen Campbell and influenced by Inigo Jones's designs. The first earl's wife had a love of grace and order, and more taste than dowry. For a century, no expense had been spared. Robert Adam had added his touch to ceilings and fireplaces throughout the great rooms. Capability Brown had designed the grounds.

And there wasn't any way in hell Fitz could restore that former grandeur.

When the chaise drew to a halt at the imposing entrance, Fitz paid the postilions and gave them directions to the stables, although he doubted there would be a grain to be found there.

At least it looked as if his creditors had given up and gone home. Or to London, where they all no doubt knew his town house address by now. He might throw off their depredations for another day or two until they found him again.

Tying his steed to a post, he assisted Abby from the carriage. Her hand was cold in his, and she gazed up at the sprawling structure with such trepidation, Fitz couldn't resist pulling her into his arms and squeezing her tight. She was round and soft and comforting, and he wanted to hug her forever, like the child's cuddly toy he'd never had. Except his Abby had a mind of her own, and that's what made her special. He adored the challenge of guessing where her thoughts flew when she went silent like this.

"It's a barn," he murmured against her bonnet. "We could ride horses through it and no one would know the difference. We could hide the children in the attic and no one would find the stairs."

She giggled a little tearily and, to his great relief, leaned against him for a moment, just enough to let him know she believed in him. That would get him through a few more hours.

The children spilled from the carriage. He had to help Tommy down from his high perch, much to the boy's humiliation. His limp was still pronounced as he wandered up the wide stairs.

The mortar between the granite blocks that made up the stairs had cracked, leaving many of the slabs loose. Vines had taken root and crept up the marble columns.

"When Penny gets here, you can take turns swatting

spiders and pulling weeds," Fitz declared with a good cheer he didn't feel.

"Penny's coming?" Jennifer asked, her frightened face brightening. "Will she bring dolls?"

"For all I know, there might be an entire nursery stuffed with dolls in there somewhere. Consider this an opportunity to explore."

Apparently hearing something in his tone that he hadn't wished to convey, Abby glanced at him with concern, then tucked her hand into the crook of his elbow. "It's late. We'll go to the kitchen and heat some water to wash up." She raised her eyebrows in question. "Will there be any servants at all?"

He shrugged and led the way up the stairs. "Depends on their patience and whether or not they had better offers of employment elsewhere. I didn't have time to warn them of our arrival."

And he still had Bibley to confront.

Perhaps his best course would be to rent out the whole sprawling dung heap, servants and all, and find a hovel to rent. His insides shriveled with fear that he would be the Danecroft to bring the earldom to an end.

Abby walked into the Earl of Danecroft's home knowing the potential of ruining her reputation if she did not accept his proposal. She suffered no illusion that she could conceal herself from the outside world for long. She must decide quickly if she should give up on marriage and return to her farm and spend her fortune on fighting through the courts. She refused to let the children out of her sight while she did so, which meant leaving London ballrooms and uninteresting suitors behind.

She'd gladly sacrifice marriage for the children, but the look of admiration on Fitz's face as he led her up the stairs made her feel as if her virtue might have some value.

Had he really meant they would negotiate marriage? How?

She gave up thinking as she entered. She felt like Cinderella on the arm of her prince passing through the castle doors. For the owner of this palace, she was glad she had learned to wear Cinderella gowns. Foolish of her, no doubt, but for Fitz, she would strive always to look stylish.

She tugged him to a halt in the entry so she might gape in wonder at the grandeur he called home. Above a marble entrance large enough to encompass her entire house, a domed skylight illuminated a rotunda of columns and marble busts.

"The dome leaks," Fitz murmured, removing her bonnet, since no servant rushed to aid her.

She bit back a smile. "Then if the children get bored some rainy day and have a stone-throwing contest, they won't be the first to break what's already broken."

"There is that." He inclined his head in approval. "I may have been the first child to drop a stone through the glass, now that I think on it."

"Drop?" She discarded her pelisse and umbrella. Fitz hung them over a bust of some important-looking Roman.

The children skated in the dust, leaving long trails in their wake as they spun around admiring the dome and taking in all the different directions in which they could scatter. Although his short legs couldn't stretch far enough, Jeremy was already testing the balustrade of the grand staircase.

"I discovered the entrance to the roof long ago," Fitz admitted. "An excellent place for hiding. We'll send the children up there should anyone stray up the drive."

She could tell by his voice that he was teasing. He didn't really mean to send the children to the roof. But she had serious doubts about preventing Tommy from repeating Fitz's youthful indiscretions. She would need to tie bells on all their necks.

"Kitchen?" she asked, hoping to distract herself from parental worries—and Fitz's proximity. He hadn't stopped touching her since she'd left the carriage, and she enjoyed entirely too much the heat of his hand at her back and on her arm. She was acutely aware of his powerful male muscles sheltering her.

She might be ruining her reputation by entering his home unchaperoned, but that didn't give him license for more familiarity with her person. Despite her pleasure at his caresses, she wasn't ready for more than kisses. She had to make that clear. Once she found her tongue.

Fitz whistled loudly, commanding the attention of her wandering tribe. He pointed to a discreet door hidden behind the stairs at the far end of the entry. "That way."

They tumbled over one another in their haste to explore the next chamber.

"Maybe we should allow them into only one room at a time," Abby mused, following her siblings across the entry. "Tell them they cannot explore the next one until the first one is clean."

Fitz snorted. "It would take an army to clean just the entry. I vote we turn it over to a museum."

"No, you don't. You were meant to be lord of all you survey. You've just been hiding in the shadows, waiting for your turn."

"Like a cockroach," he suggested helpfully.

She sent him a quizzical glance. "I was thinking more in terms of the ugly duckling who grows into a swan. You have the energy and determination to turn this into a grand palace again, where you can entertain important men and influence the path of government."

She feared she sounded wistful. She couldn't be the countess he needed to accomplish all that. Just the thought shivered her bones. Eventually, he would have to move on and leave her behind on the farm, where she belonged.

"I might have been brought up within a life of privilege, but I was never taught how to wield power wisely," he said with a negligent air. "Men of influence have educations. They've toured Europe. They sit in their clubs discussing important topics and negotiating deals. I count cards. If they'd rather gamble than vote on issues vital to our nation, I can show them how."

"Men of influence only understand the lives of people like themselves," she corrected. "You have the perspective of someone who must work for a living and use his wits to survive. Never underestimate the value of your experience."

The children raced down the dark servants' hall toward the scent of roasting venison. Fitz halted in what was most likely the cloakroom, grabbed Abby's arms, and, before she could catch her breath, swooped down to steal a kiss.

Her surprise rapidly escalated to desire. They might have only moments alone. Taking advantage, Abby slid her arms around his neck and luxuriated in the hungry warmth of kisses pressed to her cheeks, the corners of her mouth, and finally her lips.

His breath tasted vaguely of mint. Clinging to his shoulders, she fell in love just a little more, knowing he'd chewed the herb because he planned to kiss her, and he was as eager as she for it to be wonderful.

The joy bubbling through her couldn't be anything less than love. That realization alone made her both giddy and fearful as she returned his kisses with all the passion in her.

She was too caught up in the thrilling awareness of Fitz's hard chest pressed against her breasts to worry over the state of her affections. The exquisite pleasure of his big hand cupping her cheek as if she was someone precious made her heart thump so loudly she feared he would hear it.

The intimacy of his tongue dueling with hers . . . She sighed and didn't object when his fingers rode from her waist to the curve of her breast. She *wanted* his touch there. She wanted far more than his touch.

The kitchen door burst open and Jennifer shouted

impatiently, "Help! The cook is going to boil Jeremy for supper!"

Fitz snorted with laughter, ending their delicious exploration. But his chuckles forged the rude interruption into part of the bond that drew them together, and Abby relaxed against him.

They would have time for more voyages of discovery later. She needed to take this very slowly before Fitz's impulses, and her own, overwhelmed her caution.

28

"Pudding, pudding!" Jeremy chanted, pounding his little fist into Fitz's back after their country supper. It was time to find beds, but the children were too wound up to be herded. Fitz held his free arm out to Cissy, who had climbed up on the kitchen table, reaching out with chubby hands in hopes of being flung over his other shoulder. Jennifer was in the process of making a pet of the kitchen mouser, and even Tommy looked stuffed and satisfied.

The servants apparently ate well off the fat of the land while he was gone. Interesting.

All in all, Fitz counted his first dinner at home a rousing success, even if it had been conducted in the kitchen with Cook scowling in disapproval. Abby had disarmed the battle-ax by exchanging recipes with her, although even Bibley had protested when she'd attempted to help clean up after her noisy, and rather messy, brood.

"We can make up our own rooms," Abby said somewhat shyly when Bibley did his doddering best to usher them out of the servants' quarters. "If you would simply show us where to find the linens."

A stammering, scrawny maid immediately raced from

the shadows, running ahead of them at Bibley's imperious gesture. Fitz assumed that the stout housekeeper of his youth had taken a paying position elsewhere, but if she'd trained the servants she'd left behind, they'd suit him fine.

"You'll not escape my wrath by pretending you run a tight ship, old boy," Fitz murmured as he passed his rail-thin but well-fed butler in the hall. "You'll win an audience only if my guests are made happy."

"As you say, my lord," Bibley said, exuding skepticism with every palsied tremor.

Reaching the rotunda, Fitz returned the twins to their feet and let them scamper for the stairs, which their older siblings were trying to ascend with dignity—unsuccessfully, since their heads were swiveling like weather vanes in a thunderstorm.

"Do we need to bring cats with us?" Abigail called down as the twins raced to the next floor. "I'm not fond of mice."

Fitz grinned as Bibley's scrawny shoulders stiffened at the insult.

"Mice are not allowed in an earl's residence, my lady."

"Oh, earls can issue edicts to rodents? Well, you learn something new every day." With a wink, she ran up the stairs after the children.

"If you are very, very good, old man, she will consent to be my countess, and you will start receiving a salary again—if I don't push you off a cliff for pretending I killed myself." Fitz lingered at the bottom of the stairs to glare sternly at his insubordinate butler.

"Your cousin was uncommonly stubborn about loaning funds to pay the help," Bibley informed him with the same stoic tone that announced guests at dinner. "He needed to be reminded that all this might someday be his."

"And you thought faking my death would terrify him into paying you off? How well did that work?" Fitz inquired with interest.

"Your cousin is not the gentleman I hoped," Bibley replied with just the right degree of regret. "He wished to see your carcass first."

That sounded like a true Wyckerly. But if Geoff had been out here to consult with Bibley, could it have reminded his cuz of how much he stood to gain if Fitz stuck his spoon in the wall? Enough to hire scrawny ruffians in hopes Fitz would run off as Bibley wished?

"Disobey my express orders again, old man, and I will hunt down everything you ever stole and hand it over to the bankers," Fitz warned, knowing that it would do little good in a household that had run itself for decades. He had his work cut out for him.

Which included finding out if his cousin had returned from Yorkshire and coming to an understanding with his heir, just in case Geoff held out some hope that Fitz would conveniently be run over by a dray while chasing stone-slinging midgets.

But for tonight, he had seductive persuasion on his mind. To hell with heirs and titles. He'd made up his mind—he wouldn't be happy until Miss Merry agreed to marry him, and unless he was happy, restoring the earldom wouldn't be worth the effort.

Four more rowdy youngsters like Penny weren't a deterrent when he had a palace to lose them in. This could work. He would make it work.

His cock eagerly roused in approval at just the image of Abby's sunset curls and lush curves adorning his bed.

Wherever his damned bed might be. He set Bibley in search of a good one.

The children unerringly located the nursery and schoolroom on the third floor next to additional guest bedchambers. Abby did not expect a skeleton staff of servants to keep unused rooms dusted and swept, but at least the rooms contained beds, and the maid found clean linens, which was better than they'd had in the inn's parlor the prior night.

While Abby and the maid shook feather mattresses out the windows, the children prowled among the shelves and chests, exclaiming over rusty toy soldiers and beheaded dolls. Seeming somewhat dazed, Fitz turned in circles, hands behind his back, observing the abode of his youth.

Even though he'd spent the last two days in riding boots and mud, and his fashionably short-waisted coat had been rumpled and used as a blanket, he managed to look tall, square-shouldered, and breathtakingly masculine as he perused the nursery. Just the authority with which he held himself screamed of privileged aristocracy, with the power to sway men to his will. Abby had to beware that he did not use his personal magnetism to sway *her*.

"There are no books," he finally announced.

Making up a bed, Abby followed his gaze around the room. "How odd. How could your tutors teach you without books?"

"They didn't," he said absently. "Mostly, they chased us through the upper halls and grounds. After a while, they quit bothering to chase us. And after that, we had no tutors."

She returned one mattress and went on to the next bed, watching the children out of the corner of her eye but focused mostly on Fitz, who seemed to be having difficulty reconciling his past to his future. "Your tutors took their books with them?"

"I suppose they must have. I've only the one text left, and I purloined it from the vicar, before the church roof collapsed, and he moved on."

"Perhaps there are books in your library."

Fitz raised a quizzical eyebrow at the timid maid. "Do we still have a library?"

The maid quivered and pulled a sheet across her face.

"You look much too intimidatingly noble, my lord," Abby said with a laugh. "You must accept that you are an earl now, and that you do not speak to any but the upper servants."

He drew his dark eyebrows down in a scowl, which made him even more terrifying to look upon. "Tommy, ask this witless creature if we have a library."

Looking startled, Tommy glanced at Abby, who shrugged her permission.

"Miss, does Lord Danecroft have a library?"

The maid nodded, wide-eyed, keeping the length of the nursery between her and the earl. Tommy looked to Fitz for direction, but at the maid's nod, Fitz took up another mattress and proceeded to beat it against the end of a bed. At least he found constructive uses for his frustration, even if he raised more dust than he cleared.

Abby had a feeling Fitz wasn't very familiar with affection, which was frightening in itself. Having never known love, could he learn to love? For her faint, prayerful hopes, she trusted so, but she'd best not count on it. One more thing she must consider while she decided the future.

They found wearable nightshirts in the chests to clothe the children. Abby happily tucked them in and reveled in the opportunity to kiss them all. They were whispering among themselves as she closed the door and looked for a room close by so she would hear their cries if they woke during the night.

"Show us the library," Fitz commanded as the maid opened the door of the next chamber for inspection. Instead of investigating the governess's room, he caught Abby's arm and nearly dragged her toward the stairs, apparently possessing some notion of the library's direction.

She ran to catch up, observing him with curiosity. He was tense and unsmiling, his green eyes shuttered, but he was still Fitz. She had no reason to fear him, other than that he was a man and far stronger than she. And an aristocrat accustomed to commanding others. She'd not seen him in this humor before, but he was entitled to strange humors under the circumstances. It wasn't often that a man returned to a home he hadn't lived in since he was a child. She'd like to know more of the memories he harbored.

The maid scampered ahead of them so quickly that they almost lost her in the shadows.

"Bibley lied," Fitz muttered, hastening down to the ground floor after the maid. "We have mice. We've just put uniforms on them."

Abby bit back a smile at this display of the Fitz she knew. "Talk to your estate manager in the morning and find out if there are any sturdy, loud females in the vicinity available for hiring, if mousy ones are not to your liking."

"If they're smart, they won't take the position," he growled. "I'm doomed to mice. I thought I could manage all this, but I'm prone to foolish impulse."

"And a smidgen of arrogance," she pointed out.

"You're laughing at me, aren't you?" he growled as the maid hesitated outside a scarcely noticeable door at the end of a long, dark corridor.

"Maybe a little," Abby admitted. "You're an earl. You own a home far grander than many a duke's. You have servants. And no cockroaches," she reminded him. "And you're growling because you terrify a maid."

"I'm growling because I can't *pay* a maid." He turned up the light on the lantern he carried so he could examine the door. Shyly, the maid offered a key hung high on the frame.

Abby thought Fitz had forgotten she was there when he unlocked the door and stared in as if he'd never seen it before, until his fingers dug into her arm, and he tugged her in with him.

Beneath veils of cobwebs, the library was magnificent. Paneled in rich mahogany from carpeted floor to two-story ceiling, it boasted a balcony above the main chamber. Leather chairs flanked a fireplace with inlaid panels and what she assumed was the Danecroft crest carved above. Tables thick with dust invited stacks of books and sprawling atlases.

Almost every shelf was empty.

"Bibley!" Fitz roared so loudly and unexpectedly that Abby nearly fell out of her shoes. "Bibley, come in here now!"

As if conjured by magic, the shrunken butler tottered into the library upon command. "Yes, my lord," he intoned.

"Bibley, where are the books?"

The old man looked around as if just now discovering they possessed a library. "I'm sure I don't know, my lord."

"And I'm equally sure that you do. If nothing else, my spendthrift ancestors would have bought books by the yard for decoration. If you sold off the library, Bibley, I'll own you." He swung his lantern over the shelves, but the dust was too thick to discern any evidence of previous habitation. "I remember this room as being kept locked, but I thought it was to prevent us from reading inappropriate material. I should think my ancestors would have at least kept their pornography in here, even if they never read a single book."

"The earls couldn't read, my lord," Bibley stated with seeming indifference.

Fitz swung around and stared at him. Abby sank into a library chair, aware that she was watching a family drama but not totally understanding what it meant.

"What do you mean, they couldn't read?" the current Earl of Danecroft thundered. "I'm an earl. I can read. How could my father sign papers if he couldn't read them?"

"His men of business read them for him, my lord." Bibley crossed his gnarled hands in front of him. "Is that all, my lord?"

"No, that is damned well not all! My father was not a stupid man, Bibley. He was a lazy sot, but he was not stupid! And neither was George. Don't tell me George couldn't read either. He had more tutors than I ever did."

"He needed more tutors than you ever did," Bibley corrected. Adjusting his wire spectacles, he removed an invisible mote from his threadbare sleeve as if the conversation were of no consequence whatsoever. "He was afflicted in the same way as your father and grandfather."

"Afflicted?"

Fitz's voice was more dangerously menacing than Abby had ever heard it. Had she been the butler, she would have been quailing in her shoes. But the old man simply stared at the wall past Fitz's shoulders, trembling only with palsy. Or was that a hint of resignation behind the stoic facade?

"Your father used to say the letters leapt about and jumbled up worse than spillikins," Bibley explained without inflection. "He tired of picking them out to make words. When his heir suffered the same affliction, he did not demand that Viscount Wyckerly apply himself to books."

"Instead, he taught George estate management from the back of a horse," Fitz said wearily, reaching for one of the few books on the shelves. "And no one cared whether or not I was capable of learning."

"You were more interested in following your brother about," Bibley suggested with unconcern.

"Because younger children always imitate the eldest," Abby said softly, yearning to hug Fitz while he struggled with his memories. "You would have wanted to do everything your brother did, so you avoided tutors as he did, and no one saw reason to teach you otherwise."

"Bibley, you may go now," the earl said, flipping the pages of a text.

The butler nodded and doddered off, closing the door behind him.

"I'm not stupid," Fitz stated calmly. "I have no education, but I can read. I taught myself."

"You have an education. It just isn't the type most men of your rank possess. That makes you unique, not ignorant."

He set the book on the shelf, took her hands, and raised her from the seat. Abby forgot the butler and books when Fitz's gaze fastened on her face. His lips were just inches away, and she desperately desired to feel them again. The mere heat of his palms caused a tingle of anticipation.

"I'm not an insect," he declared with a triumphant grin instead of kissing her as she wanted.

Her lips turned up of their own accord at his excitement. "No, I can't think that you would be," she agreed. "A wild stallion, perhaps. A bored Corinthian, certainly. Never an insect."

Fitz wrapped both arms around her waist and lifted her from the floor, and she thrilled at his strength and closeness.

"Marry me, Rhubarbara, for I'm about to make a dishonest woman of you."

He pressed her back against the wall and smothered any protest with his kiss.

29

As if he'd finally been released from some restraint, Fitz did not give Abby time to reply. His broad frame pressed her against the wall, and his kiss melted any thought she might have. His hand on her breast ... Abby needed the wall to hold her up as shivers of expectation seeped to her womb and lower. In just that touch, she learned a very great deal of why unmarried men and women should not be left alone together.

She drank hungrily of his kisses, as if starved and thirsty and responding to sweet wine and rhubarb tarts. She couldn't get enough. She wrapped her arms around his strong shoulders, let him lift her from the floor, and only moaned a protest when he cupped her bottom and brought her too close to reality.

She was a farm girl. She knew what aroused stallions did to mares.

She tried to wriggle away, but it was like forcing water to behave once it escaped the pump. She had no backbone. She wanted his kisses to go on forever.

He fell back on one of the leather couches and cradled her in his lap. "Marry me, Abby. Please say yes. I don't think I have the strength to stop now."

And again, before she could reply, he captured her mouth with his, begging her with sweetness and rough passion. The stubble on his cheeks chafed her skin, reminding her that he was all male, as if she needed more reminding. Bay rum and masculine musk filled her senses, and the stroke of strong fingers on the curve of her breast almost made her agree to anything, had she possessed wits to speak.

She gasped as his capable fingers unfastened her bodice and slid inside her chemisette, stroking her bare flesh. Although the tips of his fingers barely grazed her skin, she could feel the sensation through every particle of her body. She shuddered and didn't fight him, needing this stimulation she'd been denied for so long. She ached for more but didn't know how to tell him.

Encouraged, he unhooked the top of her corset at the same time as his tongue swept deep inside her mouth. His fingers caressing her nipple elicited a cry of shock, swallowed by his kiss.

She could feel Fitz's arousal beneath her bottom. She desperately needed to touch him as he touched her. She wanted to lie back against the leather and let him do all the unspeakable things to her that a man did to a woman. Desire burned between her legs, and every stroke on her breast stoked the fire higher.

That was when Abby knew of a certainty that she had no choice left.

"See how right this is, my beautiful Abby?" he murmured, laying her back against the leather, just as she'd wanted.

He wants my inheritance, her logical mind protested weakly.

Hair falling in his eyes, his jaw shadowed and taut with longing, Fitz untied her chemisette and unfastened more hooks, until she spilled from her confines like a wanton. He touched her with such reverence that Abby nearly wept with gratitude that she could offer him what he wanted. Cold air brushed her bare skin, but Fitz's gaze warmed her from the inside out.

He bent over and licked one of her aching nipples, and she did weep, then slid her hand into his thick hair to hold him there while her body sang hallelujahs.

"I need you, Abby," he whispered, tugging one tight crest with his teeth and fondling the other with his hand. "You need me. We'll make it work. Trust me."

I would be giving him everything I owned to become his unpaid servant while he gambles about London, her stupid logic warned.

A strong brown hand caught her skirt and tugged it upward, caressing her stockinged leg with purpose, working its way upward.

"I'll buy a special license." He continued eager kisses from her lips down her throat. "We can marry immediately. No one can take the children away from an earl."

He's right, her weakening brain agreed. *And I want him. And he needs me. And I'm absolutely insane.*

Because by then, Fitz's fingers had found the point of no return, and Abby bit back a scream at the intimate contact with flesh no man except a husband should ever touch.

"You're going to love the magic we can make together, my Abby," he whispered with male pride. "You may throw me out on my head if I don't give you pleasure. Say yes, my precious, because I don't dare go farther until you do."

"Please," she heard herself inexplicably respond. "Please, don't stop."

Lying beside her, one leg flung over hers, Fitz propped his weight on one elbow and slowly teased the curls of her woman's place. She didn't dare open her eyes again, but she sensed him with every fiber of her being. She had never felt helpless and female so much as she did now, with his man's hand setting her mindlessly free. Forces were building inside her that she didn't understand, and all her concentration was on what he did to her. It didn't matter what he said or she said, so long as he did not stop and leave her bereft.

"Is that a yes, Miss Merriweather?" He leaned over to nibble at her breast while one finger probed temptingly.

She nearly rose up off the couch in her eagerness. "Yes, please, hurry!"

"You have made me a very happy man." His hair brushed her breasts as he suckled and, at the same time, brought his thumb to press at the place he'd aroused to throbbing.

Abby inched her legs wider, too aware of how her skirt and petticoat rode about her waist, afraid to look at herself. Afraid to look at him. She wanted to pretend this was all sensation and the rest of the world did not exist.

Fitz hesitated, and she almost stopped breathing. Her eyes flew open as he pulled his head back. Green eyes studied her with what she hoped was desire. His beard stubble and the fall of honey brown hair gave him a rakish look, but it was his slow smile that captured her heart.

"You are mine now, Miss Merriweather, to cherish and protect. And I'm going to thoroughly regret my good behavior in the morning."

Before she could question, or even think to cry a protest, he turned his persuasive lips to hers, and his tongue slid seductively between them. She dug her fingers into his wrinkled waistcoat, wishing desperately that she could peel back layers of cloth to find his skin. She needed to touch the hard muscle rippling tantalizingly out of reach.

But then he spread her thighs wider and inserted his fingers more assertively, and in the blink of an instant, her world quaked and thundered and rocked.

Squeezing her eyes closed, hanging on to Fitz's strong arms for dear life, she reveled in the astounding experience as her body came apart in sweet bliss. He eased her safely back to reality when it was over, and she wilted in his embrace. Whispering promises in her ear, he lay down beside her and cuddled her against his chest. His broad hand now stroked her bare bottom.

She was officially ruined. She thought.

"What about you, my lord?" she whispered moments later when some small portion of her rational thought returned. She knew something was lacking, but she was too lost in sensation to grasp exactly what.

Fitz hugged his beautiful Rhubarbara, selfishly admiring the bounteous breasts spilling from her bodice. He wasn't a complete scoundrel. He didn't want to tempt fate by leaving his precious Abby with child should the mad stone thrower actually hit his target before the wedding.

Just thinking about having his head stove in was sufficient to keep his arousal in check, although he ached with longing. His Abby was so sweetly responsive that he knew he'd chosen a bride who would enjoy many lusty hours in bed with him. Why marry a cold prude when he could save the expense and nuisance of a fickle mistress by having his marvelous Abby!

He pressed a kiss to her hair. "My turn will come after we exchange vows," he promised. "My villainous ways extend only so far."

"I am already ruined," she said pragmatically, or invitingly, depending on how he chose to construe it.

He was tempted, sorely tempted. His hand held a bare, firm derriere just begging for his caress. He ached to make her his, to give her what they both desperately wanted. She was moist and warm and ready. He had only to unfasten his buttons and lay her down to be in sweet heaven.

But he'd spent too many years surviving to give in to temptation now. He had a will of iron. Still holding his bride-to-be, he swung his legs over the side of the couch, letting Abby's skirt and petticoat fall down over her legs,

although he refused to cover the sight of the creamy
bosom he'd craved to behold since he'd first set eyes on
her. She was so utterly perfect that he could scarcely believe his good fortune.

"I could easily lie and charm our way out of ruin-
ation as things stand," he promised, "if that is your wish,
but I respect you too much to truly ruin you until we're
wedded."

He offered his most deceptive grin to conceal his
pain.

She narrowed her eyes as if she saw right through
him. "You are gambling again, aren't you?"

He stood, holding her firmly in his arms. "In a way, I
suppose I am. I am wagering that you will want more of
what I can offer, and that you'll not change your mind
in the morning."

Carrying her, he strode toward the stairs, hoping Bibley had left a light in whatever chamber he'd found suitable for the new earl.

"It takes time for me to make up my mind, so I don't
like changing it," she warned, leaning her strawberry
curls trustingly against his shoulder.

His, the primitive warrior inside him roared. This
intelligent, annoying, beautiful woman was *his*. He'd
never possessed such a treasure before, and he would
fight tooth and claw to keep her. His nonchalant tone
revealed nothing of his inner fierceness. "Smart people
change their minds when they realize they didn't have
all the facts the first time. Yes, I gamble, but I am not
obsessed with it. I can stop any time."

She apparently pondered that as he carried her up
the stairs. His Abby wasn't a twittering nag by any
means. She was thoughtful, which was damned dangerous. He almost wished she'd twitter instead of twisting
all his words inside her head and coming to conclusions
he wasn't prepared to counter.

"No, I doubt that you can stop any time." She stated
the conclusion he had feared she'd reach. "It's what

you're trained to do. A farmer plants fields. A seaman sails ships. A gambler gambles."

"A farmer can lay down his plow and a seaman can retire his ship," he argued.

"But unless they have other income, they will starve if they do."

Grimly, Fitz noted the light at the end of the hall and stalked toward it. The woman—or her conclusion—was becoming damned heavy. He ought to set her down right here and make her walk, but he couldn't bear to let her go. "I never owed another man in my life until I inherited this pile," he growled, as if she could follow his thought.

"And you hate being beholden to anyone," she agreed, her active mind trotting right along with his. "How much do you owe Lord Quentin?"

"Too much." He shoved the partially open door with his shoulder, swinging it wide and revealing a chamber that at least possessed a plump mattress, and pillows covered in what appeared to be decent linen, and a silk coverlet. Any draperies that might once have adorned the tester frame had been discreetly removed, probably because they were moth-eaten and filthy.

He flung her down in the center of the mattress, and when no dust rose up, he smirked in satisfaction. Propping his fists on his hips, he admired his wanton intended sprawled across *his* linens. "I wish I could have your portrait painted like this. You were made for this bed."

Abby instantly sat up and scrabbled to pull her bodice over her breasts, but Fitz fell down beside her and slid her sleeves off her shoulders, capturing her arms. He couldn't resist leaning over to suckle at her celestial bounty. He was a damned good judge of people. His farmer girl had been born to fulfill his needs.

He wasn't a stupid lovelorn youth anymore. He was a man on the brink of claiming a prize he'd worked to earn. He would prove he could take very good care of her.

"What are you doing?" she asked in surprise as he

tugged her arms from their sleeves and began unfastening her skirt hooks.

"Ruining you more," he said matter-of-factly. "Ruining you for any other man in the universe. Making you want me as much as I want you. Keeping your active mind from asking any more irrelevant questions. Is that enough for now?"

To Fitz's surprise, his Abby put her small hand against his broad chest and shoved him back against the mattress. When she began unfastening his waistcoat, he grinned hugely and helped her.

"Then we shall be ruined together, my lord," she said in the same tone as he'd just used. "And if I ask any questions, they will be very relevant. Most likely, impertinent as well."

He laughed with joy.

30

Abby had struggled to retain her chemise during the night she spent in Fitz's bed, but her new betrothed was a charmer who could talk a snake out of its skin.

And she had to admit, the self-satisfied look on Danecroft's face in the early-morning light as he lay beside her, gazing down upon her nakedness, was worth surrendering her last shred of decency.

He, the smirking devil, was still wearing his long shirt and breeches, concealing every inch of the hard body she'd stroked and tested in the dark. She'd been reduced to a complete mindless twit, and he'd maintained all his composure. Or almost all. There'd been a few moments when she'd touched him, and he'd smothered his moans by biting a pillow.

She ought to be thoroughly ashamed of herself, but Fitz had taught her lessons last night that she'd never thought to learn. And he had made every one of them seem perfectly natural, if only they could have been carried to their logical conclusion. Which they hadn't.

She had spent a night in a man's bed and was still a virgin. She picked up her pillow and smacked him across his grin.

Chuckling, he fell back against the mattress and let her pummel him with feathers. "I heard the children run past five minutes ago. They could be anywhere," he said, laughing as he caught the pillow and flung it across the room.

"You are a scoundrel," she complained, dragging a sheet over her breasts a little belatedly for decency.

"But I'm an honest one," he crowed, vaulting to his feet and searching a wardrobe for who knew what, since neither of them had any luggage.

He found a shirt and shook it out, frowning in dismay at its condition before shucking the wrinkled one he wore.

Abby stared, dumbfounded, at the remarkable broad chest he so casually revealed. And square, muscled shoulders. And taut . . . All the blood seemed to drain from her head as she admired the masculine torso she'd touched only in the dark.

John Fitzhugh Wyckerly was a stallion in his prime, with brawny arms, sculpted chest, and long, powerful limbs. No wonder he'd been able to haul her less-than-sylphlike self across halls and up stairs.

And he wanted to marry *her*? Her puny inheritance was scarcely an incentive for a man who could have any woman he wanted, should he put his mind to it.

And he'd chosen *her*. She couldn't grasp such an enormity. He really must want her, not just her money.

"Dane," she said thoughtfully. "A Viking Dane capable of carrying off entire villages of women."

Washing in the tepid water left in the pitcher last night, he swung to lift a quizzical eyebrow at her.

"You call me Rhubarbara," she pointed out, quite sensibly, she thought. Or as sensible as she could be while eyeing the hair between his masculine nipples, running down into his breeches. Breeches that bulged intriguingly, she might add. Breeches that would fill her every waking thought if she didn't find a new direction. "I think you are more a Dane than a Fitz."

"Loosely translated, *Fitz* means bastard," he acknowledged, turning back to his ablutions, rubbing his unshaven jaw as he gazed at the mirror. "I always thought my mother's surname of Fitzhugh rather rude, but otherwise, it's fitting enough."

She flung a pillow at his back and dug around for her clothing. "You're an honest scoundrel," she reminded him, dragging on her chemise, "not a bastard. And if you really meant what you said about a special license, I will have to send for funds to pay for it, and then everyone will know where we are."

He soaped his face and stropped a razor he had found in the washstand drawer. "I will ride up to London and borrow more from Quent. The matchmaker in him won't be able to resist."

She almost forgot to finish dressing while she watched him draw the straightedge across his dark whiskers. Her insides quivered in expectation when she noticed he was observing her in the mirror as much as she was staring at him.

"You'd better bring a vicar back with the license, then." She acknowledged what they both felt with that admission. She didn't think she could last another night in his bed and retain the shreds of her innocence.

His smile ran straight through her heart and left her breathless.

"And ye of little faith doubted my ability to choose my perfect countess. Don't question my judgment of people next time. I've not entirely wasted these last years."

She wasn't certain how she felt about marrying someone who could see right through her, so she turned her back on him to hook her corset. Before she knew he'd crossed the room, Fitz planted a soapy kiss on her shoulder and lifted her breast free of its confinement.

"Don't wear the corset," he murmured. "I like to touch."

"You won't be here, and I have to face your servants with some degree of respectability." But her bones melted at the prospect of stolen moments and caresses in their future.

A cry of "Abby, Abby!" in the hall ended any other intimacies they might have shared.

He sighed loudly and released her to open a door into an adjoining room. "Your boudoir, my lady, if you wish to wash and prepare yourself before the imps find you."

Daringly, she stood on her toes and pressed a kiss to the shaven spot on his square jaw. "My Dane," she said in satisfaction, before dodging his grab and darting through the open door, closing it behind her.

She was definitely a shameless hussy. The marchioness had been right. She had needed to learn who she was before she settled down in the country. Abby didn't think shameless hussy was what the lady had had in mind, but she was quite content with it if it meant she could make Fitz laugh with real enjoyment, and not just false charm. Making a man happy was even more delicious than watching the children play.

She hastily washed and wiggled into a gown that she had needed a maid to help her hook and pin the prior day. She considered asking for Fitz's aid, but she worked out the fastenings as best she could. Fearing she'd left a gap unfastened in the back of her bodice, she donned her shawl and glanced around at the beautifully curved and elegant furniture, before sailing out to meet a wide new world.

Abby hadn't realized how completely different that world was until she sat next to Fitz in the estate office after breakfast, puzzling over years' worth of dusty household ledgers. While she struggled to understand invoices for candles at twice what she paid at home, and income reading *one brace mallards,* instead of pounds or pence, Fitz was attempting to unscramble ancient banknotes.

"This isn't right." He kept shaking his head, totaling and retotaling columns longer than Abby's hand. Then he'd pull out an even older ledger and start the process over again. "I'm not the only scoundrel in the woodpile," he muttered once. "And no wonder Geoff is hiding in the outback of nowhere, afraid to show his face! If I thought he knew about this, I'd trounce the scoundrel. I still might."

Abby was a little less brave about making accusations, so she reserved her opinion until she had time to study more. "I didn't think your cousin Mr. Wyckerly had anything to do with the estate," she offered once, when Fitz was growling about *slack-brained lickspittles*.

"If there's wickedness about, a Wyckerly is at hand," he muttered even more incomprehensibly. "I'm finding banknotes aplenty, but no cash expensed to pay for improvements or debts. The notes have my grandfather's signature, but where are the deposits to go with them? And look, here, none of the writing in these ledgers matches my grandfather's execrable penmanship. If Bibley is right about the inability to read, my grandfather did not handle these accounts!" He angrily shoved still another ledger aside and looked up when Bibley announced the presence of Mr. Applebee.

Fortunately, the bell hanging at the front door intoned at the same time, and Abby gathered her skirts and hurried out with the excuse of making sure the children hadn't decided to swing from the rope. If Fitz had truly been cheated out of his inheritance, which was what it sounded like to her, she really didn't think she had the heart for listening to the steward discussing the condition of fields Fitz could not afford to repair.

"Where's my papa?" Mulish bottom lip stuck out, Penelope did not hug Abby when she opened the door to the new arrivals.

The elderly nanny who had accompanied the child gaped at the rotunda entry just as everyone always did. In this instance, Abby excused the poor woman for not responding to her charge's distress. "Your papa is in his business office, talking with his estate manager. Shall I take you to him so you may peek and wave before we find Jennifer?"

She was fairly certain the children had been making so much noise in the upper stories that they hadn't heard the carriage arrive or the bell ring down here. In a house this size, she would feel better having the extra eyes of Penny's nanny to watch over them. She hadn't forgotten Fitz's tale about stairs to the roof.

"Jennifer's here?" Only partially mollified, Penny took Abby's hand and tiptoed cautiously across the floor adorned with the family crest.

The child's obvious fear tugged at Abby's heart. She desperately wanted to cradle Fitz's daughter as she would the twins, but Penny needed reassurance first. "Yes, that's what your daddy was doing, rescuing my brothers and sisters. He didn't mean to leave you alone for so long. He missed you very much."

Nodding more confidently now, Penny hurried along beside Abby through the vast corridors leading to the back of the house. The business office was approachable by tenants—and creditors. The townsfolk had learned the earl was in residence and had been lined up at the door since dawn, but Bibley had been refusing them entry.

Not meaning to disturb Fitz, Abby intended only to let the child peek and be reassured that her father was there, but the instant Fitz caught sight of them, his face changed from hollow and cold to beaming and warm. Even the agitated tradesman standing beside Applebee looked startled by the transformation. Wide-eyed, the merchant respectfully tipped his hat to Abby as Penny tore from her grasp and ran across the room to fling herself at her father's knees.

Abby knew how villages worked. News of her presence would have gossips whispering far and wide. And she still wasn't ashamed that she was living here without a chaperone. Perhaps that came of twenty-five years of the kind of security that allowed her to know who she was, even if she didn't know this strange environment she'd been dropped into. Maybe, just maybe, she could learn to be what Fitz needed. She hoped so, because she didn't see any way out of what they'd done.

Perhaps, if she needn't entertain or go about in society pretending to be a *countess*, she could go through with this marriage. She really had no choice now. No other man would have her, and the executor would be too appalled by her behavior to consider her a suitable guardian for the children unless she married.

To the side of Fitz's desk stood the short, stout, and balding Mr. Applebee, who wore boots so old that even with a thick coat of polish the wear was apparent. Abby understood why Fitz had chosen—*gambled* on—this man to save his land. She saw only eagerness to please in the estate manager's expression as he bowed to her.

Perhaps she needed someone in her life who was willing to take chances.

While Penny planted kisses all over her father's laughing face, Abby held out her hand to the man who would have to turn Fitz's land to profit. "It is good to see you here, sir. I hope you found comfortable quarters."

"A little work, and they'll be right as rain," Applebee said cheerfully. "My missus knows how to make a penny squawk."

Abby wasn't yet mistress here, but she liked people and hoped the Applebees would stay, so she did her best to make him feel comfortable by promising a visit later.

Fitz made his excuses and, carrying his daughter, stepped outside the office. Abby followed. Placing his free hand at her back, he guided her away from listening ears.

"Now that the imp is here, I need to depart for London. I don't know how long it will take to procure a license." He planted a kiss on the top of Abby's head that she felt clear to her toes.

"You will see Lady Belden and extend my apologies

again?" Abby murmured, taking Penny from him and finally giving his daughter the hug she'd wanted to offer earlier. "I cannot imagine what she is telling the Weatherstons. And I really must find someone to take the executor to court so we needn't hide forever. I'm even afraid to write home and tell them everyone is well."

"Special license first, the toughest barrister on earth next, and the dragon lady after that," Fitz promised. "Will you mind dealing with this tomb while I'm gone? I fear you won't be able to go about without tradesmen at your heels."

"I cannot even imagine how to 'deal with this tomb' with no money," she said honestly. "I think I'll find the kitchen garden and get dirty, like the children."

"I hope you did not give away all your old clothes. I have a feeling you'll need them here far more than the pretty London ones," Fitz said with sympathy, proving he understood her too well already.

"I am not much interested in gowns," she admitted. "The children, however, grow out of their clothes faster than I can have them made. I don't think you've given full consideration to their cost."

"And I don't intend to," he said cheerfully, tugging Penny's braid and kissing her cheek. "We'll put them to work and make them earn their way, won't we, princess?"

"I'll swat spiders," Penny agreed with a firm nod.

"See, it's all settled!"

Fitz looked so confident and determined that Abby knew he was as dubious of their future as she was.

31

Avoiding his London town house, where stone throwers, along with a horde of dun collectors, might await him, Fitz strode into Quentin's home in all his travel dirt, determined to set his future on the straight and narrow. He simmered with frustrated fury over his findings in the ledgers, but he had more important projects in mind. Pounding information out of Geoff would have to wait.

Fortunately, Quent was available. He glanced up at Fitz's entrance and shook his head in dismay. "Five children, Fitz! Are you sure you know what you're doing?"

"Haven't a clue," he said cheerfully. "But I'm certain that Abby does, and that's all the assurance I need. Congratulations are in order, I believe. She has agreed to make me a happy man."

Quentin rose to reach over his desk and shake Fitz's hand. "I doubt I'll ever understand what makes a man choose one woman over another, but if you prefer Miss Merriweather to Lady Anne, then you must have your reasons. Lady Belden will not be pleased, which makes *me* a happy man."

Fitz chuckled. "She can't help it if she married an old miser twice her age and lived to regret it. Would you like to come with me when I tell Lady Bell I've kidnapped her heiress?"

"For the price of that entertainment, I'll even purchase the special license I'm sure you've come in search of."

"That's expensive entertainment, old boy." But Fitz didn't argue over the gift. His *family* mattered more than his pride. By jingo, he had a real family now. Or he would have, if he lived long enough to marry.

Of course, given the Wyckerly reputation, Geoff's family may have actually stolen the money the estate had received as loans, two generations ago. *Family* could be a two-edged sword. When had Geoff's family started its own business? Angry as he was right now, Fitz would wager they'd gone into trade on the exact date that the first banknote was issued. If that money had been fraudulently obtained and Geoff knew what had been done—then his cuz was guilty of concealing and profiting from theft.

"But I must warn you that I have to find a barrister to legally reclaim Abby's siblings, and then see if my cousin has returned from Yorkshire," Fitz now told Quentin. If Geoff were smart, *he'd* be the one heading for the Americas about now.

"Done and done," Quent said, tapping a hat onto his head and grabbing his walking stick. "After Montague warned me of what you were up to, I didn't want any delay in savoring this moment, so I did some research for you. Geoff has apparently returned to town and is consulting solicitors and bankers. He has also applied to several gentlemen's clubs to which he will probably not be accepted."

"As neither of us are, old chap," Fitz said grimly, immediately grasping the implications. "But even a disgraceful Wyckerly might be welcome if he bears a title."

"As Geoff could be, if he were earl and not you," Quent agreed.

"As much as I'd love to send the estate creditors his

way, I need to be earl to retrieve Abby's siblings," Fitz declared, suddenly glad that he had the title he would have willingly sold a few short weeks ago. "That's higher on my agenda than throttling Geoff. I'll send around a note demanding he attend me at his first opportunity. I could get used to this being head of the family."

Quent glanced at him with concern. "If he's eyeing your title, he won't be pleased to learn of your impending nuptials."

"If he's hiring stone throwers, I'll fling him over a parapet," Fitz retorted. "I'll send a message around to Montague to see if he's found the ruffian at Tattersall's."

With a nod of accord, Quent led the way out. "I've located a barrister who is eager to accept an earl as client and who will challenge the children's executor."

Although frustrated that he couldn't confront his cousin yet, Fitz happily followed Quentin into the misty gray day. With visions of his wedding night dancing tantalizingly within reach, he found it easy enough to forget everyone but Abby.

He whistled and twirled his cane as he marched off. Damn, but it actually felt *good* to shoulder his fair share of responsibility. Obviously, the need for a jolly rogering had affected his wits.

"No, no, and NO!" Abby shouted, whacking a damask sofa with a broom, sending three baby mice scurrying from the cushions and over the back, into the walls.

The mice weren't her problem. Lying, conniving Bibley was.

"You cannot rent Danecroft's rooms to any passing stranger just to put coins in your pocket! No wonder the master chamber was clean!" She whacked the sofa three more times, to be certain all the mice were gone, and to vent her frustration. No mice in an earl's residence, indeed.

Fitz had been gone for three days, and she was climbing the walls with worry. She knew he was fine. He'd sent daily notes that assured her everything was wonderful. But he wasn't *here.*

And his entire household was mad. Insane. Moonstruck and in dire need of discipline. And she was in jeopardy of falling apart at the seams with nervousness, trying to decide if she was doing the right thing after all in marrying him. She was giving up her quiet farm life for *this?*

"Yes, miss," the butler said phlegmatically. "I will tender my resignation at once, miss."

Abby swung around with the broom upraised, just missing Bibley's stuck-up nose. She shook the battered broom at him. "*You will not.* I suspect you've fared quite well here, and Fitz doesn't owe you a single shilling. In fact, you no doubt owe him. If you leave, I'll have the magistrate after you. Just tell the innkeeper to quit sending their overflow of patrons here. This is *not* an inn." No wonder the servants had kept up the linen and hadn't sold the furniture. An earl's house used as an *inn!*

On the other hand, if Fitz's family had thought of it first, maybe then they wouldn't be so far in hock.

"Yes, miss." Despite his apparent frailty, Bibley neither dodged nor blinked. "Do you foresee the earl wishing to stay through the hunting season?"

"A particularly profitable season, I assume?" she asked with rare sarcasm.

Bibley lifted the silver card platter he'd carried in before being attacked by a broom. "One must assume," he replied with feigned indifference.

Abby sighed and began to beat a velvet chair until rising dust made her cough. "Renting out rooms is Fitz's decision, not yours. Our task now is to prepare for his guests. You will be paid regularly once all the accounts are straightened out."

"His lordship reads accounts?" the butler asked, warily backing toward the door.

"*I* read accounts, Bibley." She attacked a spiderweb hanging above the Adam mantel. "I looked at Cook's just this morning. Eggs do not cost a shilling a dozen, not when you have your own hens! There are not enough people in the entire *village* to account for the number of hams for which the estate has been charged, especially when you have *pigs*. Does anyone at all in this household read invoices?"

"The bills go to the earl, miss," Bibley intoned indifferently, while casting a surreptitious glance to the escape route.

"Do you expect me to believe no one ever hunted deer and quail in winter? Or ate wild-duck eggs? I wager they did, Bibley, and that I won't find payment on the books for the privilege. I wager you paid those creditors and their inflated bills with the earl's game. Even if you meant well—and you will have to prove that, Bibley—the late earls were being robbed blind by these tradesmen who still come begging, even after being fed all year from Danecroft land! Fitz will easily discover it. You may tell them we'll see them in court if they try to collect before the accounts are all straight. They should be ashamed of themselves! I never saw such greed."

"Yes, miss." For the first time, the skinny butler's feigned unconcern developed a crack in it. He tugged at the knot in his threadbare neckcloth. "I'll send Alice to help you ready the guest chambers."

"You will send for Mrs. Worth, Bibley. That's why I called you in here. I want Mrs. Worth back as housekeeper, and I don't care if it was you or she who has been aiding and abetting the merchants, but you'll both go to prison if this house isn't back in order within the week. Mr. Applebee tells me Mrs. Worth is living quite comfortably in a cottage on the edge of town, Bibley, so do not tell me she has moved on."

"She is retired, miss," the butler said, drawing his thin shoulders straight with contrived indignation.

"She is thirty years younger than you are, Bibley." Abby shook the broom under his scrawny nose again, and his palsy instantly halted. "In fact, I have it on good word that she is your daughter, Bibley, and that you spend most of your time in *her* cottage, dining and wining well. We will need that wine when Fitz's guests arrive, do you understand me?"

"It is mere dandelion wine, miss!"

"Since it is from the estate's dandelions, then I shall send Applebee to collect it, shall I? Shall I have him look for the family silver while he is there?"

"The earls sold that. You will find the figures in the accounts." Indignant, he failed to call her *miss* this time.

"Excellent. I am glad to hear that, Bibley. And be sure I will check. And you stand warned. Lord Danecroft has a head for numbers. He will find every missing shilling and padded bill as soon as he has time to go over the books."

She halted as another unpleasant realization hit her. "*That's* why you tried to pretend Fitz was dead, wasn't it? You didn't want him going over the accounts until you had time to look at them. The previous earls never cared, but that was the first thing Fitz asked for, wasn't it? So you hoped he would stay away if you gave him a good excuse to disappear."

Bibley tried to look old and palsied again, shaking his balding head in denial.

Abby rolled her eyes. "Don't give me that helpless act. If I were you, I'd warn everyone who has padded their bills to correct the balances they claim he owes before he figures it out. Fitz does not often lose his temper, but he is very unpleasant when he does."

"Yes, my lady," Bibley said, pretending to clear his wattled throat. "I will see what I can do, my lady."

As the butler sidled from the room, Abby heard applause from the hall door. Aware she was covered head to foot in dust and that her billowing apron looked as if she'd been cleaning fireplaces, which she had, she swung around in trepidation. She would make a laughingstock of a certainty, looking like Cinderella returned to the ashes.

Blake Montague and Nick Atherton filled the opening. Atherton leaned his shoulder lazily against the doorframe and beamed with approval. Less inclined to reveal his thoughts, Montague, still clapping, sported a sardonic smile.

"That was a superb performance, Miss Merriweather," Mr. Atherton said in admiration. In his frilled neckcloth, tailored riding jacket, and polished boots, he looked every inch an indolent London dandy. "You may make an honest man of the old goat yet. I am now regretting that I did not pursue you more forcefully. If you could turn that temper on m'family, I'd be forever in your debt."

At the moment, she was still in such a state of agitation that she might have shaken her broom at the two scapegraces for letting themselves in, but her concern for Fitz overrode all else. She forgot about her disarray as she eagerly searched over their shoulders to see if he might have arrived with them.

"He's escorting the parade," Montague said, surmising where her interest lay. He, at least, looked as if he'd ridden for hours. His simple neckcloth was stained with travel dust, and his boots were well-worn and down-at-the-heels. "We're the advance party, come to warn you that Lady Belden is *en route*."

"And Quent," Atherton reminded him. "And the vicar. And a barrister and a whole host of boring twits. And Quent's sisters and maybe a niece or two," he added, thumping his cheek with one finger and idly recalling the list in his head.

"Oh, my." All the starch drained out of Abby. "We are not nearly ready."

"You've a couple of hours to find a pretty gown," Atherton said gallantly. "A lady as lovely as you needs no more than that. Why don't Blake and I round up a few of those thieving servants and see if we can whip them into a frenzy as well as you do?"

"It would be a pleasure," Montague agreed, narrowing his dark eyes.

Flustered, unaccustomed to gallantry from anyone but Fitz, but fearing his pride would be hurt if she allowed in an entire parade of guests before the house was even close to being ready, Abby dithered uncertainly.

"I do believe we've struck her speechless, Montague. Let us make good our threats before she takes that broom to our worthless hides." Atherton removed his shoulder from the wall and seemed prepared to head for the door.

"No! Wait. . . ." Abby hastily untied her apron and brushed a cobweb on her cheek, seeking words that didn't come to her easily when she was flustered. "Bibley has been robbing Peter to pay Paul for so long that he no longer knows what honesty is. Don't go threatening anyone until we have the truth of it, please."

The handsome gentlemen were looking at her with such interest that she forgot her embarrassment. "We will need some boys to help in the stables," she continued. "Talk to Mr. Applebee for me, will you? I'll tell Bibley that we have guests, and Mrs. Worth can bring some maids with her when she arrives."

Even Montague managed a grin at her curt orders. "Aye, aye, Captain. Anything else?"

"Food. We need food." Sighing, she rushed past them into the hall, wadding her apron into a ball. "Cook has kept up the kitchen garden, and we have hens, but we will need beef. Stop at the butcher, please. Invite him to the wedding, if you must."

"Pity it's not hunting season," she heard Atherton drawl as they sauntered toward the front door while she hurried toward the kitchen. "A good venison steak with a strong pepper seasoning would set me right about now."

"If we stay in the lady's good graces, maybe she will allow us to come back in the fall," Montague concluded as they departed on their errands.

She supposed she shouldn't be ordering aristocrats about, but she didn't have time to consider niceties. If tomorrow was to be her wedding day, she would have rhubarb tarts prepared for her new husband. The kitchen garden had a lovely neglected clump of rhubarb.

A childish war whoop rang out from the direction of the balcony over the portico. Remembering what she'd last seen the children doing, Abby threw up her hands, turned around, and raced back toward the front door. "Mr. Atherton, Mr. Montague, wait!"

Too late, she winced as a fall of dirty water sprayed from above onto the front steps that Fitz's friends were just crossing.

"They're helping the maids scrub the floors," she murmured apologetically as they shook dirty water from their hats and glared at the sound of small voices crying, *"Oops, sorry!"* from above.

At least the bulk of the water had drenched only the stairs, which sorely needed cleaning anyway.

"Now I remember why we would not suit, Miss Merriweather," Mr. Atherton said mournfully. "Fitz seems to have an affinity for small creatures, and I do not."

She bit back a laugh. That they were not angry proved Fitz's good judgment in choosing his friends. "But you are still welcome as guests whenever you wish to come this way," she assured them. "I hope we will have a governess in place by then."

"I know a general I could recommend," Montague said, keeping a wary eye above. "I'll send a few spare soldiers as well."

"We will return shortly, Miss Merriweather." Tipping his hat, Atherton took the stairs two at a time.

Oh dear, half London would be here shortly. How

long would they need to be housed? Would it be possible to marry quickly?

Holding her blushing cheeks, Abby raced back inside to warn Cook that hungry hordes would be upon them shortly.

32

He should have given Abby more warning, Fitz knew. He had already ascertained that she didn't like surprises. She liked to mull things over before she made decisions. And he'd pushed her. He knew he'd pushed her. And now he was springing a dozen guests on her.

He feared he would find her with bags packed, waiting on the doorstep, when he rode up.

Even *he* suffered some trepidation at hosting a wedding party on such short notice. He'd hared off to London like his usual footloose self without verifying all the guest chambers still had beds. And the village inn was very small.

"My sisters like Miss Merriweather, and they just want to help, Fitz," Quent assured him, riding beside him as the carriages rolled slowly up the hill. "And maybe they're a little curious about how an earl lives, but they won't gossip."

Remembering the long line of debt collectors and the mouse-eaten upholstery, Fitz shook his head. "They will be much disappointed."

"They're young and bored. Nothing disappoints them except their suitors. We grew up poor and know how to fend for ourselves. Set them to cleaning, and they will be quite entertained. It's Lady Belden you should worry about. She is glaring daggers at us. I don't think she intends to surrender without a fight."

Lady Belden had brought her solicitor, not a good sign. Greyson, the children's executor, had brought his partner, Sir Hunter, a barrister—an even worse sign. When they were combined with his own men—there were as many lawyers as guests.

Still, Fitz grinned. "Lady Bell isn't a problem. I'll tell the children she's their new grandmother and will set them on her as soon as she walks through the door."

Quent barked with laughter, startling all in the parade into staring. He was still chortling when they turned their mounts up the drive to the house.

To Fitz's utter and absolute amazement, a row of orderly staff garbed in stiff black and white awaited him on the steps. At the top of the stairs, the children were clothed in . . . he narrowed his eyes and tried to figure out what they could possibly be wearing, since he'd not yet succeeded in retrieving their belongings from their irate guardians. Whatever they wore, they were neat as pins, and the nanny stood behind them, assuring that they stayed so, even though they bounced with excitement. He thought the nanny held Penelope back by the bow on her dress.

He was feeling more chipper by the minute. He scanned the small assemblage for his Abby.

And couldn't find her.

She couldn't have gone far, but irrational panic filled his chest. *What if she's changed her mind?*

Abby paced the bedchamber Fitz had shown to her four mornings ago, the one meant for his countess that she'd slept in since his departure. He'd had her wardrobe sent down, so she had lots of lovely gowns from which to choose. She was wearing a pale green frock she didn't think he'd seen yet. The crisp silk rustled around her feet as she paced.

She wasn't his countess. She couldn't go down and pretend to welcome a wedding party as if she were the hostess here. Neither could she go down and stand in line as if she were a housekeeper or a servant.

She was a guest. She'd sent the children down because they wouldn't have stayed upstairs, but she simply could not go. It wasn't right. She didn't know if it would ever be right. She had no notion how to go on.

She opened the bedchamber door and tried to force her feet to march down the hall. She wanted to greet Fitz. She didn't want to greet his guests. She'd rather hide in a wardrobe.

Heavy boots pounded up the stairs.

Was he angry? She wasn't used to men being angry with her. She wasn't used to men paying a whit of attention to her.

When he reached the top of the stairs, he looked as terrified as she felt. She'd never seen her dashing Fitz look so rattled. He was usually cheerful and smiling, even when he was preparing to beat someone to a pulp. She held her hand to the base of her throat and stared at him.

He didn't pause. He raced down the hallway, grabbed her by the waist, and swept her into her chamber, slamming the door behind him.

"Don't change your mind now, Abby," he said urgently. "Please don't say you've changed your mind now. I know I've pushed you. I've been a despicable scoundrel. But I *know* this is best."

She couldn't reply for the kisses he was pelting across her face, leaving her as breathless as his words. She couldn't *think* when he pressed her like this. Her mouth eagerly sought his, and everything she had ever thought she knew flew right out of her head.

She threw her hands around his neck, and he eagerly sought her mouth, and she remembered very distinctly why she had agreed to this insane marriage that would never ever work. It evidently had nothing to do with good sense and everything to do with lust and friend-ship and her utter adoration of this man who had come to her rescue. And a modicum of convenience.

"We have guests," he finally gasped, coming up for air a few minutes later. "I'm crushing your gown. I'm sorry. Why weren't you downstairs?"

He didn't release her but let her feet touch the ground again. Abby leaned her head against his shoulder and listened to his heart beat as loudly as hers.

"Because I can't *do* this. I don't know how to be a countess," she pleaded, hating herself even as she said it, but the words came straight from her heart. She had to make him fully understand how unsuitable marriage to her would be, before his reckless impulses drove him to something he might regret later. "Lady Anne or Lady Mary would shower you in riches, pave your way through the Lords, and their families will be more use-ful than my horde of hellions. I should never, ever have allowed you to take this step."

He grasped her upper arms so tightly she feared he would leave bruises. His narrow-eyed glare was almost frightening, except that she knew it came from his own fear.

"For once in my life, I would like to have what *I* want. I don't want Lady Mary or Anne. I don't want their damned families. I don't even want the Lords. I want you. I want Penny to have you. I want this house to have you. I want your common sense. And I want this." He kissed her again.

How could she argue with a declaration like that? Her knees were already weak from the fierceness of his kiss. She couldn't have said no even had she wanted. And she was too mindless to want anything except Fitz and his wild proclamations of desire.

The sound of voices carried up the stairs. The car-riages were unloading.

He set her back half an inch but didn't release his

grip. "Marry me, Abby. I have the license and the vicar and I've even brought guests for our wedding dinner."

"Wedding *dinner*?" she said faintly, overwhelmed now that the moment had arrived.

"A special license dispenses with the need to wait until morning for the service," he said with a touch of wariness. "We can wait, if you wish, but I thought you might prefer that our guests take their leave as quickly as possible."

"Oh, yes, of course. And they will wish to leave quickly," she said with a little more certainty now that she faced practical matters and could think about breathing again. "Only a few rooms have been aired, there are mice in the walls, and although we've done the best we could, the larder is not stocked well enough for more than a meal or two."

Fitz hugged her. "Does this mean you will marry me tonight?"

As if she could answer otherwise while he held her like this. Folding her fingers into his coat, Abby nodded. "I am terrified," she whispered.

"So am I," he murmured into her hair. "I fear I will be a terrible husband and an even worse earl. But if I have you by my side, I know I'll be doing the best I can. Will you come downstairs now and pretend this is your pretty house and that we entertain only the village?"

She gulped and nodded. "Is Lady Belden very angry?"

"She would gladly lop off my head, but only because she is concerned about you. You must assure her that you have exactly what you want." He tilted her head up so he could study her carefully. "Marrying me is what you want, isn't it?"

She nodded and even managed a smile. "Yes, please."

"Then you will explain to me how you found Mrs. Worth and all the maids and made them look as if they

actually belong here," he demanded, taking her hand
and placing it on his arm to lead her downstairs to their
guests.

"That's a long story. I will explain later, although you
will see once you have time to study the household ledgers." Talking about things she understood and could
control, Abby happily followed Fitz to the guests filling
the rotunda below.

"I should spend a few days with my accounts instead
of riding back to London, should I?" he asked with a
suspicious eagerness.

She cast him a narrowed glance, but he was smiling
seductively, and her insides quivered. He was actually
thinking of beds, not accounts. And now she would not
be able to stop thinking of beds either.

"Yes, perhaps you might," she said faintly, before the
children came galloping up the stairs to grab their hands
and tug them down to see all the lovely gifts their guests
had brought.

Abby blushed mightily as they descended the stairs
and every head turned to stare, but Fitz gripped her hand
so warmly that she could scarcely think of anything else.
And the children were so happy that she let the moment
carry her forward.

Tonight, she would be a married woman.

A *countess.* She tried not to faint at the thought.

33

Bless his bride's defiant heart, Fitz thought. Instead of a formal salon, Abby had chosen the garden terrace off the glass-walled gallery for their nuptials. Flowers had apparently been dug up from all around town to adorn pots on the low stone walls outside. A few rusting lawn benches had been scrubbed and provided with cushions for the ladies in the audience. The men could pace and smoke and lean against the walls and murmur among themselves if they chose.

And the children could run rampant through the newly threshed weed field, darting in and out among the evening shadows of the hedges as they chased one another about.

Even the few straggling creditors determined to catch Fitz at home had a place to lurk near the distant corner of his office. And his *servants* lingered inside the gallery, hovering over the banquet table while remaining part of the audience.

Fitz had a hard time grasping that he actually had servants, much less a threshed field and a table with food on it. Abby had created miracles in his absence. He was eager to hear her version of how this had all come about, but he was more eager to see her walk through the French doors and into his arms.

He should have warned her that all was not well with the children's executor. And that Lady Bell was having second thoughts about handing over the inheritance. And that Montague had not found the stone-throwing scoundrel at Tattersall's. They were building a future on quicksand.

After all they'd done, he could see no other choice but to go forward with the wedding and gamble on his abilities to tilt the odds in their favor. He didn't wish to ruin Abby's pleasure in this moment with worries. She was frightened enough as it was.

Waiting for his bride, Fitz nervously smoothed his neckcloth, then forced his idle hands behind his back while his once numb heart raced in anticipation. This would work. It had to. He was gambling his life on it.

Lady Belden and Quent's youngest sisters had arranged a gown for Abby, Fitz knew. He'd even gone into personal debt to have one of his old coats refurbished for the event. He'd chosen a black frock coat to match his pantaloons, à la the Beau's recommendation, but his waistcoat was silver, with pearl buttons he hoped Abby would unfasten shortly.

He hoped she would appreciate the meager wedding gift he'd left in the chamber they would share in a few hours. He'd not had a lot of time to learn his bride's preferences, and he didn't have a great deal of money for jewelry, so he'd done what he could to please her. He wanted his beautiful Abby happy on their wedding night.

He had only to think of the night ahead for his unruly cock to grow thick and press against the tight placket of his pantaloons. His guests might as well not exist. A blithe June breeze ruffled the ladies' hats and scarves, and the men were jostling one another and joking, but his shoulders tight with tension, Fitz couldn't drag his gaze from the doors.

Even the children grew quiet when Quent escorted Abby onto the terrace. The skirt of her gown was a lovely sky blue silk to match her eyes. She wore matching ribbons instead of a cap to set off her sunset hair. A narrow azure bodice concealed the pearly flesh of her bosom. Fitz had to clench his molars to keep his tongue from hanging out at the voluptuous vision drifting across the terrace, her worried gaze fixed only on him. She was *his* now, and he almost popped his buttons in pride.

Abby drew closer, and all sensible thought departed his head. He could see straight through the translucent material barely concealing the upper curve of her breasts. Lady Belden was probably laughing up her sleeve as she watched him slaver lasciviously over his own damned bride.

The gown had almost no sleeves, and Abby wore only short gloves, leaving her firm, rounded arms and much of her shoulders bare. She might as well be wearing her shift. He wasn't going to survive through dinner without making an embarrassment of himself.

She hesitated, and Fitz banished his unruly parts to hell while he bent over her hand and planted a reassuring kiss on her fingers, dissolving her uncertainty. Curling his gloved palm proudly around hers, and holding tight, he drew her forward to face the waiting vicar.

She gripped his hand as the vicar began the ceremony. She had every right to be terrified. She was giving up everything for him. That she trusted a scoundrel like him humbled him to his very toes. He meant to take very, very good care of her.

That's what he promised to himself as he repeated the vows that would bind them as a couple into eternity.

In a daze, Abby watched Fitz unfasten the buttons of her glove so he could peel it off to place his ring on her finger. His head bent close, and his broad hand held hers gently. His caress and his proximity reminded her of the night to come . . . tingling all her nerves.

Self-consciously, she forced herself to think of the lovely ring he'd produced from his pocket rather than the mysteries of the bedchamber. How could he afford a ring? Perhaps it was part of the entailed estate.

As long as she thought of practical matters, she wouldn't expire of nervousness in front of their audience. She wished she had family here, but her father had been an only son, and her mother's few relations had always been distant. The children banging their heels against the wall were her family. She would do anything for them, and although they weren't old enough to do the same for her, Fitz would. She knew that with all her heart and soul.

He gazed deeply into her eyes as he slid his ring on her finger, leaving her breathless with desire . . . and love. She loved him so dearly, she did not even need to hear him declare the same. She had never believed she could feel like this, and she wanted to weep with joy that she had found a man to treasure.

She blinked back tears and smiled brilliantly when her new husband bent to kiss her. The vicar's blessings flew right over her head. She hadn't heard a word that was said.

Lady Sally began playing the out-of-tune pianoforte in the gallery as they turned as a married couple to greet their guests. Lady Belden bent to kiss her cheek and murmur congratulations. Released from the nanny's hold, the twins raced to grab Abby's legs.

Fitz laughed and bent over to pick up Cissy.

He'd just begun to straighten when an arrow flew past his shoulders. It bounced off the glass gallery windows with a loud crack.

Lady Belden screamed. Terrified, Abby dived to pull the children to the ground, heedless of her beautiful wedding gown. Montague vaulted over the terrace wall and melted into the shrubbery in pursuit of the villain.

With a grim expression around his eyes, Fitz merely picked up the arrow, detached the note, and read it.

With a gesture of disdain, he shoved the paper into his pocket before helping Abby up again. "A love note from an admirer," he shouted cheerfully to their audience. "The ladies will sorely miss me now that I'm off the market."

Lady Belden smacked him on the back of his head with her parasol and soared into the house in high dudgeon. Startled, not knowing whether to laugh or not, Lady Sally and Lady Margaret hastened to follow the marchioness.

Frowning, her heart still racing with fright, Abby noticed that even indolent Atherton had slipped into the shadows in the direction of the creditors, while Lord Quentin had disappeared entirely. Fitz's friends were covering his back while he played the part of host. She had seen him put up his fists and run after the stone-throwing culprit, but for her sake, he set aside his natural impulses in order to act as host and newly wedded husband.

Abby thought she understood why Lady Bell had smacked him on the back of the head. Such charm and insouciance could be infuriating—if one didn't know the depths seething beneath the surface smoothness. As Abby did.

So for Fitz's sake, she shoved aside her fear, planted a smile on her face, and helped Penny and Jennifer up from the terrace stones. Tommy glanced uncertainly from his new hero to the woods where the arrow had originated. "Cakes," she said to distract him. "And rhubarb tarts."

The older children instantly forgot their shock and raced for the door, while Fitz carried the twins. If Abby hadn't seen it for herself, she'd think nothing untoward had happened at all. His chiseled lips held a cheerful smile while he bounced the twins, then set them down inside so he could deftly catch his daughter crawling on the table before she could reach the biggest tart.

"You will show me that note later, won't you?" Abby

asked, holding his arm and wearing a false smile as the servants bobbed and offered their good wishes.

"Probably not," Fitz replied, accepting a glass of wine from Bibley. "This is our wedding night, and I mean for our minds to be on quite different matters."

Abby looked around for a parasol with which to smack him, but the innuendo had her blushing. Never in all her years had she been assaulted with such conflicting emotions.

"I can see why you did not choose a younger lady who has no experience with trying situations and perverse males," she said in frustration as they circled the tables, seeing that their guests helped themselves to the hastily prepared burgundy beef and fresh green peas and asparagus. "An hysterical bride might make consummation tiresome."

Fitz almost snorted up the wine he was sampling. "Give fair warning before you bludgeon me with salty comments next time."

"You married a farmer's daughter, not a lady. Expect it," she countered.

"My lady, we have run out of sherry," Bibley murmured, halting their parade around the room.

My lady. Abby paled and went weak-kneed at the title. Fitz gallantly held her up.

"Then bring out the nonexistent brandy, old boy," Fitz said. "We command miracles tonight."

Lady Belden waved the butler aside. "You shouldn't disturb the countess with domestic problems on her wedding day."

Countess. Abigail Merriweather, a countess. Not a farm girl. She couldn't speak *salty* anymore. She didn't even know when she should speak to butlers. She'd never had a butler.

Still, she'd shaken a broom under the nose of this butler. Abby thought perhaps their association was a little less formal than the usual between countess and servant. She would prefer general to private, and a gun with which to shoot off Bibley's palsied *toes*, the old fraud.

That thought gave her the ability to breathe again. "Lady Belden, I've not had time to thank you personally for all the joy you've given me. This gown . . ." She gestured helplessly.

"That gown is a work of art," Fitz finished appreciatively. "Even I thank you, Lady Bell. Although now that you've elevated my bride to goddess, I'm a trifle terrified of her."

Goddess? That was almost as ridiculous as countess. But for a little while, Abby's lips turned up in a smile and her fears dissipated.

Then his friends returned and Fitz abandoned her to Quent's sisters while he vanished into another room to consult about terrifying arrows.

Had someone actually tried to *kill* him?

"He had a horse. We didn't. He escaped," Montague stated bluntly. "Saddling up our mounts and tracking him didn't seem practical, as he'd be long gone."

Fitz nodded and smoothed the crudely written note on the table. *MAYT ME ET MEDNIT BY FAHTON ER DY.* He couldn't take such a preposterous threat seriously. *Fahton?* Did that mean the crumbling water hole with broken pipes that once constituted a fountain? *Dy?* In what manner? From badly aimed arrows and egregious misspellings? Or perhaps the shooter was threatening to dye his clothes, say, an elegant purple? The idea was too ridiculous to consider.

Perhaps he could send Bibley to the fountain. If one of Geoff's workers had written this note, the pair deserved each other. Nothing made sense. Frustration welled in him.

If Quent was correct, his heir had dared show his face back in town without seeking out Fitz as he'd requested. Did that mean Geoff knew nothing of the missing money—or that he was confident Fitz would come to an early demise as his father and brother had? He wanted to throttle Geoff if only for being so damned elusive.

"Well, looks as if I'll just have to die, because there isn't any way in this world or the next that I'm leaving Abby's bed tonight," he decided. Abby took precedence over idiots in his book.

Reclining on a fainting couch, admiring the painting of Diana the Huntress on the ceiling, Atherton tapped his fingers against his bent knee. "We'll tell your creditors that you mean to meet them after the guests go to bed. Then we'll assign each one a different meeting place at different doors so all entrances are covered. Free bodyguards," he said idly.

Fitz laughed at the preposterous idea of his creditors guarding his doors. It made about as much sense as meeting anyone at midnight.

"Ath and I will watch the fountain for you. We'll dunk the perpetrator and leave him tied to the mermaid statues until you decide to come down in a day or two." Montague's dark expression reflected fiendish anticipation.

Atherton sighed. "Since the house is packed full of respectable innocents, I suppose that will do for entertainment. Might we use your assailant for archery practice?"

"You may dunk him, pelt him with turnips, and hang him upside down from the portico for the children to use as a punching bag, for all I care. Just don't let anyone disturb my bride. She's nervous enough as it is," Fitz declared, relieved that the problem was temporarily in hand. "No shouting. No guns exploding. Just brutal silence."

Hands behind his back, Montague eyed the gun collection on the wall. "I think you underestimate the countess. If she comes after me with a broom, I'm aiming for the door."

Montague had faced three men in duels without quaking. Fitz grinned in pride. "Wait until you see Abby wield a hoe. I don't underestimate her at all. I simply want her to be happy and not have to take brooms to anyone's hides anymore."

He realized the truth of that even as he said it. He would do whatever it took to make Abby happy. Fitz hoped that didn't mean throttling his heir because, if his suspicions about the banknotes could be proved, Geoff had a great deal to lose if Fitz lived. Which made arrow-shooting assailants a little more worrisome than he wished to acknowledge.

34

Abby tucked the children into bed after telling them a bedtime story. She startled the nanny with the simple act of thanking her—once more proving she didn't know how to go about being a countess—then bumped into Fitz outside the nursery door.

"I've made our good-nights and left our guests well occupied," he declared, taking her arm and leading her down the hall. "I don't want you to feel as if you must hide in the nursery on our wedding night."

Which she'd been doing, she must admit. She was far more comfortable with the bouncing children than the fashionable guests drifting about Fitz's faded but elegant home.

"I wasn't hiding from you," she murmured. Or she didn't think she had been. His easygoing smile had disappeared after his discussion with his friends. She was just a tiny bit nervous of the determined man he revealed under his surface charm. She had seen that fierce focus turned to action, and she wasn't certain she wanted it turned on her.

It occurred to her that she had made a very rash decision in trusting a man she really didn't know—

No, she told herself. She had made an excellent, very wise decision, and she was proud of it. She would not second-guess her marriage or Fitz.

"Not hiding," he corrected himself, proving he understood her well, "but squirreling away and pondering and fretting until you work yourself into a state. I've hidden all the rotten apples so you can't throw them at me."

Abby chuckled as she recalled their first argument. Not having to be on her very best behavior every moment was a freedom she could easily come to love, a freedom she would never have had as a vicar's wife. "I apologize for that episode. It was very rude of me to pelt a guest with apples."

"In the face of your generous apology, I will admit that I am inclined to impulse and not much inclined to consulting anyone else about my affairs, so you had some right to be aggravated. May we kiss and make up now?"

Her *husband* lifted an expressive eyebrow in a lascivious leer that had Abby laughing even as he opened the door to his bedchamber. *Their* bedchamber.

She entered a room illumined by dozens of tall white tapers that reflected off hundreds of lamp crystals hung deliberately to produce dancing rainbows over the floor and walls. And amid all the rainbows and light sat vases spilling white blooms: elegant lilies, simple daisies, luscious roses. . . .

Abby gasped in awe and clasped Fitz's waistcoat to steady herself while she scanned the ethereal chamber. "How did you do this?" she cried, wanting to weep in response to the exquisite gift he'd given her. If she had any doubts left, they fled in this moment of awe at his thoughtfulness.

"I called in a few debts," he said with his usual confidence, before tilting her chin and studying her with worry in his eyes. "I did not have any magnificent jewels to give you, but I hoped you would understand that I would give you the world if I could."

Tears rolled down her cheeks as she lost herself in the depths of her husband's honest gaze. "No one has ever given me beauty," she whispered, choking on a sob of pure joy. "I've received many practical gifts, but this . . ." She stood on her toes and planted kisses across his freshly shaven jaw. He'd even stopped to shave just for her! "Gifts from the heart are the very best ones of all. I wish I had thought to do the same for you."

"You are the gift I claim," he murmured, swinging her up in his arms and carrying her to the bed. "You are giving me a present more precious than gold. I have waited forever for this night, so in part, the candles are pure selfishness. I want our wedding night to be perfect, to be the start of the kind of life I've never had."

She ought to be paralyzed by fear at the enormous dream he'd just laid at her feet—he was asking for the love and family he'd never known, *trusting* that she would provide it. But her brave Fitz's admission washed over her with warmth, and the unusual tenderness in his expression melted her heart. If he thought she could offer what he needed, she would be proud, not frightened.

She settled on the mattress and reached to break a daisy stem so the flower bent less formally over the side of the vase. "There is beauty in imperfection, too," she reminded him. "It's our flaws that make us special."

Standing beside the bed, Fitz peeled off his tight coat. "I am more a rutting bull than a daisy right now. I have done nothing but plot this moment for four days."

His confession that he'd been thinking of her for four days stirred the hungry desire she always felt in his presence, but she could not let him reduce her to mindlessness just yet. She hurriedly tugged up her crushable skirt and knelt on the bed. "Then you may wait a moment longer and tell me what the arrow meant. And the stone thrower last week. There cannot be secrets between us. I think it is a law of some sort."

"Not unless it's the law of just deserts." He flung himself beside her and dragged her down on top of him, planting kisses across her cheeks and tangling his hand in her hair.

Abby shoved her hands against his waistcoat and sat up again. "No, I mean it, Dane. Fitz. Jack. My wonderful husband. No secrets." She was amazed that she could find her tongue so easily. "I am much happier if I know the problem and don't have to fret over what it might be."

"You are supposed to be a shy bride," he complained, pulling her down to lie beside him and whispering kisses down her throat. "Enthralled with my lovemaking and forgetting all else."

Fighting fire with fire, Abby untied his neckcloth and kissed the taut skin revealed at the base of his throat. Finally, she had the opportunity to touch him. She began fumbling with his waistcoat buttons. "I am a farm girl aware that we will be making more children. I have no desire to raise a brood all on my own. So if you are in danger, I must know."

"And do what, my warrior queen?" He found the hidden hook at the front of her bodice and slid it open, exposing more of the translucent chemisette beneath. He trailed a seductive finger over the fabric covering her breasts. "Run scared back to Oxfordshire? Let us have a night of romance without thought to the real world."

He was right, of course, which didn't make it any easier to accept that he had secrets. But she had five children upstairs and now a husband to worry about, and she wouldn't relax until she *knew*. A countess must be strong and decisive, even if her mind washed away while her earl played a seductive game with the greedy beggars her nipples had become.

"Please," she murmured ambiguously, pushing at Fitz's unfastened waistcoat until he sat up, shrugged it off, and threw it to the floor. His shirt draped across broad, muscled shoulders and powerful arms, and she had some inkling of how ridiculous she was being. He was all huge, raw male, capable of handling mad archers, and she was mere cotton fluff in comparison. But she wasn't used to anyone taking care of her problems for her. "Tell me," she demanded; but even she'd forgotten the question.

Leaning over her, he untied her skirt and bodice and began unfastening her corset. "There is nothing to tell. Some madman keeps aiming at my hat. He holds some grudge, but I don't know about what. My friends will hunt him down if he comes near us. The house is locked up as safe and sound as a prison. The children will be fine. And if for some inane reason my heir thinks to frighten me into running away, he is sadly mistaken in my character. Tonight, I intend to beget the next earl."

Abby gulped as he divested her of corset and bodice and leaned over to suckle at her breast. She had not given her actions enough thought.

Her son would be an *earl.* How could she possibly raise an earl? This was what came of it when she rushed into something.

"And whatever you're worrying over now, don't," Fitz ordered, rolling back to the bed and carrying her on top of him. "I desperately need you, and you need me, and that's all that matters."

And he was completely, totally, irrevocably right, Abby decided as her husband tugged at her skirt until it fell below her hips, leaving her with no more than an unfastened chemise to cover her nakedness. And he was *still* dressed.

If she was to be countess and mother of an earl, then by George, she would have to learn to act with the same assurance as Fitz. Grabbing handfuls of his linen, Abby tugged his shirt up until she could finally touch his muscled waist and chest and the line of hair dipping into his breeches. "Take it off!" she ordered.

Laughing with pleasure, he did as instructed.

Fitz thought he'd surely died and gone to heaven as he lay beneath his new bride and admired the curve and bounce of her nearly naked breasts from below. No shrinking wallflower was his Abby. Once she made up her mind, the little general raced full speed ahead. And apparently, she'd finally decided he would suit.

Admittedly, she still looked a little stunned after he stripped off his shirt, but he was pretty certain that was admiration in her eyes, raising heat in his groin. Women had admired him before, but none were as special as his wise wife.

Candlelight and rainbows danced across her glorious red gold curls, and at long last, his eyes were open to the beauty of the world. Tomorrow, he might have to return to groveling for survival. . . . Tonight he had the cosmos at his fingertips.

Reverently, he grazed his fingers over the curve of her breasts to pert pink crests that furled under his touch. He coaxed her to lean down so he could kiss and lick and suckle until she moaned and no longer quizzed him about things over which he had little control.

Gently, he rolled her back to the sheets. His cock pressed into his buttons, but he wanted her awash with joy before he had to hurt her. He'd never taken a virgin before, and he almost wished she weren't so innocent. But then selfish masculine pride took over, and he was glad he didn't have to share her, that for once in his miserable life he didn't have to accept secondhand goods, and better yet, his wise Abby had chosen *him* above all others.

He eased her chemise straps off her shoulders while he kissed her throat, and she squirmed and tried to kiss him back. Her lips fluttered like butterfly wings across his thick hide, and he marveled at the tenderness she exposed in his callous soul.

Abby was the honest gem he'd sought without realizing what he'd been missing. Her loving hands stroked, and her gaze bathed him in the approval he hadn't known he needed. Tonight, he felt invincible.

When his bride daringly lifted her head to kiss his

nipple, Fitz shuddered with a desire so deep, he didn't think he could hold back much longer. He lifted her to slide her chemise up and over her head until she lay utterly exposed to his gaze. And she reached for his trouser buttons, meeting his eyes with courageous defiance. He wanted to laugh with joy that his brave Abby had emerged from behind her bashfulness. Instead, he bent and claimed her mouth.

Once he was sure he had conquered her lips and tongue and that they were fully his, he engaged her bounteous breasts until he nearly surrendered to the ecstasy of her sighs. Valiantly determined to lay claim to every inch of his new bride, he held one breast hostage with his hand, while he ran kisses southward to her navel.

His ultimate goal was moist and vulnerable, and Abby wriggled and tried to evade his intention, but tonight, Fitz was undefeatable. He settled between her firm thighs and touched his tongue to the glistening nub begging for his capture.

He'd already taught her what to expect, so she didn't shy away but dug her hands into his hair and lifted her hips in a rhythm that had him near to bursting.

He assaulted her castle, scaled the ramparts, and demanded surrender. And she gave herself completely, crying out her ecstasy as he brought her to the peaks and over. Satisfied, he teased her into urgent expectation all over again.

His turn. Finally. Kneeling, Fitz unfastened his buttons. At this point, he would gladly apply golden chains, as long as they meant he could dip into the honey his bride offered.

Weak with pleasure, Abby murmured a protest as her husband's heavy warmth moved away. Her chafed cheeks burned from his kisses. Her breasts were wet and aching from his suckling. Her bones had melted into the mattress. And even though her body hummed with the release to which Fitz had introduced her, her womb ached for more.

She reached blindly to tug him back, but her hand encountered only air. She could feel the bed bouncing with his hasty motions, and her eyes flew open to see what he was doing.

In the flickering candlelight, her husband loomed tall and muscled above her, like a Viking warrior of old. He wore his hair short at the nape, but the lock falling across his broad brow accented the fierce male pride of possession on his aristocratic face. A sophisticated Viking. She smiled at her foolishness, and he instantly leaned over to steal a kiss.

That's when she felt the heavy rigidity of the male instrument he would use on her. He was completely naked, at last.

She slid her hands into his silken hair, smothered his face with kisses, and lifted her hips, goading him to hurry. Even though she'd just been so thoroughly satisfied she thought she'd never move again, arousal swept through her with an urgency she could not deny.

His tongue penetrated her mouth, a precursor of the intimate sensations to which he meant to introduce her. At the same time, his powerful thighs spread her wide until she was exposed and open to the hard pressure of his entrance. She ought to fear the invasion to come, but she wanted Fitz with every particle of her, inside and out.

She loved him too much to ever deny him. She wrapped her arms as far as she could around his shoulders, lifted her hips to meet his, and whispered her secret desire—"Love me."

And he did, with exquisite gentleness. She gasped and wriggled when he pressed inside her. At her cry of protest over his size, he stopped to kiss her tears and apply his attention to her neglected breasts until she urged him on again.

He muffled her cry of pain with his kisses and

pushed deeper, claiming her more surely than any vows they'd spoken. And once she knew she wouldn't break in two, Abby reveled in the physical intimacy of the dashing, delightful Earl of Danecroft inside *her*. Cherishing *her*. Making mere Abigail Merriweather his wife and countess and the mother of his heir.

And then Fitz's pace increased to one of urgent insistence, and any further thought departed Abby's head. With his powerful, surging thrusts, her body spiraled out of control, seeking some height she'd never known. Her hips rose and fell, taking him deeper. She relished his groans of pleasure, the tight grip of his hand on her breasts, their mindless lack of control.

Just when she thought she might come apart, he stroked his thumb between her legs, and ecstasy swept her away. In response to her cries of joy, his body rocked harder and deeper until he shouted and flooded her with his seed. On the distant horizon of awareness, the significance of the deed thrilled her as much as the climax of sensation.

It was done, and there was no turning back. She was officially the Countess of Danecroft.

With Fitz's big body wrapped securely around her, Abby thought perhaps being a countess had its merits.

35

"Abbieeee, Abbieeee," Cissy was crying pathetically from somewhere in the distance.

"Shhhh, you'll wake them up," Penny whispered so loudly that she could probably be heard two floors below.

A feminine giggle under Fitz's armpit warned that his newly ravished bride had heard them, too. He sighed in resignation and rose up on his elbow to admire the prize he'd won last night. He couldn't be more content if he had won a pirate's golden hoard.

The candles had guttered into smoking wax, but the morning light caught the crystals, and rainbows danced merrily across the walls and ceiling and his bride's strawberry curls. Despite her initiation into sensual pleasure, or perhaps because of it, she still looked angelic and wholesome and entirely his beautiful Abby.

Fitz kissed her freckled nose.

And she lifted her shoulders from the mattress to kiss him back, placing his lips close to heaven. He pushed her to the mattress and straddled her hips and bent to claim a succulent breast.

An adult voice in the hall intruded. "Hush, now! What are the two of you doing down here at this hour?"

Fitz jerked his head up in startlement and gazed down at Abby. "Isabell?"

Abby beamed. "I placed her in the room at the head of the stairs."

"What is all this racket?" a deep male voice asked querulously as Cissy continued to cry, Penny continued to protest, and Lady Bell dealt ineptly with both.

"*Quentin.*" Realizing any thought of further conquest was futile while his wealthy guests tangled with the children, Fitz rolled back to the mattress. Now that he was more fully awake, he knew he needed to give Abby time to recover from last night. He'd tried to be gentle, but she'd been too eager for his witless cock, and the deed had been done swiftly. Twice.

He could easily envision indulging several more times this morning and wondered how long it would take her to heal. "You gave Quent the chamber next to Lady Bell's," he said with what should have been accusation but was more amusement at her conniving.

"They were the best chambers. Besides, those two manipulators deserve each other." She wet her finger and ran it down his rib cage.

Fitz almost rolled over and ravished her right there. But he'd spent most of his adult life resisting what he wanted. "Maybe so," he agreed, rolling out of bed, "but it won't put either of them in good humor to realize it."

The bare floor and cold wash water set him back quickly enough. "I'm amazed you found a stick of furniture left for them to sleep on. The only reason I could salvage your ring is because the lawyers kept it locked up. The legalities of entailments seldom deterred my family from selling off anything so common as household goods."

"Not just your family," she confirmed. "Your enterprising servants have been using your home as an inn. Apparently there is a nice profit to be had in renting out rooms they don't own, so most of the bedroom furniture and linens were kept up."

Fitz lifted his head from a towel to stare at his wanton bride. She wasn't even bothering to hide her nakedness, and he could swear there was a come-hither look in her eyes. He didn't know why he'd been blessed with this amazing woman, but he thanked the heavens. Then dunked his head in cold water again.

He had a house full of solicitors and a furious executor waiting. He would have to return to London to gamble for a living if he meant to pay his enormous debts. Perhaps he'd bang his head against the wall while he was at it.

"Maybe they have the right idea," he muttered, slathering soap across his bristles. "Maybe we should rent this place out and retire to your cozy cottage."

"You're accustomed to challenges. You wouldn't last a day in rural boredom." She dragged a sheet to her breasts and swung her legs over the side of the mattress. "If you think it might help, you could rent out the entire house during hunting season. But you need to look over your accounts first. You may not be as far in debt as you thought."

"I could be only *half* as far in debt as I thought and still be too deep for my pockets." He scraped at his face and tried not to watch her in the mirror, but having a wife was new to him, and his curiosity about her was insatiable.

She noticed, blushed, then hastily pulled the covers up over the sheets. The physical side of marriage would make her nervous for a while. He ought to stay with her until she got used to him.

But he had to secure her dowry, then pay back Quent's loan and claim his stud. Then set up race dates and stud fees. He'd have to go back to gambling just to cover expenses. Abby's small inheritance would go only so far after he paid Quent. Thank goodness he had Applebee to organize the tenants and start planting the fields.

"Still, it is better to have an accurate accounting," she continued, "and force the merchants to deal honestly with us."

Us. He was still adjusting to having a partner who understood his concerns. He stared at her in fascination.

"Your creditors are much too accustomed to dealing with Bibley," she continued, not noticing his amused delight at his countess's managing ways.

"Now, *there's* a scoundrel," Fitz agreed. "I suppose while we have a house full of solicitors, I could look through the accounts and ask them if the debts will all hold up in court." Remembering the missing cash, he wondered if he ought to present the evidence of family embezzlement while he had legal minds available, or if he should simply beat an explanation out of his heir.

A door knocker pounded loudly below. Small footsteps scampered down the hallway. Arguing voices carried up from the foyer, ending his dallying.

This was more a marriage of *in*convenience.

Abby darted back to her room and Fitz finished shaving and washing before a polite knock on his door warned him that the household wouldn't wait any longer.

"You have a visitor, my lord," Bibley announced from the other side of the panel.

"I seem to have a few dozen visitors, Bibley," Fitz called, grabbing a shirt from the wardrobe and pulling it over his head. At least he had clothes with him this time.

"Mr. Wyckerly said you expressed a wish to see him, my lord," Bibley stated solemnly.

"Geoff? Geoff is out there? Finally! Damn that bounder—" Dancing on one foot, Fitz pulled on his trousers, and in stocking feet, he jerked open the door. "Where is he?" he roared.

Abigail had a great deal of experience at dressing quickly, but this morning her head was still atwirl, and she felt too languid to move with any direction. Lady

Belden had seen that she had her new gowns, but they really required a maid and too much fuss, so after washing, she donned one of her more modest, less fashionable dresses. With all the aches and chafes in scandalous places to remind her of what she'd done last night, she didn't feel any less wanton wearing a simple gown, but she hoped she looked respectable.

She was still pulling on her slippers when she heard Fitz's angry bellow in the next room. Hastily tying the shoe ribbons so she didn't break her neck, she dashed out in the hall in time to see the top of his head disappear around the bend in the stairwell.

She ran after him, but she wasn't quick enough to halt her husband's fury from erupting.

"Where the hell have you been and who the hell do you think you are, looking at carriage crests while I'm bloody well alive?" Half-dressed in only shirt and trousers, Fitz bore down on an expensively attired, handsome gentleman standing in the rotunda, gazing around at the splendor, as all visitors must. The man glanced up in surprise at Fitz's roar of rage, and Abby screamed as her husband's fist connected loudly with their guest's jaw in a resounding crack.

The gentleman flew backward, losing his hat, but he scrambled up quickly enough to show he wasn't taking a pummeling lying down. Fitz raised his fists and jabbed a punch to their guest's midsection before he could dodge, doubling the gentleman over in pain.

"Where have you been hiding while assassins tried to kill me?" Fitz shouted, waiting for his opponent to stand up so he could swing again. "There were women and children there yesterday!" The instant the gentleman straightened, Fitz's left fist shot out, connecting with his chin, and the visitor stumbled backward again.

Was this the gentleman Fitz had been cursing as he'd perused the ledgers? Surely account books did not justify murder. Of course, if the newcomer had shot that arrow yesterday . . .

The rotunda began filling with guests and servants. And children. This wouldn't do at all. It was apparent their visitor's fists wouldn't kill Fitz, but Abby didn't want him hurt either, and she wouldn't have the men setting a bad example for the little ones. She gestured peremptorily at Fitz's friends. "Stop them!" she commanded.

Lord Quentin merely shrugged and crossed his arms over his chest while he watched Fitz try to murder a guest. Setting her lips grimly, Abby picked up a terrified Penny and shoved her into the nanny's arms. "Take the children to the nursery. I'll deal with this." Grabbing the twins, she pushed them at Lady Isabell and Lady Sally. "Take all of them."

"Abby, no, I want to stay!" Tommy protested. "I can help." Raising his fists, he prepared to leap into the fray to defend his hero.

"As you can see, Fitz doesn't need our aid. You can help by reassuring the children that everything will be fine." Abby pushed him toward Jennifer. "Go, now. I will fetch you shortly."

The two men rolled across the marble floor. She winced at the sound of a head striking stone. She would crack a few heads herself if someone didn't come to his senses soon.

Once the children and her reluctant female guests were out of sight, Abby glared at the audience circling the fight. The maids were clustered in a corner, wringing their hands, captivated by the sight of their half-dressed lord bruising his knuckles on an elegant visitor.

Even in his fury, Fitz was being a gentleman, giving his opponent time to recover before he launched into him again. They were evenly matched in size, but the other man was bleeding from the nose and lips, and Fitz scarcely looked winded.

"Brooms, Mrs. Worth!" Abby shouted at the housekeeper, around whom the maids were huddled. "Fetch your brooms. We have rats to chase from the house."

She caught the aged butler before he could escape.

"Bibley! Don't you dare leave. Do you know the meaning of this?"

"He's Fitz's heir, my lady," the old man said, as if that explained everything.

The gentlemen observers were now watching her as warily as they'd been watching the fight with enthusiasm. She seared all of them with a steely glare. All larger and broader than she, they seemed unfazed by her fury— just because she was small and female.

If this was the great London society she had dreaded, she'd set her fear aside right now. They were no better than stable lads punching noses in the hayloft. "If this unseemly situation isn't halted in three seconds, gentlemen, I shall commence screaming. It will not be pleasant," she added, in case they didn't grasp the full extent of her threat.

Fitz was obviously beyond hearing her, but she didn't think he'd overlook her screams. She had a good country voice, pitched to be heard across entire fields when necessary.

The gentlemen didn't move, obviously not understanding the danger of screams.

As the first maid ran up with broom in hand, Abigail tore it from her grip and, swinging it at Fitz's broad shoulders, simultaneously began screeching at the top of her lungs.

Her husband pitched forward, toppled more by surprise than by her blow. Her screams echoed against the hard surfaces of the rotunda as she pounded the broom between Fitz and his opponent, sending the latter shooting backward across the floor.

To Abby's immense gratitude, Mrs. Worth appeared with a basin of water. When Fitz's adversary seized the back of Fitz's shirt, seeking to take advantage of the earl's momentary shock, Abby snatched the basin and flung the water in their guest's pretty face. She continued to yell simply because it felt good to be in control for a change.

The gentlemen were no longer laughing but covering their ears. Lord Quentin shouted, *"Enough!"* in that peremptory tone of his, but smugly, Abby realized she didn't have to listen to him. She might be rustic and unprepossessing, but she had the good English privilege of rank.

Fitz rolled out of reach of the water just in time. Laughter lit his eyes at the sight of her. Abby wished she had more water with which to soak him. How could he laugh when moments ago he'd been ready to kill his *heir*? She was too furious to be coherent.

Rather than listen to any more screeching, Fitz's friends finally stepped up to grab the arms of the golden-haired man with the battered face, giving Abby some reassurance that the massacre had ended, and she might take a breath of relief and rest her voice.

"My countess, Geoff," Fitz said laughingly from the floor, where he lounged as if he were a king on his throne. "The General of Danecroft. Make your bows, Cuz, and I will call her off, but endanger her family with more assassins, and she will no doubt shoot you more accurately than the nodcocks you hired."

"Or bash his brains out and drown him," Atherton said, eyeing Abby warily while he and the others hung on to their struggling captive.

"I didn't hire any damned assassins!" the golden-haired man shouted. Or tried to shout. He winced and shook off his captors to test his jaw. Glancing over at Abby, he attempted a modest bow and almost toppled. "Good day, my lady. I did not mean to disrupt your party, but your husband has a short fuse and a few wits to let."

"Montague, stuff him in a cellar before I take his head off again." Fitz scrambled to his feet and came to stand in front of Abby. "My apologies, my dear. I will deal with the beast, if you will reassure the children that we have not been invaded by barbarian hordes."

"The only barbarian here seems to be you, but I will

assume you have your reasons." She studied him critically, noticing a bruise forming on his jaw but seeing no blood. "I think our guests must breakfast before we subject them to any further entertainment."

He grinned and planted a kiss on her cheek. "I am too accustomed to living a bachelor life, my love. Civilize me as you will."

He turned and gestured toward the dining room as if he'd always had a host of rooms and servants at his beck and call. "Breakfast, gentlemen, as my lady commands. I assume it must be loaves and fishes."

36

After breakfast, still looking sorely battered and still furious, Geoff sat with his back to the library window and his dirty boots upon a footstool. Someone had brought him a glass of brandy, and Fitz wondered where Bibley had hidden the bottle. His scoundrel of a butler was the next man he'd question.

He had to play this conversation like a hand of cards, not revealing what he held until the bets were down. "I hear you went shopping for crests for your carriage, Cuz," Fitz said genially. He took a chair and propped his boots on an empty bookshelf.

Geoffrey looked ferocious enough to chew the glass he held. "I thought you were *dead*. You can't blame me for wondering if being a bankrupt earl held some advantage."

"A crest?" Fitz scoffed. "That's not the first thing that came to my mind when George popped off." A strong drink had been. Fitz almost sympathized at the shock his cousin must have suffered.

"Unlike you, I have blunt of my own," Geoff countered. "And George didn't deliberately pop off and leave you his mess as I thought you'd done. Given our family history, I was convinced you'd faked your death, hoping this sinkhole would suck me dry."

Which he might have done if it hadn't been for his daughter, Fitz was forced to admit. Geoff had a right to believe a Wyckerly would be a dishonest dunghole, so he did not protest the insult. "Carriage crests?" he repeated in disbelief. "We have tenants starving, and you would prettify your *carriage*?"

Geoff swung his hand to indicate the house, then winced and shrugged his shoulder to work the ache out of it. "A barrel of monkeys couldn't right this place."

A *monkey* being five hundred pounds, Fitz thought that repairing the house might take a jungle full of them. Had his guts not been in turmoil, he would have laughed at his heir's terminology. He and Geoff had seldom occupied the same circles. Despite the bitterness that had developed between the two families—over money, if he was any judge—he'd never had any personal reason to dislike the man. Until now. "I remember feeling like that when I learned about George," he grudgingly admitted. "I thought he'd died to spite *me*."

Geoff glowered. "Then you know I would have to be insane to want this mausoleum and a debt deeper than Prinny's. Without a royal fortune or the aid of Parliament, there's no digging out of it. My father used to live here when our grandfather was alive, and he told me to run for the hills should it ever look as if I'd inherit the family tomb."

"So you did," Fitz said with a snort. "The lawyer said you headed for Yorkshire."

"Believe it or not, I own a pottery up there, and I had a load of woolens that needed transporting. It seemed wisest to see to them personally before your creditors came after me. Once I heard you were back from the dead, I celebrated."

"By applying to White's and courting Lady Anne," Fitz said accusingly. He might have a hard time believing his cousin would be nocked in the noggin enough to want a worthless title, but who else would want him dead?

"Why not?" Geoff retaliated. "I can't win without trying."

"And it's no coincidence that since George's death, I've been attacked by bricks and stones, and had arrows nearly take off my head? Some bounder wanted me to desert my wedding night to meet him at the *fountain.* Who besides you would have reason to want me dead?"

Fitz had already ascertained from Montague that after staking out the mermaid fountain at midnight, Blake had seen a horseman arrive, but the man had fled the garden after realizing Blake wasn't Fitz.

"The only idiot Wyckerlys are on your side of the family tree," Geoff grumbled. "I came here because I'd had some hope that you might be different."

Family history and decades of mistrust had led to this impasse. Fitz didn't want to spend the rest of his life waiting for an arrow in his back.

He dropped his feet to the floor and searched through the piles of paper on the writing desk. Finding a rumpled sheet, he produced a quill, spit into a pot of dried ink until he had enough to coat the nib, and handed them to Geoff. "Write *fountain* for me."

Geoff shot him a look but accepted the pen and rapidly scrawled the word across the paper, then handed it back.

Fountain. Spelled properly, in graceful backward script, because Geoff was left-handed. And far better educated than Fitz's own father and brother. Fitz supposed Geoff could have disguised his handwriting to some degree, but surely that wouldn't account for the extreme differences between crude and elegant, right- and left-handed.

"At least you're not as ignorant as whoever is writing those notes." Disgruntled, Fitz paced the now cobweb-free library floor. While he was quizzing this man, who didn't seem insane enough to want a penniless title, solicitors and barristers were waiting in his office, hoping to pry Abby and the children from him. They, rather than this unsolved puzzle, had to come first.

"If I wanted you dead, you'd be dead," Geoff said with Wyckerly arrogance. "In truth, I'd willingly hire bodyguards to keep you from being dead. I hastened down here the instant I heard of your nuptials. I wanted to congratulate you and rejoice that new heirs might be on the way and that I might someday be off the hook." He waited, no doubt expecting an apology.

But Fitz had Abby, not apologies, on his mind. "You don't know of any other Wyckerlys who might be insane enough to kill me, do you?" he asked, but he was already heading for the door. His family had always been too arrogant to consider keeping secrets and too brash to hide them.

Cautiously, Geoff stood. "Relations more shatter-witted than you? No. We're the last of a bad line. The lawyers would have to go back to the second or third earl in hopes of finding a line that hasn't drunk its way to perdition. Shall I hire bodyguards?"

"Wait and let's see what the solicitors have to say. If they take Abby's children away, I may have to shoot someone. You can be there to testify on my behalf, unless you want to inherit this pile after I hang."

Geoff snorted. "I *knew* there was a reason I stayed away from you."

"No, you stayed away because you were too civilized to attend Jackson's sports academy and feared my fists. I'd advise you to give boxing a try. It comes in useful when you're a Wyckerly."

Fitz rocked back in his desk chair to study the solemn men seated in front of him. The lawyers sat on wooden chairs, with spines straight, hands crossed over their paunches, while Quent sprawled on a cracked leather couch, observing with proprietary interest. Still mistrustful, Geoff watched over the proceedings from a wing chair in a dark corner.

Greyson, the children's executor, cleared his throat. "After this latest exhibition, my lord, I am more convinced than ever that you would be an unsuitable guardian for young children. I must decline your petition and that of your countess. I will be returning the children to the Weatherstons."

Fitz had learned that cautious, conservative Greyson disapproved of gambling. Of course the man would also disapprove of Fitz's beating his heir into the ground. He looked toward Pearson, the distinguished barrister Quentin had hired to defend him.

Wearing his formal court wig, Pearson harrumphed. "You are a disgrace to your profession, sir. We will take you to court for this insult! You cannot call the Earl of Danecroft unsuitable for no more reason than a fistfight."

But he probably could for owing a king's ransom. And a drawn-out court battle would see the children coming of age before it was settled. Fitz gritted his teeth. Unimaginative lawyers knew only one method of fighting.

Summerby, Lady Bell's solicitor, leaned forward. "The clause in Miss Merriweather's—Lady Danecroft's—inheritance stipulates that Lady Belden must approve of her protégée's spouse."

Damn. Fitz had had those documents in his hands when he'd examined Abby's expenditures, but he'd been too busy showing off his mathematical prowess to read them. Why must all his sins come home to roost at once?

Summerby continued. "Lady Belden can withhold the funds and leave them for the future use of the lady's children. You cannot automatically appropriate the inheritance. Lady Belden disapproves of your gambling."

As if all England wasn't gambling mad. Fitz had promised to repay Quent with the dowry. Without that, he'd have to sell Abby's farm. Or default and leave Quent with the stud. He saw Quent stiffen and frown.

He'd pushed Abby into this marriage by telling her he could get her siblings back, and he damned well wouldn't fail her. The children came first.

Fitz scowled at the roomful of conniving catch-farts. "The Weatherstons don't want those children," he said coldly. "They haven't the slightest clue how to raise them or any interest in learning. They handed them over to servants and let them run away to a *train yard*. Now, tell me whether they'd be better off neglected by lackwits or in the loving care of the sister they adore. You have seen my lady. Do you *really* think Weatherston could raise those children better than she can just because he wears trousers?"

"The fact remains, my lord," Greyson said stiffly, wiping perspiration from his balding pate, "you are not a suitable influence on young children. And given the state of your finances, the lady will no longer be able to afford to raise them. It is my duty to keep them and their father's inheritance secure, and you can make no such promise."

Pearson began to argue volubly in impressive legal terms. Fitz ground his molars in frustration. He *knew* what was right, but he had no good way of proving that he was the father the children needed.

Instead of saving the children for Abby, he'd ruined her chances. He fought with despair and his damnable temper while calculating the odds that would stack the outcome in his favor. Or Abby's. Keeping his card-playing calm, he decided this argument was more about money and control than it was about children.

Fitz interrupted his barrister's dazzling monologue to address Greyson directly. "If I sign away my rights to Abby's farm," he said, raising the stakes, "will you admit that she is the best possible person to raise the children?"

"You are still not a suitable influence in their lives," Greyson objected, although not as vociferously after being battered by the learned barrister. He eyed Fitz with suspicion, looking for the catch.

One hand down. Play the high card next. "What if Abby returned with them to her farm without me?"

"Then we are back to where we started. A single female cannot raise young boys," the executor insisted.

Refrain from punching a lawyer. Maintaining his gambler's insouciance, Fitz twirled a quill between his fingers and turned to Lady Bell's solicitor. "Will you ask Lady Belden to release some portion of my wife's inheritance for the use of a tutor for the children? A male tutor for the boys, if necessary?"

"If you will agree to sign away any claim to her inheritance, my lord, I believe the lady would be agreeable to releasing her funds. She simply wants her young relation to be happy and does not believe you are capable of protecting her future."

Fitz sensed Quentin stiffening, aware that if this term was accepted, Fitz would lose any chance of repaying his debt.

He must not reveal the depth of his despair. He was a damned *noble* and wanted to act like one. He took a deep breath and prepared to sign away his future for Abby's sake.

"Tell Lady Bell I disagree strongly with her notion of what will make my wife happy. But given your terms, I will agree to give up all of her inheritance except the sum necessary to repay my debt to Lord Quentin. Will that suit?"

Lady Belden's solicitor hesitated, considered Fitz's determined expression, and asked how much was owed. Fitz showed him his note to Quentin, and the solicitor reluctantly nodded his agreement.

One obligation down. The biggest one to go. Fitz turned to the children's executor. "Miss Merriweather is now a countess and an heiress with all the power such wealth and title entail. She can hire tutors or send the children to any school in the country. Will you allow her to keep her half-siblings?"

"Not if they are to live under the influence of a gambler such as yourself," Greyson said stubbornly.

"If they return to Abby's farm without me, until such time as you agree that I am no longer a bad influence?" Fitz thought he might choke on the words, but they had to be said.

Greyson narrowed his eyes and studied the issue before reluctantly voicing his approval. Fitz hid his relief. Not only had he won Abby her siblings, but he'd found a way to pay Quentin. At the cost of his beloved wife's company. He would deal with the crushing blow later, out of the public eye, when he could rage and storm and throw himself off a high cliff.

Quent glared at him in disapproval. Geoff crossed his arms and leaned his chair back against the wall. In all their eyes, by giving up Abby's dowry, he'd married for naught.

Only Abby could decide that. Only the *children* had to return to the farm. Fitz knew that meant Abby would go, too, but he needn't deal with that catastrophe just yet. The creditors nipping at his heels would probably hang him, if Abby didn't kill him first.

Fitz shot his heir a grim look, glanced spitefully at the wall of guns, then set his lips in a caricature of a smile. "Work up the documents, gentlemen. If it's the last thing I do, I will see my wife has her siblings home where they belong."

He took pleasure in watching Geoff squirm. Not long ago Geoff had been contemplating carriage crests after thinking Fitz had used those guns to shoot himself. Let the bastard agonize some more over the possibility of inheriting a mountain of debt.

Carrying a tray of coffee and cakes, Abby blatantly eavesdropped from the other side of the office door and gasped at the demands the lawyers were making. They would *still* take away the children? And not one soul in that room considered Fitz a fit parent? How *dare* they?

She was about to shove open the door and intrude when Fitz agreed with them and consented to send her home. Back to Oxfordshire—over fifty miles away. Without him.

Standing there, devastated, she wondered if he really hadn't wanted her siblings after all. Did she know him as well as she'd thought?

Setting aside the tray, tears streaming down her cheeks, she listened to her new husband casually dealing their futures like a deck of cards. How could she possibly believe that she or the children mattered to him when he blithely gave them up without argument? Perhaps the marriage was a sham, a gamble that only he understood. Did she mean so little to him that he could cast her off without even consulting her wishes?

She didn't think taking a broom to Fitz or the entire roomful of arrogant men would help. What good was being a countess if she was still female? She'd made enough of a fool of herself already. Shaking with fury and grief, she stayed quiet until the final agreement was reached and Fitz began signing away his life. Their life. *He was sending her away.*

She could have the children, but she couldn't have him.

She'd fulfilled her wish of so many weeks ago. She could take the children and go home. She should be ecstatic. Instead, she was miserable.

Weeping too hard to hide it, she let herself out the French doors into the side yard and raced into the maze of overgrown yews, where she flung herself on the grass and cried and pounded her frustration into the earth. She'd tried so hard . . . and wanted too much.

How could she ever have believed that a sophisticated man like Fitz would want a *rhubarb* like her? Had it always been just the money—as it had been with her previous suitor? And now that Fitz couldn't have it, he was sending her away? If so, he had gambled and lost this time. And she wept as much for his loss as hers.

The lawyers took hours to wrangle over details, writing and rewriting documents, until all were satisfied and the papers were signed and witnessed. The moment the men departed, Fitz sat down and wrote out a note to cover his debt to Quent plus interest. He shoved the paper across the desk. "I think I owe you my life and my daughter's life. This hardly covers the sum of it."

Quent dropped the ownership papers for the stud beside all the other documents and tucked the bank draft into his pocket. "I would never have loaned you the blunt had I doubted your willingness to repay me. Earlier, I questioned your choice in wives, but now that I've watched the countess feed the multitudes on almost nothing while preventing us from turning the place into a battlefield, I see that you've chosen a partner for life. She's amazing."

Fitz leaned back in his chair, still too stunned by his first act of nobility to think clearly. "She is amazing, isn't she?" he said thoughtfully, preferring to think of his brave Abby than what he would have to tell her. "I've never had a woman come to my defense before."

"You've never needed anyone to come to your defense," Quentin pointed out, logically enough. "Most men know better than to venture within range of your fists. Besides, I think she was as angry with you as she was with Geoff."

"Only because she didn't want my pretty phiz ruined." Fitz rubbed the sore spot on his jaw. "Or she thought I'd kill the bastard and didn't want me to hang. She defended me, all right. And you know, it felt damned good."

Quentin looked at him as if he were crazed. "Married life must eat at men's brains."

Fitz thought his friend might be correct, but the place

where married life had most affected him seemed to be in his heart. "I never had a family to defend me or worry about me. I never knew my mother. Never had a sister. I've had only one use for women in the past. But I'm thinking they may be far more valuable than I realized."

"If you had as many sisters as I do, you'd know how insane that sounds. But you're newly wed and I'll forgive you. What will you do now?"

"I think that will be up to her. All she ever wanted was the children."

"You have a lot to learn about women," Quent said with a snort. "I don't want to be around when you tell her. Since you don't need company eating you out of house and home, I'll gather your guests and give you and your bride time to figure out what comes next."

Fitz rose to his feet. "You're welcome to stay, although I'll admit, I have no idea how Abby is feeding us. I'm afraid to look in the larder."

"Those rhubarb tarts she served at your banquet tasted like ambrosia. Any woman who can turn bitter stalks into sweet can turn pumpkins into carriages," Quent acknowledged.

Too shattered to follow his friend out, Fitz wandered outside to stare at the land he'd foolishly dreamed of returning to productivity. With the stud papers in his pocket and all his hopes of family smashed with a few strokes of a pen, it occurred to him that he could always resort to Bibley's plan—disappear into the night. At least this time, his daughter would have someone to love her. And Abby would have Lady Bell and Quent and a host of new friends to look after her.

He didn't want to return to being a cockroach, living off others by taking their money through card games. He didn't think Abby would pack up five children and run off to the Americas to start a new life with him. And he really didn't want the earldom if he couldn't have Abby.

He had some tough decisions to make.

Patting her eyes with cold water from the broken fountain, Abby brushed the grass off her gown, feeling like something ghoulish dragged from the grave. Weeping wouldn't take care of their guests or the children, but she was in no condition to face anyone. She might yet take a broom to Fitz's head should she see him.

So she shuffled through the asparagus garden, looking for any remnants that might produce a savory dish for the evening meal. She wished she had her squirrel to talk to. Perhaps she should return to the house and shout at Lady Belden, but how could she yell at someone who had helped her gain her heart's desire? It was her own fault for not realizing that she desired love and marriage as well as the children. She was the one who had married for convenience, and then very inconveniently fallen in love with a man who did not love her.

She glanced up at a rustling in the hedge, fearing the children may have come in search of her. She'd promised to take them exploring today, and she'd left the overworked nanny alone with them for too long. The poor woman would need a nap by now.

A rock flew past her nose and smacked against the garden wall, jarring loose pebbles before tumbling under a dying rosebush. She emitted a small shriek before covering her mouth and glancing frantically around. For a moment, she thought she saw the blue cloth of Penny's dress through a break in the hedge. She shouted after her but heard no reply.

The sound of a galloping horse in the distance convinced her she'd imagined Penny. The child had many bad habits, but stealing horses wasn't one of them.

Suspecting she'd just been the victim of Fitz's incompetent assailant, she searched under the bush to see what the madman had to say this time. The rock was large enough to easily find. She dragged it from the brambles and untied the cord holding a paper wrapped around it.

*BE GEEVENG BEK MY STOD ER YELL BE
SORRY. LIV PAPPERS ET FAHTON.*

Stod?

The note was as foolish as the earlier one, but she
ought to show it to Fitz anyway. She feared she wasn't
ready to face him yet. Her knees started quaking and
her eyes filled with tears every time she thought about
losing him. But she couldn't hide in the garden forever.
Taking a deep breath, she forced her feet to turn in the
direction of the house.

Once Abby had entered through the front door,
Cissy launched herself at her from the landing. "Where's
Penny?" she demanded. "I wanna go 'sploring!"

Catching her little sister, Abby glanced up at the
nanny hovering at the railing above. An uneasy feeling
crept over her. "Isn't Penny with you?"

"The little rapscallion slipped away when my back
was turned, m'lady," the woman said. "Five of 'em at
once is more'n I can rightfully handle."

"I understand that. Do you happen to know where
the rest of our guests are?"

"Packing, m'lady. I heard them order the coaches
around. Mayhap the little one heard his lordship talking
to the others and went after him."

"Yes, I daresay so," she said calmly, not wanting to
frighten anyone. "Will you take the children walking in
the garden? I'll look for Penny."

As the children ran down the hall toward the lawn,
Abby removed the ragged bit of paper from her pocket
and studied it with more trepidation than she had earlier. The part that said *ER YELL BE SORRY* suddenly
made horrifying sense.

Then again, perhaps she was overwrought and making mountains out of molehills, as Fitz had more politely
warned her time and again.

She didn't know how she would handle these anxious

spells without Fitz to reassure her. She didn't *want* to deal with them alone any longer.

Anger rapidly filled all the hollows she'd wept clean earlier. She *wouldn't* do this alone again. He'd *promised*.

With intent purpose, Abby set out in search of her scoundrel husband.

37

Once she ascertained that Fitz had left the house, Abby's search narrowed considerably. Unlike children, who might scramble anywhere, an adult would not stomp through the knee-high bramble patches surrounding the hastily mowed lawn. Civilized Fitz would take either the gravel path to the river or the brick one leading to the kitchen garden.

Since she had been in the kitchen garden and hadn't seen him, she took the next logical course and traversed the gravel one.

Abby didn't know whether to be frightened by the note in her pocket, worried Penny might climb to the roof, or furious with Fitz for giving her and the children up without even once consulting her. Not *once*. Maybe she'd simply pack her bag and walk away without consulting *him*. Let him feel the devastation she suffered. She had so many furies exploding through her mind that she couldn't begin to put them to words. How could he sign away their future and any chance of happiness for the sake of a bunch of bullying—

Reaching the top of a hill, she spotted Fitz near the river below. In the unusually warm sunshine, he'd stripped off his frock coat and vest and folded them over a bush. He stood in billowing shirtsleeves and tight trousers, apparently contemplating the depths of the rushing waters.

The *Thames*. The river all London had feared he'd fallen into earlier. After shooting himself with one of his brother's guns.

Without another thought, Abby lifted her skirts and ran screeching down the hill.

Fitz glanced up in surprise, but fury and fear propelled her. No more timidly waiting for others to act in her place. No matter what he'd promised to the lawyers, she would not live without him.

She launched herself full square against his chest, toppling him backward into the bush. Crying, she began beating his shoulders with her small fists. "Don't you ever do that to me again! Ever! *Ever!* If I wanted to raise the children all on my own, I would have chosen some gouty old man who would pitch over dead in a year or two. But I wanted *you*, you insufferable, selfish, conceited"—she sought hysterically for just the right epithet—"smoking heap of dragon dung!"

Fitz's shoulders shook with laughter as he grabbed his beautiful bride's wrists before she beat him black-and-blue. Wherever his dire thoughts had taken him, Abby had dragged him back, and his soul exploded with joy.

"Dragon dung?" he inquired, drawing her arms behind her back and nuzzling her sweet-smelling neck. He licked her throat just below her ear and all the bluster drained out of her.

His courageous little general burst into tears and soaked his shirt. Shocked, he slid carefully out of the bush into a sitting position and cradled her in his lap, rocking her back and forth while she wept and ranted. There was a reason his banty hen didn't speak when she was upset—she cackled incomprehensibly. He pressed kisses to her temple and gave her time to calm down.

If he'd come here to make a decision, she'd resolved it for him. He could no more let her go away without him than he could give up the moon and sky. There would be no running off to the Americas and starting a new life unless she went with him. Perhaps he could disguise himself as a farmhand and hide out in her gardener's cottage again. Of course, once she learned what he'd done, Abby might pack his bags and heave him out.

Finally, he made out a word or two of her babbling, and he frowned. "Note? What note?"

"A stupid one," she said, sniveling and rummaging in the pocket sewn inside her unfashionable skirt. "And Penny is missing. And I don't want to have to do this all by myself again. I won't let you send me home. I'll camp in your attics."

He couldn't tamp down the relief swamping him. Somehow, she knew he'd signed away their happiness, and she wasn't running back to the safety of her neat little cottage. For the children's sake, he might have to persuade her otherwise, but for right now, her stubborn determination to stay with him soothed the sore places that self-doubt and the lawyers had ripped open.

Her defiance had stirred his lustful urges from the first moment she'd shaken a hoe at him. He would normally have no compunction about laying her down in the green grass and learning the joy of rural rutting, but the word *note* had fixed his attention.

"You heard about the solicitors?" he asked calmly, tugging her skirt free so she could dig deeper into her pocket. "Who told you?"

"I was coming to help you." She finally produced the paper and shook it in his face. "I was just outside the door and heard it all. And if you're considering for even one second throwing yourself in that river and leaving me with five children and a stupid tutor, I'll shove you in myself."

He snatched the paper from her waving fingers and

kissed her fiercely before attempting to read it. When he'd halted her ranting and melted her spine until she fell against him, he glared down at her. "I am not a coward," he warned her sternly. "Don't accuse me of being one."

She threw her arms around his neck and burrowed her teary face into his shirt. "You have to *talk* to me," she wailed. "I can't think things through if people keep telling me what I must do without letting me think about it first!"

"Fine, then, you think. I'll read the note. And then we'll decide what to do." He glanced at the words. *Be geeveng bek my stod er yell be sorry. Liv pappers et fahton.* What the devil?

Yell be sorry caused an uneasy shudder down his spine. "If he can call that crumbling pile of rock a fountain, it's clearly past time to meet him there and get to the bottom of this." He narrowed his eyes. "Did you say Penny has gone missing?"

"I'm afraid she's gone to the roof and it will take me forever to find the stairs and you weren't around to help me!" She wrinkled her nose a little more thoughtfully than earlier. "But I thought I saw her in the garden before the stone hit. And then I heard a horse, and surely he couldn't hurt a child. . . ."

She was babbling again. Fitz sat very still. Surely the cad wouldn't . . .

He couldn't take that chance. Very carefully, he set Abby aside, climbed to his feet, and held out his hand to help her up. "Let us go back to the house. If she hasn't shown up yet, we can start a search."

She grasped his bare hand trustingly, studying him with those big celestial blue eyes of hers. "What are you not telling me this time?"

"I can explain on the way."

She had to run two paces for each of his, but she kept up. "*Talk.* What are you thinking?"

"It's all about respect," he muttered, hauling her over

a rock on a particularly steep slope of the hill. "I'll respect your intelligence if you'll respect mine."

"Fine, then, if I'm returning to Chalkwick with the children, where are you going?"

"I'm going after an idiot first, and then I'm going wherever my family is. Is that all right with you?" he asked belligerently.

"Certainly," she retorted in the same tone. "As soon as you tell me what this stone throwing is all about."

"As soon as I know myself."

The nanny and the children were still playing in the garden when they strode up. Penny was nowhere in sight. Abby glanced at the older woman, who shook her head worriedly. "Take the children back to the nursery, will you, please?" she asked as calmly as she could.

She ignored childish protests and followed Fitz as he cursed and dragged her on to the back entrance to the estate office. They found their male guests lounging about, sipping from flasks and studying the array of guns on the wall. They glanced up in surprise at their arrival.

Fitz produced the note. "Does anyone know anything about this?"

"*Be giving back my stud?* I thought it was your stud?" Lord Quentin asked in surprise, scanning the crude missive. "What the devil does this mean?"

Montague swiped the paper from his hand and passed it on to Atherton without a word. Instead, he reached for one of the guns on the wall.

"Fitz won that stud fair and square at cards," Nick protested. "It's his, no question about it. I was there. It was one of his better performances."

"We were at the races in Cheltenham when he won it. If this came from the stud's former owner, he must have a loose screw to go after Fitz over a damned animal," Montague added.

"The man I won it from isn't the ruffian who has been chasing me about town," Fitz protested. "The nodcock with the Tattersall's posters is a half-pint."

Montague looked up abruptly. "I met Mick, the stud's trainer, at the race. He's jockey-sized."

"If Mick's the culprit, he'll be even shorter when I'm done with him," Fitz warned, shoving away from his desk.

"What do you mean to do?" Abby asked warily, watching the men remove weapons from the wall.

"Someone sending notes by way of slings and arrows is dangerous," Lord Quentin explained curtly, breaking open a rifle to check for ammunition.

"Maybe you could keep the stud and give him this useless palace instead," Geoff suggested, but he was already rummaging through drawers looking for cartridges.

"Slings? Then why are you loading guns?" Abby turned to Fitz, trying to understand what was happening here. And she thought *she* had difficulty communicating!

He grimaced and ran a hand through his hair. "I can't risk him harming Penny if he has her. We'll search the grounds. I think you need to ask the ladies to help you search the house."

"Penny? Your daughter?" Lord Quentin snapped his rifle closed. "She's missing?"

"We don't know," Abby whispered, feeling the blood leave her face. She hadn't really believed the note meant Penny would come to harm until she saw all these dangerous men with guns in their hands. "Maybe she's turned up by now."

Without another word from the men, she raced from the room to check.

She ran to the kitchen first. The servants paused in their work to stare at her disheveled state. "Has anyone found Penny yet?" she demanded. When they all stood there dumbly, she pointed at the butler. "Bibley, go help Fitz. The rest of you, come with me."

"Cook, check the cellars," she ordered as they passed that door in the passageway. "Fanny, check the rooms in this wing. Remember she is small and may have fallen asleep under furniture or behind draperies."

She led scullery maids and serving girls and everyone else they'd hired through the house, pointing out halls and passages and sending them scurrying. If Penny was simply hiding, surely someone would find her.

She sent the last of her army up to the third floor to search the schoolroom and attics, then summoned all her courage to face the party of London ladies. She had been so furious earlier that she'd feared she would say something very rude to Lady Belden. She still might. But right now, she needed all the help she could get, and that included facing a roomful of London aristocrats.

They were all in a sitting room adjacent to Lady Bell's assigned bedchamber, looking elegant, sipping tea while desultorily directing their maids in the packing of trunks. Lady Sally nearly dropped the teapot when Abby burst through the door, no doubt looking like a grass-stained bumpkin. She no longer cared that she lacked panache and she no longer feared their sophistication. A child's life was more important than her self-consciousness.

"Fitz's daughter has disappeared, and he's received another threatening note. The gentlemen are loading guns. I've sent Bibley to help them. I have servants scouring the house in search of Penny, but I fear something dreadful may have happened. I need to send Applebee, our steward, to organize a search of the tenant farms. Do any of you have acquaintances in the other big houses hereabouts? I fear I've not had time to meet the neighbors." She was running out of breath as she tried to tick off commands one by one without forgetting anything.

Lady Margaret put down her cup. "I'll run out to the stable. The men there will know how to find your steward."

Lady Sally offered to help search the attic. Lady Belden directed the Hoyts' maid to search all their bedrooms and sent her own to inquire about neighbors who might assist in the search.

"May I leave you in charge of the house, my lady?"

Abby asked, finally finding her respectful voice in her urgent desire to return to Fitz.

"I have my riding clothes with me," Lady Belden replied. "We'll leave Sally here to direct the search party indoors. I can ride to the neighbors, if necessary, and serve as messenger between parties. You go to Fitz. He must be frantic." The dark-haired marchioness looked determined.

Abby opened her mouth to say, *Yes, my lady*, then shut it again. Lady Belden was talking to her as an equal, and for the first time, she almost felt like one. She nodded, and fled back downstairs to check on the men.

Fitz hadn't gone hunting since he was a lad in knee breeches. There wasn't any blunt to be had in killing vermin. While the others prepared guns and bagged ammunition, Fitz turned to the servant Abby had sent their way.

"Bibley, where are the best hiding places?"

"There's no end to empty cottages, my lord," Bibley said, keeping his stiff upper lip. "There's none to tend them, and they're not fit for living in."

His Penny could be killed by a rotting roof falling on her head.

If the bastard harmed one hair on his daughter's head, he was going to kill him. Fitz grabbed one of the guns from his cousin and sighted along the barrel.

And immediately remembered the sprawling lodge with the stable for his father's hunters and dogs. The dogs and horses were long gone, but the lodge was solid stone.

"Bibley, draw a map of all the cottages. Gentlemen, I recommend you each choose one. Shoot your weapon if you find anything." Fitz took the ammunition Geoff handed him and stalked out with the papers for the valuable stud, his last remaining asset, in his pocket.

Losing an empty title and bankrupt estate palled beside the possibility of losing Penny's love and laughter.

38

Abby saw Fitz crossing one of the unmowed fields in the direction of the woods and raced to catch up with him, shouting until he halted. When she said nothing but continued walking in the direction he'd chosen, Fitz grabbed her arm and jerked her back. "Where the hell do you think you're going?"

"With you." She pulled her arm free and started out again. "You need me. You are prone to impulse and I am prone to dithering over decisions. We work better together."

She knew he was staring at her in incredulity, but she hurried on. She was *not* prone to saying things she didn't mean.

"I may be about to commit murder," he growled, striding beside her again. "I don't need you witnessing it."

"And you think your daughter should? See, that's one of those impulses you must learn to curb. Like giving me away."

"I did not give you away. Respect my intelligence, remember?"

"Fine, and respect mine. We need to do this together."

They walked silently after that, both too fraught with fear to continue the senseless bickering. Their silence made it easier to hear the shouting ahead.

"I need you to be cooming down from there, yih little monkey, bayfor yer after hurting yerself!" a man's voice bellowed.

Without a word, Fitz took off running down a path through the woods.

"Can't make me, you stupid tree stump!" Penny's voice taunted from somewhere ahead.

Abby thought she'd expire of fear and relief. Picking up her skirt, she raced after Fitz.

"Harm my daughter, and I'll blow your witless head from your neck," she heard her husband roar.

Coming out of the woods, Abby saw Fitz raising his rifle to his shoulder.

"And it's best if yih do!" a scrawny man shouted back. "After ye've taken my Damascus, Oi've nothing to be living for."

"This is the trainer called Mick?" Abby asked, gazing in dismay at the roughly garbed countryman, before turning her attention to the dilapidated hunting box and locating the child on its roof. "Penny, come down here at once!"

Although quite dirty, Penny didn't appear to be harmed. She crossed her arms and glared down, looking for all the world like her father in a snit. "I saw him in the garden. He threw a rock at you! So I threw one back at him."

"A rock? You threw rocks at my *wife*?" Fitz thundered, priming his weapon.

"Jaysus, it's not as if *yih* were paying attention to the lahks of me! Yer man did not hayre a word I said when Oi tried to see yih."

"Unless you learn to speak the King's English, *no one* will hear a word you say! We bloody well can't understand you," Fitz shouted in frustration.

Mick glared. "Oi was after standing in line with all ta

tradesmen, but what with bailiffs on yer doorstep and yih raising that nasty cane or fists every time Oi be coming near, Oi couldn't talk to yih. Oi can't fight yih, much as Oi wanted to beat ta snot from yih."

"So you nearly take my head off with slings and arrows?" Fitz asked in incredulity.

"Oi was just after getting yer attention to make yih feed my Damascus. But a fancy earl is too busy geeving parties and running about the countryside to listen to ta lahks of me."

"How could I listen when you shouted gibberish and threw rocks instead of meeting me like a civilized man?" Fitz was torn between blowing the head off a madman and watching in trepidation as his daughter crawled down roof shingles while his bullheaded wife looked for a way to climb up. But Mick's size didn't allow Fitz to go after him with his fists.

"Look at may!" the horseman growled. "Yih treated may like a beggar. Oi sold my fancy clothes to pay fer ta stud's feed, even after yih took his pappers. Otherwise, he'd be after starving because yih haven't paid a farthing toward his upkeep! Do yih think horses feed and stable themselves? Renting that stall costs ta earth!"

"Why would you do that when the horse isn't even yours?" Abby asked in what sounded like exasperation when she couldn't find a foothold to reach the roof.

"Because Oi figured if nobody else wanted him, Oi'd keep him," the would-be villain protested. "That horse would have proved Oi can win races, and yer man stole it from me! And then he mistreated a valuable stod by not paying his upkeep! Oi was that angry, Oi was thinking he desarved shooting. But mostly, Oi wanted to be heard."

"Of all the babbling blockheads . . ." Fitz fired the gun into the air, hoping the others would come running to save him from the temptation to murder a midget. "So you meant to *threaten* me into paying for the feed?" he asked in disbelief.

"Yih could have found may at Tattersall's if yih'd read ta bloody notes! Oi'm not after having fancy learning for sending long letters, and from what Oi hayre from them men at yer doors, Danecrofts don't read their letters anyway. Oi had to do someting *different* than them."

Apparently his family's ignorance had become a matter of public knowledge. Charming.

"Are you such a self-centered lackwit that it never occurred to you that I might have other enemies breathing down my neck and little time for solving your silly puzzles?" Fitz demanded. Flinging the weapon into the shrubbery in disgust, he swung up on a tree branch, climbed to the next one, and crawled over to the roof. "Did that man hurt you?" he demanded of his daughter, who watched him with wide-eyed amazement while Abby voiced protests from below.

"He chased me when I threw stones at him," Penny said indignantly.

Fitz needed to teach her not to throw stones like a little heathen. He needed to get them both off the roof. He needed to regain his sanity. Or maybe he was better off without it.

"The little brat followed may here," Mick cried from below, apparently ready to spill all his grievances now that he had an audience. "Oi've been trying to bring her down. Now that yih're finally hayre and listening, Oi challenge yih to a game of cards!"

The poor dolt had worse control of his impulses than he did, Fitz concluded.

From up on the roof, he could see riders responding to his signal, galloping across the fields in this direction. He had only to lie here and bask in the sun and wait for half the countryside to lynch the fellow. Fitz sprawled along the tiles, crossed his arms behind his head, and hoped the roof wouldn't cave in. "Abby, why don't you look inside the barn and see if you can create any miracle meals for the audience currently approaching. We should offer sustenance with the entertainment."

"I'm a countess now," she argued, responding to his sarcasm with impatience. "I let Cook create miracles. Do you have a list somewhere of people you'd like to invite to your funeral if the roof collapses with you on it?"

Fitz grinned. His wife's bossiness was making a comeback. All would soon be right with the world.

"Ye're both crazy as bedbugs!" Mick exclaimed.

"I'm a gambler," Fitz called down to him. "I calculate odds. And the odds of you winning against me are pretty bad. I'm not a horseman, I admit. I didn't think about who was taking care of the stud while I hocked it to Quent. But I've seen the list of races that horse has won. I calculate that the odds of Damascus winning regularly are pretty damned high."

"If yih won't be playing me fair and square, then Oi'll be stealing him from where he's stabled. Oi'll hunt yih down to get his papers," the clod threatened. "Oi need them papers before Oi can collect ta stud fees to feed him."

No doubt tired and hungry, Penny crawled over Fitz's knees and out on the tree limb. Fitz kept an eye on her, poised to leap if she seemed in danger of hurting herself. But he'd seen cats with less grace than his urchin daughter. He needed to stay here and imitate Abby by taking time to sort through this muddle.

Relieved that no one wanted him dead, Fitz was almost inclined to be reasonable. He truly was at fault for neglecting a valuable piece of horseflesh.

"I'll see you hung if you endanger my wife or children again," he shouted down, more or less thinking aloud. "If you love your horse more than life, then you'll understand how I feel about protecting the ones I love."

"What?" he heard Abby squeak from below.

Fitz had to run his careless words through his head before he realized what he'd said, and then he wanted to weep at her astonishment. She ought to know she was loved and worshipped and respected by everyone who knew her. But his silver tongue hadn't learned phrases he'd seldom heard spoken. He needed practice. "How could I not love you?" he asked, knowing exactly what he'd said to startle her. "You're my heart. You're the reason I exist. Without you, I am a cockroach."

He loved her giggles, too.

"You could never be a cockroach," she assured him. "You are a true gentleman, and I am almost afraid to love you. But I am learning to be fearless."

Before Fitz could catch his breath at that announcement—she might *love* him?—Abby's affectionate words turned practical. "Neither of you will be able to race Damascus without entry fees, and neither of you can even pay his feed bill or stable rent."

"Now is not the time to negotiate, my love," Fitz protested.

But Mick lingered, listening to Abby as if he hadn't just called her crazier than a bedbug.

"Let us buy your first stud fee," she told the dolt.

"What?" Fitz sat up and scrubbed tree seeds out of his hair. "Where will we find a groat for more than hay? And we have no mares for breeding. Besides, I already own the damned horse!" He caught the tree branch and swung down. Once on the ground, he swatted Penny's filthy skirts for good measure, sending her to cling to Abby. "No more climbing roofs and throwing stones at strangers without me, understood?"

Penny glared back at him, unharmed and undaunted. She had the wisdom to bite her tongue, which showed progress since their first meeting. He was aware that they now had an aristocratic audience surrounding them, halting their mounts to listen, but he no longer cared what the *ton* thought. He was a damned earl and didn't have to toady to anyone anymore.

Fitz circled his wife's waist with his arm, and Abby stood on her toes to kiss his jaw until it tingled. "I can sell all my crops," she murmured in his ear, "and make my wedding gift to you a pretty mare. That is one of your dreams, isn't it? A stable of your own? That's why you took the stallion off a man who didn't care for it."

"Gambling on races is a fool's or a rich man's game," Fitz said in scorn, although he thrilled at the amazing realization that Abby understood him so well. "I just wanted the income from the stud fees."

"He's a winner, my Damascus is." The nodcock sense-lessly stood there quibbling. "Ye have all ta empty sta-bles. House him between races, and yih can be putting him to yer mares in exchange. Yih'll get good prices for ta foals, yih'll see."

Abby smiled up at Fitz with a confidence he loved see-ing. "You can gamble that your mares will bring higher prices than the grain you feed them," she suggested.

Fitz began calculating costs of grain and labor and actually saw profit signs for a change. "He's insane," he whispered for her ears alone. "We can't deal with a madman."

"Is he really?" she asked. "Or is he just desperate, as we were?"

"If desperate is what yih are," the madman added, not in the least diplomatically, "then we're in ta same boat. May name is Mick Black, m'lady, and Oi'm a damned fine trainer."

Fitz sighed in exasperation. He was supposed to trust this scoundrel to be honest with his last remaining asset? As Abby had trusted him with hers. Well, *damn,* she was right. He was a gambler; he would always be a gambler. "I hope you're a better trainer than speller," he told Mick. "We've got rotten stables for housing the beast, the stud fees will have to feed him, and you'll have to earn your keep from the winnings because I haven't a bloody cent."

In actuality, he was too relieved to have Abby's for-giveness to care if he dealt with devils or sapskulls. He drew her fully into his arms until her lovely eyes could see only him. "I love you," he repeated, thinking it was past time to let her know how he felt. "I love you when you're being unreasonable. I love you even if you think I can't defend myself."

Abby snuggled closer and began kissing wherever she could reach. "Just as I love you even if you think I ought to be roped and tied just like Penny."

"I heard that." Lady Belden rode out of the trees. Behind her rode Lord Quentin, who appeared less concerned about the newlyweds and more interested in the belligerent villain.

"And misunderstood every word, I vow," Fitz told her. "If you want to meddle in lives, meddle in his." He jerked his head in Mick's direction. The trainer appeared rightfully confused by the crowd. "But one of these days, I shall make you pay for trying to separate me from my Abby."

"No, I meant I heard what you said a minute ago about gambling." Lady Bell leaned down to shoo Penny away from her horse's nipping teeth. "Quent has almost convinced me I was wrong about you. You really don't wager on horses?"

Cradling Abby closer, Fitz favored the marchioness with a look of annoyance. "Do I look like an idiot? Have I done one damned foolish thing to make you think me stupid enough to risk the roof over my head on a wager that can only be won by an act of God, and only then if an animal isn't crippled, its jockey isn't drunk, or its owner hasn't been bribed? I gamble only on what I can control."

Abby leaned her head trustingly on his shoulder and gazed up at her benefactor. "I appreciate all you have done, Lady Belden," she said, "and know you've only had my best interests in mind, but I'm not a silly young miss either, and I don't appreciate that you've treated me as one. I'm not giving up my husband, no more than I gave up on getting the children back. And if Fitz wants to set his home to rights, then I shall do all within my ability to help him, even if we must do it from Oxfordshire to honor his promises."

Stiffly, Lady Bell nodded. "I was mistaken. I often am, it seems. If you wish to slave away in this monstrosity to make a home of it, then I shall talk to the solicitors, and you shall have full access to your funds to use as you please. I apologize for doubting both of you."

"Your apologies are accepted," Abby said with gracious gravity.

To Fitz's glee, his less-than-timid bride lifted Penny, hugged her, and then maliciously swung the grubby urchin into the dowager's lap. Both urchin and marchioness warily studied each other.

Which left Fitz free to swing Abby into his arms, and stride toward home.

His grandiose home. His bankrupt estate. He was a fortunate man who had apparently just acquired a new trainer as well as a stud for his nonexistent mares. A fine madness this was, indeed.

By the time his cousin and friends straggled back from racing all over the countryside, Fitz was comfortably ensconced in his office with Abby by his side. She jotted down the numbers he gave her into a list, while occasionally helping Penny sound out a word in one of the children's books the maids had found in the attic.

As he had suspected earlier, he was uncovering an amazing sequence of events within the pages of these dusty tomes that his father apparently couldn't read.

The twins were napping, as Penny ought to be, but they'd given the older children permission to stay up this once, if they behaved. Jennifer had found a kitten in the kitchen, and Tommy had grown bored with accounts and gone exploring. The nanny was taking a well-earned rest.

Fitz couldn't bear to let Abby out of his sight. Since it was too late in the afternoon to send everyone out on the road today, and he'd rather have Abby with him than entertain his guests, he'd allowed Quent's penny-pinching Scots sisters to prowl about the neglected mansion alone. They were currently rearranging rooms and discussing economical refurbishing with the housekeeper. Maybe they knew how to get rid of mice.

He didn't want to know what Quent and Lady Bell were doing with his new horse trainer. Lady Bell knew more about animals and stables than Fitz did, and if it kept her out of his hair, he'd let her supervise them all, including Mick, who obviously needed managing.

Rather than rearranging rooms or stables or even kitchens, Abby seemed content to be with him, which was a marvel he might never get over. He'd sat in this office a few weeks ago, wondering if a bullet to the head might be his only salvation. He leaned over and kissed her.

He'd been alone all his damned life. Abby was meant to be with him forever, like the trees and the clouds. Abby was a goddess among women, timeless and omniscient. And he would steal every moment he could with her.

"I love you," he murmured for the umpteenth time. "I can never say that enough."

"As I can never tire of hearing it," Abby admitted. "We are both in dire danger of becoming maudlin, I fear. And it gives me such a thrill every time you say it, it is hard for me to behave respectably. So unless you wish to retire upstairs . . ."

She gazed expectantly at him, and Fitz nearly carried off his Lady Temptation right there and then. Had it not been for the sound of several sets of boots stomping down the hall, he might have. But he had things to say to his cousin that he needed others to hear. This business of being earl stood to be damnably inconvenient on occasions like this.

He took the ledger from Abby with the notations he'd dictated, set it neatly on the desk in front of him, and waited for the door to slam open now that the stragglers had returned. He glanced to his daughter and noted with satisfaction that she'd curled up on a pillow and fallen asleep.

"Poor mite has spent so much of her life being wary, it's a wonder she can trust us enough to sleep so easily," Abby murmured, tucking her shawl around her new daughter. "I'll warn them to be quiet."

She stepped into the outer room and the racket of big noisy clods approaching was instantly silenced. Fitz grinned like a fiend at the thought of his pocket Venus quelling big, lordly men like Quentin, who liked to throw his weight around. He stopped grinning and rose when his disheveled guests entered with Lady Belden in tow.

He gestured for Lady Bell to take a padded chair near the empty grate.

Quentin filled the center of the room, impatiently tapping his boot with a riding crop. The small estate office wasn't large enough to contain all the restless energy building inside it, but Fitz needed the ancient ledgers scattered across the desk.

"I'm an earl," Fitz informed them, reinforcing what he had only just come to accept.

Montague, with his usual grasp of intense situations, swung a wooden chair around, and straddled it, prepared to fight or defend as needed. He was no doubt lining up the various puzzles of stone throwers, reluctant heirs, and tottering ledgers in his head and running detailed analyses on the answers. He would probably work out Fitz's announcement before Fitz could seat everyone.

With languid grace, Atherton propped his wide shoulders against the doorframe. Gazing from beneath hooded eyes, he appeared bored, but Fitz knew his friend was studying the room's occupants in the same way Fitz studied cards.

Geoff was the mystery here. His heir prowled the edges of the office, examining the gun collection and the portrait of Fitz's mother with interest.

"I outrank the lot of you," Fitz declared, once his visitors were settled. "I want to make that perfectly clear. I don't have to explain a damned thing. But for Abby's sake, I'll prove that I won't endanger her inheritance or that of her siblings any more than I have."

The marchioness waited without her usual air of suspicion. With a knowing smirk, Geoff abruptly grabbed another wooden chair and straddled it as Blake had.

Once Abby was sitting again, her busy hands resting in her lap for a change, Fitz opened the ledger to her notes. "I have only had time to trace the largest of my outstanding debts."

Geoff nodded encouragingly, and Fitz narrowed his eyes in his cousin's direction.

"The largest ones are bank loans obtained ostensibly to cover improvements on this sinkhole, as my cousin so rightly calls it. They date back to my grandfather's time and have multiplied over the years of nonpayment."

"Those weren't bankers hanging about the door out there," Quentin observed.

"No, they're just the tradesmen who provided my family with food and clothing and whatever it pleased them to buy without payment. Over the years, the tradesmen must have learned that if they harassed Bibley sufficiently, he would find means to cover some portion of what was owed. In consequence, they padded the bills, regularly sent old ones that looked like new ones until they were tumbling stacks of invoices, and otherwise used whatever method they could to pry blood out of turnips. Their accounts are vastly inflated at this stage. Once we settle on the corrected sums, I will arrange payments at harvest time."

"It will take years just to calculate Bibley's method of payment," Abby said, biting back a smile. "He often traded estate assets for necessary items. We need to discover who has been paid in such manner, then negotiate their recompense in price per pound of deer and duck meat or whatever commodity he exploited."

"Threaten Bibley with a broom until he straightens it out. That seems to work." Fitz leaned over and kissed her again, just because he could. Then he turned to glare at Geoff. "But judging by how far back these ledgers are in disarray, and from Bibley's assessment, it seems my father and brother inherited their inability to read from my grandfather. They could not adequately decipher invoices and ledgers and relied on people *they trusted* to handle the details for them—family members who could *read*, like Geoff's branch of the family. My family wasn't as self-indulgent and incompetent as I believed, and I owe their memories a great apology."

"And you have worked this all out by yourself in these few days?" Geoff asked in amazement. "How?"

"Danecroft is a mathematical genius," Abby said cheerfully. "Really, I don't understand why no one has seen that. That little book in front of him is the sum total of years of ledgers. He did them all in his head these last few hours."

"Like my father," Geoff said, surprising them all. "He could sum ledgers in an instant. My grandfather—Fitz's great-uncle—had a genius for investment. Our pirate ancestor was actually a brilliant navy captain when England had no navy. The Wyckerlys weren't just wicked. They were geniuses. Unfortunately, only a few of them learned to put their brains to good use instead of bad."

"Education and a few morals might have made a difference," Quentin said dourly.

"That's all beside the point," Fitz interceded. "The point is ..." And here he glared at Geoff, who smirked as if he already knew the point. "To keep his accounts, my grandfather relied on family members who did not suffer his reading difficulties—which apparently included my grandfather's youngest brother and his son, Geoff's father, may they rest in peace."

"And my branch of the family robbed the old man blind," Geoff concluded for him. "I feared as much. My father and grandfather were thick as thieves. When I was little, I thought it was because they were forced to go into trade to keep food on the table, thus putting us beyond the pale. But once I took over the various enterprises they operated, I started wondering about the source of the capital that originally built them. I could have expanded several times over if I could have had access to that kind of blunt."

Quentin straightened, his financial acumen allowing him to catch on faster. "Because Fitz's grandfather, the fourth earl, relied on his younger brother and nephew to take care of the estate accounts, they had the ability to siphon funds from Danecroft's branch, who thus unwittingly financed *your* family's holdings?"

"That's the way it looks to me." Geoff didn't appear shocked or angered by the accusation. "You're the mathematical genius, Fitz. What say you? Aside from despising you and yours, did my side of the family rob the earldom blind?"

Fitz tapped his pen against the ledger and looked around at the friends who had stood beside him through thick and thin over the years. He might not have survived without their guidance and aid. Now that he had some modicum of influence, he would return their respect and support in any manner necessary.

Geoff didn't fall under that umbrella, but he was family, and he was being honest. Fitz was learning the hard way that family was important. He could take Geoff to court and ensure a lifetime of enmity, or he could find a means of mending family bridges.

Abby placed a loving hand on his arm, encouraging him to do as he thought best. He had five children and perhaps more on the way. He needed to give them a future. And a family. And friends. Ones who wouldn't cheat his son and heir if he should inherit the family affliction.

"I think my grandfather placed his trust in men who knew how to invest more wisely than he did," Fitz said cautiously, watching Geoff's expression. Apparently, the estrangement between his cousin's branch and the earldom had begun in his grandfather's time. Somehow, the fourth earl must have twigged to the theft that had drained his coffers and, in consequence, severed the family relationship. Fitz might never know why the matter hadn't been resolved then, but it was up to him to lay the groundwork of reconciliation now. "Your father and grandfather provided the time and labor in developing the investment. My grandfather provided the funds."

Geoff's forced smile faded, and he straightened, placing a hand to his back and stretching as if relaxing for the first time since he'd arrived. "I was hoping that was the conclusion you would reach. Otherwise we were in for a rather nasty court fight, and I don't trust the courts."

"No point in paying barristers for family matters," Quent agreed, looking interested.

Lady Bell frowned in puzzlement. "Does this mean Danecroft is not bankrupt?"

"Oh, I am a thread away from Newgate still," Fitz said cheerfully. "But a share of Geoff's substantial investments should provide a more reliable income than gambling."

He raised an eyebrow at Geoff, who already seemed to be tallying mental lists. "We'll have the solicitors draw it all up," Geoff agreed. "Put you on the board, give you a share of the stock. Then you can approach the banks and negotiate payments with collateral in hand."

"And perhaps I can use my mathematical abilities to increase the company's profit." Fitz glanced at Abby. "Would you mind if we rented out the town house for a few seasons, my love?"

Her face lit up like a chandelier. Had it not been for their guests, he'd have carried her off to bed right then.

"Not at all, dear Dane," she said in delight, gently mocking his endearment. "I will even contribute toward hiring someone to clean up the town house, if you wish. And how will you employ yourself if you don't have card games to attend?"

"Acquiring an education in crop production, I believe. And convincing an executor that I no longer gamble—at cards, at least." Fitz tugged Abby from her chair, swelling with pride that he'd put that joy in her eyes. "If you'll excuse us," he said to dismiss their company, "I think we need to peruse the library."

"Your daughter, Danecroft," Lady Bell said sharply, glancing at the sleeping Penelope. "You cannot leave her there alone."

He and Abby laughed. Lady Bell needed someone to manage. Far better that she start with a child. He allowed his bride to do the honors.

Abby smiled at her benefactor. "She's one of the brilliant Wyckerlys, my lady. Not only can Penelope read, but she taught herself to do so. Given her genius, I'd advise you to treat her as the child you've never had, and if she has inherited any of Fitz's gift, you could train her to look after your investments. Your kindness to me will be returned threefold."

All of which would give his illegitimate daughter a secure place in society someday.

Chuckling, Fitz swept his blushing bride into his arms and carried her away. They'd provided sufficient amusement for the day. His guests could entertain themselves for a while.

He had a countess to please and an heir to beget.

39

Abby slipped from the nursery late that evening to find Fitz leaning against the wall, arms crossed and wearing an expression of bemusement. He cocked an eyebrow and glanced down at her. "Are they finally asleep?"

Odd noises rose from the rotunda two stories below, but Abby addressed the important question first. "Penny is hiding under the covers with Cissy and telling her a story that involves some rather colorful language, but they're being quiet."

"You do not mind that my daughter is teaching her an inappropriate vocabulary?" He took her arm and strolled toward the railing overlooking the front entrance.

"Children learn from example. They will soon grasp when it's suitable or not to use their newly extended vocabulary," she said in amusement, before giving in to curiosity. "What is going on down there?"

Wrapping his arm around her waist, Fitz leaned over the upstairs railing. "I believe I've given our guests the wrong impression. They seem to have decided the rotunda is a boxing ring. I fear Bibley will soon post flyers and invite the public—for an admission fee, of course."

Abby stared in astonishment at the mat of bedcovers stacked on the marble floor below. Mr. Wyckerly and Mr. Montague were already circling each other, fists raised, while the ladies hastily lined the "ring" with the mouse-eaten cushions from the salon. Whether they meant to sit on the cushions or use them to prevent cracking heads was not immediately evident.

The other gentlemen were lounging about the walls, talking among themselves, exchanging wagers, and keeping an eye on the action.

"Whatever on earth are they fighting over?" she whispered. "Shouldn't we stop them?"

"Geoff needs to learn to fight, and Blake's volatile temper needs an outlet. He knows his strength—he'll hold his blows. I question their wisdom in allowing Bibley to hold the wagers, though."

Abby shook her head in dismay at the sight of Lady Isabell glaring at Lord Quentin, who was insouciantly handing gold coins to the wily butler. "I may never understand the *ton.* Lady Bell hates gambling. Why is she down there?"

"Lady Bell hates losing. As I understand it, she and Quent had a wager. Once she gave you control of your dowry, she lost, so she's now obligated to send off Lady Sally this season. I do not question as long as she and Quent have agreed to tackle Greyson so that I might have you and the children here with me."

"They are generous benefactors. We must find some way of returning their generosity someday. It is a pity Lord Quentin is in trade and only a younger son with no land of his own."

"Do not underestimate the man. I'd say from the way he's hanging about, he may be raising the stakes. Quent is a bit of an enigma." Fitz gently steered her from the fascinating spectacle below.

Abby glanced uncertainly over her shoulder at the first thuds and shouts of the gathering. "Lady Bell is an independently wealthy marchioness who has no desire to marry. He cannot hope to win her. I'm not at all certain why she wagers and argues with him."

Fitz tucked her hand into the crook of his arm and led her down a corridor. "Because she is a woman and he is a man. Really, all the rest does not matter when it comes right down to it, does it?"

"Oh." Abby blinked at the image he raised. "Roosters will do what roosters do. And here I have been so very terrified of society when they are no different than a farmyard."

"Precisely," Fitz responded with glee, opening a narrow door at the far end of the passage that she'd not noticed before.

"Where are we going?" Curiosity overcoming her concern about their guests' entertainment, she peered up a dark staircase but could not see its end.

"To the roof. I thought you might like to know how to find Tommy or Penny if they disappear. The temptation to explore up here is much too great for independent minds like theirs." He lit a candle and held it high so she might precede him upward.

She had rather hoped to spend the second night of their marriage in a different manner, but after the day's terrors, Abby supposed it was wise to know the sprawling mansion's hiding places.

She turned a bend in the staircase and a silver light lit a path upward. "Oh, my, is that the moon?"

"It's full tonight," Fitz said with a decided purr of pleasure deep in his throat.

Abby shivered in anticipation at the sound. A man who had learned to survive on his wits had many advantages, such as planning ahead. She appreciated her new husband's many talents. She could easily come to rely on his calculating ways.

He held her elbow as she stepped through an open door, onto the roof, and into an ethereal fairyland. "Oh, my," she whispered in delight, spinning in a futile attempt to take it all in at once.

The glass dome skylight of the rotunda rose at the front of the vast expanse of roofline, illuminated by the chandelier below. Beyond that, minarets, domes, spires, and towers gilded in moonlight and wrapped in wisps of fog created an enchanted playland. "I never knew anything like this existed," she murmured in awe.

"Less practical than a rhubarb bed," he admitted, "but sometimes life needs a little splendor. I believe with a bit of work, we could honeymoon in a different location every night and never leave the house."

She laughed, and the sound floated toward the stars. "If the roof leaks in a storm, we could call the leak a waterfall, add sand, and pretend we're at the beach."

Catching her in his arms, Fitz swirled her across the rooftop to the music of a waltz only they could hear. "Who needs wealth when we have each other and our imaginations?" he crooned in her ear, before sweeping her up in his arms—and depositing her on a very wide, mattress-filled hammock.

Abby gasped in startlement as the bed swayed, and even more so when he climbed on with her. "Are we on a ship sailing a moonlit sea?"

"A rope bed tied between two chimneys, but the effect is the same." He leaned over and kissed her and the mattress rocked gently.

Abby wrapped her arms around his neck and held on tightly for the ride. "My wonderful, wicked Wyckerly," she murmured as his kisses moved to her ear. "Whatever did I do to deserve you?"

"Take in a wayfaring stranger?" He laughed and proceeded to divest her of earthly attire and wrap her in moonlit gossamer.

Author's Note

Depending on the economic standard used, my heroine's inheritance of a thousand pounds in 1807 might *very* roughly approximate $70,000 in today's dollars. That might be sufficient to provide a comfortable home, but certainly not the standard of living of nobility at the time, where a thousand pounds could easily be lost on the turn of a card.

Don't miss the story of Blake Montague,
the dark, dangerous duelist with a warrior's heart.
He'll be starring in

The Devilish Montague

the next book in the Rebellious Sons series
by Patricia Rice.
Available from Signet Eclipse in July 2011.

Standing in a field outside a duke's mansion, in a drenching predawn downpour, surrounded by a crowd of equally drunken young men, Blake Montague decided that getting shot by a drunken imbecile over a rude parrot possessed potent symbolism, if only he could fathom what it might be.

Perhaps he should not have partaken of that last glass of brandy while attempting to ignore a vivacious Venus—damn the woman and her haunting eyes.

Blake examined the assortment of weapons being offered to him. For whatever reason, the perfumes of the ladies had disturbed him since his prior encounter with Miss Carrington. He hadn't the looks or the blunt to be a ladies' man, so he needed another outlet for his many frustrations. Shooting anything would help.

Hair unfashionably tied at the nape, whiskers in need of scraping, and torso stripped to shirtsleeves, embroidered vest, and loosened neck cloth, Blake was aware that he looked the part of disreputable highwayman. Perhaps if he accidentally killed Bernie, he'd take up thievery for a living.

"'He's a most notable coward,'" he pronounced, the words tripping effortlessly off his well-oiled tongue while he held up a pistol and checked the length of the barrel. "'An infinite and endless liar, an hourly promise breaker, the owner of not one good quality.'"

Oblivious of his terrified opponent huddled with friends farther down the hedgerow, Blake pointed an ornate Manton at the moon. "'I desire that we be better strangers.'"

"Damnation, he's quoting Shakespeare," Nicholas Atherton said to the man acting for Blake's opponent in settling the rules of this meeting. Staying dry beneath the spreading branches of an oak, he did not seem overly anxious about Blake's impending confrontation with death. "We could all drown out here before he's done."

Blake would miss his callous friends if he took up thievery. He wouldn't, however, miss Miss Carrington's infectious laugh. Or that riveting cleavage she'd flaunted this evening. Ladies be damned.

Bernie's second sounded more concerned than Nick did. "We're supposed to resolve this dispute, not let them further insult each other."

"I didn't do anything!" Bernard Ogilvie, the Duke of Fortham's nephew, protested, as he had done ever since the drunken party had whooped its way from the mansion to this distant pasture.

Ogilvie ignored the proffered box of weapons while he affixed the duke's molting parrot on a perch he'd planted in the ground.

The wet creature flapped its wings and squawked a bored protest. "Acck! Stick it up her bum! Roger her, boyo!"

The very words that had set Blake off this evening.

"You stated the rules, Bernie—you said I might shoot the bird over your dead body," Blake reminded him, aiming the still-empty pistol in his host's direction.

"The beast don't mean nothing by it!" Bernie burped prodigiously and didn't look as if he knew which end of the pistol to take when the box was offered again.

"'Methinks thou are a general offense, and every man should beat thee,'" Blake quoted, filling his weapon with powder.

Shoulders propped against the oak, Nick sighed in exasperation. "You're not on the battlefield anymore, old friend. Let the poor boy toddle to bed and sleep it off. You may not mind fleeing the law for a stint on the Continent, but it's a damned poor way to treat your host."

"It is my duty to defend the delicate sensibilities of the ladies. How can I marry a rich one, and return to the battlefield, if I allow them to be insulted?" Blake said calmly.

Bernie's second lifted a questioning eyebrow.

"Blake needs a dowry to buy colors. He thinks he can run the war better than the current crop of hen-hearted rattle-pates," Nick explained

"You're serious?" the other man asked in disbelief.

Nick shrugged. "He possesses the intellect to run the country but hasn't a ha'penny to his name. What do you think?"

"War heroes get titles." Bernie's second nodded in understanding.

"Acck, tup her good, me lad!"

Ignoring Nick's idea of repartee, Blake aimed the loaded pistol at the half-featherless creature, which was barely discernible against the backdrop of yew. "'Scurvy, old, filthy, scurry lord.'" He fired a test shot in the general direction of the bird and hedge. A flurry and scuttle of night creatures shook the evergreen branches, and the parrot squawked incomprehensible curses.

"Not the bird, Montague!" Bernie cried, in more fear of the parrot's life than his own. "His Grace will disown me! Someone move Percy behind the hedge."

One of Bernie's companions obligingly pulled up the perch and moved the scurvy lord out of sight, if not out of hearing. Obscenities and squawks screeched against the silent dawn, raising songbirds into protest.

"The ladies are already packed and prepared to leave," Nick called from his position beneath the oak, making no effort to verify the safety or accuracy of the next pistol Blake hefted. "Shooting Bernie won't do you any good now."

"'Twill satisfy my soul." Blake again sighted along the

length of a barrel, in the direction of the hedge where the bird resided.

The shrubbery rustled as if retreating from his aim.

"Shakespeare?" Bernie's second asked.

"Montague," Nick concluded, "although one never can be quite certain. His brainpan is stuffed with an encyclopedia."

As the two combatants finally primed and loaded their chosen weapons, Bernie's second said dolefully, "Books don't stop bullets."

Since Blake still limped badly from a mending bullet wound, he didn't think that observation deserved a reply.

Eager to escape the chilly September rain, one of the onlookers herded the duelists into position, back to back, and gave the signal for them to begin pacing off their distance. The tension of the final count dispersed at a demonical shriek from the hedge. "Ackkkk, kidnapper, murderer, help. Hellllppppp!"

Ignoring the cries, Blake swiveled steadily at the count of ten and aimed his pistol. But Bernie was no longer in position.

Instead, coattails flapping, the duke's nephew was racing for the shrubbery. "She's stealing Percy!" he shouted.

Sure enough, a dark, cloaked shadow could be seen darting through the deluge away from them, up the hill, and into a grove of trees.

In disgust, Blake fired at Bernie's hat, sending the expensively inappropriate chapeau bouncing across the saturated grass with a hole through its middle. The rain had stopped as suddenly as it had begun, and a glimmer of dawn appeared on the horizon. His opponent's balding pate glistened as he fought his way through tangled yew branches in hopes of reaching his pet.

The bird screamed again from the field beyond the hedge.

Jumping up and down and pointing, Bernie shouted, "A thousand pounds to anyone who catches her. Devil take the damned witch!"

"I say, did he promise a thousand pounds for that paltry poultry?" Blake asked, reloading the smoking pistol.

"He did, old boy, he did." Nick pushed himself away from the oak trunk. "But everyone knows Ladybyrd took him. She's been sniffing around Percy, complaining that he's ill treated. He'll never see the creature again."

Blake snorted. "For a thousand pounds, I'll follow her to the Outer Hebrides." Chasing Jocelyn Byrd Carrington, commonly known as Ladybyrd, anywhere was exactly what he needed. He could still smell the damn woman's exotic scent. Her laughing violet eyes and her molten silver tears haunted his sleep. Shooting her would be good for the soul and would relieve the world of a silly, annoying widget.

"For all your education, you have ale for brains, professor," said Nick. "With that game leg, you can barely walk. You're supposed to be recuperating. Haring after a crackbrain will only get you killed sooner."

"She's carrying a damned squawking parrot. How far can she get?" Donning his coat, Blake tucked the pistol into his pocket and trudged toward the hedge.

Blake had despised his enforced idleness. The last fumes of liquor evaporated with the exhilaration of action priming his blood. He didn't know a woman alive who would travel without bags and boxes, and the lady in question had only recently acquired loads of both. If she was fleeing with the parrot, she wouldn't part easily with them. *Voilà*, she and the parrot could be found with the baggage.

A thousand pounds would buy his colors and free him from the need to marry for money. For the first time in recent memory, his spirits soared, and the thrill of the chase was on.

"Methinks he thinks too much," Jocelyn crooned to the parrot, stroking it beneath the dark cloth covering the warm, dry box she'd provided for the mistreated creature. The parrot batted its head against her soothing finger, then settled into sleep.

Shivering in her wet cloak, Jo tried not to think too

hard about Blake Montague. Tonight, aiming a pistol in her direction, he had looked the part of a dangerous rogue.

She tucked the bird's box among the rest of the baggage in the wagon. Hearing the crunching of gravel up the carriage drive, she glanced toward the ducal mansion nearly a quarter mile from the stable where she stood. She had hoped the combatants were all too drunk or involved in the duel to follow her, but she didn't underestimate the provoking Blake Montague.

Montague was a lethal weapon. His cynical wit had a cutting edge she couldn't hope to match. And for all his education, he didn't seem to like anyone very much. She'd seen scorn in his eyes each time he looked at her. Men disliked rejection, and she had rejected him.

With no hope of reaching the house before Montague caught up with her, she abandoned the wagon and slipped into the shadows of the stable. Nickers and whoofs and the pungent odor of manure permeated the early-morning air as the animals stirred in anticipation of their breakfast.

She'd learned the value of stealth and diversion very early in life, while avoiding her half brother Harold's rages. Spreading her thick cloak, Jocelyn settled in a rear stall, where a barn cat fed her newborns.

"I know you're in here," a husky baritone called from the entrance. "You have disappointed me. I had hoped to have to hunt you down."

Jocelyn wanted to ask what he intended to do to her, shoot her? But she saw no reason to disturb the kittens.

She suffered a nervous chill at the thought of being alone with an enraged man, but for all his brooding gloom, Mr. Montague was widely reported to be an honorable gentleman. He might scald her with his acid scorn, but a gentleman would never lay a hand on a woman. Behind him, dawn was lightening the sky, silhouetting his square shoulders. She wished she didn't admire his strength so much.

She'd stationed herself so she could see the length of the barn and knew when he approached. When his tall outline loomed close, she looked up so he could see her white face against the stall.

Good soldier that he was, he spotted her instantly. She could almost swear he growled as he limped forward. She held a finger to her lips to indicate quiet.

"Quit posturing and admit the bird is better off free," she whispered.

"Free?"

If he'd worn a hat, she thought he might have stomped on it. He really was a dashingly dangerous figure of a man—and regrettably not at all suitable for her purposes. But then, no man she'd met these last six months had a care for her purposes—only her money. Picking up a kitten, she returned Montague's glare. "What else could be done with such a rude creature than set it free?"

"You did not let a tropical bird loose in chilly England. You may be nicked in the nob, but no one ever said you were stupid."

She slanted her eyes thoughtfully. "Actually, Harold said it quite often. And my brothers-in-law have had occasion to mention it once or twice. Lord Bernard certainly said it over these past days. I think I prefer *nicked in the nob*. What, precisely, does that mean?"

He ignored her effort to distract him. "The bird belongs to the duke. You cannot keep it. It's theft. Just tell me where you've hidden it, and I'll see it's returned without question." He crossed his arms over his soaked waistcoat and glowered.

Jocelyn beamed at him in return. "Nature cannot be owned, sir."

He blinked as if he'd just realized she truly was dimwitted—the reaction she was most accustomed to receiving.

He recovered more quickly than most, unfortunately. He reached down, grabbed her arm, and hauled her to her feet, much to mama cat's consternation. "That's the most preposterous idiocy I've heard all week, and I've heard a lot. *Where is the bird?*"

"Really, sir, you'll ruin the drape of my gown." She probably ought to be afraid. Blake Montague was more raw male than she normally encountered. He didn't stink of perfume or hair pomade but of male musk, perspiration, and damp wool. His hands on her weren't the polite escort of a gentleman. She sensed he was passionately determined for reasons she could not perceive, but she couldn't believe he would harm her over a bird.

"Would you like me to summon an audience?" he asked maliciously. "What will Lady Bell have to say to the scandal if we are discovered here alone at dawn?"

Jocelyn cocked her head thoughtfully. "Oh, something pithy and intelligent like *birds of a feather flock together.* Or *dross sinks to the lowest depths.*"

She thought she almost caught a quirk of humor in the curl of his lip, and a thrill of totally unjustified pride swept through her. She really ought to be concerned about her reputation, but he was a baron's youngest son, and until recently, she had been no more than the impoverished daughter of a deceased viscount. Their families were Quality, but not of vast import to most of society.

But Lady Belden—Lady Bell, as they called her—had been more than kind to her, and Jocelyn tried not to disappoint her hostess. She set the kitten down and left the stall so the mama cat might rest easy. "Wouldn't you rather explain your concern for a half-dead old bird than cause a scandal?" she asked.

"Personally, I'd wring the foulmouthed featherbrain's miserable neck, but Bernie has placed a thousand-pound reward on its return."

"Surely you cannot still be set on buying colors!" Jocelyn declared in dismay. "You've already been grievously injured. It would be suicide to return to the battlefield."

Blake Montague bared his considerably white, strong teeth and hauled her past the stalls. "What I choose to do is no concern of yours. Now tell me which of these stalls contains the damned bird, or I shall open them all."

"Then I hope you enjoy chasing the duke's cattle," she agreed merrily.

Montague shot her a disgruntled look, studied her amused expression, and withdrew a pistol from his coat pocket. He aimed it carefully at the luggage cart clearly visible through the barn doors. "What if I proceed to shoot those boxes?"

Jocelyn shrieked, jerked his arm downward, and the delicate firing mechanism of the expensive firearm exploded.

In dismayed horror, Jocelyn covered her mouth to prevent crying out, as Montague lifted his boot to reveal a smoking hole through the toe.

New York Times
Bestselling Author

PATRICIA RICE

MYSTIC GUARDIAN

Off the coast of France and guarded by Trystan l'Enforcer lies the sun-kissed isle of Aelynn. Its people use magical abilities to protect a sacred chalice. An ambitious Trystan intends to marry for convenience, but when a sultry beauty washes up on shore, she stirs in him a carnal hunger—and his plans take a confounding turn. Now he must work with her to recover Aelynn's most sacred object before chaotic forces can lead to devastating destruction.

Available wherever books are sold or
at penguin.com

New York Times
Bestselling Author

PATRICIA RICE

MYSTIC RIDER

Ian Olympus, skilled fighter and visionary, has left the isle of Aelynn for the Outside World to retrieve a sacred chalice. He finds it in the hands of Chantal Deveau, who plans to use it to buy her family out of prison.

But her outrage at his demand that she hand it over is nothing compared to her powerful, sensual response to his presence—and the startling conviction that their lives are irrevocably entwined.

Available wherever books are sold or at penguin.com

New York Times
Bestselling Author

PATRICIA RICE

MYSTIC WARRIOR

As Europe is torn by revolution, the fate of the
Mystic Isle of Aelynn also falls into question—
its survival dependent on recovering the elusive
treasure known as the Chalice of Plenty. Only the
daughter of Aelynn's spiritual leader and a renegade
warrior can accomplish the dangerous mission.

Available wherever books are sold or
at penguin.com